Please renew or return items by the date shown on your receipt

www.hertfordshire.gov.uk/libraries

Renewals and enquiries: 0300 123 4049

Textphone for hearing or 0300 123 4041
speech impaired users:

L32 11.16

Also available from S. Jae-Jones and Titan Books

Wintersong

SHADOWSONG

S. JAE-JONES

TITAN BOOKS

Shadowsong
Print edition ISBN: 9781785655463
E-book edition ISBN: 9781785655470

Published by Titan Books
A division of Titan Publishing Group Ltd
144 Southwark Street, London SE1 0UP

First Titan edition: January 2018
10 9 8 7 6 5 4 3 2 1

Hand-lettering and title page art courtesy of the author.

A CIP catalogue record for this title is available from the British Library.

Printed and bound in Great Britain by CPI Group Ltd.

For the monstrous,
and those who love us

AUTHOR'S NOTE

All books are mirrors of the author in some way or another, and Liesl's journey to the Underground and back perhaps reveals more about me than I first realized. If *Wintersong* was my bright mirror, reflecting all my wish-fulfillment dreams about having my voice recognized and valued, then *Shadowsong* is my dark one, showing me how all the monstrous parts of the Underground were really another facet of me.

I would like to offer up a content note: *Shadowsong* contains characters who deal with self-harm, addiction, reckless behaviors, and suicidal ideation. If these subjects are triggering or otherwise upsetting to you, please proceed with caution. If you are struggling with suicidal thoughts, please know that there are resources and people who can assist you at the Samaritans, 116-123. Please call. You are not alone.

In many ways, *Shadowsong* is a far more personal work than its predecessor. I have been open and candid about writing Liesl as a person with bipolar disorder—much like her creator—but in *Wintersong*, I kept her diagnosis at arm's length. Part of that is due to the fact that bipolar disorder as a diagnosis wasn't really understood during the time in which she lived, and part of it is due to the fact that I did not want to face her—and therefore my—particular sort of madness.

Madness is a strange word. It encompasses any sort of behavior or thought pattern that deviates from the norm, not just mental illness. I, like Liesl, am a functioning member of society, but our mental illnesses make us mad. They make us arrogant, moody, selfish, and reckless. They make us destructive, to both ourselves and to those we love. We are not easy to love, Liesl and I, and I did not want to face that ugly truth.

And the truth is ugly. Liesl and Josef reflect both the manic and melancholic parts of myself, and they are dark, grotesque, messy, and painful. And while there are books that offer up prettier pictures, windows into a world in which things are healthy and whole, *Shadowsong* is not one of them. I kept the monster at bay in my first book; I would claim it as my own for my second.

Again I leave you with the phone number for the Samaritans, 116-123. There is no need to suffer alone. I see your monstrosity. I am not afraid. I have faced my own demons, but not alone. I had help.

116-123.

Remember me when I am gone away,
Gone far away into the silent land;
When you can no more hold me by the hand,
Nor I half turn to go yet turning stay.
Remember me when no more day by day
You tell me of our future that you plann'd:
Only remember me; you understand
It will be late to counsel then or pray.
Yet if you should forget me for a while
And afterwards remember, do not grieve:
For if the darkness and corruption leave
A vestige of the thoughts that once I had,
Better by far you should forget and smile
Than that you should remember and be sad.

— CHRISTINA ROSSETTI,
Remember

To Franz Josef Johannes Gottlieb Vogler
care of Master Antonius
Paris

My dearest Sepperl,

They say it rained on the day Mozart died.

God must see fit to cry on the days of musicians' funerals, for it was pissing buckets when we laid Papa to rest in the church cemetery. The priest said his prayers over our father's body with uncharacteristic swiftness, eager to get away from the wet and the muck and the sludge. The only other mourners aside from family were Papa's associates from the tavern, there and gone when they realized no wake was to be held.

Where were you, mein Brüderchen? Where _are_ you?

Our father left us quite a legacy, Sepp—of music, yes, but mostly of debt. Mother and I have been over our accounts again and again, trying to reconcile what we owe and what we can earn. We struggle to keep from drowning, to keep our heads above water while the inn slowly drags us down to oblivion. Our margins are tight, our purses even tighter.

At least we managed to scrape together enough to bury Papa in a proper plot on church grounds. At least Papa's bones would be laid to rest alongside his forefathers, instead of being consigned to a pauper's grave outside town. At least, at least, at least.

I wish you had been there, Sepp. You _should_ have been there.

Why so silent?

Six months gone and no word from you. Do my letters reach you just one stop, one city, one day after you leave for your next performance on tour? Is that why you haven't replied? Do you know that Papa is dead? That Käthe has broken off her engagement to Hans? That Constanze grows stranger and more eccentric by the day, that Mother—stoic, steadfast, unsentimental Mother—weeps when she thinks we cannot see? Or is your silence to punish me, for the months I spent unreachable and Underground?

My love, I am sorry. If I could write a thousand songs, a thousand words, I would tell you in each and every one how sorry I am that I broke my promise to you. We promised that distance wouldn't make a difference to us. We promised we would write each other letters. We promised we would share our music with each other in paper, in ink, and in blood. I broke those promises. I can only hope you will forgive me. I have so much to share, Sepp. So much I want you to hear.

Please write soon. We miss you. Mother misses you, Käthe

misses you, Constanze misses you, but it is I who miss you most of all.

Your ever-loving sister,
Composer of <u>Der Erlkönig</u>

To Franz Josef Johannes Gottlieb Vogler
care of Master Antonius
Paris

Mein liebes Brüderchen,

Another death, another funeral, another wake. Frau
Berchtold was found dead in her bed last week with frost about
her lips and a silvery scar across her throat. Do you remember
Frau Berchtold, Sepp? She used to scold us for corrupting the
good God-fearing children of the village with our terrifying tales
of the Underground.

And now she is gone.

She was the third this month to pass in such a manner.
We all grow fearful of the plague, but if it is plague, then it is
like no pestilence we have ever known before. No pox, no bruises,
no sign of the disease, none that we can see. The dead appear
unharmed, untouched, save for the silver kisses about their
mouth and neck. There is no rhyme or reason to their passing;
they are old and young, male and female, healthy and infirm,
sound and unsound altogether.

Is this why you do not write? Are you healthy, hale, whole?
Are you even alive? Or will the next letter with your name
upon it contain nothing but heartbreak and another funeral to
arrange?

The elders of the town mutter dire portents under their breaths. "Elf-struck," they say. "Goblin-marked. The devil's handiwork. Mark our words: we are headed for trouble soon."

Goblin-marked. Silver on the throat. Frost on the lips. I do not know what this betokens. I once believed that love was enough to keep the world turning. Enough to overcome the old laws. But I have witnessed the slow unraveling of reason and order in our boring, backward little village, the rejection of enlightened thought and a return to forgotten ways. Salt on every threshold, every entrance. Even the old rector has warded the steps of our church against evil, unbroken white lines that nevertheless blur the boundaries between what is sacred and what is superstition.

Constanze is no help. She isn't much for conversation these days, not that our grandmother ever was. But in truth, she worries me. Constanze emerges from her quarters but seldom nowadays, and when she does, we are never certain which version of our grandmother we will meet. Sometimes she is present, sharp-eyed and as irascible as ever, but at others, she seems to be living in another year, another era altogether.

Käthe and I dutifully leave her a tray of food on the landing outside her room every evening, but every morning it remains untouched. A few bites may be taken of the bread and cheese, drops of milk scattered on the floor like fairy footsteps, but

Constanze seems to take no sustenance beyond fear and her faith in Der Erlkönig.

Belief is not enough to live on.

There is madness in her bloodline, Mother would say. Mania and melancholy.

Madness.

Mother would say that our father drank to chase away his demons, to dull the maelstrom inside. His grandfather, Constanze's father, drowned in it. Papa drowned in drink first. I hadn't understood until I had demons of my own.

Sometimes, I fear there is a maelstrom swirling within me. Madness, mania, melancholy. Music, magic, memories. A vortex, spinning around a truth I do not want to admit. I do not sleep, for I fear the signs and wonders I see when I wake. Thorny vines wound round twigs, the clack of invisible black claws, blood blooming into the petals of a flower.

I wish you were here. You always could straighten my wandering, rambling thoughts and prune my wild imaginings into a beautiful garden. There is a shadow on my soul, Sepperl. It is not just the dead who are goblin-marked.

Help me, Sepp. Help me make sense of myself.

Yours always,
Composer of Der Erlkönig

To Franz Josef Johannes Gottlieb Vogler
care of Master Antonius
Paris

Beloved,

The seasons turn, and still no word from you. Winter is gone, but the thaw is slow to come. The trees shiver in the wind, their branches still bare of any new growth. The air no longer smells of ice and slumber, but neither does the breeze bring with it any scent of damp and green.

I have not stepped foot in the Goblin Grove since summer and the klavier in your room has lain untouched since Papa died.

I don't know what to tell you, mein Brüderchen. I have broken my promises to you twice over. The first by being unreachable, the second by failing to write. Not words, but melodies. Harmonies. Chords. The Wedding Night Sonata is unfinished, the last movement still unwritten. When the sun is high and the world is bright, I can find a myriad excuses for not composing in dusty corners, in accounting ledgers, in stores of flour, yeast, sugar, and butter, in the quotidian minutiae of running an inn.

But the answer is different in the dark. Between dusk and

dawn, the hours when kobolds and Hödekin make mischief in the woods, there is only one reason.

The Goblin King.

I have not been honest with you, Sepp. I have not told you the whole story, thinking I would do so in person. This is not a story I thought I could commit to words, for words are insufficient. But I shall try anyway.

Once there was a little girl, who played her music for a little boy in the wood. She was an innkeeper's daughter and he was the Lord of Mischief, but neither were wholly what they seemed, for nothing is as simple as a fairy tale.

For the span of one year, I was the Goblin King's bride.

That is not a fairy tale, mein Brüderchen, but the unvarnished truth. Two winters ago, Der Erlkönig stole our sister away, and I journeyed Underground to find her.

I found myself instead.

Käthe knows. Käthe knows better than anyone just what it was like to be buried in the realm of the goblins. But our sister doesn't understand what you would: that I wasn't trapped in a prison of Der Erlkönig's making, but became Goblin Queen of my own free will. She does not know that the monster who abducted her is the monster I claim. She thought I escaped the Goblin King's clutches. She does not know he let me go.

He let me go.

In all our years of sitting at Constanze's feet and listening to her stories, not once did she ever tell us what came after the goblins took you away. Not once did she ever say that the Underground and the world above are as close and as far as the other side of the mirror, each reflecting the other. A life for life. How a maiden must die in order to bring the land back from death. From winter to spring. She never told us.

But what our grandmother should have told us was that it isn't life that keeps the world turning; it is love. I hold on to this love, for it is the promise that let me walk away from the Underground. From him. The Goblin King.

I do not know how the story ends.

Oh, Sepp. It is hard, so much harder than I thought to face each day as I am, alone and entire. I have not stepped in the Goblin Grove in an age because I cannot face my loneliness and remorse, because I refuse to condemn myself to a half-life of longing and regret. Any mention, any remembrance of those hours spent Underground with him, with my Goblin King, is agony. How can I go on when I am haunted by ghosts? I feel him, Sepp. I feel the Goblin King when I play, when I work on the Wedding Night Sonata. The touch of his hand upon my hair. The press of his lips against my cheek. The sound of his voice, whispering my name.

There is madness in our bloodline.

When I first sent you the pages from the Wedding Night Sonata, I thought you would read the through-line in the music and resolve the ideas. But I must own my own faults. I walked away, so it is up to me to write the end. Alone.

I want away. I want escape. I want a life lived to the fullest—filled with strawberries and chocolate torte and music. And acclaim. Acceptance. I cannot find that here.

So I look to you, Sepp. Only you would understand. I pray you will understand. Do not leave me to face this darkness alone.

Please write. Please.

Please.

Yours in music and madness,
Composer of <u>Der Erlkönig</u>

To Maria Elisabeth Ingeborg Vogler

Master Antonius is dead. I am in Vienna. Come quickly.

EVER THINE

I can only live, either altogether with you or not at all.

—LUDWIG VAN BEETHOVEN,
the Immortal Beloved letters

THE SUMMONS

"absolutely not," Constanze said, thumping the floor with her cane. "I forbid it!"

We were all gathered in the kitchens after supper. Mother was washing up after the guests while Käthe threw together a quick meal of spätzle and fried onions for the rest of us. Josef's letter lay open and face up on the table, the source of my salvation and my grandmother's strife.

Master Antonius is dead. I am in Vienna. Come quickly.

Come quickly. My brother's words lay stark and simple on the page, but neither Constanze nor I could agree upon their meaning. I believed it was a summons. My grandmother believed otherwise.

"Forbid what?" I retorted. "Replying to Josef?"

"Indulging your brother in this nonsense!" Constanze pointed an accusing, emphatic finger at the letter on the table between us before sweeping her arm in a wild, vague gesture toward the dark outside, the unknown beyond our doorstep. "This . . . this musical folly!"

"Nonsense?" Mother asked sharply, pausing in scrubbing out the pots and pans. "What nonsense, Constanze? His career, you mean?"

Last year, my brother left behind the world he had known to follow his dreams—our dreams—of becoming a world-class violinist. While running the inn had been our family's bread and butter for generations, music had ever and always been our manna. Papa was once a court musician in Salzburg, where he met Mother, who was then a singer in a troupe. But that had been before Papa's profligate and prodigal ways chased him back to the backwoods of Bavaria. Josef was the best and brightest of us, the most educated, the most disciplined, the most talented, and he had done what the rest of us had not or could not: he had escaped.

"None of your business," Constanze snapped at her daughter-in-law. "Keep that sharp, shrewish nose out of matters about which you know nothing."

"It is too my business." Mother's nostrils flared. Cool, calm, and collected had ever been her way, but our grandmother knew how best to get under her skin. "Josef is *my* son."

"He is *Der Erlkönig's* own," Constanze muttered, her dark eyes alight with feverish faith. "And none of yours."

Mother rolled her eyes and resumed the washing up. "Enough with the goblins and gobbledygook, you old hag. Josef is too old for fairy tales and hokum."

"Tell that to that one!" Constanze leveled her gnarled finger at me, and I felt the force of her fervor like a bolt to the chest. "*She* believes. *She* knows. *She* carries the imprint of the Goblin King's touch upon her soul."

A frisson of unease skittered up my spine, icy fingertips skimming my skin. I said nothing, but felt Käthe's curious glance upon my face. Once she might have scoffed along with

Mother at our grandmother's superstitious babble, but my sister was changed.

I was changed.

"We must think of Josef's future," I said quietly. "What he needs."

But what did my brother need? The post had only just come the day before, but already I had read his reply into thinness, the letter turned fragile with my unasked and unanswered questions. *Come quickly.* What did he mean? To join him? How? Why?

"What Josef needs," Constanze said, "is to *come home.*"

"And just what is there for my son to come home *to?*" Mother asked, angrily attacking old rust stains on a dented pot.

Käthe and I exchanged glances, but kept our hands busy and our mouths shut.

"Nothing, that's what," she continued bitterly. "Nothing but a long, slow trek to the poorhouse." She set down the scrubbing brush with a sudden clang, pinching the bridge of her nose with a soapy hand. The furrow between her brows had come and gone, come and gone ever since Papa's death, digging in deeper and deeper with each passing day.

"And leave Josef to fend for himself?" I asked. "What is he going to do so far away and without friends?"

Mother bit her lip. "What would you have us do?"

I had no answer. We did not have the funds to either send ourselves or to bring him home.

She shook her head. "No," she said decisively. "It's better that Josef stay in Vienna. Try his luck and make his mark on the world as God intended."

"It doesn't matter what God intends," Constanze said darkly, "but what the old laws demand. Cheat them of their sacrifice, and we all pay the price. The Hunt comes, and brings with them death, doom, and destruction."

A sudden hiss of pain. I looked up in alarm to see Käthe suck at her knuckles where she had accidentally cut herself with the knife. She quickly resumed cooking dinner, but her hands trembled as she sliced wet dough for noodles. I rose to my feet and took over making spätzle from my sister as she gratefully moved to frying the onions.

Mother made a disgusted noise. "Not this again." She and Constanze had been at each other's throats for as long as I could remember, the sound of their bickering as familiar as the sound of Josef practicing his scales. Not even Papa had been able to make peace between them, for he always deferred to his mother even as he preferred to side with his wife. "If I weren't already certain of your comfortable perch in Hell, thou haranguing harpy, I would pray for your eternal soul."

Constanze banged her hand on the table, making the letter—and the rest of us—jump. "Can't you see it is Josef's soul I am trying to save?" she shouted, spittle flying from her lips.

We were taken aback. Despite her irritable and irascible nature, Constanze rarely lost her temper. She was, in her own way, as consistent and reliable as a metronome, ticking back and forth between contempt and disdain. Our grandmother was fearsome, not fearful.

Then my brother's voice returned to me. *I was born here. I was meant to die here.*

I sloppily dumped the noodles into the pot, splashing myself with scalding hot water. Unbidden, the image of coal black eyes in a sharp-featured face rose up from the depths of memory.

"Girl," Constanze rasped, fixing her dark eyes on me. "You know what he is."

I said nothing. The burble of boiling water and the sizzle of sautéing onions were the only sounds in the kitchen as Käthe and I finished cooking.

"What?" Mother asked. "What do you mean?"

Käthe glanced at me sidelong, but I merely strained the spätzle and tossed the noodles into the skillet with the onions.

"What on earth are you talking about?" Mother demanded. She turned to me. "Liesl?"

I beckoned to Käthe to bring me the plates and began serving supper.

"Well?" Constanze smirked. "What say you, girlie?"

You know what he is.

I thought of the careless wishes I had made into the dark as a child—for beauty, for validation, for praise—but none had been as fervent or as desperate as the one I had made when I heard my brother crying feebly into the night. Käthe, Josef, and I had all been stricken with scarlatina when we were young. Käthe and I were small children, but Josef had been but a baby. The worst had passed for my sister and me, but my brother emerged from the illness a different child.

A changeling.

"I know exactly who my brother is," I said in a low voice, more to myself than to my grandmother. I set a dish heaped high with noodles and onions in front of her. "Eat up."

"Then you know why it is Josef must return," Constanze said. "Why he must come home and live."

We all come back in the end.

A changeling could not wander far from the Underground, lest they wither and fade. My brother could not live beyond the reach of *Der Erlkönig*, save by the power of love. My love. It was what kept him free.

Then I remembered the feel of spindly fingers crawling over my skin like bramble branches, a face wrought of hands, and a thousand hissing voices whispering, *Your love is a cage, mortal.*

I looked to the letter on the table. *Come quickly.*

"Are you going to eat your supper?" I asked, glancing pointedly at Constanze's full plate.

She gave her food a haughty look and sniffed. "I'm not hungry."

"Well, you're not getting anything else, you ungrateful nag." Mother angrily stabbed at her supper with her fork. "We can't afford to cater to your particular tastes. We can barely afford to feed ourselves as it is."

Her words dropped with a thud in the middle of our dinner. Chastened, Constanze picked up her fork and began eating, chewing around that depressing pronouncement. Although we had settled all of Papa's debts after he died, for every bill we paid, yet another sprung up in its place, leaks on a sinking ship.

Once we were finished with supper, Käthe cleared the plates while I began the washing up.

"Come," Mother said, extending her arm to Constanze. "Let's get you to bed."

"No, not you," my grandmother said with disgust. "You're useless, you are. The girl can help me upstairs."

"The girl has a name," I said, not looking at her.

"Was I talking to you, Elisabeth?" Constanze snapped.

Startled, I lifted my head from the dishes to see my grandmother glaring at Käthe.

"Me?" my sister asked, surprised.

"Yes, you, Magda," Constanze said irritably. "Who else?"

Magda? I looked at Käthe, then at Mother, who seemed as bewildered as the rest of us. *Go,* she mouthed to my sister. Käthe made a face, but offered her arm to our grandmother, wincing as Constanze gripped it with all her spiteful strength.

"I swear," Mother said softly, watching the two of them disappear up the stairs together. "She grows madder by the day."

I returned to washing the dishes. "She's old," I said. "It's to be expected, perhaps."

Mother snorted. "My grandmother remained sharp until the day she died, and she was older than Constanze by an age."

I said nothing, dunking the plates in a clean tub of water before handing them to Mother to dry.

"Best not indulge her," she said, more to herself than to me. "Elves. Wild Hunt. The end of the world. One might almost think she actually *believes* these fairy stories."

Finding a clean corner of my apron, I picked up a plate and joined Mother in drying the dishes. "She's old," I said again. "Those superstitions have been around these parts forever."

"Yes, but they're just *stories,*" she said impatiently. "No one believes them to be true. Sometimes I'm not sure if Constanze knows whether we live in reality or a fairy tale of her own making."

I said nothing. Mother and I finished drying the dishes and put them away, wiped down the counters and tabletops, and swept up what little dirt there was on the kitchen floor before making our separate ways toward our rooms.

Despite what Mother believed, we were not living in a fairy tale of Constanze's own making, but a terrible, terrible reality. A reality of sacrifices and bargains, goblins and

Lorelei, of myth and magic and the Underground. I who had grown up with my grandmother's stories, I who had been the Goblin King's bride and walked away knew better than anyone the consequences of crossing the old laws that governed life and death. What was real and what was false was as unreliable as memory, and I lived in the in-between spaces, between the pretty lie and the ugly truth. But I did not speak of it. Could not speak of it.

For if Constanze was going mad, then so was I.

the boy's playing was magic, it was said, and those of discerning taste and even deeper pockets lined up outside the concert hall for a journey into the realms of the unknown. The venue was small and intimate, seating but twenty or so, but it was the largest gathering for which the boy and his companion had ever played, and he was nervous.

His master was a famous violinist, an Italian genius, but age and rheumatism had long since twisted the old man's fingers into stillness. In the maestro's prime, it was said Giovanni Antonius Rossi could make the angels weep and the devil dance with his playing, and the concertgoers hoped that even a glimmer of the old virtuoso's gifts could be heard in his mysterious young pupil.

A foundling, a changeling, the concertgoers whispered. *Discovered playing on the side of the road in the backwoods of Bavaria.*

The boy had a name, but it was lost amidst the murmurs. *Master Antonius's student. The golden-haired angel. The fair youth.* His name was Josef, but no one remembered, save for his companion, his accompanist, his beloved.

The companion had a name as well, but there were none

who thought it worth noting. *The dark-skinned boy. The Negro. The servant.* His name was François, but no one bothered to use it, save for Josef, who held his beloved's name on his lips and in his heart.

The concert marked Josef's introduction to cultured Viennese society. Ever since France had beheaded or expelled the nobles from their borders, Master Antonius found his coffers growing lean in his adopted Parisian home, with wealthy patrons emptying their funds into Bonaparte's army. So the old virtuoso left the city of revolution and returned to the city of his greatest triumphs with the hopes of hooking golden fish with younger, prettier bait. At present they were hosted by the Baroness von Schenk, in whose salon the performance was to be held.

"Do not fail me, boy," the maestro said as they stood in the wings, waiting for their entrance. "Our livelihood depends on you."

"Yes, maestro," Josef said, his throat hoarse. He had slept ill the night before, his stomach knotted tight with nerves, his dreams broken by the half-remembered sound of thundering hooves.

"Keep your head together," Master Antonius said warningly. "None of this whining and crying for home. You are a man now. Be strong."

Josef swallowed and looked to François. The youth gave a slight reassuring nod, a gesture not lost on their teacher.

"Enough," Master Antonius growled. "You," he said, pointing to François, "stop indulging him, and *you*"—he pointed to Josef—"pull yourself together. We cannot afford to lose our heads now. We will start with a few selections I have composed, then we will move on to the Mozart as planned, *ça va?*"

Josef shrank beneath his master's glower. "Yes, maestro," he whispered.

"If you are good—and *only* if you are good—you may play Vivaldi for the encore." The old virtuoso pinned his pupil with a beady glare. "None of that *Der Erlkönig* nonsense. This audience is used to the music of the greats. Do not insult their ears with that monstrosity."

"Yes, maestro." Josef's voice was scarcely audible.

François took note of the boy's flushed cheeks and clenched jaw, and wrapped his warm hand around his beloved's tightened fists. *Be patient,* mon coeur, the touch seemed to say.

But the other boy did not reply.

Master Antonius parted the curtains and the boys walked out before the audience to polite applause. François sat himself down at the pianoforte while Josef readied his violin. They shared a look, a moment, a feeling, a question.

The concert began as planned, with the pupil playing selections composed by the master, accompanied by the youth at the keyboard. But the audience was old, and they remembered how divine the master's playing, how transporting the sound. This boy was good: the notes were clear, the phrasing elegant. But there was something missing perhaps—a soul, a spark. It was like hearing the words of a favorite poet translated into a foreign tongue.

Perhaps they had expected too much. Talent was fickle, after all, and those who burned brightest with it often did not last.

The angels take Antonius if the devil does not get to him first, they once said of the old virtuoso. Such gifts were not meant for mortal ears.

Age had gotten to Master Antonius before either God

or the Devil, but it did not seem as though his pupil were graced with the same divine spark. The audience dutifully clapped between each piece and resigned themselves to a long evening of little significance, while from the wings, the old virtuoso fretted and fumed at his pupil's diminishing returns.

Another set of eyes watched the performing pair from the opposite wing. The eyes were the startling, vivid green of emeralds or the deep waters of a summer lake, and in the dark, they glowed.

Selections finished, Josef and François moved on to a Mozart sonata. The room fell quiet, dull, laden with the inattentive lull of genteel boredom. A soft snore rose from the back of the salon, and in the wings, Master Antonius silently seethed. Yet still those green eyes watched the boys from the shadows opposite. Waiting. Wanting.

When the concert was over, the audience rose to their feet, perfunctorily calling for an encore. Josef and François bowed, while Master Antonius gripped his wig, sending plumes of powder into the air. *Vivaldi save us,* he thought. *The Red Priest hear my prayer.* Josef and François bowed once more, sharing another private look, the answer to an unspoken question.

The youth settled himself back by the keyboard, dark fingers and white-laced wrists poised over black sharps and natural ivories. The boy tucked his violin under his chin and raised his bow, the horsehair quivering with anticipation. Josef gave the tempo and François responded in kind, the two of them weaving a tapestry of melody between them.

It was not Vivaldi.

The concertgoers sat straighter in their seats, their attention sharpened on the edges of their confusion. They had never heard such playing before. They had never heard such *music* before.

It was *Der Erlkönig*.

In the wings, Master Antonius buried his face in his hands with despair. On the other side of the salon, the green eyes gleamed.

A chill wind seemed to blow through the room, though no breeze ruffled the lace or feathers at the audience's necks. The scent of earth, of loam, of deep, dark places seemed to grow around them, a cavern of sound and sensation. Was that the *plink* of a dripping cave or the distant rumble of a wild stampede? Beyond the corners of their eyes, the shadows began to writhe, the cherub-faced *putti* and ornately carved flowers on the columns in the corners of the salon taking on a sinister aspect. They did not look too closely, for fear that the angels and gargoyles had transformed into demons and goblins.

All save one.

The vivid green eyes observed the changes wrought by the music and disappeared into darkness.

When the encore was done, there was a moment of silence, like the world holding its breath before a storm. Then the thunder broke to raucous shouts and applause, for the audience would cheer lest they cry for the tumultuous anxiety and elation that roiled through them all. Master Antonius ripped the wig from his head in disgust and left the scene in a huff.

He passed a beautiful green-eyed woman on the way, carrying a silver saltcellar in the shape of a swan. They tipped their heads in passing as the old virtuoso retired to his rooms and the woman limped toward the salon. He did not see her begin to pour a line of salt on the threshold to the concert.

He did not hear the hooves for the praise raining down upon his pupil, and missed the postman arriving with a message.

"Master Antonius?" the courier asked when the green-eyed woman answered the door. A bright scarlet poppy was pinned to her bodice.

"He has retired for the evening," the woman said. "How may I help you?"

"These are to be delivered to his pupil, a Herr Vogler?" The postman reached into his satchel and removed a bundle of letters, each written in the same desperate hand. "They are addressed to his old residence in Paris, but it wasn't until now that we were able to find him here in Vienna."

"I see," the woman said. "I shall see that they are delivered to the proper person." She tipped the courier a gold coin, who tipped his hat in response before riding off into the night.

The green-eyed woman stepped over the salt into the salon, taking care that her skirts did not break the line of protection. Back in the shadows, she scanned the letters for a signature.

Composer of Der Erlkönig.

She smiled and tucked the letters into her bodice before hobbling off to congratulate the boy and his black friend.

And upstairs, Master Antonius tossed and turned in his bed, trying to drown out the sound of hooves, howls, and hounds, wondering if the Devil had come for him at last.

The following morning, the scullery maid was turned out for stealing salt and the old virtuoso was found dead in his room, lips blue, with a curious silver slash at the throat.

THE PRICE
OF SALT

the next day dawned bright and bitter as I woke to the sound of Mother and Constanze arguing. Their voices carried all the way from my grandmother's quarters down to Josef's room where I slept, and if I could hear their shouting from this tucked-away corner of the inn, then all of the guests could as well.

"*Guten morgen*, Liesl!" my sister cried when I emerged from the kitchens into the main hall. A few guests were already gathered there, some to eat, others to grumble and grouse about the noise. "Will breakfast be ready soon?"

Käthe's voice was full of forced cheer, her cheeks pulled tight in a conspicuous smile. Behind her, I could see the disgruntled faces of our customers. If Papa were still alive, he would have smoothed tensions over by making merry with his violin. If Papa had been alive and sober, that is. If he had ever been sober.

"What is the meaning of this?" Mother's words were as

clear as shards of glass. "Look at me, Constanze. Look at me when I'm speaking to you!"

"Ahaha," I tittered nervously, trying to match my sister's smile, but it sat ill upon my face. "Soon. Breakfast will be ready soon. I just—I, ah, I need to, um, ask Mother about something."

Käthe glared at me, although her pleasant expression never faltered. I squeezed her hand and nimbly sidestepped her grasp, making my way upstairs to the dragon's lair for a reckoning.

The door to Constanze's room was shut, but Mother's anger was loud and sharp. She never lost her skill for projection from her days as a singer in a troupe, and knew how to make her voice a force to be reckoned with. I did not bother to knock and turned the handle instead, bracing myself for the scene inside.

The door didn't budge.

Frowning, I jiggled the handle and tried again. The door remained stuck fast, as though there were something blocking the entrance. Whatever it was seemed braced against the bottom of the door, a chair or a dresser, perhaps. I shoved my shoulder against the jamb.

"Constanze?" I called, trying to modulate my voice so the guests wouldn't overhear. "Constanze, it's Liesl." I knocked again, and pushed harder. "Mother? Let me in!"

There was no sign that either of them heard me. I put more weight against the door and suddenly felt it give a little, moving inward with an unexpected scraping sound. I pushed harder and harder, winning inch after inch against an invisible opponent. Finally, there was enough room between the door and the jamb for me to squeeze through.

I immediately tripped upon entering, stumbling over an

enormous mound of dirt, twigs, and leaves, scraping my knees in the process. "What on earth—"

I was hands-deep in a pile of soft loam, freckled with bits of rock and stone. I looked up. Constanze's room was in a shambles, every corner of it covered in dust and detritus from the woods outside. For a brief moment, I had the disorienting sense that I was not inside, but standing in a winter forest, the ground dusted with a light covering of snow. Then I blinked, and the world rearranged itself back into its proper order.

It was not snow. It was salt.

"Do you know the price of salt?" Mother cried. "Do you know how much this will cost us? How could you do this, Constanze?"

My grandmother crossed her arms. "For protection," she said stubbornly.

"Protection? Against *what*? Goblins?" Mother gave a bitter laugh. "What about debtor's prison? What can you do to protect us from *that*, Constanze?"

With a sinking heart, I could see that Constanze had somehow dragged bags of salt up from the cellar the previous night and upended them, dumping several pounds'—several months'—worth on to the floor. This was more than the lines across every threshold and every entrance we had drawn together on the last nights of the year. My grandmother had not spilled salt as a precaution, but as insurance.

Mother caught sight of me by the door. "Oh, Liesl," she said hoarsely. "I didn't hear you come in." She ducked her head, fishing about her apron pocket for something I could not see. It was only when the light of the late morning sun struck her cheek that I realized she had been crying.

I was thunderstruck. Mother, who had suffered twenty-odd years of emotional abuse from Constanze, never once cried before her children or her mother-in-law. It was a point of pride for her to endure with stoicism the very worst excesses of my father and my grandmother, but this had broken her. She was sobbing over spilled salt, agonized tears of anguish.

I did not know what words of comfort to offer, so I reached into my pocket for my handkerchief and silently handed it to her. The only sound was Mother's wretched weeping, a sound which terrified me more than any screaming match. Mother was resilient. Resolute. Resourceful. Her hopelessness more than her hiccoughs frightened me.

"Thank you, Liesl," she said thickly, dabbing at her eyes. "I don't know what came over me."

"I think Käthe needs some help with the guests downstairs, Mother," I said quietly.

"Yes, yes, of course," she said. And then she was gone, unable to stand another moment in Constanze's presence. For a moment we stood there, my grandmother and I, staring at each other, at the salt and filth on the floor between us.

"Girl," she rasped.

I threw up a hand. "I don't want to hear it, Constanze." I yanked open the broom cupboard in her room, roughly shoving a bucket and washrag in her hands. "Either you help me clean up this mess or you march straight on downstairs to help Käthe with breakfast."

Her lip curled. "You would leave a fragile old woman to make her way down those rickety stairs by herself?"

"You were obviously fine carrying all this salt from the cellar by yourself," I said shortly. "Get started, Constanze, or make yourself useful in another way. Clean this up." I grabbed the broom and dustpan and began sweeping.

"And leave us vulnerable to the Hunt?"

I resisted the urge to grab my grandmother by the shoulders and shake some sense into her. "The days of winter are over. We'll be fine."

To my surprise, Constanze stamped her foot like a petulant child. "Do you not remember the stories, child?"

In all honesty, I did not. While Josef and I had delighted in our grandmother's gruesome tales of goblins and gore, it was always stories of *Der Erlkönig* to which I returned over and over as a child. My hand went to the ring I wore on a chain about my throat. The ring was silver, wrought into the shape of a wolf with two mismatched gemstone eyes, one blue, one green. The Goblin King had ever been more than a myth to me—he was a friend, a lover, a man. I released the ring, and lowered my hand.

"The Hunt are . . . spectral horsemen," I hedged. "Riders who galloped before death, disaster, or doom."

"Yes." Constanze nodded. "Harbingers of destruction and the unraveling of the old laws. Do you not see, girl? The signs and wonders?"

I vaguely remembered now what she had told me of the Wild Hunt. It was said *Der Erlkönig* himself rode at their head. I frowned. But I thought he only ever wandered the world above during the days of winter. Was it with the unholy host? To search for a bride? Yet it took a sacrifice from a maiden to bring the world back to spring. Every year? Once a generation? What exactly were the old laws that maintained the balance between worlds?

"Bettina?" Startled, I glanced at Constanze, whose dark eyes were fixed on my face with a faraway expression. "Do you see?"

I took a deep breath, trying to calm my racing mind, trying to catch up to the present moment. "See what?"

"In the corner," she croaked. "It watches us. It watches you."

I blinked, wondering if it were me or my grandmother who had lost the plot. I could not grasp her thoughts, could not follow, could not understand, but was Constanze alone in her tower of nonsense, or was it me?

I shook my head and glanced over my shoulder. "I see nothing."

"Because you do not choose to see," Constanze said. "Open your eyes, Bettina."

I frowned. Constanze occasionally called me by my given name, Elisabeth, but more often I was merely *girl* or *child*. Never Liesl, and certainly never Bettina. I watched my grandmother carefully, wondering if she were with me, or in the midst of one of her flights of fancy.

"Well?" she harrumphed.

With a sigh, I turned to look again. But as before, the corner was empty of anything save dust, dirt, salt, and filth.

"It's on your shoulder now," Constanze went on, pointing to a spot by my left ear.

I swear, she grows madder by the day.

"A strange little homunculus, with hair like thistledown and a pinched expression." She leered, a spiteful smile on her thin lips. "It doesn't seem to like you very much."

A chill ran down my spine, and for the briefest of moments, I felt the weight of tiny black claws on my back. *Thistle.*

I whirled around, but the room was still empty.

A cracked cackle came from Constanze behind me. "Now you begin to understand. You're just like me. Beware,

Bettina, beware. Heed the horn and the hound, for something wicked this way comes."

I snatched the wash bucket from my grandmother's hands and shoved the broom and dustpan at her. "I'm going to fetch some water from the well," I said, trying to hide the shaking of my voice. "You had better start straightening up before I come back."

"You can't escape it." A wide grin plastered itself across Constanze's face, and a flame of recognition lit her dark, dark eyes.

"Escape what?"

"The madness," she said simply. "The price we pay for being *Der Erlkönig's* own."

Giovanni Antonius Rossi was dead. Plague or poison, the Viennese weren't sure which, but when the old virtuoso's pupil and servant were found missing, they suspected the latter. But the body was untouched when the Baroness's valet discovered him—his golden-buckled shoes still on his feet, his silver fob-watch still in his pocket, his jeweled rings still pinching the base of his gnarled and weathered fingers. No thieves they, those two boys, but their absence was damning, for if they had nothing to do with their master's death, then why disappear?

The city guards came for the body, to be borne away and dumped in an unmarked grave like all the rest. The Viennese no longer buried their dead within city limits for fear of spreading disease, and highborn and low, rich and poor, moldered together in common. No party followed the funereal wagon that left the city gates down the road to St. Mark's Cemetery, for although Master Antonius had been a famous virtuoso in life, he was just another poor musician in death.

From darkened alleyways, François watched the sad pine box grow smaller in the distance. When he came to dress the old man and found a body instead, he knew he would have to make himself scarce. He had seen what happened to other men his color once their masters died under mysterious circumstances. They were not around to tell their side of the tale. The youth knew his skin would make him a target, just as he knew his master's death would be the cause of his doom.

François had known this day would come ever since he was torn from his *Maman's* arms and thrust like so much baggage onto the ship that bore him away from Saint-Domingue to France. No shelter, no security would ever be his, not when he was the only black pearl among a dozen ordinary ones. So he went to ground after Master Antonius's death, vanishing into the foxholes where he could blend in with the shadows and dregs of the underworld. And so he would have stayed with the madams and mistresses of the brothels and pleasure dens were it not for his one weakness: his heart.

He had always known that Josef was not meant for his world. The trading of flesh and favors, the crass, the carnal, the dirty, the vulgar: such things made his companion wilt and wither, but it was more than a distaste for the common and the low. The love François bore for the other boy was sweet and tender, hot and fierce all at once, but Josef never evinced anything more than a polite disinterest in such affairs. François knew that Josef's love for him was more metaphysical than physical. He understood that their bond was not of the body, but of the mind and of the soul.

It was what made their treatment at the hands of their former master so unbearable. So when François found Josef that fateful morning, standing over the body of their teacher with a glazed expression on his face, he held no blame, only fear in his heart.

In the immediate aftermath of their flight from Vienna above, François and Josef took shelter with L'Odalisque, one of the grand dames of the underworld. Unlike several of the girls in her employ, she was not a Turk, but peddled fantasies of the Orient with cheap silk and opium. There were many things François regretted about staying with L'Odalisque, but it was the laudanum he regretted most.

Josef had always been delicate, different, dreamy. He was moody and melancholy, and François had learned to temper those tempests with patience and compassion, but the girls of L'Odalisque were not so caring. Most were lost in an opium haze, their dilated eyes large and lustrous, their language lush, their movements languid. When they first arrived at L'Odalisque's, Josef had been quiet and withdrawn, but as the days, weeks, and months went on, François watched the blue of his beloved's eyes slowly become swallowed by the black of dreams and delirium.

He tried hiding the bottles of laudanum. He took over managing L'Odalisque's ledgers, painstakingly accounting for each trip to the apothecary, the doctor, the midwife. He never saw a single drop of the opium tincture cross Josef's lips, but the blond boy grew hazier and more distant by the day, speaking in cryptic riddles, half-finished thoughts, words twisting in upon themselves like a labyrinth, *mise en abyme*.

At first François thought it was his imperfect grasp of German that was the source of his confusion. The girls of L'Odalisque often spoke of a tall, elegant stranger who approached them in their poppy-laced stupor.

"What is the tall, elegant stranger?" François asked.

The dark and the danger, the fear and the fury, they would reply. *He rides with horse and with hound, but beware! It is madness to stare into his eyes.*

And so François believed it was merely a fanciful turn of phrase for laudanum dreams, until one day, they found Josef standing over the body of the youngest girl, Antoinette. She had been discovered dead in her room, lips blue, and a silver slash on her throat.

The tall, elegant stranger! the others cried. *The stranger strikes again!*

But Antoinette had not been a lover of the poppy. Not for her was the endless sleep of one more sip, one more taste, one last oblivion.

"Who is this stranger?" François demanded of Martina, Antoinette's best friend in the house. "What does he look like?"

"He looks like me," Josef said dreamily. "I look in the mirror and the tall, elegant stranger is me."

It was then that François knew his beloved had gone where he could not follow. He thought of the promise he had made Josef's sister in another time, another life.

Take care of him.

I will.

And he would.

Later that night, he stole paper, ink, and Josef's prints of the suite known as *Der Erlkönig*, scribbled with notes and markings in the blond boy's inimitable, unpracticed hand.

"I'm sorry, *mon coeur*," François whispered. *"Je suis désolé."*

Slowly, carefully, he lifted letters and rearranged them into a plea for help.

Master Antonius is dead. I am in Vienna. Come quickly.

François hoped his beloved's sister would come soon.

He could no longer do this alone.

THE MAD, THE FEARFUL,
THE FAITHFUL

there was no more salt to be had.

The food was bland and the guests complained, but we had neither the time, the funds, nor the credit to replenish the stores Constanze had ruined. Still, we managed for a while yet, but when Käthe privately told me that there wasn't even enough salt for baking, I knew things had become quite dire.

"What do we do?" my sister whispered as we took stock of the stores in the cellar. We had enough flour, root vegetables, and cured meats to carry us over for the next few weeks, but little else. Ever since Papa died, the butchers, the bakers, and the brewers of town had been unwilling to extend his widow and daughters the same credit, and demanded payment in hand.

"I don't know." I rubbed at my temples, trying to soothe away a headache growing there. I had not slept well, troubled by dreams I could not remember upon waking. Images melted away like snowflakes when I opened my eyes, but unease remained like a bitter chill long after I had risen. "Are you sure the money is quite gone?"

Käthe fixed me with an exasperated look. I knew as well as she that our coffers were long since gathering dust. The inn held on to profit like a sieve held on to water.

"Perhaps we can ask Hans if we could borrow some salt," I suggested.

Käthe stiffened. Ever since my sister had ended their betrothal, we had seen little of our erstwhile family friend. He had since married a distant cousin from Munich, and they were expecting a babe come next spring. No, we could not ask Hans. Not anymore.

"What of . . . what of the parish?" Käthe said slowly. "Surely someone at the church could help us."

I frowned. "You mean accepting charity?"

My sister fell silent. "What other choice do we have?" she said gently.

"We're not paupers!"

"Yet." Although her voice was soft, I felt the words like an arrow to my chest.

"Josef could—" But I did not finish the sentence.

"Josef could what?" Käthe's eyes flashed. "Send us money? How? By what means?" She shook her head. "He has no position, no job, and no master now. We can't afford to bring him home, nor can we afford to go to him. Our brother is stranded, Liesl, just like us."

Sepperl. My heart tightened with pain at the thought of my brother so far away. Was he alone? Afraid? Lost? Hurt? Josef was fragile, frightened, and friendless but for François. What would happen to them both without Master Antonius's protection? Perhaps I could find a way to get to them. To Vienna. Shed our names, our pasts, and start anew. Find jobs. Play music.

"Liesl."

The ideas came one after another, bubbling up to the surface of my mind faster and faster, fizzing my blood with possibilities. After all, did we not have gifts? Were we not talented? Perhaps I could find work as a music teacher. Perhaps my brother would find a position in a nobleman's orchestra. Why struggle to keep our heads above water when the present was dragging us down to debtor's prison?

"Liesl."

My mind was on boil, the thoughts drifting into steam. We could cut ourselves free and float away. Burn down the inn, dance in the embers, revel in the ashes. We could, we could, we could—

"Ow!" I looked up, startled. Käthe had pinched me. "What on earth was that for?"

Instead of spite, there was an expression of worry on my sister's face. "Liesl, have you heard a single word I've said?"

I blinked rapidly. "Yes. Going to the church. Accepting God's charity."

She studied me. "It's just . . . you had a strange look in your eye, is all."

"Oh." I absently rubbed at the red pinch mark on my arm, trying to rally my thoughts into some semblance of order. "Well, you can't blame me for being a little reluctant to go begging."

Käthe's lips tightened. "We can't feed ourselves on pride, Liesl."

As loath as I was to admit it, she was right. For a long time, we had managed on our creditors' goodwill and Papa's promises to pay. Anything remotely valuable we had owned had disappeared into Herr Kassl's pawn shop to cover our debts, and we had nothing left to give. The weight of the Goblin King's ring lay heavy on my breast, strung on a simple length of twine. Whatever the ring's true value, it was worth infinitely more to me. My austere young man had given it to me when we made our vows, and again when we broke them. The ring was a symbol of the Goblin King's power, but more than that, it was a promise that his love was greater than the old laws. One could not place a price on a promise.

"I can go if you'd like," my sister offered. "I can speak with the priest." -

The memory of the church steps lined with salt rose suddenly in my mind. I remembered then that the rector was the oldest person in our village—the oldest save for Constanze, perhaps. A man of the church, but I suspected he was also a brethren of the old faith.

"No, I'll go," I said quickly. "I'll speak with the rector."

"The rector?" Käthe asked, surprised. "That creepy old bat?"

"Yes." Dimly, I recalled seeing the rector leaving leftover communion wafers and wine out on the back steps of the church when I was a child. *For the fair folk,* he had said. *Our little secret,* Fräulein. I was certain he was one of *Der Erlkönig*'s own.

Käthe looked skeptical. "Are you sure?"

I nodded.

"All right," she sighed. "I'll let Mother know."

I nodded. "Wish me luck."

"It's not luck we need," my sister said grimly. "It's a miracle."

The village seemed deserted when I arrived. While the unseasonal cold was keeping most people indoors, the town seemed diminished. Chastened. There was hardly anyone out and about their business, and what few folk I did meet kept their heads down and their gaze averted. There was a touch of tension in all their faces, an anxiety that seemed to permeate the air and make it difficult to breathe. I told myself this wasn't strange; after all, we had just buried several members of the town, lost to that mysterious plague.

Elf-struck, the voices of the elders whispered in my mind.

I shook off my unease and wrapped my red cloak tighter about me.

The village church stood on the eastern edge of town, its western façade opening directly onto the market square. It was easily recognizable by its crooked belfry, built and rebuilt over the years. Our little town had never been big or grand enough to warrant a more beautiful place of worship; its whitewashed walls were plain and dirty, the nave and altar unadorned. It was, as the stories went, the oldest structure around for miles, built when Charlemagne was still a pagan king.

The church doors were closed between services, but unlocked, open to any pilgrim in search of solace. I had never been much for grace or God, for if I had any holy place, it was the Goblin Grove. I gripped the ring at my throat, feeling a bit as though I were about to do something illicit or naughty. I stared at the wooden doors before me, noticing for the first time that the panels on its face were covered with carvings. They were odd, the figures misshapen and bent, but the details lovingly and intricately carved. My eye fell on the bottom right panel, which depicted a tall, thin figure with curling ram's horns growing from his head standing in a field of flowers. Roses? Poppies? The . . . devil? I squinted. Something seemed to be scratched along the edges, less purposeful than the rest. Writing? A message?

I knelt for a closer look. There, in Gothic script, were the words: *Ich bin der umgedrehte Mann.*

I am the inside-out man.

Foreboding ran its icy finger down my spine. I shivered, the hairs standing up along my arms.

"The stranger comes, the flowers leave."

I jumped, tripping on the edge of my skirt with a startled yelp. The old rector stood beside me, popped up out of nowhere like a toadstool after spring rain. I recognized him by the tufts of wispy cotton that patched his crown and his large, oversized black robes. He was a familiar sight in these parts, usually perched on the steps of the church like a strange little gargoyle, peering at passersby from beneath bushy white brows.

"I'm s-sorry?"

"The inscription. That's what it says. *The stranger comes, the flowers leave.*" The rector pointed to panel before me, where the phrase HOSTIS VENIT FLORES DISCEDUNT was carved in Roman letters.

Gone was the horned figure, and in its place was a young man with hands outstretched. A corona haloed his head, while around him lambs frolicked and played. An image of our Lord and Savior, not the devil. Not *Der Erlkönig.*

I wasn't going mad. I wasn't.

I wasn't.

"I—I see," I stammered.

The rector's dark eyes glittered. Up close, I could see that cottony hair sprouted from his ears, along his jaw, and the tip of his chin, giving him the appearance of a new-hatched chick. "Do you? You see what is before you, but can you see past the nose on your own face?"

"Beg pardon?" Bewildered and self-conscious, my hand flew up to cover my nose.

But he seemed to take no notice. "You learn much by reading the old histories," he continued. The old rector maintained the church register, recording the births, marriages, and deaths of the town. "You begin to see patterns. Cycles. You understand that what has come before will come again."

I had no response to such a cryptic statement, so I held my tongue. I was beginning to regret my visit to town.

"But I don't imagine you are here to study the old histories, *Fräulein*," the rector said with a wry smile.

"I, er, no." My fingers twisted in the folds of my apron and I steeled myself to ask. To beg. "I have come . . . I have come to ask you for a favor."

"A favor?" Those tufty cotton-white brows lifted with interest. "What can the house of God do for you, my child?"

I kept my eyes on my feet. "Our—our stores of salt are . . . depleted, *Herr Rektor,* and I—I would be most grateful for your assistance . . . and your charity." My angry flush of shame heated the air around my cheeks.

"Ah." The old man's voice was neutral and expressionless, but I dared not meet his gaze. "Is it Constanze?"

The question startled me into looking at him. His dark eyes were unreadable, but I sensed a hint of pity in his features. Pity . . . and sympathy.

"Not precisely," I said carefully. "But she is, in a manner of speaking, involved."

"Let me guess. She was trying to protect herself from the Wild Hunt."

I stared at the line of white crystals at my feet. "Yes," I whispered.

The old rector sighed and shook his head. "Come with me, *Fräulein*." He turned and led me to the north side of the church. Unlocking a small door, he held it open and bade me enter. I took care not to disturb the unbroken line of salt on the threshold, stepping into the dimly lit transept.

"Follow me."

I flinched at the feel of his dry, spindly fingers on my right elbow, but the rector carefully guided me down a small flight of steps as my eyes adjusted to the gloom. At the foot of the stairs, he unlocked yet another door and gestured inside. I frowned, wondering where we were headed. The church cellars?

The door slammed shut behind me, sealing me in complete darkness. I thought of stories of maidens and lovers buried alive in crypts and catacombs, and the creeping sensation of having been locked in a tomb crept up and around my throat.

"*Herr Rektor*—" I began.

A snap, and then a flame blazed to life, hovering in midair before me like a fairy light. I squinted against the brightness and saw the old rector with a lantern in hand, although I could not guess how he had lit it so quickly with no taper or candle to kindle it.

"We are in the old vestry," he said in answer to my unasked question. "Priests used to get robed in here before coming up to the chancel through there." He gestured toward a door on the far side with a tilt of his head. "But Father Abelard prefers to dress in the choir. Says he finds it unsettling down here."

I found myself rather sympathetic to our priest. "What are we doing here?" I asked.

"We discovered that our cellar had flooded during that

brief period of spring warmth last week, so we moved our stores here."

He cast his light over the space, which was much larger than I had thought. In addition to the barrels of foodstuffs brought up from their cellars, the room was stocked with several shelves, all laden with reams upon reams of dusty paper, parchment, and portfolios. It was only then that I realized that these were the records and history of our little backwoods village.

"Ah yes, my life's work." The flickering light of the lantern cast deep shadows, carving strange shapes into the planes of the old man's face. His nose grew long and sharp, his lips pinched and thin. His cheekbones protruded painfully, giving him a rictus grin. "I have traced the descent of every man, woman, and child in this town," he said proudly. "The fruits grown from the bed of blood and seed from whence this village had sprung. But there are some families that disappear into time. Stories with beginnings and middles, but no ends."

"Such things happen in a village as small as ours," I said. "Mothers, sons, fathers, daughters, sisters, brothers, aunts, uncles, cousins, neighbors—over time we all become hopelessly tangled."

The rector shrugged. "Perhaps. But there are mysteries not even I can unravel. Lives and lines cut off in the middle, vanished, unfinished. Yours is one such family, *Fräulein*."

I shot him a sharp look. "Excuse me?"

He smiled, showing the tips of his yellowed teeth. "Did Constanze ever tell you about her sister, Magda?"

Magda. I thought of my grandmother calling Käthe by that name the other night. Mother had dismissed it as yet another sign of Constanze's deteriorating mind, but I had not known she had had a sister. "No," I said slowly. "But I have heard the name."

"Hmmm." The rector lifted the lantern to a shelf a few inches above his head. He ran his fingers along the spines of years bound in calfskin leather, searching for the right book, the right generation. His fingernails were overgrown and black with dirt and ink. "Ah, here we are."

He pulled down an enormous tome, nearly as large as he, setting it on the desk with a dusty slam. The book immediately fell open to a page, the leaves settling down on either side of a well-worn seam in the spine. The rector held the lantern aloft and pointed at an entry in the middle with a long, clawed finger.

MARIA MAGDALENA HELOISE GABOR

Magda. Constanze's sister. My grandmother had been a Gabor before she married.

"Your grandmother's family was one of the oldest, if not necessarily the most respectable," the old man said. I bristled. I might not have been a Gabor, but the slight still stung. "Strange and queer, the lot of them. *Elf-touched,* they were called in the old days."

I frowned. "Elf-touched?"

The rector's yellow smile slowly spread wider across his face. "The mad, the fearful, the faithful. Those who dwell with one foot in the Underground and another in the world above."

All the hairs rose at the back of my neck. *There is madness in her bloodline.* But was it madness? Or an unseen connection to something greater, something beyond mortal ken? Many of the beautiful and broken branches of my family tree were touched with genius, a drive to create that turned them inside out and upside down. There was my great-great-great-uncle Ernst, a talented woodcarver and carpenter, whose unearthly and transformative figurines were deemed heretical and destroyed. They still told stories of my distant cousin Annabel, whose poetic and twisted ways of speech cast her first as a prophet, and then a witch.

And then there was Papa. And Josef.

And me. Guilt throbbed in me at the thought of the klavier in my bedroom, untouched and unplayed since I had returned from the Underground.

"Magda was the youngest of Eleazor and Maria Gabor's children," the rector went on, handing the tome over to me to read. I staggered under its unexpected weight, heavy with heritage and history. "There were three: Bettina, Constanze, and Magda."

Bettina. I understood better now why my grandmother had called me that. "What happened?"

He gestured to the book before me with his chin. Turning the pages, I moved back and forward in time, the parchment growing thinner with age. Agnes, Friedrich, Sebastian, Ignaz, Melchior, Ilse, Helena, generations upon generations of Constanze's family. My family. Entire lives sprouted, then withered away beneath my fingers. They were born, got married, had children, died. All recorded in an impersonal hand.

"I don't understand," I said. "What am I looking for?"

The rector's dark eyes bored into mine. "The ending. Magda's ending."

Frowning, I returned to the book. Babies were born and, if they were lucky, grew old. Some never made it out of infancy; others lived to see several generations of their own children predecease them. There was no rhyme or reason but chance. I didn't understand why Magda's ending was so important.

Until I couldn't find it.

Constanze and Bettina's lives were well-recorded: their births and baptism, their marriages, their children. Bettina's story seemed to end with her marriage to Ansel Bergman, but Constanze's continued on through her children: Johannes, Christoph, Constanze, another Constanze, Georg, another Constanze, Josef, and Franz. Every single one of my aunts and uncles had their deaths written alongside their births, indelibly inked into history.

But not Magda.

I went backward and forward in time, searching for an exit, an ending. But no matter where I looked, there was no further sign of Magda, no marriages, no children, not even a death. Her life was unfinished, and if it weren't for the fact of her birth, recorded by the rector several decades before, she might have never existed.

"There is—there is no ending," I whispered.

The rector folded his hands into his voluminous sleeves. "Yes," he said simply.

"Do you know what happened to her? Did she die? Move away? People don't just . . . disappear." I looked up from the tome, spooked and unsettled. "Do they?"

"People don't disappear, but their stories become forgotten," he said in a soft voice. "It is only the faithful who remember."

"And you remember."

The rector nodded his head. "She was taken. Stolen." He swallowed. "By the Wild Hunt."

The world narrowed to a single point of focus before me, the small, steady light of the lantern flame. All else was dark, and I felt myself falling, spiraling down, down, down into the abyss of fear. I tried to recall everything I knew of the Wild Hunt—what they were, who they were, and why they rode abroad—but a cold void of anxiety spun at the heart of my swirling mind. My hand went to the ring at my throat, feeling the comforting bite of the wolf's head in my palm.

"How?" I croaked. "Why?"

It was a long moment before the rector replied. "No two stories of the unholy host agree. It is said their appearance presages some unspeakable catastrophe: a plague, a war, or even"—he flicked his gaze at my clenched fist—"the end of the world."

I tightened my grip on the Goblin King's ring.

"Others say the Hunt rides abroad when there is an imbalance between heaven and hell, between the Underground and the land of the living, sweeping through the world above to claim what is rightfully theirs. The old laws made flesh: given steel and teeth and hounds to reap what they are owed."

The void at the heart of me was threatening to engulf me whole. "A sacrifice," I said hoarsely. "The life of a maiden."

To my surprise, he gave a dismissive snort. "And what sort of sacrifice would a maiden's life be? A heartbeat? A breath? A touch?"

Think you your beating heart the greatest gift you could give? No, mortal, your heartbeat is but the least and last.

"Then what . . ." But I could not finish. *Then what was my sacrifice for? What was* his? What was the price to be paid by my austere young man for letting me walk away?

"Oh, child," the rector said with a sigh. "Life is not the body"—he tapped my hand, the one curled around the Goblin King's ring—"but the soul."

"I don't—I don't—"

"You don't understand?" He shook his head. "The queer, the wild, the strange, the elf-touched—they are said to belong to the Goblin King. Their gifts are fruits of the Underground, their genius, their passion, their obsession, their *art*. They belong to him, for they are *Der Erlkönig's* own."

Der Erlkönig's own. It was what Constanze had always called us, me and Josef, but I had always thought she meant those of us who believed in the Underground.

"And Magda was taken because of her . . . gifts?"

The rector's face was grim. "Magda was taken because she believed. It is madness to bear witness to the Hunt, and she was already mad."

A sudden, chilling thought crossed my mind. "What happens to those who do not believe?"

Through the haze of the flickering lantern light, our gazes met. "I think you know, *Fräulein*."

I did.

Elf-struck.

a king stands in a grove, hooded and cloaked, a tall, elegant stranger. His back is turned, his face gazing into the formless mist around him, both defiant and sorrowful, as the sound of thundering hooves and the bell-like bays of hunting hounds fill the air.

His features are hidden by shadow, but wisps of feathery-white hair peek out from the depths of his hood, a glint of pale eyes mirroring the strange, depthless light around him. In the distance, shapes begin to coalesce, the passing tatters of fog into banners, mist into cresting waves, into horses' manes, into men. Men with spears, men with shields, and men with swords. An unholy host.

They are coming, Elisabeth.

The king throws up his arm in a violent gesture, as though shielding himself from attack. The force of the movement knocks back his hood, revealing a face both terrible and beautiful. His skin is stretched tight across his cheekbones and patterns of darkness swirl about his hairline, ears, jaw, and neck, shadows staining the skin there an inky black. The darkness crawls up his throat and around his chin, and on his head, rams' horns grow from a ragged nest of silver hair.

He is both a man and a monster.

His faded eyes held color once, a mismatched blue and gray-green, but now they are pale, so pale his pupils are but a pinprick in a sea of white. But it is not only the colors of his mismatched gaze that are fading; it is his memories, his manhood, his music. He tries to hold on to them with hands that have changed, hands that were once slender and elegant. A musician's hands. A violinist's hands.

Elisabeth.

But these memories slip through his fingers, fingers that are now broken, mangled, and strange. His nails are blackened into claws, and there is an extra joint in each finger that had not been there before. He can no longer remember the sound of her voice, the feel of her skin, the scent of her hair, only the smallest snippet of song. A melody, a tune. He hums it to keep sane, to keep human.

What are monsters but mortals corrupted?

The clatter of hooves grows louder, along with the clang of steel and the crack of the whip.

Don't look, don't look. Don't look or you shall go mad.

The king holds his hands before him and covers his face. The host surrounds him, both there and not there. A dangerous company. A wild hunt.

Her name, they say, their voice as one.

The king shakes his head. To give her name to the old laws would be to give up the last of the man he had been, so he swallows it down, feeling it warm the space where his beating heart used to be. He had made her a promise.

Her name, the host repeats.

Still he holds it close, refusing to yield. He will pay the price. He will bear the cost.

The host does not ask a third time. A snap, a lash, and

the king throws his head back in a wordless roar of pain. His eyes go pure white, the inky shadows staining his skin, consuming it utterly. The rams' horns atop his head grow twisted, and his face stretches in an expression of pure, monstrous menace. He climbs atop a stallion, which rears and screams in a hellish cry, its flaming eyes two stars in a night sky. Then he turns and bolts off into the heavens, to claim his own—*Der Erlkönig's* own—and bear them back to the Underground and the old laws.

And as he rides, his heart still beats her name.

Elisabeth. Elisabeth. Elisabeth.

THE USE
OF RUNNING

i had been sent home with a measure of salt, enough to last us through the month, if we didn't let Constanze get her hands on it. And yet the old rector's tale of Magda, the old laws, and the unholy host haunted me on my way back to the inn, ghostly hoofbeats thudding in my ears. Snippets of story floated across the surface of my mind, and I tried to gather them into something I could hold. When wisps of clouds blew themselves across the face of the moon, Constanze used to say they were the souls of the departed, joining the eternal hunt in the sky. What became of the stolen? What became of my great aunt? I thought of the circle of alder trees we called the Goblin Grove, the suggestive shapes of the trunks and branches, like limbs frozen in an eternal dance.

The shivers that wracked my body had nothing to do with the icy wind blowing through my cloak.

They say the Hunt rides abroad when there is an imbalance between the Underground and the land of the living.

I had crossed the barrier between worlds, had walked away from the Goblin King and my vows last summer. Had my leaving caused a rip in the fabric of the world, allowing the spirits and ghouls and denizens of the Underground to escape? Was I in danger from the Wild Hunt?

My hands were full of salt, but I felt the weight of the Goblin King's ring against my chest, bouncing with every step like the beating of my heart. If I had upset the ancient balance, then what was his promise worth?

Don't look back, he had said. And I hadn't. And I wouldn't. But now I wasn't so sure.

On my way back home, I searched for any sign of new life, faint traces of green among the gray. Nothing yet, for the freeze after nightfall was sure to kill any tender shoot struggling to grow, but the days were growing warmer. Mud squelched beneath my boots as I walked along the path. Surely the seasons still turned as they always had and ever would.

Yet I could not shake off the sound of hooves.

Elf-touched. Elf-struck.

I did not know what to tell Käthe. Or Mother. For all that my sister had crossed the veil dividing the worlds, she was not one of *Der Erlkönig's* own. She believed, but her faith was simple and uncomplicated. For her, reality and unreality was as starkly divided as the barrier between the land of the living and the realm of the goblins. There were no maelstroms lurking in my sister. She was all calm waters and smooth sailing. I envied her.

It was in moments like these I missed my brother most.

I thought of the cryptic letter we had received. *Master Antonius is dead. I am in Vienna. Come quickly.* I would have doubted the letter was from Josef at all, if it weren't for the unmistakable handwriting on the page. The shapes of the words were half-formed, the letters improperly joined up, the hand of a boy who practiced his scales far more than he had his penmanship.

There were so many things I wanted to say to Josef. So many things I had tried to say in the myriad letters I tried to write and the few I had actually sent. So many drafts, so many sheets of paper consigned to the flames, searching for words, finding them, excising them, losing them, muddling them. So many questions I wanted to ask, wanted to know, wanted to complain, wanted to explain, only to end up with a tower of nonsense.

In the end, words had been insufficient. Music was the language my brother and I shared down to our bones. Melodies were our sentences, movements our paragraphs. We spoke best when we let our fingers do the talking—mine over my keyboard, his over the strings. It was in our playing, not my letters, that I could make Sepperl understand.

How I could make myself understand. The restlessness, the anxiety within me. The feeling of incompleteness and dissatisfaction, my frustration with my inability to execute my ideas on the page, either in words or in song. I could not catch my own mind, my thoughts racing past in a blur, like fingers rushing through sixteenth notes without regard to tempo.

The hoofbeats grew louder.

With a start, I realized that the hoofbeats weren't in my mind, but the sound of an actual horse riding down the road. I glanced over my shoulder and beheld a rider in black, his dark cloak streaming out behind him like wings. Beneath the brim of his hat, his hair was pale, the planes of his face narrow and sharp. His horse was a large black stallion, its eyes wild and teeth bared, a creature running straight from the mouth of hell.

My heart stopped. It couldn't be—could it?

As the horseman drew nearer, I saw that his eyes were a simple twig brown, not a mismatched green and gray. The white hair was nothing but a wig between the tricorn hat. And still my excitable heart leaped and trembled like a skittish thing, searching for the familiar in every unknown, every unfamiliar thing.

It was not the Goblin King.

Of course it wasn't the Goblin King.

The rider rushed past, and I jumped out of the way to avoid being splattered. I watched the horseman and his steed disappear around a bend in the road, feeling a strange combination of relief and disappointment. I had not been sleeping well, of course my mind would conjure specters where there were none. And yet the expectation—the *hope*—that I might see my Goblin King again was the dagger with which I stabbed myself. It couldn't be. It cannot be. I must move on.

Then, to my astonishment, the horse and its rider came galloping back.

I paused by the side of the road, waiting for the horseman to pass again, but instead he slowed at the sight of me, bringing his steed from a gallop to a trot, a walk, a stop.

"*Fräulein* Vogler?" the rider asked.

I was stunned. "Y-yes?" I managed. "I am she. How can I help you?"

The rider did not answer, but reached into the satchel at his side. *A courier*, I realized. A postman. Then my heart lifted. *Josef!*

He pulled out a small leather pouch, leaning down to hand it to me. The pouch was rather heavy for its size, and clinked musically as I accepted it. Mystified, I was about to open the pouch to examine its contents when the courier handed me a letter.

All else was forgotten as I snatched the letter from his hands, not caring whether or not I bent or battered the edges. I had been waiting for word—for an explanation—from Josef for so long that I was past caring about such trivial matters as polite manners or social niceties.

The weight of the paper was heavy and expensive, faintly perfumed with a sweet scent that lingered despite the many miles it had traveled. The letter bore an official-looking wax seal, a crest with the image of a flower pressed into it. A rose, or a poppy perhaps? It did not seem like something my brother would send—the paper, the ink, the scent were all wrong—yet I clung to hope, because I wanted to believe my brother would send for me. Would write—*really write*—to me, instead of leaving me behind.

"Who sent this?" I asked.

But the postman, having delivered his message, merely tipped his hat to me and rode off. I watched him disappear down the road, then returned to the letter in my hand and turned it over. My heart stuttered, tripping over its excitement and dread. There, written in an unfamiliar, elegant, educated hand, was an address:

To the composer of Der Erlkönig.

"Is everything all right?" Käthe asked once I got home. A pile of chopped root vegetables and salt pork lay on the sideboard, while a pot of water bubbled away above the stove. "You look as though you've seen a ghost!" She laughed, but sobered at my expression. "Liesl?"

With trembling hands, I handed the small leather pouch out for my sister to hold.

"Is that the salt?" she asked with a frown.

"No." I set the salt down on the table, then set the leather pouch down beside it. It clinked musically. "But it might just be our miracle."

Käthe sucked in a sharp breath. "What is it? Who's it for? And who's it from?"

"I think"—I swallowed—"I think it's for me."

I held up the letter, with the words *To the composer of* Der Erlkönig clearly visible in stark, black ink. Its faintly sweet, cloying scent perfumed the air, clashing horribly with the onions and herbs my sister was prepping for supper.

"But it must be from a very important person," Käthe observed. "Look at the paper! And"—she squinted—"is that a crest?"

"Yes." Upon closer examination, I thought the seal might be a poppy, not a rose. A strange choice.

"Well, are you going to read it?" My sister went on with making supper. "Let's see what this mysterious nobleman wants with the composer of *Der Erlkönig,* eh?"

I broke the wax sealing the letter and unfolded the page. "Dear Mademoiselle Vogler," I read aloud. "Forgive me for this most unconventional and improper method of correspondence. You and I are strangers to each other, but pray do not be alarmed when I write that I feel as though we have already been acquainted."

"Ooh, a secret admirer?" Käthe teased. "Liesl, you sly thing!"

I shot her a stern look. "Do you want me to read this or not?"

"Sorry, sorry," she said. "Do go on."

"Last month, I happened upon the performance of an unusual piece of music, played on the violin by an unusual young man. I cannot adequately express the extent to which the music moved me, a profound and deep resonance, as though the notes touched upon a nerve of fire in my very soul."

I caught my breath. An unusual piece of music, played on the violin by an unusual young man.

Josef.

When my sister harrumphed impatiently, I coughed, willing myself to continue for her benefit.

"I confess I was possessed of an obsession with your work. Not a single person in Vienna could tell me the name of the composer, only that the piece had been published in an obscure collection of curated works by Giovanni Antonius Rossi before his death. I knew the old man well, and do not hear much, if anything, of his voice in the piece."

Josef must have taken my strange little bagatelle and had it published under Master Antonius's name. In fairness, the decision made sense, for the old virtuoso was a known musician with an established output. Yet as grateful as I was to have found an audience for my work, the knowledge that *Der Erlkönig* was not published under my own name niggled at me, a worm of discontent burrowing its way through my heart.

"The young violinist has been as mysterious as you, my dear genius," I went on. "After the old virtuoso's passing, he and his companion vanished entirely. Unfortunately, I am afraid I was forced to take matters into my own hands."

The feeling of vague disquiet sharpened into one of foreboding. The creeping sensation of trespass, of violation, of having my privacy invaded rose up like vines from the author's words, threatening to strangle me with dismay. I read on in silence.

After Master Antonius's death your correspondence was discovered among the old virtuoso's effects. I saw that the letters were addressed to a Franz Josef Vogler and I managed to preserve them before they were discarded, unread. The letters were dated these several months past, with a most curious signature in each one: Composer of Der Erlkönig.

I went utterly still. I thought of Josef's anguished summons, the plea for me to join him in Vienna. Guilt twisted my heart into knots. I should have answered him sooner. I should have found a way to get to him. I should have tried harder to get in touch, I should have, I should have, I should have—

"What, Liesl?" Käthe said. "What is it? Don't leave me hanging."

Shaking, I cleared my throat and continued reading aloud.

"I—I do not take pride in my next actions, but I simply had to . . . had to know the identity of the composer of the work. I . . . I . . ." But my voice failed me, trailing into nothing.

I read one of the missives, the letter went on. *Forgive me, mademoiselle, for this gross trespass upon your privacy, but I discerned immediately the nature of your relationship with Herr Vogler—namely, that you are his sister and his muse.*

My hands were trembling so badly I could barely make out the words on the page.

Fearing that they were friendless and alone in this world, I went through great pains to discover the whereabouts of your brother and his companion. Never fear, mademoiselle, for they are safe and well provided for by yours truly, a most devoted patron and sponsor of their careers. Now if you could find it in your heart to forgive an overeager enthusiast of your music for this breach in confidence, I write you now to urge you to join us in Vienna. A talent such as yours must not be wasted in a backwater Bavarian town and should be celebrated to great acclaim. Funds, influence, power: I lay all that I possess before you as your kindly benefactor. I will take no offense should you decline my offer, but can only urge you to accept, as I look forward to hearing more from the remarkable mind behind such otherworldly music.

As a token of good faith, I present to you a payment of fifty florins, to be spent at your discretion. Spend them as foolishly or as wisely as you choose, for they are my gift to you in thanks for the gift of your music. However, should you choose to spend them by purchasing coach fare to Vienna for yourself and your family, give my name to the factor in your town and he will advance whatever additional funds you need to make a new life here.

Yours faithfully,

Graf Procházka von und zu Snovin

"Liesl?" Käthe prompted. "Liesl!"

The letter slipped from my numb fingers, fluttering to the floor. Dropping her knife with an exasperated sigh, Käthe snatched it up before it touched the ground and read the words of our unknown benefactor for herself.

"I just—my goodness—how—" My sister could not properly string her words together, the strand connecting her thoughts breaking, scattering them everywhere. She looked up at me, her blue eyes alight with joy and relief and . . . hope. It shone brighter than the sun and I had to look away, lest I be blinded. My eyes watered, and I told myself it was due to my sister's radiance, not the rush of relief. "Could this possibly be real?"

Numbly, I picked up the leather pouch and opened it. Gold glinted in the late afternoon sun, and I poured the coins out over the table. Käthe gasped.

"What does this mean?" she cried.

What did this all mean indeed? I tried to smile, but felt strangely removed from the matter. Surely beneath the numbness of shock there was a wellspring of excitement and anticipation, but everything seemed as though I were in a dream. The scene unfolding around me had a slow, surreal feel, as though I were still asleep, caught between waking and slumber. A path had opened before me that I had not seen before. I had wanted to compose music. I had wanted to escape. There was a time when I was the Goblin Queen, when my wishes had weight, when I could twist and shape the world to my will, and now opportunity lined itself up like dominos before me.

But if there was anything I learned from my time as *Der Erlkönig*'s bride, it was that nothing came without a price.

"This . . . this is a godsend! Think of all we could do for the inn!" Käthe counted the fifty florins with all the meticulous exactitude of a miser. ". . . forty-seven, forty-eight, forty-nine"—she laughed with delight—"fifty!"

I realized then I had not heard that laugh in an age, the halls of the inn silent of its musical peals, as bright as a bell. I had not known then how I had relied upon her laugh to chase away the storm clouds in my heart.

"You'll come with me to Vienna, of course," I said. It wasn't a question.

Käthe blinked, surprised by my sudden turn in conversation. "What?"

"You'll be coming with me to Vienna," I repeated. "Won't you?"

"Liesl," she said, eyes shining with tears. "Are you sure?"

"Of course I'm sure," I said. "It'll be just like the Ideal Imaginary."

She laughed again, and the sound was as pure as a spring morning. The what-if games my little sister and I had played as girls had been ways to pass the time, a space we created untouched by the grime and grief of ordinary drudgery. A world where we were princesses and queens, a world as beautiful and as magical as any my brother and I had made together.

"Just imagine, Käthe." I took her hand in mine. "Bonbons and handsome swains waiting on us hand and foot."

She giggled. "And all the silks and velvets and brocades to dress ourselves in!"

"An invitation to a different ball every night!"

"Masques and operas and parties and dancing!"

"Schnitzel and *Apfelstrudel* and Turkish coffee!"

"Don't forget the chocolate torte," Käthe added. "It's your favorite."

I laughed, and for a moment, I allowed myself to pretend we were little girls again, when our wants and our dreams were as closely entwined as our fingers. "What if," I said softly.

"Not a what-if," my sister said fiercely. "A when."

"When," I repeated. I could not stop smiling.

"Come," Käthe said, rising to her feet. "Let's go tell Mother. We are going to Vienna!"

Vienna. Suddenly, the words on our lips were no longer a wish, but a possibility. I was excited . . . and frightened. I thought of the manic, frantic fantasies I had spun for myself and told myself it was the uncertainty of what we would find there that scared me. I told myself it was the fear of not knowing anyone save for Josef and François, of being lost and alone in a big city without our friends and family to guide us. What I did not tell myself was that it was a warning I had heard from a face wrought of goblin fingers, and a promise I was not sure could be fulfilled.

You cannot leave the Underground, mortal, not without paying the price.

I stared at the broken wax seal, the poppy flower torn in half, and wondered if we were running down the wrong road.

there was a kobold in the house, or so the girls of L'Odalisque claimed. A spiteful little sprite, it liked to play pranks on them—stealing trinkets, switching shoes, sullying their silks and ribbons with dust and dirt from the gardens. In close quarters in a house full of women, such things often went astray. A slit stay here, a slashed gown there, bits of tit for tat as they settled scores and slights with one another.

But these tricks were not the ordinary tallies of mundane retribution borne of a jilted lover, a disinterested client, an unpaid favor, the girls of L'Odalisque would protest. They were the cruel and capricious whims of an invisible spirit. No rhyme or reason but chance and discord, not mischief but malice. When Elif lost her mother's pearl ring. When Aloysia's perfume was switched for cat piss. When the miniature portrait of L'Odalisque's late husband in her locket was defaced. The kobold seemed to know exactly where each person's sore spots were and spared no one. Personal, pitiless, precise.

Maria and Caroline began carrying iron in their pockets. Edwina and Fadime made charms warding off the evil eye.

L'Odalisque herself began lining the thresholds with salt, but no spell or superstition kept the sprite at bay.

It's no use, Josef said in a distant, misty voice. *The monster is in the mirror.*

By now they were all used to the blond boy's queer turns of phrase. He never quite seemed tethered to the present, seeming to trod on ether and air instead of earth and soil. Josef was neither innocent nor pure—he lived in a bawdy house, after all—yet there remained an aura of untouchability or distance to him that was both charismatic and off-putting. He was often seen wandering through the receiving rooms and reception halls of L'Odalisque's at odd hours of the night, silent as a *geist* floating from chamber to chamber. The rarc times he was heard to speak seemed like prophecy from on high, just as cryptic and just as obtuse as the words of an oracle.

Not a kobold, but a king. He rides ahead of the end. My end.

The girls shook their heads with affection and pity. *Lost,* they said. *Laudanum-addled.* And then, in lowered voices. *Lacking.*

Indeed as the days went on, Josef seemed less and less present. François watched with despair as time seemed to whittle his companion down to his essence, a being not meant for his world. The sunshine in Josef's hair faded to the colorless gold of dusk or dawn, the blue in his summer-sky eyes dimming to a cloudy winter gray. He had grown tall and lanky with his height, his skin stretched pale over hollow bones. He was a wisp, a wight, a waif, and François wanted nothing more than to breathe life and love back into his beloved's lungs.

Music was their only connection now, a tether growing thinner and more tenuous by the day. At first they would play suites by Vivaldi and concertos by Haydn, Mozart, and even the upstart Beethoven, much to the enjoyment of the patrons of the house.

I'm a fancy establishment now, L'Odalisque would say.

As long as you don't raise the prices! the johns would reply.

But even in his playing Josef seemed to be drifting away. His notes were as exact and as clear as ever, but his soul was not in the moment or the melodies. His music was no less beautiful than it was before, only now it was less weighty, less . . . human. François closed his eyes, and turned his head away.

Late at night, the house could hear Josef play the melancholy airs and tunes of a childhood lost and left behind. The girls of L'Odalisque kept ungodly hours, but such was the nature of their trade. The spaces between transactions, the quiet between breaths, this was where Josef lived. He liked to stand before the mirrors in the girls' quarters, watching the smoothness of his bowing arm, the movement of his fingers across the neck of his violin. Sometimes he wondered which was the reflection and which was the reality, for he felt as though he lived under glass, on the other side of emotion, the other side of home.

Until the glass disappeared.

Josef had not played *Der Erlkönig* since his last public performance, since the last time he had been seen in the world of Vienna above. He was frightened of the feelings the piece wrought in him—not just longing and homesickness, but rage, despair, frustration, futility, sorrow, grief, and hope. On the road with Master Antonius, he had played the bagatelle in secret, sharing the music with François like contraband. Then, *Der Erlkönig* had seemed both like shelter and an escape, the sensation of his sister's arms enfolding him in a protective embrace.

But now it felt like a rebuke. Or perhaps a bruise. Having emotions at all felt tender, sore, and Josef was comfortably numb. He saw François's sadness but did not share it. He was living under glass, and it was safe.

That night, he decided to open up old wounds.

As he was wont to do, he stood before the mirror and began to play. The instant his bow touched the strings, the world changed. The scent of pine and damp filled the room, the deep green of sleeping woods and earth. Shadows deepened the mirror-blue night with depth, and before him stood the tall, elegant stranger, also playing a violin.

Josef felt no fear or surprise, only a distant sense of recognition. He remembered this figure from his dreams, as familiar to him as an old friend. The stranger was cloaked and hooded, his face lost to darkness, but those long hands matched his bowing and fingering, phrase for phrase, the music matched in perfect unison.

And then, little by little, note by note, Josef felt the lightening of his spirit. A door had been opened, and for the first time in a long time, he was present. A faint, persistent drumming filled his ears. Hoofbeats? Or his heart?

The stranger stood in a room much like the one in which Josef was standing. He watched with fascination as the figure turned and explored the room, picking up a hairbrush here, a ribbon there. He pocketed a ring, a coin, a slipper. He unraveled a scarf, tied knots into corset strings, and hid a powder box on a shelf where no one could see. The stranger turned to Josef, and a slash of light illuminated the sharpened tips of a wolfish grin. He pressed his finger to his lips in a quiet gesture, and Josef found himself mirroring the movement. Up close, those long, elegant hands were twisted and odd, and Josef saw that there was an extra joint in each finger.

"Who are you?" he whispered to the stranger in his reflection.

The figure cocked his head. Blond curls peeked out from beneath the hood, a quizzical tilt of the chin. Josef nodded and the stranger's grin widened. Slowly, deliberately, he raised those extra-jointed fingers to the edge of his hood and pushed it from his head.

It was his own face that stared back at him.

The kobold, the monster in the mirror, was him.

The thundering of Josef's heart grew louder and louder, until it drowned out all sound and sense. He collapsed onto the floor, as shadows passed over the face of the moon, spectral riders on a spectral chase.

And outside, a woman with green eyes that glowed in the dark watched the clouds quake and quiver as they passed over the house of L'Odalisque, the small, satisfied smile of a hunter curling about her lips.

A MAELSTROM
IN THE BLOOD

i sent our reply to our mysterious new benefactor the
following day. Mother had been delighted by the news,
and for the first time in an age, I saw her smile. The
years fell away from her face, smoothing the furrow that had
taken up permanent residence between her brows since Papa
had died. Her blue eyes sparkled, her cheeks glowed, and I
was reminded that our mother was still a beautiful woman.
Several of the guests must have agreed, for they gave her
appreciative sidelong glances when they thought she
wouldn't see.

Count Procházka must have been very wealthy indeed, for
when we presented his name to the factor in town, we were
advanced an ungodly sum of money. After the coach fare,
luggage, and wardrobe were taken care of, we still had funds
left over. I made good with our vendors in town, establishing
new lines for credit for Mother and the inn, but Käthe and I
allowed ourselves one small luxury each. My sister bought

trimmings for a pretty new bonnet while I bought myself paper and a fresh set of quills, neatly trimmed. It did not matter that I had not composed or touched the Wedding Night Sonata since I had returned from the Underground; I could write in Vienna. I *would* write in Vienna.

The next few weeks passed by in a blur, a flurry of preparations that seemed to take up every waking minute of our days. I was mostly focused on packing what few belongings we had that would travel easily: our clothes, our shoes, what few trinkets we had left that weren't sold to the pawnbroker to pay off Papa's debts.

"What will you do with your klavier?" Käthe asked. We were in Josef's room, sorting through my things. "Will you have the Count send for it once we are settled there? Or do you intend to sell it ere we depart?"

I hadn't given the matter much thought. In truth, I hadn't given music much thought at all.

"Liesl," Käthe said. "Are you all right?"

"Of course," I said, making a conspicuous show of sorting and organizing my notes. "Why wouldn't I be?"

She ran her fingers over the faded ivory keys. I could feel her watching me as she pressed a note here, a note there. F-G-E-D sharp. A-A-A-F sharp. As she played tunelessly, aimlessly, I felt an inordinate sense of jealousy at her freedom, her nonchalance, her indifference. For my sister, music was just noise.

"It's just," she said after a moment, "I haven't heard you play in a while, that's all."

"I've been busy."

"You're always busy," she observed. "But that's never stopped you before."

I felt a pang—of guilt, of shame, and not a little frustration.

Käthe was right, of course. No matter how tired I was at the end of the day, no matter how full my hours had been with cooking and cleaning, I had always managed to find time for music, magic, and the Goblin King. Always.

"I'm surprised you noticed," I said tartly. "I didn't think you cared."

"Just because I don't have your gifts doesn't mean I don't notice or care," she said. "I know *you*, after all."

To my horror, my eyes welled up with tears. I had pushed aside and made excuses for my reluctance to sit down and compose for so long that I hadn't realized my music was a weeping wound that would not heal. Käthe's kindness was an antiseptic, and it stung like hell.

"Oh God, Liesl," she said, stricken. "I didn't mean—"

"No, no." I surreptitiously wiped at my cheeks. "It's all right. You didn't do anything. I'm just overwrought, is all. It's been a long week."

Käthe's penetrating blue gaze was patient, but I did not elaborate. There was a part of me that wished I could confess and confide everything to her. How I hadn't played or composed in an age because I was unable to face the enormous effort it would take to sit, to work, to labor. Because whenever I worked on my magnum opus, I felt another's presence beside me—his touch, his kiss, his caress. Because I was afraid she wouldn't believe me; or worse, that she would.

"It's nothing," I insisted, a sudden, absurd urge to giggle bubbling up my throat. "Come, why don't we play the Ideal Imaginary World to while away the tedium of cleaning and packing? I'll start. Once we arrive in Vienna and are settled in our new apartments, Count Procházka will throw a ball in our honor. Josef will be there, of course, playing my newest concerto. Perhaps his friend François will be there also, and they will play a duet. And you—you shall be decked out in the finest jewels, with all of Vienna's most eligible bachelors vying for your hand, plying us with chocolates and sweets and— Ow!"

My sister had pinched me. Again. It seemed to be becoming a habit. Käthe pushed the hair from my face, frowning as she peered into my eyes. "When was the last time you slept?" she asked

I glanced down at my hands. I clenched them into fists, resisting the urge to hide them in my apron pockets.

"Liesl."

I closed my eyes.

"Is it . . . is it the Goblin King?" Her voice was soft.

I flinched. "No," I said quickly. "No, of course not." It may not have been the truth, but neither was it entirely a lie.

Käthe was quiet, but I could feel her eyes upon me. "I wonder," she said after a moment, "if it's not Vienna you're running toward, but a kingdom you're trying to outrun."

I sucked in a sharp breath and opened my eyes. It was as though my sister had pulled a splinter from my heart that I hadn't even known was there. "Käthe, I . . ." But my voice faded to nothing at the look of pity on her face.

"You can be running toward something or running from something, but you cannot do both at once," she said gently.

Tears burned along my lashes, but I refused to let them spill. "Who says I'm running at all?" I said, forcing a laugh. Käthe's laughter came more easily now, and I wanted her to smile, to joke, to look away from the dark corners of my soul so they would not be subject to the sunshine of her sympathy.

But my sister did not laugh. "Ah," she said softly, "but what's the use of running"—she lifted her eyes to mine—"if you are on the wrong road?"

As the weeks went on and our time at the inn wound down to a close, my sister's words needled me, pinpricks of guilt and resentment poking holes in my comfortable avoidance. I hated how Käthe had made me confront my lack of composing, my inability to sit down and *play*. It had been easier to believe the pretty lie that I had been too busy, too tired, too preoccupied, too *anything* but scared to revisit the Wedding Night Sonata.

But the truth was far uglier.

I did not *want* to work on the Wedding Night Sonata.

The fear was easy to face. So much was lost in translation from my mind to the page, and I was afraid the music I played would fail to do justice to the music I heard in my head. I was not skilled enough, not trained enough, not good enough.

But I had vanquished these fears before. I had spent an age Underground cracking open my ribs to lay my insecurities bare before me, to face them without flinching. I had the courage and fortitude to conquer my doubts, and I would not back down now.

It was the hope I could not bear.

Don't look back, the Goblin King had told me. And I hadn't. But in the moments between sleeping and waking, the hollows that loneliness carved from my soul were large enough to swallow me whole. Playing the Wedding Night Sonata conjured up ghosts, both literal and metaphorical.

I could have let it rest. I could have passed the time with my klavier in other ways, with other composers, other compositions. Yet the abyss always beckoned at the sight of those black and white keys, the temptation to break my promises and run back and back and back.

The coach that would bear us to Vienna was arriving in three days. Nearly all was in readiness, and all that was left was to pick up the flotsam and jetsam of our lives. For Käthe, those were her ribbons and trimmings and other pieces of finery and frippery, and for me, it was the klavier.

We had managed to sell the instrument to a merchant in town, who had amassed enough wealth to want to enrich it with musical accomplishments. He had even managed to hire a tutor all the way from Munich to teach his wife and daughters how to play The young man would be arriving after we had gone, but the merchant would be bringing along a hired wagon and some hired hands to bring the keyboard back to his home on the morrow.

It would be my last night with the klavier; I ought to say goodbye to it like a proper friend.

After the inn had settled down for the evening, I sat down at its bench, feeling both awkward and not. The feel of the wood beneath my thighs was the same as it had always been, yet somehow different, somehow new. I was relearning the instrument, experiencing it with fresh fingers and fresh eyes. I had forgotten how to take it for granted.

Moonlight edged my world in silver, illuminating the yellowed keys of the klavier, turning them a dull gray. I ran my hands over the keyboard, and hesitated, my fingers poised with notes unplayed. A prickle skittered along the side of my neck, invisible spiders crawling up my spine, an unseen breeze stirring my hair against my skin. I shuddered, trying to brush away the cobwebs of doubt. The weight of a promise sat heavy on my breast, hung from a chain about my throat. A wolf's-head ring. His ring.

I played a few chords, softly, quietly, although I was far enough removed from the rest of the inn in Josef's old room that the guests would not overhear. I ran through a few scales, warming up my fingers before settling into some exercises by Clementi. I was avoiding another song, another melody that was fighting its way to the forefront of my mind.

The longer I played, the easier it began to feel. There were no ghosts in my home, no regrets or longing made flesh. But it wasn't only my mind that carried memories; it was my muscles, my fingers, my heart. Slowly, but surely, the music began to change.

The Wedding Night Sonata.

No. I wrenched my thoughts away from the past and toward the future, my brother, Vienna.

Vienna. Where one could attend a concert of the newest symphony by Haydn, see the latest play by Schikaneder at the Theatre auf der Wieden, or mingle with the greatest minds of our generation in a myriad of coffeehouses and salons. Vienna, where artists and philosophers flooded the streets, conversation flowing like wine. Vienna, where there were no sacred spaces, no places where the worlds above and below existed together.

Where Josef was free.

Where I might be free.

I clenched my fists, wringing sour notes from the klavier. *No.* I will not. I would not.

Yet like a boat borne backward along the current, I found myself sinking back into the music. My music. In my memory and in my mind, a violin began to play the second movement, the adagio. I closed my eyes and let myself be swept out to sea.

I let myself drown.

Elisabeth.

Images rose up behind my closed lids. Long, elegant fingers across the neck of a violin, the smooth motion of a bowing arm, the rise and fall of a body in thrall to a musical tide.

I played.

Working on the sonata was as easy and as difficult as falling asleep. My body instinctively knew how, even if my mind had forgotten. My fingers found their places on the keyboard, occasionally forging new paths, new combinations. Composing was the process of working through an idea, the gathering of snippets of melody, of sound, of rhythm, of harmony. The refinement of phrases, counterpoint, and supporting lines. Drafts upon drafts upon drafts until a theme emerged, a story, a resolution.

I did not have a resolution.

Elisabeth.

A weight settled onto the bench beside me. The scent of pine and deep woods filled the room, tinged with the edges of ice and winter, though the spring rains had already begun outside. My breathing grew shallow and quick as I tried to silence the thudding of my racing heart.

Elisabeth.

A cool breeze, the barest breath, a whisper against my ear. The Goblin King had always called me Elisabeth.

"Be, thou, with me," I whispered to the listening dark.

My skin tingled as a tender touch brushed the hair from my face, the softest press of lips against my cheek. My hand flew up to my face, as though my fingers could capture his kiss in my grasp.

"*Mein Herr,*" I said, voice trembling. "Oh, *mein Herr.*"

There was no answer.

I wished I had a name to call him. *You cannot love a man with no name*, he had said. He had thought he was doing me a kindness. The man he had been was nothing more than a shadow now, his name irrelevant, lost to the old laws as the price he paid to become *Der Erlkönig*. But it was not a kindness. It was cruelty—cruel to be here in the world above, alone, alive, and apart, our story abandoned.

"Please," I said hoarsely. "Be, thou, with me. Please."

A sharp intake of breath. A gasp of pain. The weight on the bench beside me shifted, and I waited for the feel of the Goblin King's arms around me once more.

But when I opened my eyes, the room was empty.

It was always empty.

I buried my face in my hands, and cried.

A soft, shushing sound, the sound of branches rubbing together in a winter wind filled my ears. I thought of Twig and Thistle, my goblin handmaidens, of their long, crackling fingertips brushing against their dry, scaly palms. Goblin applause.

I rose to my feet. "Hullo? Is anyone there?"

Silence answered, but it was not an empty quiet, not as it had been before. I fumbled my way across the room, thrusting my hands out before me. Grotesque, otherworldly creatures resolved themselves into drapes, chairs, and other mundane, everyday objects.

I was alone.

And yet.

I should sleep. Fatigue wore down my defenses like a rising tide against a dike, leaving me vulnerable to the vortex at the heart of me. I undressed down to my chemise and quickly climbed into bed, shivering against the night.

Darkness doused my eyes, but sleep did not come. I

reached for its shores, straining and swimming toward slumber, but it remained out of reach. I desperately wanted to rest, to shut my eyes and my mind and my heart.

Don't think. Feel.

"Oh, *mein Herr*," I sighed. "I wish I could. I wish I could."

As my mind drifted into slumber, I felt the weight of a name upon my heart. I wrapped my hand around his ring at my throat and tried to wake up, tried to remember, but it was gone before the dreams came.

S he calls to him.

A monster lifts his head as the sound of music filters down from the world above. The Hunt has ridden him hard, and his hands and teeth are stained silver with the souls of the disbelieving. His eyes are blue-white and glow with pleasure, remembering how the taste of life, of sunshine, of breath, of passion had burst like bubbles on his tongue. Even now they tickle his throat until he throws his head back with laughter, joy, frenzy, and wild abandon.

It is a cry for help.

Several more have joined his immortal company since they began their eternal ride across the sky. The dancer in the grove, the singer in the wings, the painter in the studio, the prophet in the alley. The Hunt bore them away on undead horses across the veil, but the living cannot bear the crossing. The barrier becomes a weapon, a blade, a dagger in his hand. Innocent blood is spilled as *Der Erlkönig*'s own join the unholy host. The drops fall to the ground and blossom into scarlet petals, like poppies in a field. The last vestiges of the living, they are all that remain of the humans they once were.

The music is all that remains of the human he once was.

Passing through endless, empty halls, the monster slips from shadow to shadow, a train of goblins in his wake. His hands have carried the sword and shield on the long night, but now they hold the violin and the bow. The Underground rearranges itself as he pleases, but for the first time in an age, he finds himself in a room lined with mirrors, a klavier at the center. A receiving room.

The hearth is dead, the mirrors cracked, the instrument dusty and out of tune, but still she calls to him through the veil.

Be, thou, with me.

He presses the horsehair to the strings, letting the warm, grainy voice of his violin fill the space between them. The mirrors around him reflect not the receiving hall, but a cramped, dingy space, crowded with trunks and papers and odds and ends.

And at the center of the room, a girl. A woman. She sits at the klavier with eyes closed, playing their song. Their story.

Elisabeth.

Her image flickers, wavers, a reflection seen on the edges of a candle flame. The shadows wriggle and writhe with curiosity, and with tremendous effort, the monster holds them back.

Please, he whispers. Please, let me have this one thing.

As he plays, the darkness recedes. From his skin, from his hair, the weight of the rams' horns on his head lightening. Color returns to the world and to his eyes, a mismatched blue and green as the monster remembers what it is to be a man.

Elisabeth.

He sits down on the bench beside her, begging her— beseeching her—to open her eyes and see him. Be with him.

But she keeps her eyes closed, hands trembling on the keyboard.

Elisabeth.

She stirs. He sucks in a sharp breath and lifts his hand to stroke her cheek with fingers that are still mangled, broken, strange. His touch passes through her like a knife through smoke, yet she shivers as if she can feel the brush of his fingers in the dark places of her soul, her body, her heart. She is as insubstantial as mist, but he cannot resist the urge, the itch, to kiss. He closes his eyes and leans in close, imagining the silk of her skin against his lips.

They are met.

A gasp. His eyes fly open but hers are still closed. Her hand lifts to her mouth, as though the tingle of their unexpected caress still lingered there.

"Mein Herr," she sighs. "Oh, *mein Herr."*

I'm here, he says. Look at me. Be with me. *See* me. Call me by name.

Yet when she opens her eyes, she stares through him, not at him. The darkness hisses and crawls, the shushing sound of branches in an icy wind. She drops her head into her hands, her shoulders hunched, and the sound of her crying is more bitter than even the coldest winter night.

No! he cries. He wants to comfort and caress her, but he cannot hold her, cannot touch her. He is a ghost in her mind, voiceless, silent, and incorporeal.

The shadows have had enough of his wallowing, and the inky black twines itself about his hands, his arms, and his face once more. But even as the old laws have him in their grip, the man he is struggles against the monster he is becoming. He closes his thoughts and falls away, holding the last bit of himself uncorrupted and pure. He reaches out for her one last time, pressing his name onto her heart.

Keep me safe, he thinks. *Keep me human. Keep me whole.*

And then he is gone.

A KINGDOM
TO OUTRUN

The coach was to arrive in the morning.

To my surprise, that evening, several folk from the village paid a visit to send us off with gifts, well-wishes, and unsolicited advice. The baker and his wife brought sweets, the butcher brought meats, and the brewer delivered several kegs of beer to toast our departure. The inn's guests mingled with the rest of the crowd, and before long, there was an impromptu celebration. I was touched by everyone's coming and appreciated their gestures of goodwill, even if their advice was not quite as well received.

"Mind you watch after your sister, Liesl," Frau Bäcker said. "Beauty has its own blindness, and we don't want our Käthe falling in with a bad crowd."

"You've got a good head on your shoulders," her husband chimed in. "And we needn't worry about any men trying to take advantage of you."

My grin tightened into a grimace, but I thanked them for

the cake, which was a glorious confection of moist white sweetness. We did not have sugar to spare for such luxuries at the inn, so it had been an absolute treat, even if it did leave a bad taste in my mouth.

But before long, one by one, our well-wishers slipped out the door and into the deepening night, leaving our hearts heavy with anticipation, apprehension, and not a little affection for the tiny town Käthe and I were so eager to escape. Mother insisted we retire to bed early and not worry about the chores, for we needed our rest for the morrow. By the glitter in her blue eyes, I suspected our mother wanted to retreat to the refuge of the kitchen to spare us the sight of her tears.

Constanze had passed the evening locked upstairs in her bedroom. Although I knew it was probably for the best, her unsociability stung. She had deigned to make an appearance for Josef's farewell celebration, after all.

I was being unreasonable, of course, but a strange sort of melancholy had taken hold of me on our last night in the inn. I should be happy. I should be excited. My life was stretching out before me, a golden path lit by opportunity, a shining city of possibility on the other side. Yet I felt a curious sort of detachment from the prospect, as though I were experiencing my joy at a degree of remove.

There was a shadow on my soul. I could see the sensations I should be feeling, the consequences that I should be fearing, but everything was dark, murky, vague. A veil was between me and my inner heart. I thought of the old rector's dire warnings and of Constanze's terror of the Wild Hunt. I knew I should worry. I knew I should care. But all I felt, this night before the rest of my life, was exhaustion and fatigue.

Even Käthe noticed my unusual reticence. "Would you like to pass the night with me, Liesl?" she asked, once everyone else had retired. We were sitting in the main hall before the fire, watching the flames burn down into embers. "I know I could use the company. It would be like old times, yes?"

As little girls, my sister and I had shared a bed while my brother had his own quarters downstairs. Back then, I had thought privacy the height of all luxury, wondering what it would be like spend a night without another treading on my dreams. And while I cherished having my own retreat, there were times when solitude had more weight than the feel of another's limbs crowding my sleep.

"No, it's all right," I said, staring without seeing into the fire. "You go on ahead, Käthe. I'll . . . I'll retire soon."

I could see her reach out, then withdraw, her mouth twisting as it struggled to find words of comfort. I wanted to lift my hand, to meet her concern with reassurance, but I could not. My shadow enveloped me in a shroud, and I could not move.

My sister rose to her feet and made to head up the stairs up to her bedroom, when she paused. "Liesl," she said quietly.

"Yes?"

"Go to the Goblin Grove."

Even the astonishment that knifed me felt dull. "What?" I asked.

"Go to the Goblin Grove," she repeated. "Make your peace and say your farewells. You cannot have a new beginning without an ending. Go, and be free."

I toyed with the ring on its chain about my throat. "I'll consider it."

"What is your problem?" Käthe's eyes flashed, her voice filled with sudden vehemence. I was taken aback by the force of her anger, but more than that, I was envious. I wanted the strength of her convictions because my own resolve was weak. "What is it you're afraid of? I am tired of bearing your emotional burdens, Liesl. I cannot carry them forever. I am not your crutch."

I blinked. "Excuse me?"

She began pacing back and forth before the fire. "Ever since you came back from—from where you'd been, you've been barely holding yourself together." Before I could protest in my defense, she went on. "You're hot, you're cold, you're up, you're down, you're fast, you're slow. I can't keep up with you sometimes, Liesl. You're like a top spinning out of control, and I'm continually watching—waiting—for any wobble that might topple you."

I was stunned. Was I so changed by my time beneath the earth? I was a different Liesl—no, Elisabeth—than I had been before I entered the realm of the goblins, but I was still the same me. Still the same soul. Still self-indulgent, selfish, selfless, savage. I had shed my skin to emerge anew, more me than before. But had I always been this insufferable? Had I always been so tiresome?

"I—I—" Words withered on my tongue. "I didn't mean— I'm so sorry, Käthe."

Her expression softened, but I could see that even my apology wearied her. She sighed. "Don't apologize, Liesl," she said. "Do. Stop wallowing and go find closure. Absolution or resolution or whatever it is, I am tired of holding your heart. Give it back to the Goblin Grove if you must. I can no longer carry it."

My eyes burned. I could feel Käthe's pitying glance, but

did not look at her. A hot tear slipped from beneath my lashes, and I tried very hard not to sniff. *Stop wallowing,* she had said. It was hard.

My sister leaned over and pressed a kiss to my brow. "Go to the Goblin Grove," she said. "Go, and make peace."

I went.

The night was clear as I made my way into the heart of the wood.

It had rained earlier that day, and a few clouds lingered, but the bright, full face of the moon shone down on me, touching the forest with silver frost. But I would have been able to find my way to the Goblin Grove even if the night had been as black as pitch. The woods and the legends surrounding it were etched into my bones, a map of my soul.

The walk was both longer and shorter than I remembered. The distance from grove to inn seemed to have shortened, but the time it took to reach it seemed to have grown. I came upon the Goblin Grove almost by surprise, the circular ring of twelve alder trees jumping out of the shadows like children playing peekaboo. I hesitated on the edges of the grove. The last time I stood here, I had crossed the barrier between worlds. The Goblin Grove was one of the few places left where the Underground and the world above existed together, a sacred space made holy by the old laws and my memories. I stood on the edge, waiting for a sense of trespass to overcome me as I crossed from one world back to the next.

It did not come.

I entered and sat down with my back against a tree, wrapping my cloak tighter about me.

"Ah, *mein Herr*," I said softly to the night. "I am here. I am here at last."

There was no answer. Even the forest was unwontedly quiet, without its usual sense of patient waiting. I felt awkward sitting here in the dark, like a child who had left home, only to return to find it not as they remembered. The grove was like and not like how I remembered it, but it wasn't the minute and minuscule failings of memory that made it different; it was the emptiness.

I was alone.

For a moment, I considered going back, returning to the inn where it was warm, where it was bright, where it was safe. But I had promised my sister I would make peace, even if I did not know how. Even if there was no one to hear me.

"I am leaving for Vienna on the morrow," I said. "I am leaving the Goblin Grove behind."

I couldn't help but pause to wait for a reply, even though I knew not to expect it. I wasn't talking to myself; I was having a conversation, even if I was the only one participating.

"I should be happy. I *am* happy. I have always wanted to go to Vienna. I have always wanted to see the world beyond our little corner of Bavaria."

It was getting easier now to speak as though to an audience and not myself. I wondered then if I wanted the Goblin King to respond, or if I merely wanted to leave my heart here before him, before the old laws.

"Is it not what you taught me, *mein Herr*? To love myself first instead of last?" My words hung before me in a cloud of mist. My wistfulness turned breath, my longing made visible. I was growing colder by the minute, the damp chill seeping through my cloak and into my bones. "Are you not happy for me?"

Again, no response. His absence was nearly a presence, a noticeable, unavoidable void. I wanted to close that void, to seal that abyss, and heal the fractures in my heart.

"I know what you would say," I said. *"Go forth and live, Elisabeth. Live and forget about me."* I heard his voice in my memory, a soft, expressive baritone as rich and warm as a bassoon. Or was it a powerful tenor, as sharp and clear as a clarionet? Time had blurred the details and edges of the Goblin King, turning him from a man back into a myth, no matter how hard I had tried to hold on. To remember.

"Forgetting is easy," I whispered to the empty air. "Easier than I thought. Easier than I want to admit. Even now the exact colors of your eyes are no longer clear to me, *mein Herr.*"

I ran my fingers over the still-frozen ground. "But living?" There was nothing beneath my feet or fingers. No sense of thaw, no sleeping green waiting to burst forth. Dead, hollow, lifeless. "Living is hard. You didn't tell me it would be so hard, *mein Herr.* You didn't say a word."

My limbs were growing numb from the chill, so I got back to my feet, stamping away the myriad prickling needles in my skin. I began to pace throughout the Goblin Grove, agitation and frustration keeping me warm.

"You didn't tell me living would be one decision after another, some easy, some difficult. You didn't tell me living wasn't a battle, but a war. You didn't tell me that living was a choice, and that every day I choose to continue was another victory, another triumph."

It was more than agitation keeping me warm now; it was anger. It coiled within me, winding me tighter and tighter. My fingers curled, my jaws clenched. I was a spring ready to be sprung. I wanted to tear each alder tree from the earth by its roots, I wanted to claw and dig my way back to the

Underground. I wanted to rip and scream and tear and shriek. I wanted to hurt him. I wanted to hurt myself.

"I wish you were dead," I said vehemently.

My voice did not echo in the woods, but the force of my emotions rang in my ears.

"I do," I repeated. "Do you hear me, *mein Herr*? I wish you were dead!"

At last the forest took up my cry, a hundred mouthless voices repeating *dead, dead, dead*. I thought I heard the otherworldly giggles of Twig and Thistle, their high-pitched titters crawling up my skin. The old Liesl would have felt guilty for her uncharitable words, but the new Elisabeth did not. The Goblin King had taught me cruelty, after all.

"You would agree, of course," I said with a bitter laugh. "No one could punish you harder than you punish yourself. You could have been a martyr. Saint Goblin King, willing to die for me, willing to die for love.

"But I'm not like you," I continued. "I am not a saint; I am a sinner. I wish you were dead so I could live. If you were dead, I could bury you—in my heart and in my mind. I could mourn you, then let you go."

I stopped pacing and wrapped my arms about myself beneath my cloak. Now that my anger was fading, the cold began to creep in. I drew the wolf's-head ring out.

"You live an unlife instead," I said. I held the ring before me and looked at it. It was old, tarnished, and even a little ugly. "An unlife, a not-death. You exist in the in-between spaces, between sleep and waking, between belief and imagination. I wish I could wake up, *mein Herr*. I wish I were awake."

I undid the clasp and removed the chain with his ring from my neck. With a trembling hand, I set it down in the middle of the Goblin Grove.

"I won't look back," I said in a choked voice. "Not this time. Because you won't be there to hold me back. I relinquish you, *mein Herr,* just as you let me go." A sob hitched in my throat, but I swallowed it back down, straightening my spine with resolve.

"Goodbye," I said. I did not turn around. "Farewell."

I half expected, half hoped I would feel a ghostly hand upon my shoulder as I left, as I stepped foot from the Goblin Grove. But as it had been when I left the Underground, there was no touch, no half-whispered plea to stay. I couldn't help but look for him anyway, my Goblin King. I gasped, my hand going to the ring I no longer wore at my throat. I could not be sure, but I thought I saw a tall, dark figure standing among the trees, watching me as I walked away.

Then I blinked and the figure was gone. Perhaps he had never been there, my madness made manifest from the mournful yearning of my muddled mind. I turned away and walked back home, toward my future, toward the mundane.

I almost made it to the inn before the tears fell.

Interlude

ate one morning, in early spring, a coach bearing passengers en route to Vienna arrived at an inn in Bavaria.

Two girls waited hand in hand to join them, one dark, one fair. Their clothes were simple, their belongings few, and though one was pretty and the other plain, they had the look of sisters. They bore mirrored expressions of hope and hollowness, like two halves of a whole. The passengers shuffled and grumbled, groaned and shifted, making room for the girls—one plump, one thin. The sisters took each other's hands as the dark-haired one stared straight ahead, unwilling to acknowledge the demons only she could see.

Meanwhile, over the mountains and a country away, two boys—one dark, one fair—walked the streets of Vienna side by side, en route from one home in the gutter to another in a finer part of the city. A footman dressed in poppy red had been dispatched to ferry their belongings to their new apartments, but their only possession was a single, slightly battered violin. Passersby shifted and shuffled, avoided and averted their gaze from the sight of the boys' hands intertwined—one black, one white.

The dark-skinned boy knew that luck did not smile upon those of his color or class, and distrusted the sudden good fortune that brought a green-eyed woman to the house of L'Odalisque, searching for him and his beloved. The woman had come bearing gifts: an offer of patronage and a letter written in a hand unfamiliar to François, but precious to his fair-haired companion.

I am honored by your faith in my work and humbly accept your generous offer. Please convey all my love and affection to my brother, Herr Vogler. I implore you reassure him that his family have not abandoned him, just as his ever-loving sister prays that he has not forgotten her.

Yours most gratefully,
Composer of Der Erlkönig

François did not trust the green-eyed woman. He had learned long ago that nothing came without a price. But Josef still had faith, still believed in fairy tales and hope, magic and miracles. Josef took the letter.

And accepted.

It was late in the afternoon when the coach from Bavaria drew through the city gates and later still when two sisters stood before a set of apartments off Stephansplatz, near Vienna's great cathedral at the heart of the city. The dark-haired one shivered in her red cloak as she stood outside, but not from the unseasonable spring chill. She was watching—waiting—in the darkened doorway for blue eyes, blond hair, and a shy, sweet smile. She was waiting for a little boy. She was waiting for her brother.

But the brother that emerged was not the child Liesl remembered. At sixteen, he could not properly be called a boy any longer. Josef had come into his full height, towering a head taller than both his sisters. Yet neither was he fully grown, for his chin was still bare, his limbs still gawky and gangly with unexpected growth. He was both a man and a child, and neither.

For a moment, Liesl and Josef stared at each other, doing nothing, saying nothing.

And then they broke.

She opened her arms and he ran into her embrace, just as they had when they were young and each other's shelter from their father's worst excesses. When they listened to scary stories at their grandmother's knee. When the world was too much for them, and not enough.

"Liesl," he murmured.

"Sepp," she whispered.

The tears that fell from each other's cheeks were warm and tasted of joy. They were together. They were home.

"Oh my goodness, Josef, how you've grown!" the fair-haired sister exclaimed.

Josef startled, surprised to see her. "What are you doing here, Käthe?"

He did not see the spasm of hurt that crossed her face. "Didn't Liesl tell you?" Käthe huffed. "We've come to join you in Vienna!"

"Join me?" Josef turned his blue-eyed gaze to his sister, eyes that were paler and icier than Liesl remembered. "You're not—you're not here to take me home?"

"Home?" Käthe said incredulously. "But we *are* home now."

The coachman had unloaded their things and driven away, leaving the makeshift family with nowhere to go but through the threshold and up the stairs to their new domicile. François and the landlady emerged from the shadows to help Käthe carry their belongings to the two-room apartments on the second floor. First the landlady, then François, then Käthe disappeared through the doorway, leaving Liesl and Josef on the street together, but alone.

"Home," the blond boy said in a remote voice.

"Home," the dark-haired sister echoed softly.

It was a long time before either of them spoke. She had traveled hundreds of miles—through forests and woods, over mountains and plains—to be with him, yet the distance between them had grown.

"Sepperl," she began, then stopped. She did not know what to say.

"Liesl," he said coldly. There was nothing to be said.

And then the fair-haired boy turned around and vanished into the darkness of their new life without another word, leaving his sister to finally understand—to know—that she had spent miles upon miles upon miles running down the wrong road.

EVER MINE

Why this deep grief, where necessity speaks?

—LUDWIG VAN BEETHOVEN,
the Immortal Beloved letters

STRANGE
PROCLIVITIES

It all began with an invitation.

"Message for you, *Fräulein*." Frau Messer accosted me at the door as I returned from Naschmarkt with the week's groceries in tow. "Looks like it's another one from your"—her lips twitched—"*mysterious* benefactor."

It wasn't often our landlady emerged from her hidey-hole on the ground floor, but nothing flushed city folk from their dens faster than the possibility of good gossip. Any bit of information about our anonymous patron was too delicious a morsel for her to ignore.

"Thank you, ma'am," I said politely. I reached for the letter, but she held it just beyond reach. Frau Messner was not tall; she was a short, stout woman with sharp features that brought to mind a plump, well-fed ferret, but I could not retrieve my message without stepping in closer than I was comfortable.

"'Twas brought over by a liveried servant this time." Her

beady eyes darted from the letter to my face and back again, inviting me—taunting me—to say more. "Queer little fellow. Small as a child, dressed in red with his white wig all tufty 'bout his head like dandelion fluff."

I gave her a tight smile. "Was he?"

"Not many noble families in Vienna outfit their liveries in red," she mused. "But fewer still mark their correspondence with the sign of the poppy." Frau Messner held the letter up before me, where I could clearly see the image of the flower pressed into the wax seal. "Your benefactor is quite unusual, *Fräulein*. I understand better now how you came across your good fortune in the city."

I stiffened. I had been in the city long enough to know that luck was merely power in another guise. While I had not expected our lives to be easy, what I hadn't expected was just how dependent we would be on another's kindness, another's whim. The apartments in which we lived were already leased in our names when we arrived, introductions and invitations to influential members of society penned and received, lines of credit established with shopkeepers, every need anticipated, arranged, and attended to. Our rude and rustic ways were already the subject of much ridicule, but what we could not be forgiven for was our good fortune. Our luck had little to do with success, and everything to do with access.

"I see," I said, schooling my features into a neutral expression.

"I meant no disrespect, my dear," she said, but her sneer belied her words. "Count Procházka is richer than Croesus, and how he chooses to spend his money is his own affair."

A flush crossed my face, betraying my agitation despite my best efforts to keep calm. "If you please," I said, holding out my hand. "My message."

Frau Messner hesitated. "A word of warning before you go." She absently fiddled with the edges of the letter, almost as though she were reluctant to speak. "You are young and so very innocent in the ways of the world. Know that there are unsavory predators in this town who would prey upon that naïveté."

"I am not so credulous as all that," I said, a trifle defensively.

"I know, *Fräulein*," Frau Messner said. "Only . . . I was like you once. Homely, hungry, and eager to make something of myself." Her eyes fell to the letter in my hand. "Your patron is said to be rather eccentric, and prone to . . . strange proclivities."

Ice trickled down my spine. "I beg your pardon?"

Strange proclivities. I thought I could hear the snicker beneath her sugary-sweet demeanor, the questioning, judgmental glances that lingered on my sister's buxom figure, on François's dark complexion, on Josef's choirboy face.

Seeing my misgiving, my landlady went on. "They say the count and his followers are lovers of the poppy," she said in a conspiratorial tone.

I glanced at the red crest on the letter with the image of a flower pressed into the wax. "Do you mean . . . opium? Laudanum?"

"Aye," she said. "Theirs is a house of madmen and dreamers, of smoke and visions. Laudanum loosens the mind and"—the smirk was back on her face—"loosens other things as well." Her gaze trailed down my rail-thin figure, my sallow skin, and overlarge eyes, and a prurient glint lit their beady depths.

I went rigid. "How dare you?" I asked in a low voice.

Frau Messner lifted her brows. "Gossip spreads through this city faster than fire, *Fräulein*," she said. "And the tales that come out of Procházka House are more incendiary than most."

I had had enough. "I appreciate your advice," I said shortly, snatching the letter from her hand. Turning, I made my way up the stairs to our apartments.

"I don't say this to be mean or cruel, Elisabeth," she called after me. "The last young woman the Procházkas took under their wing disappeared under . . . mysterious circumstances."

I paused on the stairwell.

"She was a poor, plain little thing from the country," she went on. "A distant relation of theirs, or so they claimed. From what I heard, she was a particular favorite of the Countess. 'Like a daughter to them,' they said."

After a moment, I succumbed to my curiosity and turned to face Frau Messner. "What happened to her?"

My landlady grimaced. "There was . . . an incident. At their country home. In Bohemia. Details are scarce, but there are reports of some sort of . . . ritual. The next morning the girl was gone and one of their friends was dead."

"Dead?" I was startled.

"Aye." She nodded. "They claim there was no foul play"— she snorted—"but the young man was found out in the woods, his lips blue with frost and a strange gray mark across the throat."

The bottom fell from my stomach, that sickening lurch that accompanies an unexpected misstep. *Elf-struck*.

"They're only rumors, of course," she said quickly, seeing the expression on my face. "It's just . . . you are a clever young woman with a good head on your shoulders, Elisabeth. Use your judgment and take heed, is all."

I ran my thumb over the wax seal on the letter, tracing the shape of the poppy petals. For all that I did not want to admit it, my landlady was merely voicing my doubts about our patron aloud. We had not met with Count Procházka or seen him since we had arrived in Vienna. Not once. Messages were few and far between, mostly concerned with our domestic details—clothing, groceries, rent. For someone who had been so eager to bring us *to* Vienna, he seemed considerably less interested in seeing us *in* the city. It was getting harder and harder to ignore my unease the longer we were here.

"I thank you for your warning," I said slowly. "And will take your advice into account." I picked up the folds of my skirts and started to make my way to the landing above when Frau Messner called my name one last time.

"Elisabeth."

I waited.

"Beware." Frau Messner's face was hard. "It is not the wolves you need fear, but the sheep skins they wear."

Käthe and François were home when I returned to our apartments. She sat on the bed surrounded and swathed by yards of fabric, her fair head bent over her sewing, while François carefully cut and basted patterns on the nearby table. Of the four of us—my sister, my brother, François, and me— only Käthe had a practical skill that could be leveraged to bring us some extra income. My sister assisted the dressmaker down the street with simple needlework, constructing basic gowns for the tailor to finish for each of his clients.

"Where's Josef?" I asked, hanging my hat and bonnet on a peg by the door and setting down the week's shopping. François rose from the table to assist me, all too eager to leave his sewing behind.

"What took so long?" Käthe snapped. Carnival was fast

approaching, and the Viennese celebrated with balls and masques before the Lenten season put an end to all luxury and frivolity. Herr Schneider was overwhelmed with work and had given much of it—along with his irritability—over to my sister to manage in his stead. "I need to finish these gowns by tomorrow and could use all the help I can get."

I looked to François, who shrugged apologetically. His German had improved by leaps and bounds since we first met him, but his gestures were just as eloquent as his words. *I do not know where Josef is, mademoiselle.*

I sighed. "I was waylaid by our meddlesome Frau Messner."

Käthe rolled her eyes. "What did the old busybody want?"

"The usual." I held up the message from Count Procházka. "Any bit of gossip about our esteemed benefactor, of course."

"A letter?" François asked. "From the *comte*?" We corresponded so rarely with our patron that any contact between us was a source of both fascination and fear.

"Yes," I said. A sickly sweet perfume stained the air, cloying and close. I glanced at the message in my hand, trying to identify the scent. Not roses. Violets? Lilac? The poppy on the wax seal stared back at me.

Käthe squinted a little as she looked up from her work. "Is that an invitation?"

"An invitation?" I frowned. "To what?"

"His masked ball, of course. For Carnival." Käthe tilted her head toward the pile of dresses around her. "It's what half these gowns are for. The Count's parties are *infamous*." A sigh of longing escaped her lips. "Invitations are extremely difficult to come by, and the guest lists are kept secret, so no one knows who is to attend."

"What is *infamous*?" François asked.

"It is, er"—I struggled to find the French word and failed—

"it means *well-known,* though not necessarily in a good way."
Frau Messner's words returned to me. *The tales that come out of Procházka House are more incendiary than most.*

"*C'est mal?*" His brows knit together. "Bad?"

"Infamous isn't necessarily *bad.*" Käthe returned to her needlework. "People want to go to the Count's parties."

"Why?" François turned to me.

I shook my head. I wanted to know the answer as well.

"*Because,*" Käthe said exasperatedly, "it's the mystery that makes it exciting. No one knows exactly what happens at these parties, for the Count binds all his guests to secrecy."

"What?" I had never heard of such a ridiculous notion. "What on earth do they get up to at these soirees?"

She shrugged, pushing a blond curl out of her eyes. "Oh, the clients tell all sorts of stories at Herr Schneider's dress shop. The Procházkas sacrifice goats to a dark god in occult rituals. They drink laudanum to induce visions. They call upon sinister forces. There are also"—her cheeks pinked—"other, ah, *salacious* tales that emerge. Everyone is masked and anonymous, after all. People are keen to shed their inhibitions along with their identities."

Theirs is a house of madmen and dreamers.

"Salacious?" François asked.

Neither Käthe nor I answered him. "And you want to go?" For a brief moment, I thought of another masked ball my sister and I had attended, deep Underground, where I had seen her dance and laugh and party to wild excess on the arm of several comely young changelings. A flutter of anxiety and excitement flickered in my stomach.

"Of course!" Käthe snorted. "You don't think I truly believe those stories, do you? And besides, even if the Procházkas participated in arcane blood magic rituals, anything would be more exciting than being cooped up in these apartments, waiting for our lives to begin."

As apprehensive as I was about our benefactor, I could not gainsay her. Ever since we arrived in Vienna, we existed in a liminal state, always waiting for the next audition, the next chance, the next opportunity. Opportunities for musician work came in fits and starts, either feast or famine. For all that the Count could provide us with funds to live in Vienna, we were as dependent on public opinion as we were his generosity. What passed as talent in our small, provincial town in Bavaria was ordinary in here, for musicians in the city were as common as beer, and twice as cheap. Every week there was another concert, another salon, another gathering, another audience, and it was hard to make ourselves heard above the din.

I held the message out before us. There was nothing to be gleaned from the letter itself; it was faintly perfumed in the same scent, written in the same elegant hand, and sealed with the same poppy seal as the first correspondence we received from our patron. All my misgivings and doubts rose to the fore. When we first heard from Count Procházka, I had been so eager to read news of Josef and so distracted by the un-expected windfall of fifty florins that I had overlooked troubling signs. The lengths to which he had gone to satisfy an obsession with my music. My stolen letters to my brother. The Count's complete and utter disregard for my privacy. They all pointed to a man who seemed to have little consideration for boundaries.

"Mademoiselle?" François lifted his brows. "Will you read or no?"

With some hesitation, I turned the message over. For the first time, I noticed text printed in Roman type beneath the seal. HOSTIS VENIT FLORES DISCEDUNT. Latin. A motto? The words seemed vaguely familiar, but my Latin was rudimentary at best, useless outside the Mass.

Printed on weighted card stock in Gothic black letter were the words BLACK & WHITE CARNIVAL.

And then, in that flowing, flawless hand:

Mlle Elisabeth Vogler is requested to attend the BALL *at Prochàzka House, on the night of Shrove Tuesday, at* FIVE O'CLOCK IN THE EVENING.

An invitation. Four of them, each addressed to a different person. Me. *Mssr François Saint-Georges. Mlle Katharina Vogler.* My heart clenched. *Mssr Josef Vogler.*

"Well?" Käthe bit off her thread and tied a knot. "Don't keep us waiting, Liesl."

"You were right, Käthe," I said softly. I handed her the invitation with her name. "We've been invited to one of Count Prochàzka's infamous balls."

My sister squealed in excitement. "I knew it!" She tossed aside the gown on which she had been working. "Take *that,* Frau Drucker," she gloated to the crumpled silk. "I *am* personally acquainted with Count Prochàzka!"

I gave François his invitation. He met my gaze. "Josef?" he asked.

I closed my eyes. "I don't know," I said in a small voice. "I don't know . . . I don't know if he would want to come."

François sighed, and in the depths of his sigh, I heard what he did not say. *I don't know what Josef wants these days.*

I didn't either. Not anymore. I wasn't sure if I ever had. I opened my eyes. The rooms were small, cramped, crowded, but I felt my brother's absence from this scene as acutely as a missing tooth. He should have been here. He should have been with us, part of the new family we were building here. An irrational surge of anger and irritation spiked my blood. Josef should at least *try* to make a new life. I was trying. François was trying. Käthe was trying and seemed to have nearly succeeded. Even if my brother and I were both struggling to take root in Vienna, we used to struggle together when we were children. Now we were alone. Isolated.

"The Count could have invited us sooner," Käthe grumbled. "We'll have no time to make our own costumes." She was already furiously sketching her ideas for our fancy dress onto a spare bit of foolscap. An old draft of the Wedding Night Sonata that I had discarded in a fit of frustration and fury. I waited for the sharp stab of jealousy or resentment to see my sister turn my failure into a new work of art, but there was nothing. Only a sense of emptiness.

"What of your work for Monsieur Schneider?" François asked Käthe.

She turned an imperious blue gaze on each of us in turn. "I fully expect the two of you to pull your weight around here," she said primly. "And leave me to my genius."

I would have laughed if I didn't feel so bereft of my own creative spark. "Yes, ma'am." I gathered the discarded gowns and moved them to the table in the next room where François joined me, resigned to another long night by the candle.

"And if Josef comes back," she called after us, "tell him he's not exempt!"

François and I exchanged another glance. Not when Josef came back.

If.

FAULTLINES

the third candle was halfway gone when Josef finally returned.

I had sent François to bed a candle and a half ago and moved my work to the front room. All those hours of mending and sewing I had neglected in favor of music had come back to haunt me, for although my fingers were nimble enough on a keyboard or strings, they were hopeless with a needle and thread. But while I was determined to help my sister in any way I could, I had been even more determined to confront my brother the moment he came home.

"Where have you been?" I kept my voice low, so as not to disturb François. Käthe and I shared the other room while the boys slept in the front.

Josef paused in unlacing his boots. "Nowhere," he said. His tone was expressionless, but it was a calculated sort of neutral that spoke volumes.

Although the light of the candle did not reach far, I thought I could see the dark tracks of mud on the soles of his shoes and at the hem of his greatcoat. "Liar," I said calmly, keeping my head bent over my needlework. "You've been to the cemetery again, I see."

My brother stiffened. "Yes," he said. "It is the only place in this godforsaken city where I can breathe."

St. Marx Cemetery was some two and a half miles from the outer city walls. It was also the only bit of wildness within any easy distance, with stretches of open space and trees and grass and nary another person in sight but the dead underfoot.

"I know," I said quietly.

And I did. No matter where you turned, you were never more than a half step away from your neighbor and your neighbor's business. Horses, pedestrians, and gutter refuse lined the streets, alleyways, and boulevards. Everyone trod the same mud, muck, and filth, breathing the same sour-smelling air, and around every corner was another stranger, another potential for danger that was to be avoided. There was no room, no space, no place to be alone, to think, to *be*. I was as hemmed in by the ring of stone that encircled the city as I had ever been trapped Underground as the Goblin King's bride.

Josef's shoulders relaxed, but his posture was still wary. "It feels like . . . it feels like home out there."

Home. Until we arrived, I had never given much thought to the idea of home. For most of my life, home was where I lived and the people I loved. Home had been the inn and my family.

Home had been the Goblin Grove and a soft-eyed young man.

"I know," was all I said. It was all I could say.

Josef said nothing. The silence between us was pointed, its jabs meant for me. I had no defense against my brother's coldness, and I felt each and every absent word like a knife between the ribs. Vienna had become our Tower of Babel, our speech broken by my mania and his melancholy. But it was more than communication that was missing between us; it was communion. Once Josef and I would have spent the quiet hours together without speaking, simply *being* with each other in the moment. Once he would have picked up his bow and I my hands, and we would have spoken across sound, across melody, across music. Once, once, once.

All was silent.

I watched my brother set down his violin case by the door. "You've been playing, I see."

Talk to me, Sepp. Look at me. Acknowledge me.

He did not turn to face me. "And you haven't been composing, I see."

I hissed as I stabbed myself deeply with the needle. A drop of blood blossomed across the surface of the silk on which I was working, looking like poppy petals in the snow. I cursed under my breath. Several hours of work ruined. I did not know what I would tell Käthe when she awoke.

Josef's face was unreadable beyond the edge of the candle flame. "Soak it with cold salt water," he said. He made his way to the cabinets where we kept our spices, and returned with a rag and a bowl filled with a bit of salt. He retrieved the pitcher of water from the washstand and poured a measure into the bowl. Taking my sewing from me, he dipped the tip of his rag in the solution and began dabbing at the stain.

How did he know to do this? Where? So much of my brother's time away from me was a complete mystery. What he had learned under Master Antonius. What he had done in those weeks after the old virtuoso died and he had disappeared into the depths of Vienna. I had asked François once, but it was the only time our shared understanding had ever failed. Neither boy could tell me what had happened to them. Could not. Would not.

The faintest trace of healing red welts flashed across the skin of my brother's pale forearm as he worked. I sucked in a sharp breath. "Sepperl . . ."

The use of his childhood nickname made him pause, but when he caught me staring at his wrists, he was quick to pull down his sleeve. "You can do the rest," he said shortly, shoving my sewing back at me.

"Sepp, I—"

"Do you need anything else, *Elisabeth*?" he asked. "If not, I will be off to bed."

The use of my given name was a slap to the face. I had always been Liesl to him, only and ever Liesl. "I need . . ." I began, but trailed off. *I need you to come back to me. I need you to be whole. I need you in order to be whole.* "I need you to talk to me, Sepp."

He looked me squarely in the face. "What could I possibly have to say to you?"

A sob caught in my throat. "How could you possibly be so cruel?"

"Me, cruel?" He laughed, and the sound was a little feral, a little wild. "Oh, Liesl. It is you who are cruel. It is you who lie. Not me. Not I."

I blinked the tears from my eyes. "How have I been cruel, Sepperl?"

The light in his icy blue gaze shone with something like contempt, even malice. I was taken aback. The youth who stood before me was no longer the child I knew. Since being reunited, I had marked how my brother had grown: lean and lanky with his height, the last of his baby fat withered from his smile to reveal sharp cheekbones and an even sharper chin. But it was more than the visible changes time had wrought upon him that made him unfamiliar to me; it was the invisible ones that turned him into a stranger. I wondered then what my real brother—the one stolen by changelings—would have looked like now. I immediately quashed the treacherous thought, furious with myself for even thinking it.

"Is this where you want to have our reckoning?" Josef's voice was quiet. It was an unquiet quiet, the hush before a winter storm. "Because we can have it now. Right this moment. With both François and our sister to overhear."

I glanced to the sleeping boy in the bed beside the table. François's eyes were closed, but there was a waiting stillness to every line of his body. He was listening. The door to the room I shared with Käthe was cracked open a sliver, and I caught the reflected gleam of her summer-blue eyes before they winked out into darkness. I looked away.

"I thought so." Josef's face was hard.

"Fine," I said. "Be off to bed then. I shall see you in the morning." I shoved my sewing to the side and made to blow out the candle when I felt my brother's hand about my wrist.

"Liesl." His voice cracked, leaping several octaves as it hadn't in several months now, unexpectedly young and vulnerable. "I . . . I—"

I held my breath. A gossamer-fragile truce, a filament of peace, and I dared not exhale lest I disturb it altogether.

The moments stretched on, and beneath and between us, a growing chasm.

"I wish you good night," my brother said at last.

I shut my eyes. "Good night, Josef."

He blew out the candle. I made my way to my own bed,

stumbling through the dark.

And then a voice from the shadows, so soft I could have imagined it:

"Sweet dreams, Liesl."

I did not dream.

The following morning I awoke late. Käthe was already gone, the gowns I had finished vanished along with her. The boys too were missing, but François had left me a note stating that he and Josef had left with my sister to run errands and prepare for Carnival. The Procházkas' black-and-white ball would be held in two weeks, and there was no time to lose.

It had been a long time since I had had any space to myself. The solitude felt strange, like an old dress I had not worn in a year. It sat oddly on my shoulders, as though I had forgotten how to fill it out, how to wear it. Back at the inn, any bit of time alone had been rare and therefore precious. I had been cautious not to spend my minutes and seconds carelessly, instead choosing to place all my waking moments by myself to that which I held so dear.

My music.

The table in the front room was a mess of papers, blunt quills, and spilled ink. I could see where my sister had spent the morning refining her ideas for our costumes for the black-and-white ball—half-finished sketches of lace and ribbons and silhouettes scribbled onto any bit of blank space—on bills of fare, torn pages from our accounting ledger, on the backs of abandoned compositions. One could trace the progression of Käthe's thoughts from page to page, as her vision became sharper and clearer. These endless attempts at perfecting and refining were both foreign and familiar to me. I understood this process of creation and genesis. This genius. Or I had once.

One of the first things we acquired once we were settled in our apartments was a klavier. François and I had spent days hunting through shops selling all sorts of keyboards: harpsichords, virginals, and even the newer pianofortes that seemed to be all the rage in town. We had marveled at the nuance and tonality of these modern instruments, the control in sound just the subtlest of touches could wring. I could see the longing in François's eyes, the hunger in his strokes, but unfortunately there was no room in our apartments for a pianoforte.

In the end we decided upon a clavichord, small enough to fit in our cramped home and discreet enough not to bother the neighbors. It was not an instrument to practice performance on, but one to compose and write upon. A tool for me rather than for François, who was the better musician.

It had lain untouched ever since we purchased it.

You've been playing, I see.

And you haven't been composing, I see.

I ran my hands over the keys. A fine layer of dust had already settled over the instrument, and my fingertips left questioning trails in their wake. I waited for some mood or inspiration to strike me, for the desire to play to overtake me, but there was nothing. Solitude around me and silence within me. I had not dreamed once since we came to the city. The voice inside me—*my* voice—was gone. No ideas. No drive. No passion. My nights were quiet. Blank. The dullness was seeping into my days.

I had thought that by leaving home—leaving *him*—I could escape my own inability to write.

I wonder if it's not Vienna you are running toward, but a

kingdom you are trying to outrun.

Excuses were easy to find for my lack of composing and creativity. Here in Vienna, it was easy to hide my cracks behind the everyday tumult and turmoil of city living. Eruptions of mania or melancholy could be attributed to ordinary, quotidian frustrations: the price of bread, the backsplash of an emptied chamber pot, the shouts and screams of joy, sorrow, rage, and surprise of complete strangers, the calculated indifference of casual acquaintances. I was overwhelmed by the variety of sights and sounds we encountered on the streets—musicians, artists, noblemen, beggars, cobblers, dressmakers, grocers, merchants, landlords—people of every shape, every size, every creed, every color.

But in a city of thousands, I had never been more lonely.

It wasn't just my relationship with Josef that had grown tenuous and fragile. Käthe was by turns tender and frustrated with me, for I was a beast to be around. I trailed regrets and reproach in my wake, my moods as mercurial as quicksilver. I strained even François's infinite patience—pleasant and productive one moment, sullen and snarling the next. I knew I was insufferable, yet my irritability was a force both beyond and beside me. Even I found my own whining exhausting at times. I vacillated between rage and despondency, furious I couldn't force happiness on myself. I had everything I had ever wanted. I was here. In Vienna. At the start of my career.

That wasn't going anywhere.

If I hadn't spent any significant time working on the Wedding Night Sonata since I walked away from the Underground, it was because I didn't want to look at the monsters in my mind. Think of that spectral touch upon my hair, my cheek, my lips. That sigh across my skin. That murmur, that whisper of my name across the veil. I had been terrified of what those echoes of memory had meant. A breaking down of barriers, but between what? The veil between worlds? Or my sanity?

So I had abstained. Refrained.

I understood better then why Papa had always needed just one more drink, just one more. The temptation to open those wounds, to call upon those feelings and sensations, to indulge in the Goblin King's presence—whether real or imagined—by working on the Wedding Night Sonata had been nearly irresistible.

I had been so, so good.

But I was so, so lonely.

It was easy—too easy—to imagine the Goblin King as my savior from sorrow. The keys of the clavichord beckoned, like the sight of laudanum to an addict. Just one taste. Just one more. Just enough to dull the pain.

I sat down and began to play.

The notes of the clavichord were dampened, for the mechanism wasn't built to carry sound. I warmed up by running through the scales, then with a few agility exercises. My fingers were stiff, my mind fatigued. I played by rote, the music as soulless as I felt.

Practice makes perfect. I heard Papa's voice from the past, the discipline he imposed on my brother that he could not impose upon himself. *Feeling can be feigned, skill cannot.*

But what was music without emotion? Without sentiment, without conviction? Notes into noise, merely tones arranged in a pleasing manner. I heard the rise and fall of pitches, the varying intervals of sound and silence as I worked, but what I did not—could not—hear was my music. I did not know where to go. I did not know what to write next.

So much of my inability to compose had been bound up

in my fear of my fragile mind, but perhaps I had had it all wrong. Perhaps I was afraid I had nothing left to say. That my inspiration and my muse were buried Underground, for what was my art without *Der Erlkönig*? The hours we had worked together on the Wedding Night Sonata had been some of the best and most productive of my life. What if I was the musician I was because of *him*?

The Underground, the Goblin Grove, and the Goblin King were all behind me. I was Elisabeth, entire, even if I was Elisabeth, alone.

It was such cold comfort.

"Be, thou, with me," I murmured. An ache echoed in the empty chambers of my heart, returning nothing but hollow loneliness. Whatever connection I had to music, to magic, to whatever mysterious force that drove me to create was gone.

"Be, thou, with me," I repeated. "Please."

There was something buried deep in me, a seed, an acorn, but it was smothered, stifled, strangled. I was cut off from the sun, the loam, the woods, and the Goblin Grove that had nurtured me my entire life and I was withering in Vienna, unable to take root in foreign soil. My hand went to the place at my throat where his ring had hung, feeling its loss like a missing limb.

"Please," I said hoarsely. "Please."

I could rise above this. I *would* rise above this. This life was what I wanted. This was the culmination of all my wishes, all my desires. I just needed time. I would be myself, whole and entire, once again. I would.

I would.

But no matter how much I played, how much I called, the Goblin King did not come.

I was alone.

THE HOUSE OF MADMEN
AND DREAMERS

arnival festivities in Vienna grew to a fever pitch in the week leading up to Ash Wednesday. Back home, we had celebrated *Fasching* the old way, with players and townsfolk donning monstrous masks to drive away the spirits of winter. Here, there seemed to be a ball or concert or three every evening, a riotous swirl of color and costume, shouts of *Ahoi!* and *Schelle schelle!* sounding late into the night. These were not the spirits of winter to be driven away until the following year; they were the idols of excess and extravagance to be purged before Lent.

On Shrove Tuesday, the night of our benefactor's ball, François hired us a coach to drive us to the Count's home. Procházka House was not a *Stadthaus* in the city proper, but a manor on the outskirts, where haphazard human habitation gave way to tame, cultivated wilderness. It would have taken no great effort to walk the mile or so to the house, but François told me that these things were not done.

Sometimes living in Vienna felt as though I were dropped in the midst of a game where everyone but me knew the pieces, the moves, and the rules.

"Oh, I do hope we look respectable," Käthe said, fretting with her handkerchief as we drove past rolling lawns and stately homes.

Unlike the other parties hosted throughout Vienna's fifth season, Count Procházka's soiree required that we be attired only in black and white. An odd constraint that Käthe had initially balked at, but quickly rose to the challenge. She had dressed François and Josef in matching yet opposite costumes as Night and Day, with François in white and gold, my brother in black and silver. Sober woolen coats, brocade waistcoats with gold and silver thread, and well-tailored breeches were paired with knee-high leather boots, simple but striking. Their masks were simple silk dominos—Josef's patterned with stars, François's with a golden sunburst.

"*Magnifique*," François assured her. "*Très belle, mademoiselle.*"

"You are a genius," I added.

We glanced expectantly at Josef, but he was determinedly looking out the carriage window. Sparks of irritation ignited my blood. Käthe had worked her fingers to chafed calluses and her eyes to watery wrinkles to stitch us all new apparel in time for the ball, so the least we could do was congratulate her on her hard work.

"We look amazing," I repeated, as if I could make up for our brother's rudeness.

And we did look amazing. Käthe and I were dressed as an angel and demon, but to my surprise, my sister had chosen to be the devil. She looked majestic in her gown of black velvet, her golden curls draped with black silk and lace, cleverly twisted together and pinned to resemble horns growing from her head. She had rouged her lips a bright red, and her blue eyes looked imperious from behind her black mask. For a moment, the image of moldering gowns on dress forms rose up in my mind, a polished bronze mirror reflecting an endless line of faded Goblin Queens. I swallowed.

The dress my sister had made for me was nearly innocent in its simplicity. Yards and yards of fine white muslin had made a floating, ethereal gown, while Käthe had somehow fashioned a brocade cape into the shape of folded angel wings, which grew from my shoulder blades and cascaded to the floor. She had braided gold into a crown about my head for a halo, and I carried a lyre to complete the picture. The four of us stared at each other through our dominos, our faces made strange and unfamiliar by our masks.

Tonight would be our formal introduction to Viennese high society. The invitations we all carried marked us as Count Procházka's peers, and to say we were all a little nervous was to understate our anxiety. Käthe and I had had no real exposure to the well-heeled members of town; we were innkeeper's daughters. Our only exposure to money was whatever coin we had managed to keep in our coffers. François had grown up among the wealthy, but he, too, had never been one of them. The color of his skin forever marked him as an outsider to the noble class, even if he had learned their manners and ways.

I looked to Josef, but he was ignoring us. He betrayed little, his expression schooled to careful indifference. It was a greater mask than the one perched upon his face, and I hated how he never took it off, not anymore.

Käthe gasped. "Look!" she said breathlessly, pointing out the window. "Procházka House!"

We all leaned outside for a better look as we pulled up

the drive. Past the ivy-wound wrought-iron gates was an old manor built of gray stone, dark wood, and diamond-paned glass. It had the look of an abbey, or a castle, tall pointed arches forming the peaks and gables of its roofs. A fountain played in the courtyard, where a fish-tailed woman sat and played with water flowing from the rocks. It did not resemble any of the great houses or palaces we had passed on our way here; it looked far older, built in a different century, a different world.

A footman opened the carriage door for us as we pulled in front of the entryway. He was rather small for a footman, and there was something of a shriveled and disheveled look about him. His wig was mussed and askew, bits of white hair flying away into a puff of cloud about his head. He was old, much older than any of the other footmen I had seen around town.

"Thank you," I said as he helped me down.

The footman returned my smile, and I tried not to recoil. His teeth were yellowed and sharp, and in the flickering torchlight, his sallow skin seemed tinged with green. "Welcome to Procházka House, *Fräulein*," he said. "Home of madmen and dreamers. I hope you enjoy your stay with us." He pulled a flower from seemingly nowhere and presented it to me with a flourish. "I think you will."

I took the flower from his crabbed fingers. It was a common poppy. "Thank you," I said shakily.

"Wear it," he said. "For faith."

Faith? It seemed an odd reason, but I tucked the bloom behind my ear to humor him. I noticed then that a few of the guests arriving for the ball were wearing scarlet flowers pinned to their lapels and gowns, bright spots of crimson blooming like splashes of blood against their black-and-white costumes. The footman bowed and I hurried to follow the rest of my family to the house, eager to extricate myself from the situation.

Madmen and dreamers. I stood in line with Käthe, Josef, François, and the other guests waiting to be received by the hosts. Behind our masks, we were all anonymous, but the press of partygoers clad in only black and white heightened the sense of surreality. It was not a parade of fantastic monsters or beautiful creatures. We were all scraps of light and darkness, and standing among them in the fading twilight made me feel as though we would all disappear at any moment.

Your patron is said to be rather eccentric, and prone to . . . strange proclivities.

Dread clenched my stomach with icy fingers. We were nearly at the door.

"Ready?" Käthe asked, squeezing my hand. The blue of her eyes was intense amidst the sea of black and white. Her nervousness was edged with excitement, while mine was limned with fear. I tried to draw strength from my sister's gaiety, her sunshine humor, relying on them to burn away my shadows of doubt.

I smiled and returned her squeeze. I handed our invitations to the footman at the door and stepped inside, crossing the threshold from twilight into darkness. Something gritty was ground underfoot, and it was only when I glanced at my shoes that I noticed the small, white, crystalline grains.

Salt.

I didn't know what I was expecting. Gargoyles leering at me from cramped corners, perhaps, or derelict and decrepit furniture, the glamor of decay laid over rooms and caverns as vast as the Underground. Instead, we were greeted by an enormous marble entryway, the inside of Procházka House more like the great halls and galleries of Schönbrunn Palace and other fashionable Viennese residences. The interior was so at odds with its gothic exterior that I wondered if we had entered the wrong house by mistake.

A grand staircase led up to a second floor, the ballroom doors thrown open. Beneath the curve of the stairs, a tunnel disappeared into shadow. Above us, I could hear the faint strains of a minuet above the susurrus of a crowd, the muffled shuffling of footsteps treading the boards. At the top of the staircase, a stone crest was mounted, showing the expanded arms of the Procházka family. A poppy was embraced by vines at the center of a quartered shield, the top left filled with a burg atop a hill, the bottom right with a melusine on a rock, her fishtail trailing in the waters of a lake, very much like the fountain outside. Above the shield, carved into marble, was their motto: HOSTIS VENIT FLORES DISCEDUNT.

A servant came by and made to collect our things as we waited with the other guests to enter the ballroom upstairs. We relinquished our cloaks and heavier garments, but Josef shook his head, holding his violin case closer to him like a child. Or a shield. I had brought my folio of music and my brother his instrument in case we were called upon to perform for the Count.

"Don't you want to dance?" Käthe asked.

"No," Josef said petulantly. "I do not want to dance."

"We're here as his *guests*, Josef, not his hired musicians." She rolled her eyes. "Try and enjoy yourself, will you?"

Our brother gave an exasperated sigh and stalked off, disappearing into the crowd. François and I exchanged glances. He closed his eyes and gave a slight shake of his head. I grimaced. It was going to be a long night and we hadn't even entered the ballroom.

We were crowded in on all sides by partygoers. The uncomfortable proximity of so many anonymous strangers was beginning to get the better of me and I flinched and twitched at the slightest touch like a skittish thing. The last time I had attended a ball, I had been surrounded by goblins and changelings, but these black-and-white-clad guests were no less frightening. In many ways, Vienna was a place far stranger and more dangerous than the Underground. I broke out into a sweat, despite the gooseflesh pimpling my skin.

"Mademoiselle?" I turned to see François offering me his arm. A corner of his lips quirked up in a sympathetic smile, and I accepted his arm with a smile of my own. He did not flinch when I tightened my grip as we entered the ballroom, my palms slick with nervousness. I was grateful for his steadiness, for the room was beginning to rock and sway like a boat upon the waves.

There was the slightest pause in the constant hum of conversation, a breath, a beat, when we entered. A myriad eyes turned their gazes upon us, and an icy-hot sensation prickled over my skin. So many faces, so many people, so many expectations. I began shaking, dropping François's arm and trying my best to fade into the shadows. It was only then that I noticed that the guests weren't staring at me; they were staring at François. The darkness of his skin against the stark white of his costume. The contrast of my arm upon his. Whispers rippled in our wake as we made our way across the ballroom. Guilt crawled up from my stomach, and I felt as though I were going to be sick.

"Oh, François," Käthe said, loud enough to be clearly heard by all those in attendance. "I do hope you reserve a dance for me."

The murmurs stopped. Käthe smiled, her sunshine curls twisted into devil horns gleaming a burnished gold in the candlelight. She was the most beautiful girl in the room, and her beauty cast a halo as much as the glow of flame about her head. Her hand was held out to François, a queen of the night extending an alliance to a prince of the sun.

He did not flinch or falter. Bowing deeply, he took her hand. "I would be honored, mademoiselle."

The two of them beamed at each other, their grins grimaces in disguise, teeth bared at the room at large. Käthe and François both glanced sidelong at me, concern and a question writ upon their brows. I nodded at them both, and they swept onto the floor, joining the other couples in a lively quadrille. Black and white skirts swirled over black and white marble tiles arranged in a checkered pattern, and I retreated to the edges of the room, dizzy with nervous lightheadedness. I needed a drink. I needed air.

I left the dance floor, looking for a place to gather and compose myself. I wandered from room to room in the eccentric and fantastic house of my mysterious benefactor, but everywhere I stepped and everywhere I went was another person, another crowd, another stranger. Banquet tables were laden with food and ice sculptures carved into fantastic shapes—winged beings and horned creatures melting into water. At the center of a room was an automaton, a silver swan that "swam" in a silver stream teeming with fish. It moved its neck and caught one of the fish jumping from the water to the delighted gasps of its audience. The swan did not move with the herky-jerky motion of other automata I had seen displayed in great houses throughout the city, and its incredible, lifelike movements reminded me a little of Constanze's stories of goblin-made wonders. Magical armor, exquisite metalwork and artistry, jewels possessed of a blessing or a curse, wars had been fought, blood had been shed, and an incalculable amount of money had been spent for the privilege of owning a single one of these treasures. I wondered how much this silver swan cost.

The oddities did not end there. This unexpected house was full of such unexpected trinkets. In one corner, a pair of silver hands pouring an endless stream of champagne into an endless flute. In another, a pair of whimsical bronze sculptures without form or meaning . . . until one passed them just so and realized the emptiness between them created a screaming face. I threaded my way in and out of these rooms, past bright young things and respectable elders resting their feet and working their lips, looking for peace, looking for calm.

But there was none to be had. Gossip and speculation filled the space like the buzz of insect wings, rising along with smoke from candles and powder from wigs. The scent of sweat and perfume lay heavy on the air, coating the back of my throat with a warm, moist slickness. Heat rose in waves from damp necks and heaving bosoms, the musty musk of human flesh, close and choking. I thought I caught a glimpse of black, beetle-carapace eyes and twig-like fingers out of the corner of my eye, but it was only the shiny jet buttons of a man's waistcoat and the spidery embroidery of a woman's bodice. The sick feeling rose up again, stronger than ever.

"Looking for someone, child?" said a rich, melodious voice.

I turned to find a tall woman dressed as a winter spirit.

She was dressed in all white, her gown cunningly worked with beads to mimic the glitter of falling snow. She carried a spindle in one hand and wore the withered mask of an old woman, which sat strangely atop her long, swanlike neck. The only thing marring this vision in white and silver was the scarlet poppy pinned to her bodice, a drop of blood in the snow.

"N-no," I stammered. "I mean yes, I mean, no, I think my brother might have—" My words tumbled over themselves before I could catch them, spilling out ahead of my racing mind. The sounds of the house seemed garbled, muffled, the music from the other room warped and twisted beyond recognition, as though heard underwater. My vision wavered and narrowed, tunneling down so that near seemed far and far seemed near.

"Here." The woman flagged down a passing server and took two glasses filled with a rich, ruby red wine. "Have a drink, my dear. It will calm your nerves." She handed me the drink.

Through the haze of my whirling thoughts, I remembered that I wasn't much for spirits or wine of any kind anymore. I couldn't help but remember the last time I had been at a ball such as this, the last time I had drunk from a goblet handed to me by a mysterious stranger. The same uncertainty, the same precarious feeling of unbalance between unease and excitement overcame me, but out of politeness, I accepted the drink. I gingerly took a sip, trying not to grimace at the unexpected flowery aftertaste. To my surprise, the drink did soothe me, the liquor a balm to my raw and exposed nerves.

"Thank you," I said, dribbling a bit. I sheepishly wiped at my mouth. "Beg pardon, ma'am."

The woman laughed. "It is an acquired taste." Her eyes through the mask were a pale grass green, startlingly vivid in this color-starved room. "Is this your first ball here?"

I gave a self-conscious laugh. "Is it so very obvious?"

She only gave me an enigmatic smile in response. "And how are you enjoying yourself, my dear?"

"A little overwhelmed," I admitted. "I was looking for a place to catch my breath. Get some air."

The winter woman smoothed a stray bit of hair behind my ear and my hand flew up to catch the wilting poppy still tucked there. It was an uncomfortably intimate gesture from someone I did not know, and the queasy feeling arose again. Glancing about the room, I noticed that all those in attendance—save François, Käthe, and Josef—wore a scarlet bloom pinned to their costumes.

"Are you sure? It's quite chilly outside," she said. "I can escort you to one of the private rooms upstairs if you need a moment to yourself."

"Oh no, I couldn't possibly," I said, my cheeks flushing. "I—I think I'm overheated. Perhaps a walk outside will do me some good."

Those extraordinary green eyes regarded me thoughtfully. "The Count and Countess have a hedge maze in their gardens if you would like to wander."

"Oh yes, please," I said.

She nodded. "Follow me."

I handed my goblet to a waiting server before turning to follow the woman in white through the rooms and corridors to the gardens. She walked with a limp, a clubbed foot peeking out from behind the hem of her skirts as we made our way outside. I knew exactly what her costume was meant to portray. Frau Perchta of the swan-foot, the Christmas spirit who made sure we had spun our allotted amount of flax the previous year. But Christmas was long past and we were nearly to spring with the start of the Lenten season tomorrow. An odd choice.

We arrived at a set of glass doors in an empty room that led onto a terrace. "The gardens need tending," she said, a bit apologetically. "They've grown a bit unruly. Unsightly."

"I'm not afraid of ugliness," I said. "I rather enjoy a little bit of wildness."

Those green eyes studied my face, as though searching for an answer to a question she had not yet asked. "Yes," she said, placing a hand upon my cheek. "There is the air of the uncanny about you."

I coughed, opening the door and stepping out onto the terrace to further avoid her touch.

"Don't tarry too long, Elisabeth," she warned. "The night is long, and it is not yet spring."

Elisabeth. The hairs rose all along my arms. "How did you know—"

But the woman was already gone, the doors closed behind her. A shining, unbroken line of white lined the terrace, gleaming faintly in the moonlight. I swallowed hard, then stepped over the salt and into the darkness beyond.

THE LABYRINTH

I was not alone.

A handful of guests were also gathered outside, clustered in dribs and drabs around torches planted in intervals about the gardens. A few gentlemen were smoking pipes while their female companions fanned at the blue haze gathering about their faces, huddled close for warmth. Although the days in Vienna had grown almost warm, the nights still nipped at any bits of uncovered flesh like spiteful icy sprites. The cold air felt good against my flushed cheeks, but I wished I had brought my cloak.

Low laughter and soft murmurs rose in conversation as I descended from the terrace to the gardens, a persistent yet inescapable buzz that followed me like a swarm of flies. I resisted the urge to swat at the words catching at my ears.

"Have you heard about poor old Karl Rothbart?" I overheard one of the women say.

"No!" one of the men exclaimed. "Do tell."

"Dead," the woman replied. "Found in his workshop, lips blue with cold . . ."

Their voices faded away as I pressed myself farther and farther into the garden's murky retreat, searching for the entrance to the hedge maze. For all that I could not bear my own silence, I wanted the voices of the world around me to disappear. Solitude was different from loneliness, and it was solitude I was seeking.

At last I came upon the hedge maze. Far from the warm circles of light cast by torch and lamp, the leaves and twigs here were edged in a silver lacework of starlight and shadow. The entrance was framed by two large trees, their branches still bare of any new growth. In the darkness, they seemed less like garden posts marking the way into the labyrinth than two silent sentinels guarding the doorway to the underworld. Shapes writhed in the shadows beyond the archway of bramble and vine, both inviting and intimidating.

Yet I was not frightened. The hedge maze smelled like the forest outside the inn, a deep green scent of growth and decay, where life and death were intermingled. A familiar scent. A welcoming scent. The scent of home. Removing my mask, I crossed the threshold, letting darkness swallow me whole.

There were no torches or candles lit upon the paths, and neither moonlight nor starlight penetrated the dense bramble. Yet my footing along these paths was sure, every part of me attuned to the wildness around me. Unlike the maze at Schönbrunn Palace, a meticulously manicured and man-made construction, this labyrinth *breathed*. Nature creeped in along the edges, reclaiming groomed, orderly, and civilized corridors into a twisting tangle of tunnels and tracks, weeds and wildflowers. Paths grew vague, roots unruly, branches untamed. Somewhere deep in the labyrinth, I could hear the giggles and gasps of illicit encounters in the shrubbery. I was careful of my step, lest I trip over a pair of trysting lovers, but when I came upon no one else, I let myself fall into a meditative state of mind. I wandered the recursive spirals of the hedge maze, turn after turn after turn, feeling a measure of calm for the first time in a long time.

Somewhere at the heart of the labyrinth, a violin began to play.

It was as though some part of me that had been asleep was waking up after a deep slumber. Every part of me opened and unfurled toward the sound, my eyes clear, my ears alert. The thin, high wail of the instrument's voice seemed distant, yet each note was as clear as a dewdrop, the sound surrounding me from every direction: from north, south, east, west, up, down, behind.

"Josef?" I called.

I had not seen my brother since he vanished into the crowd earlier that night; he had not been on the dance floor, nor in any of the other rooms I had seen in my efforts to find a way out. I imagined he felt as out of depth as I had and had run to the first place that had felt comfortable, safe. The hedge maze possessed a waiting quality that reminded me of the Goblin Grove, an in-betweenness that reminded me of the long-forgotten sacred spaces of the world.

A swift breeze rustled the twigs and branches around me, raising the hairs at the back of my neck. The night grew even colder, and I wrapped my arms about me for warmth. There was a strange, metallic smell like the air before a thunderstorm, although the wind that knifed through my flimsy gown was keen-edged and bitter. Dead leaves skittered about me like rats through walls, and the darkness deepened as clouds raced across the face of the moon.

I reminded myself that I was not alone in the labyrinth, that somewhere beyond these bushes was a pair of lovers enjoying the salt-sweat of each other's company.

As I continued on, the voice of the violin changed. It grew deeper, weightier, the sound rich with emotion and resonant with feeling. This was not my brother's playing. The lightness, the transcendence, the ethereality that characterized his performance was missing. It was another musician.

And then I recognized the piece.

The Wedding Night Sonata.

My teeth chattered and I began to shiver uncontrollably. Fear and frost froze my blood. How could this be? I had never properly shared this piece of music with my brother; the letters containing drafts I had sent him had vanished, unread, into the Count's clutches. To my knowledge, he had never even heard the piece, for although his ear and his memory were good, not even Josef could recall in perfect detail every note, every pause, every phrase. There was only one other person who knew the Wedding Night Sonata.

"M-mein Herr?"

It could not be. It shouldn't be. There was no crossing the veil, no breaking the barrier between worlds. What could this possibly mean? The skittering around me escalated into a frenzy of scratching. It no longer sounded like leaves skipping across still-frozen ground, but fingernails—claws—scraping over stone.

Mistress.

I startled and glanced over my shoulder. I could make out no familiar shapes in the darkness of the hedge maze corridors. No human shapes. Branches and brambles reached for me with grasping hands as I passed, bursting forth from the walls like sudden shoots and saplings. Stone urns and marble benches warped and shifted into leering gargoyles, and I tried not to look at them, tried not to imagine beetle-black eyes and cobweb hair.

Your Highness.

It was but the whispering wind. The same wind that brought with it an unseasonably wintry chill, the scent of ice, of pine, of deep waters, and underground caverns. It was a memory, a ghost, my longing made manifest, not my mind gone awry. But as the underbrush shivered and danced, it unfolded itself into the shape of a girl.

"No," I said hoarsely.

A face grew from the ragged leaves, a long nose, pointy chin, narrow cheeks. It was a familiar face, a face I had thought I would never see again.

"Twig?" I breathed.

The goblin girl nodded, dipping her branch-and-cobweb-laden head at me in acknowledgment. In respect. Spots of granite dotted her green-brown arms like bruises, patches of stone crawling up the side of her face like a disease. She scratched at the patches as though they pained her, and she looked as though she were in agony. The only time I had ever seen Twig turn into stone was when she had violated one of the old laws to tell me what had happened to the first Goblin Queen. My heart twinged with pity—pity and fear and longing—and I reached for her, hands trembling.

My goblin girl held out her hands to me in turn, but our fingers passed through the other's like smoke. Her lips moved but no sound emerged but the sighing of the mistral breeze.

"Twig?" I rasped. "Twig? What is it?"

She opened her mouth to speak, then choked, the patches of stone on her skin seeming to writhe and grow.

"Twig!"

The covenant is undone. There was terror in her depthless black eyes, the first human emotion I had ever seen on a goblin's face. *It is corrupting us. Corrupting him.*

Him. The Goblin King. My austere young man.

"Twig!" I grabbed her hand, but got nothing but a fistful of thorns. "Twig!"

Save us. Twig cried out in silent anguish, her body cracking, popping, snapping in unnatural ways as she resisted crumpling back into bush and brush. *Save him.*

"How?" I cried over the screaming wind. "Tell me!"

My goblin girl's eyes rolled back in her head as vines burst from the ground, crisscrossing her body like chains around a prisoner. With tremendous effort, she lifted a hand and pointed a many-jointed finger at my feet.

The . . . poppies . . .

Looking down, I saw that I was standing in a river of red, a trail of blood leading away from me like a guided path of scarlet petals.

"Twig?"

Nothing remained but stars, winking at me through bramble branches. I thought I could hear the rumble of thunder in the distance, a gale howling just beyond the edges of the hedge maze. Hoofbeats and the baying of hounds in a hunt. The Wild Hunt.

The old laws made flesh: given steel and teeth and hounds to reap what they are owed.

Heart hammering, I raced along the path of poppies, trying to outrun and outpace the clang and the bang of alarm bells ringing in my mind. Behind me, I thought I could hear heavy breathing, the thudding footfalls of a pursuer. Turn after turn after turn, until I lost sight of the flowers and understood too late that I had become lost in the labyrinth.

And still the violin played on.

I pressed a hand to my breast, trying to catch my breath. A name came to my lips—Josef? Käthe? François?—but who would find me here, alone and anonymous? I thought of the Goblin King, and the burn in my chest intensified to a soul-deep ache.

The bushes rustled behind me. I turned to look, and gasped.

Looming in the shadows was a figure, skin night-black and eyes moon pale. Fingers broken and gnarled like desiccated vines curled around the neck of a violin, the resin cracked and peeled with age. A crown of horns grew from a nest of cobwebs and thistledown, but the face that stared back at me was human. Familiar.

Him.

"M-mein Herr?"

No sound from his lips, no movement of his head. The face that stared back was dear to me for all that it had changed, but it was like gazing into the eyes of a stranger. The mismatched irises had faded entirely to a blue-white that glowed in the dark, and there was no hint of recognition in their depths.

"Mein Herr?" I said again.

But no glimmer or spark of love warmed those icy eyes. I did not know if I could bear the weight of my shattered heart.

"Oh, *mein Herr*," I said, voice catching. "What have they done to you? What have *I* done?"

Slowly, carefully, so as not to startle a frightened forest creature, I lifted my hand, fingers outstretched. I reached for his cheek, to press my palm against his skin, to feel his flesh beneath my touch. The Goblin King held himself still as I drew just a bit closer, a bit closer, our eyes locked as I pushed and tested the new edges between us. His pupils grew dilated, and the pale ring of color around them deepened to a gray-blue, a muted green.

"Elisabeth?"

His head snapped up at the sound of someone calling my name.

"Elisabeth!"

"No," I whispered. "No, please, be, thou, with me—"

But he was gone in the next blink. The face I had been so close to caressing was the wind-smoothed wood of a cherry tree, the crown of horns its branches, his eyes a pair of stars in the night sky, winking at me in cruel jest. A wave of resignation and despair nearly overwhelmed me to my knees. Of course this had all been nothing but a bad dream. Nothing but my longing and loneliness giving life to the shadows in my mind.

"Elisabeth? Ah, there you are!" said an unfamiliar, faintly accented voice.

Glancing over my shoulder, I nearly fainted when I saw a skull hovering beside me, its teeth bared in a ghoulish grin.

"My dear? Are you all right?" The skull tilted back, and it was in that moment I realized I had not been staring at a disembodied skeleton, but a plump little man draped in a black cloak with a death's-head mask perched atop his face. An incredibly realistic and detailed death's-head mask.

"I-I'm sorry," I stammered. "Who are you?"

"I am *Der Tod*," the stranger chuckled. "I thought the costume was obvious." He beckoned toward me with the tip of his toy scythe. "And you, my dear, are my lost little angel of music. We have been looking for you for over an hour."

I held myself close, not wanting to make any sudden movements lest I spook this odd little man into doing something unpredictable. *"We?"* I asked. "Who's been looking for me?"

"My wife and me, of course," he said blithely, as though it were the most obvious answer in the world. "We've been waiting for you a long time. Now, my dear, let us make our way back to the party."

I had no response to such a cryptic statement. When I made no move to follow the stranger in the death's-head mask, he tilted his head in a quizzical expression.

"Fräulein? Are you coming?"

"You must forgive me," I said stiffly. "I don't know *who* you are, Master Death."

"Hmmm? Oh!" He laughed then, lifting his mask to reveal a surprisingly cheerful, apple-cheeked face. "I do beg your pardon." He swept forward in an elegant bow. "I am Otto von Procházka und zu Snovin, at your service." He straightened and fitted his death's-head mask over his face again, becoming anonymous once more. "The host of this infamous soiree, the proprietor of this magnificent house, and if I'm not mistaken"—dark eyes twinkled at me from the depths of the skull—"your most excellent new benefactor."

SHEEP SKINS

ount Procházka was . . . unexpected.

My mysterious benefactor was a rotund little man of indeterminate age. What little hair he had about his crown and side whiskers was a wiry gray, but his cheeks were rosy with the glow of youth and good humor. His waistcoat crinkled around his shiny brass buttons in much the same way his skin crinkled about his eyes when he smiled. Aside from the skull mask, his costume as Death seemed hastily put together, a black silk cloak thrown over what appeared to be ordinary apparel—a pale satin waistcoat, dark woolen jacket, dun-colored breeches, white stockings, black shoes with brass buckles glinting dully in the moonlight. A bloodred poppy was pinned to his lapel.

I hadn't realized until that moment that I had had a certain impression of my host from the elegant and educated hand on the letter he had sent me, as well as the salacious stories I'd heard from Frau Messner and the ladies of Herr Schneider's shop. I wasn't entirely sure what

I had been expecting—someone tall, beautiful, and languid, perhaps—but I certainly hadn't thought my patron—the subject of so many misgivings and incendiary rumors—would be a cheerful little cockatiel of a man twittering about in Bohemian-accented German.

"Terribly sorry if I gave you a fright," said the Count. "But your brother, your sister, and your friend were worried about your whereabouts, and when my wife told me you had come out to the gardens, I knew I had to come find you. Very few people have solved this labyrinth, you see."

Indeed, my unexpected host was making his way confidently through the twists and turns of the hedge maze while I tripped and skipped in order to keep up.

"It was my grandmother's idea," the Count went on, carrying on his half of the conversation whether I responded or no. "The hedge maze, I mean. She had a mind for mathematics and puzzles, but they say the labyrinth follows no logic anyone can decipher." He chuckled. "They say you must either be magical or mad in order to solve it."

Magic. I remembered the path of poppies blooming before me in the dark, a pair of glowing eyes blinking and winking in the night sky. *Madness.*

"I think it's pretty clear which one I am," the nobleman said. He grinned, a manic expression, and I had the suspicion I knew the answer.

"Both, obviously," the Count continued. "Although my wife would beg to differ." His smile widened, but it did nothing to lessen my discomfort. "Ah, but listen to me prattle on like a foolish girl just out of the schoolroom. Come, come, let us make haste, for the night is cold and full of horrors that might snatch you up and steal you away."

My ears pricked. "Steal me away?"

He paused then, turning to stare at me through the holes of his mask. "Haven't you heard the stories, *Fräulein?*" His voice was soft, sweet. "There are those"—he gestured toward the house, toward the city proper—"who would say that these disappearances are a regrettable consequence of the, ah, pleasures in which I and my associates are known to indulge."

I stiffened, thinking of what my landlady Frau Messner had told me: of the nameless girl the Procházkas had taken under their wing, the plain country maiden who had vanished under suspicious circumstances. Other bits of rumor and gossip flickered through my thoughts, wavering and dancing in and out like candle flame. *Laudanum. Rituals. Secrets.*

My host broke the tension with a laugh. "I jest, my dear. You have nothing to fear from me! Ah, I see we've found them," he said, waving to someone in the distance. "Or perhaps we have been found."

We emerged from the labyrinth. Standing outside, silhouetted by the lights from the house, were two figures: the swan-masked woman in white and a tall, thin youth holding a violin case, dressed as the night.

Josef.

"There you are," said the woman in white. "I was beginning to worry about you." Her green eyes were vivid, even in the shadows of her mask. "The night is cold and you have been gone quite some time."

"*Fräulein,*" the Count said, turning to me. "May I introduce you to my wife, Countess Maria Elena von Procházka und zu Snovin."

His wife. Suddenly, our earlier encounter made more sense, her overly familiar manner, how she seemed to have known me. The two of them made an odd pair; she all grace and cultured elegance, while he seemed put together by an absentminded puppeteer.

"Charmed," she said. "But we've met before."

Too late I remembered my manners and dropped into an awkward curtsy. "M-madame."

"The title is properly styled Your Illustriousness," the Count said kindly.

"Oh." My cheeks flamed with shame. "Beg pardon."

The Count waved his hand dismissively. "Let's not fuss over such piddling details. Do call me Otto, or *mein Herr*, if you prefer."

Reflexively, my hand went to the bare spot at the base of my throat, but no one seemed to notice.

"I would you stop embarrassing our guests, Otto," the Countess admonished, but there was fondness in her voice. "You must forgive my husband, children," she said, turning to me and Josef. "His enthusiasm rather runs away with him."

I looked to my brother, but he was resolutely not returning my gaze.

"Shall we return?" he asked in a dull voice. "I would need some time to warm up."

"Your brother has offered to grace us with a performance," the Countess said. Those startling green eyes were fixed on my face. "A selection which includes some of your work, as I am to understand it."

"Ah, yes, the composer," Count Procházka said. "What a rare and magnificent gift you have, *Fräulein*!"

I tried to smile, but my face felt as frozen as the air outside. "It's not much of a gift, Your Illustriousness."

"Nonsense," the Countess said. "The gift of creation and genius is the only one we share with God. Embrace your talents, Elisabeth, for they are rare indeed. Now"—she glanced over her shoulder at the labyrinth—"let us get back inside quickly. It is not a night to be caught outdoors without protection."

Josef frowned. "Protection?"

"From frostbite." The Count gave us a disarming smile.

The Countess shook her head. "Oh, an old superstition, child, nothing more. It is Shrove Tuesday, a night of transition from one season to another. As the days of winter draw to a close, hostile forces ride about."

This time my brother did meet my gaze. There was a question in those pale blue depths, one I did not quite know how to answer. While Josef and I had grown up on tales of goblins, Lorelei, and *Der Erlkönig*, there were myths and tales we had yet to remember. The Wild Hunt. Elf-touched. Elf-struck.

The Count shivered. "Let us head inside, my dears; I'm freezing my unmentionables off." He offered his wife his arm, not merely out of courtesy, but to help her hobble back inside.

"Otto!" The Countess gave her husband an affectionate slap on the arm, but the expression in those green eyes was anything but playful. Instead they seemed almost worried, darting back and forth from us to the hedge maze, as though she, too, could hear ghostly hoofbeats trailing us from another world.

Inside the house, the ball was still in full swing, the music filtering in along with the rhythmic patter of feet and the shushing swish of shoes and skirts across the floor. The Count and Countess brought Josef and me into a side gallery, away from the crowd in the ballroom, but the gallery was far from empty. A handful of guests were gathered there, drinking and smoking and laughing with the comfort and ease of long-standing acquaintances and friends. Behind their masks, there was an eerie similarity to all of them, although I did not know them from Adam. They all had the plump, placid look of those who had never known a moment's hardship, the easy, generous manner of those who had never lacked for aught, yet there was a hunger about them, a want, a desire. My brother and I were no more than mayflies in their privileged sphere, but whenever their gazes alighted on us, they lingered with interest—with covetousness—at our bare faces. Their curiosity scratched, and I itched with discomfort.

"Where are Käthe and François?" I asked. My teeth chattered with more than cold.

"You're shivering!" the Countess exclaimed. "Come, warm yourself by the *Ofen,* the two of you."

She led Josef and me to what I had taken for a tall ceramic ornament or wardrobe set into a stone nook, radiant with heat. It looked a little like an oven, with poppies carved across its face.

"Shall I fetch you a shawl, my dear?" the Count asked me. His skull mask was perched atop his head, his cheeks red with overexertion and cold alike, sweat streaming down his temples.

"Oh no, Your—Your Illustriousness," I said. "I'm quite all right. Have you seen my sister and our friend?"

But the Count paid me no heed. He waved down a servant and murmured something into his ear.

"Is there a place I might warm up in private?" Josef asked the Countess in a quiet voice. His eyes darted from corner to corner, side to side, taking in the number of people in the gallery.

"Of course, my child." She gestured to another servant, who nodded his head and disappeared into the crowd. "We have a klavier in the drawing room downstairs," she offered. "I'm afraid it's nothing fancy; just an old harpsichord that belonged to Otto's grandmother. Will that suffice?"

Josef looked to me, brows lifted. It was a bit surprising that the Count, a professed lover of music—my music—did not have a more modern instrument in his house. Nearly all performances were made on the fortepiano these days.

"We would have to ask François, Your Illustriousness," I said. "He is my brother's usual accompanist."

"Not you?" the Countess asked. Her tone was neutral, but she seemed surprised.

"No, ma'am."

"But I thought you were a musician."

I bit my lip. My brother had once called me the genius of our relationship, the creator, not the interpreter. I wrote the notes, Josef gave them life. But many of Vienna's well-known composers performed their works as well—the late, great Mozart and this upstart Beethoven among them. I was no prodigy of performance, a fact I learned almost immediately after hearing François play for the first time.

It was in these moments that I wished my brother would come to my defense, to speak for me, to explain our process, to be the one holding me up for once. But he stayed quiet and withdrawn, nearly invisible despite his golden curls, sharp features, and lean height.

"I am a musician," I said quietly. "But my talents lie in the creation of music, not the execution of it. You will find my playing a very poor substitute for François's indeed."

Those grass green eyes glinted—with amusement? annoyance?—as the Countess studied me closely. "Nevertheless," she said. "You are the composer of *Der Erlkönig,* are you not? It is *your* execution of your own work that interests me, not someone else's interpretation of it."

I looked to Josef again, but he was fiddling with his violin case, his feet shuffling back and forth nervously. A sudden surge of irritation burned the unease from my gut. If my brother would not speak on my behalf, then I would say nothing on his either. François was by far the better partner for Josef; they had had months of practice together on the road, and he knew how to shape their playing into a singular performance rather than a display of individual talents.

"As you wish, Your Illustriousness," I said.

"Please." The Countess smiled. "We are among friends. Call me Elena."

I tried not to let my discomfort show. "Yes, ma'am," I said, unable to bring myself to use her Christian name.

Her eyes twinkled in the depths of her wintry mask. "That's settled then," she said. "Come, we shall adjourn downstairs." Yet another servant reappeared with a tray with glasses of sherry. Or was it the same as the first? I could no longer tell. "Ah, thank you. Have a drink, my dears. It shall keep you warm as we move you away from the *Ofen.*"

Josef and I accepted the glasses out of politeness, but neither he nor I were much inclined to take a sip.

"Drink, drink," the Countess urged. "Drink and we shall begin."

Seeing no other way to avoid being rude, we both downed our sherry and returned the glasses to the tray. Josef coughed, his face reddening.

"Fra-François," he choked out, but our hostess did not appear to hear him. She held her arm out to her husband, who took it in his grip and helped her limp downstairs.

Josef and I watched them go.

"Well," he said after a moment. "Shall we?" He absentmindedly scratched his neck, as though the sherry he had drunk could be rubbed away. It was then I noticed the scarlet poppy pinned to the lapel of his costume.

"Sepperl," I said, pointing to the flower. "What is this?"

"Hmmm?" He dropped his arm and glanced down at his lapel. "Oh. The Countess gave it to me. 'For faith,' she said."

My hand reached up to touch the wilted poppy tucked behind my own ear. I hadn't lost it in the labyrinth.

"Sepp," I whispered. "What have we gotten ourselves into?"

It was a long while before he answered. "You tell me, Liesl," he said. His eyes were hard beneath his black domino mask. "After all, isn't this what you've always wanted?"

DER ERLKÖNIG'S OWN

the parlor downstairs was small, more like the vestry of a church than receiving room. It looked a bit like a sacristy as well, the walls lined with dark wood panels resembling a choir and the granite floor covered with a tapestried Persian rug. The acoustics were strange in the space, both echoing and muffled at once, and I thought again it was an odd place for a professed lover of music like the Count to hold an impromptu concert.

The Count and Countess were already comfortably seated on plush red velvet chairs on opposite sides of the room from each other when Josef and I entered. The harpsichord lay between them, and they looked like guardian deities to a musical underworld. Neither had removed their masks; the Countess as Frau Perchta in her swan's feathers, the Count as *Der Tod* in his death's-head guise. Mirrors and opposites: black and white, night and day, save for the poppies pinned to their clothing like a drop of blood.

"Welcome," the Countess said. "Make yourselves comfortable. Once you feel sufficiently warmed up, we can bring the other guests in for the performance."

"And my sister?" I asked. "François?"

The Count smiled. "I'm sure they shall come in with the others."

His wife gestured to the harpsichord. "Your kingdom awaits, my children."

My brother and I exchanged glances before making our way to the instrument. My brother set his case down and took out his violin while I sat down at the harpsichord. I lifted my hands to black and ivory keys, the inverse of all the other keyboards I had played before. The major keys were black, the minor white, and for a stomach-churning moment, I thought that I had forgotten how to play. The inverted colors gave me a sense of vertigo, making me unsure of my fingering and even the notes.

"Liesl?" Josef held his bow poised over his strings, ready to tune his violin.

Shaking off my disorientation, I found my place. I played a few chords; old as it was, the harpsichord had been relatively well cared for, the plucking mechanism smooth, the strings in tune. Josef nodded to me as I played G, D, A, and E, repeatedly plunking the notes until Josef had tuned his violin to me. Then he diligently ran through his exercises: scales, thirds, fourths, fifths, repeating rounds of musical phrases to warm up his hands.

I did the same on the harpsichord, trying to acquaint myself not only with an entirely new instrument, but to reacquaint myself with the attitude of playing for performance and not in private. I had long since stopped the agility drills and exercises Papa had made us do every day, and my fingers felt thick and leaden.

"Are you ready?" The Countess watched us with avid interest, but the Count's attention seemed elsewhere. For someone who had been so keen to bring me here—to Vienna, to his very home—because of my music, he evinced remarkably little interest in our playing. I had initially taken his bumbling eccentricity for charm or possibly the product of a laudanum-addled mind, but my feelings about my patron quickly returned to their initial dread.

"If you please," I said a trifle sheepishly. "I left a folio of sheet music upstairs with my cloak and other things. If someone could—"

Another red-clad servant entered the room before I could even finish my thought, carrying my leather-bound folio on a silver platter. My dread deepened. The room, my hosts, the entire *house* made for an eerie company, and the strange sameness of the liveried members of the house contributed to this growing sense of unreality.

I thanked the servant with a tight smile, and opened the folio to sort through the pages until I found *Der Erlkönig*. I tried to ignore the press of the Countess's eyes upon my skin. There was something about her scrutiny that went beyond mere curiosity; there was a sort of hunger or desire that pulsed from her like waves of perfume, and it made me both ashamed and excited at once.

I settled the pages of the score on the music stand of the harpsichord and sat back down upon the bench. I looked to Josef, who was silently running his hands along the neck of his violin, practicing his fingering in an almost perfunctory manner. This casual indifference toward performance struck me more than his coldness toward me; Josef was sensitive and shy. Or at least, he was once.

"Shall we call your guests, Your Illustriousness?" he asked in a dull voice.

The Countess smiled, leaning back in her chair. "I was rather hoping you would indulge us both with a private rendition of *Der Erlkönig*, Herr Vogler," she said. "I hope you don't mind."

Josef shrugged, but gave a quick, polite bow. "As you wish, my lady."

He settled his instrument against his shoulder, his bow in hand loose by his side, and raised his gaze to mine, waiting for me to join him. A low, insistent throb pulsed at the base of my skull, and I regretted not having a bite to eat upstairs at one of the myriad banquet tables. I felt as though I had swallowed gravel, but I smiled at my brother, and nodded. He straightened his back and rested his chin against his violin, while I poised my hands over the keyboard, awaiting his cue. Josef gave me the tempo, counting us in with the bounce of his bow, and the two of us began to play *Der Erlkönig*.

The sound of the harpsichord was initially jarring when paired with the violin. The plectra plunked and plucked, the strings shivered and did not resound, and the piece took on an ominous overtone that was not normally present when played on a more modern instrument. I tried to find my footing in the midst of this new aural sensation, trying to focus on the *notes* and not the *sound*. I was distracted by a sudden desire to experiment, to improvise. To *play*. To frolic and gambol and race within the music the way the Goblin King and I had done when I was a child. I shook my head and tried to focus on my brother instead, to listen, to follow, to support.

But he was not there.

Josef was not present in his music. His notes were

precise as always, but we were missing something, a connection that ebbed and flowed between us as easy and intimate as conversation. We were playing at each other, not with each other.

The Count shifted in his seat, lifting his hand to stifle a yawn.

Oh, mein Brüderchen, I thought. *Oh, Sepp, what is happening to us?*

I tried desperately to make eye contact with my brother, trying to find that vein, that lifeline that bound us together. *Play with me, Sepp,* I begged. *Play with me.*

I had not been lying when I told the Countess that I was not a performer. I had the skills but not the touch. I wondered if my brother had become so used to playing with François that he could not remember how to find me, how to dance together in the music we shared. Or was this disconnect a symptom of a deeper estrangement? How had it come to this, we who had been as close as two halves of one heart now as distant and careful as strangers? Sadness bled from my face down to my fingertips, weighing down the notes with grief.

And Josef . . . he played on with that ruthless, exacting clarity. He was ether and air and void, while I was earth and root and rock. Resentment burned through my sadness, followed by the wash of anger. *Meet me, Sepp,* I thought, and then changed the accompaniment.

The change in the room was immediate. A lifting of pressure, an intake of relief, the waiting lull before a rainfall. Josef was too practiced a musician to falter when I took him by surprise, but for the first time in a long time, a spark crackled between us, lightning jumping from cloud to cloud. My brother was here. With me. He was present, and listening.

A game, Sepperl, I thought. *A game like we used to play.*

I improvised on the structures I had established, finding new shapes in the chords. My brother followed, his playing growing sharper. The melody was the same, but the color different. This version of *Der Erlkönig* had keen edges that sliced and cut you with its beauty, its otherworldliness. It was not the version of the bagatelle I had in mind when I wrote it. I had written it to be dreamy, melancholy, nostalgic. I had written it as a farewell to my family when I first ventured Underground, leaving behind a piece of the girl I was.

Now that I had taken the music and molded it, my brother took the lead. The notes grew angry, and it was as if he were saying, *You want a reckoning? We shall have it now.* We were speaking to each other once more, and I hadn't known until that moment how little we had heard one another. We transitioned back into the original arrangement, and I understood what it was he was trying to say at last.

Discontent. Unfulfillment. A hollow emptiness. A constant questing, searching, seeking, only to find himself right back in the place he began. Trapped. My brother felt trapped. Hemmed in by expectation, by pressure, by the weight of my desires crowding in on him so that his own wants had no room to breathe.

Oh, Sepp, I thought.

I listened. I listened and listened and listened, letting my accompaniment support my brother the way I had not since we came to Vienna. Josef played, adding trills and embellishments that were practically Baroque in complexity and flourish, but were also an expression of his frustration. He nearly rushed a set of sixteenth notes, but even in the midst of this uncharacteristic outburst of emotion, my brother was controlled, years of rigid discipline keeping his tempo even.

Something changed.

There was a strange, hushed quality to the room that had nothing to do with the rediscovered connection between us nor the reverent rapture of the audience. The smell of pine and loam and ice filled the air, but faintly, like the whiff of perfume caught in passing. I drew in a clean, clear, alpine breath, the crispness of mountain breezes and stony caverns filling my lungs. The skull's head and the swan pressed in closer.

Elisabeth.

My fingers skipped a few notes, and I almost stumbled out of the playing, startled out of the piece. But my hands still held on to the hours of practice to which I had subjected them, the muscles moving automatically as though they held memories of their own.

Elisabeth.

I kept my eyes on my brother, attentive to his cues, but I sensed a presence in the room that was neither human nor mortal. I thought of the vision I had in the labyrinth, the glowing eyes and the crown of horns and kept my eyes grimly focused on Josef, trying to blot out the other voice in my mind.

Then the music ended.

The bagatelle was not a particularly long piece, and it finished on an uncertain note. Josef did not hold that last fermata with any sort of conviction, only a resignation that shattered me even more than his despair. His bowing arm went limp, his head drooping as though the weight of his isolation was too much for him to bear. Despite our momentary connection, my brother seemed unchanged, untouched by the magic we had created together. Now that the music was over, my head felt thick, the beginnings of a headache crowding my mind.

Our hosts broke into applause, the Count most enthusiastic of them all.

"Capital, capital!" he said, beaming with delight. "I have never heard such playing! It was so beautiful. So pleasant!"

I frowned. He *had* heard such playing before; he had written of it in his letter to me. While I was flattered by his remarks, the music my brother and I performed tonight could hardly be called *pleasant*. My heart slowly sank into my stomach like a stone. I was beginning to realize that the Count was not a man of discerning taste. And although I was grateful for his attention and his desire to elevate us, I couldn't help but wonder if he were merely looking to be fashionable. Countess Thun and Prince Lichnowsky were both patrons of Mozart and Beethoven; perhaps this Bohemian nobleman was looking for his own pet musician with no standard of quality or aesthetic. I could have been any other composer as far as he was concerned. I rubbed at my temples, the throbbing moving up my skull to push at my eyes. I needed to stand up. I needed to sit down. I needed to lie down.

"*Bravi, bravi.*" The Countess clapped, two sharp claps of approval. "It was everything I had hoped for and more."

Everything *she* had hoped for? That niggle of doubt, that trickle of suspicion about the Count suddenly flowed together in a flood of understanding.

"It was you who wrote me the letter that brought me here." I did not use her proper courtesy. I was too dizzy to be concerned about rudeness.

It all made sense. The elegant hand on the invitation, how

she addressed me as *Mademoiselle* like the writer of the letter, not *Fräulein* like her husband. I thought of the Count's unsophisticated ear and his lack of enthusiasm or education about either Josef or me, save for when we interested his wife.

Her green eyes sharpened as though in a smile. "Have I been so transparent?"

I shook my head, but not in answer to her question. My head felt thick, my eyelids heavy.

"I have heard extraordinary rumors about you, young lady," she continued in a soft voice. "Rumors about the . . . *otherworldly* nature of your music."

I laughed, but it sounded twisted, warped. "I am merely mortal," I said hoarsely. "Not magic."

"Are you so certain of that, my dear?"

I flushed both hot and cold at once. I shivered uncontrollably, small, tiny tremors all over my body although the room was too close, too warm. I broke out in a sweat, but my skin felt clammy. "What . . . what . . ." I thought of the glasses of sherry my brother and I had drunk before we came down to perform. "What have you put in my drink?" I slurred.

A soft *thud*. Josef crumpled to a heap on the floor, his violin jangling as it struck the ground, his bow arm outstretched and pointed toward the Countess, an accusatory finger.

"Sepperl!" I cried, but the words were dampened, deadened, numb. I pressed my fingers to my lips, but I could no longer feel them.

The room was growing smaller, the air was stagnant around me, dank and rank with the sickly sweet smell of rotting flowers. I could not breathe, I could not get out. My limbs felt thick and heavy, and there was an iron band of pressure at my brow. I turned to the Countess.

"Why?" I asked weakly, trying in vain to keep my balance

through the room swaying and tilting around me.

"I'm sorry, Elisabeth," the Countess said, and there was genuine sorrow in her voice. "But I promise this is for your own good."

"Käthe—"

"Your sister and the dark-skinned young gentleman are taken care of," she promised. "They shall come to no harm."

I was falling, falling through the ground, an endless void opening up beneath me. "Who are you?" I croaked.

"You know who we are." I heard the Countess's voice as though from far away, miles or years distant. "We are the mad, the fearful, the faithful. We are those who keep the old laws, for we are *Der Erlkönig's* own."

Elisabeth.

I open my eyes but I do not know where I am. The world around me is hazy, murky, formless, as though seen through mist, or fog, or cloud. My breathing echoes strangely, both echoing and muffled at once, and my heart beats louder than a gong.

Elisabeth.

My pulse quickens, the drumbeats of my blood rising in pitch. I turn around, a name on my lips, an ecstatic shout in my heart. *Mein Herr, mein Herr!*

Elisabeth.

His voice is far away, coming from a great distance. I wander aimlessly through the flat gray, searching for shapes, for light, for shadow, for anything to give my surroundings weight and depth. Where was I? Was I dreaming?

Howling rises all around me, the bell-like baying of hounds. It rings in my rib cage, resounding in my chest. I feel it crawling up my throat, a ripping, tearing sound, silver-sweet and sharp. I want to scream, not in pain, but in stark, raving madness. I scratch at my neck, hard enough to draw blood, but whether to free my voice or keep it trapped, I don't know.

Elisabeth!

When I pull my hand away, my fingertips are not stained red, but silver. I stare at my nails, trying to make sense of what I see when out of the formless gloom, a monster emerges.

I do scream when a pair of blue-white eyes appear, a pinprick of black in their center. Slowly a shape coalesces into being—a long, elegant face, whorls of inky shadows swirling over moon pale skin, ram's horns curling around pointed, elfin ears. He is more terrifying and more real than the vision I experienced in the labyrinth. But worst of all are the hands, gnarled and curled and with one too many joints in each finger. With a silver ring around the base of one. A wolf's-head ring, with two gems of blue and green for eyes.

My ring. His ring. The symbol of our promise I had returned to the Goblin King back in the Goblin Grove.

Mein Herr?

For a brief moment, those blue-white eyes regain some color, the only color in this gray world. Blue and green, like the gems on the ring about his finger. Mismatched eyes. Human eyes. The eyes of my immortal beloved.

Elisabeth, he says, and his lips move painfully around a mouth full of sharpened teeth, like the fangs of some horrifying beast. Despite the fear knifing my veins, my heart grows soft with pity. With tenderness. I reach for my Goblin King, longing to touch him, to hold his face in my hands the way I had done when I was his bride.

Mein Herr. My hands lift to stroke his cheek, but he shakes his head, batting my fingers away.

I am not he, he says, and an ominous growl laces his words as his eyes return to that eerie blue-white. *He that you love is gone.*

Then who are you? I ask.

His nostrils flare and shadows deepen around us, giving shape to the world. He swirls a cloak about him as a dark forest comes into view, growing from the mist. *I am the Lord of Mischief and the Ruler Underground.* His lips stretch thin over that dangerous mouth in a leering smile. *I am death and doom and* Der Erlkönig.

No! I cry, reaching for him again. *No, you are he that I love, a king with music in his soul and a prayer in his heart. You are a scholar, a philosopher, and my own austere young man.*

Is that so? The corrupted Goblin King runs a tongue over his gleaming teeth, those pale eyes devouring me as though I were a sumptuous treat to be savored. *Then prove it. Call him by name.*

A jolt sings through me—guilt and fear and desire altogether. His name, a name, the only link my austere young man has to the world above, the one thing he could not give me.

Der Erlkönig throws his head back in a laugh. *You do not even known your own beloved's name, maiden? How can you possibly call it love when you walked away, when you abandoned him and all that he fought for?*

I shall find it, I say fiercely. *I shall call him by name and bring him home.*

Malice lights those otherworldly eyes, and despite the monstrous markings and horns and fangs and fur that claim the Goblin King's comely form, he turns seductive, sly. *Come, brave maiden,* he purrs. *Come, join me and be my bride once* more, for it was not your austere young man who showed you the dark delights of the Underground and the flesh. It was I.

His words send a thrill through me, galvanizing me from the top of my head to the tips of my toes, and my body responds to the honey in his voice, even as my mind finds it bitter, rancid. *No,* I say. *Never.*

Der Erlkönig's eyes narrow, and the mist between us thins and retreats. But it is not cloud or fog in the distance; it is the spectral forms of ghostly horsemen, scraps of clothing hanging off shriveled flesh and ancient bone. The unholy host. Their eyes are milky, shining with an absence of light, of life, and at their feet are hounds made of darkness, their eyes the red of blood, of hell, of . . . poppies.

Poppies.

A sickly sweet smell begins to fill my senses, causing me to cough and gag and retch. A heavy, cloying scent, it clouds the world around me again, pulling me away from *Der Erlkönig,* from the hellhounds, from the Hunt.

No! Der Erlkönig is furious, lunging for me before I disappear into a purple haze. But those gnarled hands pass straight through me, spearing me with ice and cold and death. I scream with pain, gasping out a name, but that ghostly embrace is keeping me in this dream, this nightmare.

At once those blue-white eyes warm, filled again with color. *Elisabeth!*

The Goblin King wrenches himself away and I fall to my hands and knees, breathing hard. *Mein Herr!*

Elisabeth, he says, and I can see him struggling to hold on, to fight back the darkness threatening to subsume him. *Go. Run. Get away from here, lest the Hunt claim you.*

No, I say. *Stay with me. Be with me!*

But the Goblin King shakes his head. The intense,

flowery smell grows stronger, and the world wavers, as though seen underwater.

The old laws seek to redress the ancient balance. I made you a promise, Elisabeth, and I intend to keep it. He holds his hand out to me, and in his palm I see the ring I had left for him back in the Goblin Grove. His ring. A symbol of his power and our troth. I reach out and for the briefest of moments, we touch. Our palms brush each other's, and I am swept up in a tide of longing so intense, I fear I will go mad.

Hold me, kiss me, take me, ravish me, steal me away—

No! The Goblin King's eyes go wide, and he shoves me away.

Oh please oh please oh please oh please—

Go, Elisabeth! he cries. *Go, before I am lost, before—*

And then he is gone, those mismatched eyes drowned in a sea of white.

Mein Herr!

Elisabeth!

Still he calls my name. I search for his, digging, clawing, tearing at the corners of my mind, scratching at the corners of sanity to find it.

Elisabeth!

Elisabeth!

I wake up.

THE END
OF THE WORLD

"Elisabeth!"

I struggled to open my eyes, feeling as though they were each weighted down and sealed shut with iron. I was overwhelmed by the strong smell of ammonia, my lungs involuntarily seizing as I try to draw in large breaths of stale, flat air. Nausea roiled my stomach, and I rolled over, retching out my guts.

"Ugh!" Someone made a disgusted noise beside me, but nothing but bile burned my throat.

"She's awake," said another voice. Female. Familiar. "Put that away, the smell is quite putting me off my supper."

Slowly, as the waves of nausea subsided, my senses began to return. I was lying on something soft and plush, a luxurious velvet rubbing against my cheek. Whatever I was lying on was moving, rocking me back and forth, back and forth, like a boat on the sea. A rattling noise filled my head, *clop-clop-scritch, clop-clop-scritch.* My fingers were curled around something small, hard, and round. I cracked open my eyes, my vision blurry and hazy, hand unfurling to reveal something glinting silver in my palm. Two chips of blue and green winked at me.

A ring.

His ring.

It was then I recognized the rattling noise as the *clop-clop-scritch* of horseshoes on gravel, the swaying beneath me as the bouncing of a carriage. I quickly closed my hand over the Goblin King's promise as I sat up with a start, wincing as a sharp pain lanced through my skull.

"Liesl?" It was my brother's voice, unstrung and ragged with worry.

"Sepp?" I croaked. He did not answer, but I felt his hand wrap around my closed fist, clammy despite the cold. "Where—what—"

"How are you feeling, my dear?" asked a kindly voice. With a herculean effort, I looked up to see the plump form of Count Procházka sitting before me, his skull's-head mask still perched atop his head.

My throat was on fire, my mouth stuffed with cobwebs and cotton wool. "Like I've just been drugged," I rasped.

"We did apologize," said another. The Countess, her white dress gleaming in the darkness, her face in shadow. Only her vivid green eyes were visible, catching the dim light filtered through the curtains like a mirror. "The methods were uncouth, but we didn't have time to explain."

"Then explain now," Josef said tersely. "Explain where you're taking us and what you've done with François. And Käthe."

Alarm rang in my chest, waves of fear resonating in my bones like a bell. It cleared away the remnants of fog from my mind and I leaned forward, yanking at the draperies that concealed us from the world outside. Moonlight poured into the carriage along with the cold, illuminating unfamiliar farms and fields wreathed in mist. We were hours—miles—from the city, judging by the empty, desolate, sparsely populated landscape rushing past.

"Do close those curtains, child," the Countess said. "You'll catch your death of a chill."

"What have you done with my sister?" I demanded. "Our friend?" I thought of the stories circulating around the Procházkas, the mysterious disappearance of the young woman in their care, the suspicious death of a young man of their acquaintance.

"They're fine," the Count said. "I promise you they are alive and well. They are at Procházka House at the moment. Our friends and associates shall care for them."

"Have you drugged them too?" I asked sharply.

"They shall come to no harm," he repeated.

"Forgive me if I don't believe you."

"You are forgiven."

I turned my head to face the Countess, startled by the sight of her distinctive eyes in an unfamiliar face. Then I realized that she had removed her Frau Perchta mask, at last revealing her countenance entire. The Countess was not a young woman, perhaps ten or so years older than Mother. Her hair was dark and liberally streaked with gray, but her complexion was bright and clear, the bones of her face strong, giving her an ageless quality. She was not beautiful, exactly, but her features held the same old-fashioned elegance of many of those in the rural villages where I had grown up. It was not a delicate, refined face; it was the solid, high-cheeked, heavy-jawed face of a dairy wife or farm *Frau*.

"Your sister and your friend shall come to no harm," the

Countess said. "But the same cannot be said for you or your brother."

Josef's grip tightened, and the Goblin King's ring bit into my palm. "Is that a threat?" I asked.

"No, Elisabeth," she said. "Not a threat, but a warning. We are en route to our summer estate in Bohemia at the moment, a stronghold of our family. There are forces in the world that wish you harm, and it is our duty to protect you."

"Protect us?" I was incredulous. "Why?"

"A covenant has been broken," the Countess said, her face grim. "The old laws have been cheated of a proper sacrifice, and they have let the unholy host loose upon the world."

Scraps of spectral flesh hanging on skeletal frames, eyes white with death, silver blood on my hands and a voice urging, *Go. Run. Get away from here, lest the Hunt claim you.*

"And you believe we are in danger?" I asked.

Her green gaze grazed my skin, stinging like the rays of the sun. "No. I *know* you are," she said in a low, hard voice. "Goblin Queen."

The words thudded in the thick air, heavy and portentous and accusatory. Silence came down like a curtain between us, muffling all thought, all feeling, all sensation. Josef hissed in surprise, drawing away from me as though he had been burned. Betrayed. The Count's eyes darted between his wife and me, shrinking like a nervous rabbit caught between a hawk and a wolf.

"No," I whispered. "How did you . . . I'm not . . ."

"Yes," she hissed. Those green eyes were lit with fervor, crackling like St. Elmo's fire. "Did you think you could walk away without facing the consequences?"

I shook my head. "He let me go." My voice was small, remembering the last time I had seen the Goblin King, whole and entire, standing in the Goblin Grove with his hand upraised in farewell. "He let me go."

The Countess scoffed. "And you believed him?"

I thought of the ring in my hand, but I dared not turn it over to study it, to verify that I had pulled a promise from a dream. "Yes," I whispered.

"He is not the Lord of Mischief for nothing," she said.

I thought of mismatched eyes fading to white, the image of a young man turning into a monster, his beautiful violinist's hands contorting into claws, horns growing from the crown of his head. "He is so much more than that."

"Liesl," Josef said. "What is going on? What is happening? Goblin Queen? Unholy host? What does this all mean?"

I said nothing. I did not—could not—face my brother at the moment. I had once tried to tell him of my fantastic past, of my time beneath the earth as *Der Erlkönig*'s bride. I had bared my soul in writing, in words if not in notes, but Josef never received them. That letter had never reached him, along with the countless others I had sent, stolen by the woman before me. And now the rapport between my brother and me was broken. Muffled. Stifled. Silenced.

"It means nothing good, lad," the Count said gently. "It means that we need to get you and your sister somewhere safe as soon as possible, away from the unholy host."

Josef narrowed his eyes. "The unholy host?"

"They have many names." The Count was the very picture of a bumbling, absentminded man, the kind people were apt to dismiss due to his amiability. Yet his black-button eyes were sharp, and a canny intelligence gleamed there, nearly lost to the smiling chubby cheeks. "Some know them as the Wild Hunt. Back home in Bohemia, we call it *divoký hon*. Your dark-skinned friend would know them as *le Mesnée d'Hellequin,* I should think."

"Hellequin?" I thought of the figures of the *commedia dell'arte,* those black-and-white-masked players onstage as Columbine, as Pierrot, as Harlequin. I'd seen those costumes at the Procházkas' ball. "Like the trickster?"

"Hellequin, Harlequin, the Italian Arlecchino, Dante's devil Alichino, whom the Anglo-Saxons called *herla cyning,*" he said. "They are one and the same. You know him best, *Fräulein,* as *Der Erlkönig.*"

Josef sucked in a sharp breath. "The Goblin King."

"Yes," he said solemnly. "The ruler Underground."

The ring in my palm. A promise made, a marriage troth broken. I curled my fingers even tighter, feeling the impression of the wolf's-head dig into my hand like a brand.

"Then it's true," Josef whispered. He trembled in the seat next to me, but not with fear. With excitement. Eagerness. "What the legends have said. What our grandmother always told us. *Der Erlkönig* calls to us, beckons us to his side. It's all true?"

The longing in my brother's voice tugged at me, tangling the threads of guilt and love that were wound around my heart. *We always come back in the end.* Twin spots of red stained his cheeks, and his blue eyes shone like gems in the dark.

"Yes, young man." The Countess looked grave. "It is all true. Which is why we have brought you here, so we can watch over you."

The letter. The fifty florins. The apartments, the appointments, the auditions, the audiences. All arranged by the Countess. Everything, down to the even, elegant handwriting that gave no clue as to the intentions of its author, was calculated for this. To bring me to Vienna. To bring me before her.

To the composer of Der Erlkönig. It was not my music the Countess had been after. I did not know whether to be disappointed or relieved.

"But why?" I asked her. "I am not the Goblin Queen, not anymore. I gave up that power. That responsibility."

The Countess's eyes glittered. "The old laws have not given you up, Elisabeth. Think you can remove the taint of the uncanny so easily? You have a gift, child. It makes you vulnerable."

I frowned. "What gift?"

It was a long moment before she replied. "When I first heard your brother play that queer little bagatelle you both performed tonight, I sensed it," she said softly.

"Sensed what?"

She turned her head away. "The thinning of the barrier between worlds."

All the hair stood up on the back of my neck.

"At first, I thought it was your brother who had the gift," she said, giving Josef a sidelong glance. "He certainly has a marvelous talent for music, but no, it was not his playing that parted the veil between us and the Underground. It was the notes." She laughed, without humor, without mirth. "Those of us who have been touched by *Der Erlkönig* can reach across worlds, in sight or sound or sense. We can hear things, see things, feel things that no other mortals can witness. My gift is sensation, but yours, Elisabeth, is sound."

The air around us grew heavy, stale, thick, as though we were trapped in a burrow. A barrow. A grave.

"Touched by *Der Erlkönig*," I breathed. "What do you mean? Have you . . . have you met . . . *him*?"

The Count and Countess exchanged glances. "Not all of us," he said, shaking his head. "Some of us merely wish to be graced with the gifts of the Underground."

"You keep saying gifts," I said. "What gifts?"

"Why, a connection with the unseen currents of the world," he said, opening his hands and spreading them wide, palms turned up as in supplication. "They say the greatest artists, musicians, philosophers, inventors, and madmen were elf-touched."

Elf-touched. Magda. Constanze. Me. Those broken, beautiful members of our family with one foot in the Underground and one in the world above. Straddling the here and there had turned them inside out.

"Madness is not a gift," I said angrily.

"Nor is it a curse," the Count returned gently. "Madness simply *is*."

The Countess shook her head, but bestowed a small, tender smile upon her husband when she thought the rest of us didn't see. I looked to my brother, but Josef kept his gaze averted. Instead he was staring at the Procházkas, his face a picture of hunger, want and desire honing the features of his face into an almost predatory sharpness.

"You say my gift is sound," I said to the Countess. "But you fail to convince me that it is of any significance."

"It is," she said, "when you are the only one who can speak with *Der Erlkönig* himself. When your music creates a bridge between worlds."

"A bridge between worlds? What does that mean?"

The Procházkas looked at each other again. A silent conversation passed between them, an argument held and resolved within the space of several heartbeats. Then the Count closed his eyes and nodded, before turning to me with a hard expression on his face that was at odds with his cheerful, friendly countenance.

"It means, *Fräulein*," he said, "that you are the only one who can save us."

"Save you from what?" I asked.

His face was grave. "The end of the world."

Interlude

no one heard the sound of hooves above the music.
The horn and the hound were drowned out by the pipe and the viol, the drumming of horseshoes muffled by the shuffling of dance steps. Black-and-white-clad guests spun over black-and-white-checkered floors, black, white, black, white, red. Scarlet poppies pinned to silk and brocade winked in and out of sight, appearing and disappearing like bloody fireflies against a night-and-day sky.

And outside, the unholy host began to gather.

The dancers twirled and whirled as the hours stretched longer and longer into the evening. Wine-loosened lips and laudanum-muddled laughs came together in dreamy kisses, hands meeting and parting in the minuet like moths to flame. Anonymous strangers behind masks, intimate friends behind closed doors. The murmur of names exchanged only under the cover of darkness, to keep secret and tucked away with one's discarded stockings and stays.

No one noticed that the Count and Countess had disappeared.

But throughout it all, a pair of dancers kept themselves apart. One dark, one fair. A prince of the sun and a queen of the night. Their fingers intertwined, black skin against white, as they made their way across the ballroom, their steps measured, their movements precise. They were order amidst chaos, logic amidst madness. Slowly, resolutely, they drifted toward the edges of the dance floor and to the gardens, stately and serene, neither betraying a hint of the anxiety and discomfort roiling inside their hearts.

They had noticed their beloved and sister were missing.

And inside, the gathering of gaiety continued on, oblivious to the currents that moved within and without the house. It was the night before Ash Wednesday, when the barriers between this world and the next were thin. Uncanny doings happened at the turning points, at the thresholds, at the twilights and dawns. It was a time of transition, neither night nor day, winter nor spring. It was the nothing hour, when horrors and mischief-makers came out to play.

It wasn't until a scream pierced the air that the revelries came to a halt.

They're dead! someone cried. *Oh someone help, they're dead!*

A pair of bodies were discovered in the gardens: one dark, one fair. Their eyes were glassy, their lips blue-gray, but most curious and disturbing of all were the twin slashes of silver at their throats.

Elf-struck, the guests whispered in terror and in awe.

Who were they? they asked one another.

For although the assembly was anonymous, each in attendance could guess the person to whom the eyes peering through their masks belonged. Yet even without their disguises, the victims could not be identified. A man and a woman. Neither young nor old. Their respective states of deshabille pointed to their amorous activities when their bodies were discovered in the labyrinth, a respectable pursuit at one of the Procházkas' infamous and incendiary soirees, yet the clothes of this trysting pair lacked the scarlet poppy that marked them as one of *Der Erlkönig's* own.

One of the protected.

Käthe and François stood over the dead, hands pressed to their hearts in relief. They were not Liesl and Josef. If their sister and beloved could not be found, at least it was not their remains that had been discovered.

"You must leave," said a cracked voice behind them. "You must go."

Behind them stood a liveried servant of the house, small, sallow-skinned, and frizzy-haired. He had greeted them all upon arriving at the ball, had gifted their sister with a poppy to wear. Käthe remembered him, so starkly different from the other footmen whose features blended into each other's, utterly indistinguishable despite their bare faces.

"Beg pardon?" she asked.

"You must leave," the footman repeated. "You are not safe."

"But Josef—Liesl—" François began, but the servant shook his head.

"It is not their lives that are in danger; it is yours." His pinched and sallow face was grim. "Come, follow me, *meine Dame und Herr.* We must get you someplace secure."

"What are on earth are you talking about?" Käthe snapped. Fear and anxiety made her short-tempered. "What about my brother and sister? Why should we trust you?"

The footman's dark eyes were grave. "Your brother and sister are long gone," he said. "And beyond your help."

Käthe's brows lifted in alarm. "You haven't harmed them!"

"No, *Fräulein.*" He shook his head. "They are with the Count and Countess. Their well-being is no longer your most pressing concern."

François looked bewildered, eyes darting from the fair-haired girl on one side and the beetling servant on the other. "Käthe," he said, *"qu'est-ce que c'est . . . ?"*

She narrowed her eyes at the footman. "Who are you?"

"I am no one," he answered softly. "A friend. Now hurry, we must get you back inside lest the Hunt return."

"The Hunt?" François asked.

Käthe paled. "The unholy host?"

The footman turned to her in surprise. "You believe? You have faith?"

She set her lips in a tight line. "I have faith in my sister. She believes in the old stories."

He nodded his head. "Then have faith in the old stories, if you will not have faith in me. All the tales are true, and believe me when I say that you are not safe here."

Käthe looked to the bodies of the lovers at her feet. Their eyes were open, staring at the night sky. What sights had they seen before they died? Had they taken ghostly scraps of rotting fabric for wisps of mist? The dull gleam of rusted armor for moonlight upon stone? Had they not believed? Was this why their lives were lost?

"All right," she said. "Where are you taking us?"

"Home, *Fräulein*," the footman said. "Where the Faithful can watch over you."

She did not think he was referring to their apartments near Stephansplatz. Käthe turned to François. If neither were fluent in each other's tongue, then they shared a language down to their bones nonetheless. The language of trust, and of faith in their loved ones. After a moment, François nodded and offered his arm to Käthe.

"Mademoiselle," he said with a bow.

She took his arm with a nod and faced the footman.

"Lead on, Herr . . . ?"

The footman grinned, showing row upon row of crooked, yellow teeth. "You may call me Bramble." He laughed at their confused expressions. "It was what the villagers called me when I was a babe, found abandoned and tangled in a blackberry bramble."

"Ah." Käthe was embarrassed.

The edges of Bramble's smile twisted, turning sinister, sad. "It's all right, *Fräulein*. I am one of the lucky ones. They gave me a name. And a soul."

François knitted his brow. "A soul?"

"Aye, Herr Darkling," Bramble said. "A changeling has no name and no one to call him home. But I do. I do."

Part II

EVER OURS

*Can our love persist otherwise than through
sacrifices, than by not demanding everything?*

—LUDWIG VAN BEETHOVEN,
the Immortal Beloved letters

SNOVIN HALL

The Procházka family estate was a shambles.

If I had thought their home in the environs of Vienna had been odd, it was nothing compared to Snovin Hall, the majestic, tumbledown manor that was the seat of their house. We had driven through the night on the evening of our flight from the city, stopping only to change horses. We slept on the road, ate on the road, and drank on the road, leaving no time to catch our bearings.

Or write a letter.

"Why such haste?" I had asked the Countess. "Surely men and women of your stature could afford more luxurious accommodations and modes of travel."

"Oh, Otto detests traveling," she replied. "The food disagrees with him, poor lamb."

It was true the Count seemed to be a pampered, petted creature, but I couldn't help but suspect that the Procházkas had other reasons for speed. No time for Josef or me to speak to anyone at a tavern or inn, no opportunity to pass along a message or a note to my sister and François, no chance to . . . escape.

We spoke little on the journey, preferring to doze or watch the surroundings change. The countryside grew colder the farther from the city we drew. The smells and scents of human habitation, barnyard stock, churned mud and trampled hay and woodsmoke gave way to sharp pine, wet stone, deep loam, and dark spaces. Farmlands eventually began to grow more mountainous, more forested, more like . . . home.

Despite my distrust of the Procházkas, I felt a lightening in my chest the closer we drew to Snovin, as though I were letting go of a breath I'd been holding ever since I left Bavaria. Although my brother had kept mostly mum our entire carriage ride, I sensed that he, too, had been waiting to exhale. The quality of his silence shifted as we approached our destination, taking on a waiting, listening quality. Before he had been a fortress, a castle, a burg, but now there was a door in the wall. It could be opened, when the time was right.

Bits of snow drifted lazily like ash, settling on the road as we crested the hill and began our descent into the valley. As the path opened up before us, I gasped as the vista came into view.

Spindly turrets and towers of what appeared to be an ancient castle rose out of the earth like stony fingers reaching toward the sky. A forest encircled the house like a crown of thorns, a tangle of bare branches and the colorless gray-brown of sleeping green studded with gemstones of granite, while waiting clouds heavy with snow rested atop the hills in the distance. Twin waves of homesickness and homecoming overcame me at once, and a queer emotion floated in my chest, as though my heart had become unmoored from my ribs. There was something familiar about the sight before me. It wasn't the forests or the hills or the dark unknown that was both similar to and dissimilar from the woods around Bavaria where I had grown up; it was the sense that I had seen this exact landscape before, although I could not remember where.

"Beautiful," Josef murmured. I gave him a quick, sidelong glance; it was the first word he had said in days.

The Count beamed. "Isn't it? The castle has been in my family for over a thousand years. Each generation of Procházkas has added to or subtracted from the original foundations, so hardly a single stone from the old building remains. Unusual and one of a kind, but not everyone appreciates its unique beauty as you do, young man."

I did not think it was the castle my brother found beautiful, but the Count was right; the old castle was indeed one of a kind. I thought of the burg I had seen represented on the Procházka crest, but this castle seemed less like a fortress and more like a wattle-and-daub cottage made of borrowed bits from bigger, better buildings. The crenellations and parapets undulated along uneven slopes like the spine of a sleeping dragon, the manor towers and turrets were thrust out at tipsy angles, and gables jutted forth in unexpected places. Yet despite its oddities, there was a picturesque charm about it: a wild, untamed house for a wild, untamed landscape.

"What is that?" Josef pointed across the valley to a large building set into the hills before us, a crumbling ruin looking down upon us like a priest sneering down his nose at the populace.

"That is the old monastery," said the Count. "It belonged to the order of St. Benedict before it was destroyed several hundred years ago. It's been empty ever since."

"What happened?" I asked.

"It burned down in a fire."

As we drew closer, I could see scorch marks painted onto the stones, traces of oily black tears streaming from hollow-eyed windows. "What caused the fire?"

He shrugged. "No one knows. There are stories, of course. There are accounts there was a lightning storm of biblical proportions the night it burned down. Still others say that the ghost of a restless wolf-spirit started it. More likely than not"—he shrugged—"some poor hapless monk fell asleep at his desk while transcribing something and knocked his candle over."

"Wolf-spirit?" Josef asked.

"There have been tales of spectral wolves and hounds in these parts for as long as I can remember," the Count said. "The villagers still speak of D'ábel, a monstrous beast with two different-colored eyes like the Devil."

His eyes fell to the ring on my finger, two mismatched gems winking from a wolf's silver face. Without thinking, I quickly moved to cover it, not thinking how that gesture would betray its importance to my . . . hosts? Benefactors? Captors?

"An interesting piece of jewelry you have there, *Fräulein*," he remarked. He and his wife exchanged glances. "May I see it?"

"I—I . . ." I did not know what to say, or how to decline without calling more attention to it. I myself didn't want to think too hard about how it had been returned to me. "It—it does not belong to me," I finished. "It is not mine to share."

"Curious," the Countess said. "Is it so precious that you must guard it with your own life?"

I looked down at the ring, scuffed and tarnished with age. The mismatched gemstones—one blue, one green—were small, hardly enough to be considered worth much. Yet whatever its value, it was worth infinitely more to me. I thought of the dream—vision?—I had of the Goblin King, of the shadows crawling over his skin, the crown of horns growing from his head, and remembered his vow.

"One cannot place a price on a promise," I said shortly. "And that is all I will speak of the matter."

I felt Josef's eyes upon me then, a questioning touch. It was the first hint of interest—of engagement—I had felt from my brother in a long time.

"Strange, what weight we place on such trinkets," the Countess murmured. "What meaning we imbue our possessions. The ring is but a bit of silver, wrought in an unusual shape. Yet it is more than a piece of jewelry. A symbol? A key?"

I said nothing and turned my head to gaze out the window. I watched darkness fall as the sun set behind the clouds, casting long shadows across the valley and across my heart.

By the time we pulled up the long gravel driveway to the manor house itself, night had fallen entirely, and a thin layer of snow had settled along the roads. The dark was oppressive in these parts, the sort of dense black that had depth and weight, familiar to those of us who had grown up in the wild. Our only source of light aside from the lantern hanging on its pole before our driver were twin torches blazing in the distance, held by two silhouetted figures waiting at the door for our arrival.

"Too late for supper, I suppose," the Count grumbled. "I wanted some of Nina's cabbage soup before bed."

"I'm sure the housekeeper will feed you until your waistcoat pops tomorrow, dear," said his wife.

"But I want it now," he said petulantly.

"We'll see if Nina can send us some trays after we turn down for the evening," the Countess sighed. "I know you get cranky when you're hungry. Apologies, children," she said, turning to Josef and me, though it was too dark to see our faces inside the coach. "We shall have a proper dinner and introduction to Snovin tomorrow."

"And why you've brought us here?" I asked.

I felt the touch of her green eyes on mine. "All shall be revealed. Tomorrow."

The two torch-wielding silhouettes in the distance resolved themselves into the shapes of a man and a woman; one short, stout, and dumpling-faced, the other tall, thin, and craggy-cheeked. They opened the carriage door as the Count introduced them as Nina and Konrad, the housekeeper and seneschal of the estate.

"Nina will show you both to your rooms," the Count told us. "Konrad will be along with your things."

"What things?" I said shortly. We had fled Vienna so quickly, neither Josef nor I possessed anything beyond the clothes on our backs, my brother's violin, and my portfolio of music scores.

He had the grace to look sheepish in the flickering light. "Ah, yes. Well, could you send for the tailor to take their measurements tomorrow, my love?" The Count turned to his wife instead of his housekeeper, and she looked displeased to be asked.

"As you wish," she said stiffly. "I shall send for my uncle in the morning."

Uncle? The Countess had rather low relations for such a lofty position as lady of the estate if her uncle was a tailor.

"Capital," said her husband. "Now, children"—he turned

to us—"I bid you both good night. If there's anything that makes me grouchier than an empty stomach, it's lack of sleep. We've been on the road a long while and I look forward to laying my head upon an actual pillow. I shall see you in the morning. Sweet dreams."

And with that, he and his wife swept indoors with Konrad, leaving us alone with the housekeeper.

"This way," Nina said in thickly accented German. We followed her past the great entrance hall and toward the east wing of the house, down a flight of stairs, up another, through a set of doors, around a corner, then up and down and around and around again until I was thoroughly lost. If I thought solving the hedge maze in the Procházkas' garden was difficult, it was nothing compared to this.

Our path through the estate was silent, for Nina's grasp of German seemed to be limited to the two words given earlier, and Josef kept his own counsel. Although he seemed less closed off and withdrawn than before, I still had no idea of what he thought or felt of our strange adventure. Whether he was frightened. Nervous. Excited. Relieved. That face I had known and loved his entire life was opaque to me, as though he wore a mask of his own features.

We passed no one else on our way to our rooms—no footmen, no maids, no gardeners—a stark contrast to the liveried servants at Procházka House. The grounds at Snovin Hall were extensive and would have required a great deal of care, more than what a middle-aged housekeeper and seneschal could provide. The neglect showed in a myriad ways: in the warped wooden window frames, the cobweb-dusted furniture in empty rooms, the birds' nests and rodent burrows tucked into the exposed eaves and moldering couch cushions. The world outside crept in through the crevices, vines crawling up rotted wallpaper, weeds working their way through the cracks in the floor.

I am the inside-out man.

Soon we emerged into a nicer—or at least, better kept—part of the house. As with their domicile in Vienna, the Procházkas possessed a number of exquisite curios at their country estate: tiny pewter farmers threshing wheat, a herd of bronze sheep leaping over fences, a beautifully ornate clock with golden rings that circled the hours of the heavens. Each of these trinkets were mechanical like the swan in their banquet hall, moving with fluid motions almost too smooth to be real.

We walked up another flight of stairs until we arrived at a long gallery. Nina unlocked one of the doors and we followed her into our quarters, a suite of connected rooms. A large, double-sided fireplace divided our sleeping quarters, with doors on either side that could be shut to maintain our privacy. The fires were already lit, and the rooms pleasantly warm and dry—almost toasty—compared to the drafty corridor just beyond the threshold. The rooms themselves were comfortably appointed, if a bit threadbare. There was a secondhand quality to all the furniture, although they all seemed to be heirloom pieces. A washbasin and pitcher of water stood on the bedside table in the room, but there was no mirror atop the vanity. I thought of the fifty florins the Countess had gifted me in order to lure me to Vienna and wondered why their ancestral seat was in such shabby condition. They had the funds to maintain Snovin Hall, surely.

"Is good?" Nina smiled, her dark eyes nearly lost in the crinkle of dumpling cheeks.

"It's fine, thank you," I said.

She nodded and pointed to a cupboard full of linens and candles. "Is good?" she asked again. Then she said something in Bohemian I couldn't figure out. The housekeeper mimed eating, and after some back and forth, I understood that trays of food would be sent to our rooms.

"Thank you, Nina," I said.

The housekeeper glanced at Josef, who had kept sullen, silent watch during the entire exchange. He did not offer his gratitude, either genuine or perfunctory, and Nina left us, looking a little disgruntled. Her footsteps tapped out *rude, rude, rude,* growing fainter in the distance.

We were alone.

For a long time, neither my brother nor I said a word. We had not yet decided whose room was which, but neither of us made a move to claim either as our own. The crackling of the fire filled the space between us, making conversation with the shadows on the wall. There was so much I had to say to Josef, and yet there was nothing to be said at all.

"Well, *mein Brüderchen,*" I said softly. "Here we are."

He met my gaze. "Yes," he said. "We are."

And for the first time in an age, I saw my brother, really and truly saw him. Until that moment, I had seen Josef as the little boy who had left me behind—sweet, sensitive, shy. My Sepperl. Sepp. But the man who stood before me was not that child.

He was taller, certainly, and lean with his height, towering over me by a head. His golden curls were overgrown, not in the manner that was currently fashionable in the cosmopolitan places of the world, but in the absentminded way of a genius who had more pressing concerns on his mind than his appearance. Time had honed all the softness from his cheeks and chin so that he was no longer the cherub-faced sprite of our childhood, but a gangly-limbed youth. His blue eyes were harder, less innocent, his gaze distant and dispassionate.

Yet there remained that ineffable ethereality in those clear depths that had stirred my protective heart ever since he was a babe in the cradle. Since he had been changed for the child that was the brother of my blood, if not the brother of my heart.

"Oh, Sepp," I whispered. "What are we doing?"

It was a while before he answered. "I don't know," he said, his voice breaking a little. "I don't know."

And just like that, the wall he had constructed around him came crumbling down. The mask fell, and the brother I loved, the gardener of my heart, appeared.

I held my arms open for a hug as though he were still a boy and not a man near full-grown. But Josef walked into my embrace without a second thought, wrapping his arms around me. The tears that had been simmering beneath my lashes ever since I walked away from the Goblin Grove slipped down my cheeks. I had missed my brother, yes, but it wasn't until this moment that I understood just *how much*.

"Oh, Sepp," I said again.

"Liesl." His was a man's voice now, deeper and fuller. It carried all the rich resonance of his experiences, and would only grow richer with time, acquired with knowledge like a violin resined with age. My heart beat a painful tattoo, *Don't grow up, Sepp, never grow up.*

"How did we get there?" I asked in a muffled voice. "What are we to do?"

I felt Josef's shoulders lift in a shrug. "What we've always done, I suppose. Survive."

A sober stillness fell over us. We both knew how to

survive. We had done it our entire lives, in different ways. It wasn't just the long cold nights and empty bellies we endured to make ends meet; my brother had long suffered under our father's crushing expectations. *My* expectations. I thought I had been helping him shoulder his burdens, yet I had done nothing but add to the weight with my resentment. My arms tightened around him. I did not know how to tell him I was sorry. Not with words.

"Are you frightened?" I asked, unable to look at him. "Of . . . the Wild Hunt? The Procházkas? Of . . . everything? I am."

There was no reply but the steady beating of his heart. "I'm frightened," he said at last. "But I think I've been frightened ever since I left home. Fear has been my constant companion for so long I think I've forgotten how to feel anything else."

Guilt squeezed my ribs in a painful grip, and fresh tears started in my eyes. "I'm sorry, Sepperl."

He extricated himself from my embrace. "It's over and done now, Liesl," he said in a dull voice. "This is where I live. This never-ending haze of fear and longing and dissatisfaction. Vienna or no, it is all the same to me."

Worry pierced through my remorse. "What of Käthe? And François? Don't you want to go home?"

Josef gave a bitter laugh. "Do you?"

I was about to respond that of course I did when I realized I wasn't sure what my brother meant by *home*. Vienna? Or the Goblin Grove? Or, I thought with a stab of alarm, the Underground?

We all come back in the end.

"I don't know," I admitted. "I know now that Vienna was perhaps a mistake. But to go back . . ." I trailed off.

"Would be an admission of failure?" Josef asked softly. His voice was gentle.

"Yes," I said. "And . . . and no." I thought of the words of the old rector. *The queer, the wild, the strange, the elf-touched— they are said to belong to the Goblin King.* I had tried so long and so hard to move on that I was afraid of returning to the places where his ghost still lingered. To return to the Goblin Grove would be returning to a self I had outgrown, trying to tuck who I had become back into the seams of another girl. Then I thought of the vision I had had, of *Der Erlkönig* transformed, tortured, treacherous.

His ring weighed heavily on my finger.

Josef studied me. "What happened?" he asked carefully. He gestured vaguely toward the world outside, toward the forest beyond, the roads back over the Alps to the Goblin Grove. "Did you—did you meet . . . *him*?"

Him. *Der Erlkönig.* The Goblin King. My nameless, austere young man.

"Yes," I said, the word forced from me in a choking laugh. "Yes, Sepperl, I have."

He sucked in a breath. I could see his pulse fluttering at the base of his throat, his eyes dilating to a depthless black. Interest honed his features to sharp edges. Interest, and envy.

"Tell me," he said. "Tell me everything."

I opened my mouth, then shut it. Where to begin? What did he want to know? What could I tell him? That the stories Constanze told us were real? That there was a fantastic world just below and beyond our mortal ken? The glowing lake, the Lorelei, the glittering cavernous ballrooms, the skittering beetle-eyed goblins, the needle-whiskered tailors? What of the chapel, the receiving room, the mirrors that were windows into another world? How could I reveal that the magic was real . . . without revealing the truth of who—or what—he was?

We all come back in the end.

"I—I don't know if I can, Sepp," I said. "Not yet."

His eyes narrowed. "I see."

Something about his tone niggled at me. I frowned. "See what?"

"No, no, I understand," he continued, the corner of his upper lip lifting in a curl. "Special Liesl. Chosen Liesl. You've always wanted to be extraordinary, and now you are."

My mouth fell open and I blinked. It was as though my brother had punched me in the gut; I could barely breathe for the pain. We had been circling each other for a long time, Josef and I, taking swift swipes at each other with razor-keen comments, enough to sting but not enough to wound. A dance of provocation, not injury. We might have been cold and cruel to each other, but this was the first time my brother had been actively malicious.

"Is that what you think of me?" I whispered.

He turned his head away, refusing to answer. Refusing to dignify his underhanded move with an explanation, taking the coward's way out. Well, two could play at that game. If my brother wanted to fight dirty, then I would gladly oblige him.

"Fine," I said, my voice hard. "I'm selfish and self-absorbed. But I don't take my life—my very existence—for granted." Josef started, and my eyes slipped to his wrists, where he was hastily pulling down his sleeves. Guilt seized me. "Oh, Sepp, I didn't mean—"

"Enough," he said softly. And like that, the mask of indifference he had worn before this moment slipped back into place, perfectly still and perfectly blank. "Enough,

Liesl. I cry uncle. Let's go to bed."

"Sepp, I—"

"I'll take the other room." My brother bent to pick up his violin and walked through the open door connecting our quarters. "You should get some rest. It's been a long journey. I'll see you in the morning."

I did not know what to say. I knew that the wound I had dealt him was far greater than the one he had given me and I did not know the extent or depth of the damage. I did not know how to fix it. I did not know how to fix *us*. So I said the only thing I could.

"Good night," I said, my throat tight. "Sleep well, *mein Brüderchen.*"

Josef nodded. "Good night," he said, slowly shutting the door between us. "Sweet dreams . . . Goblin Queen."

he villagers called it a demon, *der Teufel* in wolf form as it prowled the woods at night. An enormous, monstrous beast, it harried the edges of the town and its surrounding environs for months, slaughtering the sheep and carrying off the cattle.

Two eyes like mismatched gems, the villagers said. *One as green as sin, the other blue as temptation. The Devil, the Devil!* they cried. *Come to plague us all!*

So they brought in the *Wolfssegner,* the wolf-charmers, they brought in the hunters, they brought in the priests. They brought in anyone and everyone they thought could rid them of their fear.

Four hundred Gulden *for the pelt of* der Teufel! the villagers shouted as they papered the town square with rewards. *Four hundred* Gulden *for bringing us his head!*

The giant wolf had been terrorizing their sheep and goats for months, but as the winter set in, as the livestock died of hunger and of cold, they felt its ravenous teeth upon the napes of their necks. They were next, the villagers knew. They were next.

A little girl was the first to disappear. She was the youngest daughter of a shepherd, disappeared from the hills one after-noon when the clouds hung low with frost. The crags and crevices rang with her name as the villagers went searching, but it was only after they found bloodied ribbons in the snow that they gave her up for lost.

Next was a youth of fifteen, sweet on the dairy maid.

Then was an old man, of years long uncounted.

Slowly but surely, the Devil circled in on them, picking them off one by one. The priests sprinkled holy water, the *Wolfssegner* hung charms, and the hunters went searching, but as the winter deepened, so, too, did the Devil's bite.

A sacrifice, the wolf-charmers said. *Let a sacrifice be made to the Devil to appease his black heart.*

The priest protested, but the villagers persisted. They scoured their homes for the appropriate victim, a willing lamb to be led unwitting to the slaughter.

First, the idiot with his tongue thick in his mouth. *No,* said the priest. *That would be callousness beyond measure.*

Then, the harlot with all her wares on display. *No,* said the hunters. *That would be cruelty beyond bearing.*

At last they found a little infant boy, scarce a year out of his mother's womb. *Yes,* said the wolf-charmers. *This is a sacrifice worth giving.*

The little infant boy was an orphan, his mother and father lost, gone, or forgotten. No name, no baptism, no record. This was a child to whom Heaven and earth had turned a blind eye, a child meant for damnation. A ward of the church, the boy had been a foundling placed in a basket before the altar. Unclaimed and unloved, it would be no great crime to give this child up to the Devil, for he was surely shunned by God.

The proof was in the eyes.

The little boy's eyes were of two different hues; one as green as spring grass and the other as blue as a summer's lake. *Witch eyes. Cats' eyes. Like* Der Teufel's, the villagers said. *Like the Devil's. Cast the little demon back into the fires of hell from whence it came!*

The village priest refused to give up the child. He was a pious, God-fearing man, but it was his goodness that would be his damnation.

They came with pitchforks, they came with knives. They came with torches and flame and purpose. They brought their rage and fear to the doorsteps of the church and built a pyre to the unknown. As the walls of God's house crumbled into smoke and ruin, the bones of the village priest melted into char and ash. They found his remains three days later, when the haze had cleared and the embers had grown cold at last.

But of the little boy, they found nothing. No swaddling cloths, no hair, no precious baby fingers. No earthly remains, almost as though he had vanished into thin air, blown away like mist with the bitter wind.

As the spring rains melted away the winter ice, the wolf attacks on the village ceased.

Praise be! the villagers cried. Der Teufel *has accepted our sacrifice.*

Over the course of the next few weeks, the villagers saw no trace of the blue-and-green-eyed demon, or indeed, any traces of wolf at all. Only footprints remained in the frozen mud, great padded paws and the haunting imprint of one tiny, perfect human foot.

THE KINSHIP
BETWEEN US

i awoke the next morning with my hand wrapped about the Goblin King's ring. Despite the rough journey and the restless, turmoil-laden sleep, my head was clearer than it had been in a long time. The wisp of a dream returned to me, and I clung to it, trying to remember what I had seen, felt, experienced. But it was gone, leaving nothing but the sensation of fullness, as though my mind were a well that had refilled in the middle of the night.

The door between my brother's room and mine was still shut. I wondered if it would ever be open again, or if I had locked us up and thrown away the key. I wanted to apologize. I wanted to demand an apology. I hated what we had become. I hated how Master Antonius and the Goblin King had come between us, and I hated even more that my brother could make me resent what had been the deepest and most transformative time of my life. I wanted to yell at Josef. I wanted to break down that door between us. I wanted to throttle him. I wanted to coddle him.

I shoved off my linens and threw myself forcefully from my bed.

Nina had left me a tray of food and some clothes outside my door. The food was cold, but the clothes were clean, and I gratefully changed out of my travel-stained clothes into something more comfortable. I washed my face and did my best to tidy my hair without the use of a mirror. By now I was ravenous, having barely eaten since we left Vienna. I supposed I could have eaten the bread and cheese left for me last night, but it was cold and stale, and I was more of a mind to wander and explore . . . and potentially find someone who might help me get word to my sister and François.

The twisting, labyrinthine corridors and passageways of Snovin Hall were no less confusing by day than they had been by night. I knew we were in the east wing of the house, having marked it when we arrived. I headed back toward what I assumed was the entrance, figuring it would be easier to orient myself from there.

The neglect and decay were far more noticeable in the light. Although the wing where Josef and I were staying was relatively sound, a large part of the house had completely and utterly fallen apart: the roof collapsed in one room, brambles and vines climbing through empty window frames in another. I passed by portraits of Procházkas past, their stern faces looking down upon me from tattered hangings, an interloper in their midst.

"I know," I muttered to one particularly grim-looking fellow. "I don't know what I'm doing here either."

The Count and Countess told me that I was in danger from the Wild Hunt, that they had abducted me and my brother in order to protect us. But Snovin Hall hardly seemed a refuge with its dilapidated walls and desolate halls. There seemed to be no staff, no personnel, no armed guard at the Procházka ancestral seat. It didn't seem as though Josef and I were any better protected here than we had been in Vienna. It led me to believe that we had been brought here for other reasons.

The warning from my old landlady Frau Messner swirled about my mind, the story of that young woman who had disappeared, the young man who had died. *An incident. At their country home.* Käthe's voice, too, rose up in my memory. *The Procházkas sacrifice goats to a dark god in occult rituals. They call upon sinister forces.*

But it was the Countess's words from the night we were abducted that echoed the loudest. *Your music creates a bridge between worlds.*

I looked down at the Goblin King's ring on my finger. Incontrovertible proof that the veil between us and the Underground was thin. The Procházkas claimed that I could save us all from the end of the world, but I did not understand how. Not without going back. Not without giving up everything I had left for in the first place. My music. My life. Myself.

And then I thought of mismatched eyes and a mouth tender with love. I thought of the Goblin King as I had seen him that last night as husband and wife, not entwined in our marriage bed, but playing a sonata in the chapel. Perhaps going back wasn't giving up. Perhaps it was giving in.

Then I remembered blue-white eyes and inky-black skin stretched over hollow bones, a voice hissing, *He that you love is gone.*

Before long, I realized that I had come to an unfamiliar part of the house. I thought of my time as the Goblin Queen, when the pathways of the Underground rearranged themselves to suit my whim. I hadn't paid much attention the night before, but I did not recall coming across a gallery this size. What seemed like portraits or paintings were hung high on the walls above me, covered with sheets. Curious, I reached up to look under the sheet when there was a gasp and a crash.

I jumped and whirled around to see Nina on her hands and knees. She must have dropped another tray at the sight of me, and was hastily trying to gather the broken crockery. I got down to help her clean, apologizing profusely for the fright.

She tried to wave me off, but I insisted, pretending not to understand her Bohemian, even though her emphatic gestures were perfectly clear. It appeared as though the housekeeper had been coming to bring my brother and me our breakfast, but now that I had ruined the service, she seemed amenable to bringing me to the kitchens.

Only it wasn't the kitchens she brought me to. Instead, Nina led me to a small, brightly lit room with large windows, where the Count was sitting before a large, roaring fire.

"Ah, *Fräulein!*" he said when he saw me. "You are up, I see. Please, come join me for breakfast."

By the looks of things, he had already been up for hours, his dark eyes bright and beady, his cheeks pink with health and good humor. He rose and offered me his seat, walking to a sideboard I had not seen laden with pastries, fruit, an assorted selection of cured meats and cheeses, as well as a large silver carafe.

"Do you take coffee?" he asked.

"I, uh, yes, thank you," I said, a bit flustered. Coffee was a popular beverage back in Vienna, brought to the city by the

Turks, but I had never developed much taste for the bitter brew.

"Cream? Sugar?"

"Both, please."

The Count made me a cup before pouring himself one as well. He drank his without anything to cut the acrid bitterness, smacking his lips with relish. His chipper countenance this morning suddenly made much more sense.

"I trust you and your brother slept well," he said. "Alas, you must excuse my wife. She is not an early riser, nor is she much for breakfast. It looks as though it will be just you and me this morning."

The Countess and I had this much in common at least. In Vienna, I had grown accustomed to rising late; without the pressure of chores and other duties to perform around the inn, the luxury of lying abed when I could had been too sweet to resist.

We sat in silence with our coffees for a while, me sipping gingerly, the Count gulping his down. I wasn't much for breakfast either, but felt I had to eat for courtesy's sake. I set my cup down and walked to the sideboard to fill a plate with a few small, cookie-sized pastries topped with a sweet poppy seed paste. The room in which we sat was one of the few better-maintained parts of the house, the furniture sturdy if shabby, the rug of high quality if threadbare. Two sets of windowed doors framed the fireplace, opening onto a terrace that overlooked wildly overgrown lands. Like the dining room, a painting or a mirror was hung above the sideboard, and as with the rest of the framed objects in the house, it was covered with a sheet.

"If you don't mind me asking," I said, pointing to the framed object, "may I ask what it is you keep covered under there?"

The Count coughed, choking a bit on his coffee. "Now, now," he said, face reddening. "Mustn't touch."

Another voice from another time returned to me, whispering the same words. *No, no, mustn't touch.* I thought of the mirror in my chamber Underground, my enchanted window to the world above.

After a few more minutes of coughing and clearing his throat, the Count continued. "It's not a painting or a portrait, my dear," he said. "It's a mirror."

I was surprised. "A mirror?"

"You may consider it a silly old superstition," he said sheepishly, "but around these parts, it is ill luck to keep mirrors uncovered in empty rooms and while the house is sleeping."

"Why?"

He gave a nervous laugh. "Oh, it's an old wives' tale, but they say that if the mirrors aren't covered, a dreamer's soul may accidentally wander through them to the shadow world and become trapped." The Count gave the one hanging above the mantel a sidelong glance. "One never knows where one's soul might end up. The realm behind the reflection may or may not be true, and they say the fey and the spirits of the restless dead travel through the shadow-world paths created by mirrors."

I shivered, thinking of how I had spied upon my brother and sister through the enchanted mirror in my chamber Underground. Suddenly, I understood the why of it. One never knew just who was staring back as you gazed into your reflection.

"Are you frightening our guests, Otto?" The Countess emerged from the hall, limping into the room on Konrad's arm. "Don't believe everything he tells you," she said.

"Otto does love a good story."

He gave his wife a tender smile. "Especially ones with happy endings."

The Countess rolled her eyes. "My husband is a sentimental fool, I'm afraid," she said, but she could not keep the smile from her voice. "I myself prefer the old tales. Wouldn't you agree, mademoiselle?" Konrad helped the Countess to her seat while her husband rose to his feet and made his wife a cup of coffee.

"I would prefer it if we dispensed with the storytelling and went straight to truth seeking, if you don't mind," I said tartly. "What are we doing here? Why? How?"

She sighed and set down her cup after a sip. "I had hoped to get settled in before all that."

"Get you acquainted with Snovin," the Count added. "You are our guest, so please make yourself comfortable and at home here."

I lifted my brows. "And how long will my stay be?"

"Until the danger to you is passed," the Countess said. "And in order to make sure you're safe, we need your help, Elisabeth. You are far more precious to us than you know."

"Precious?" I laughed incredulously. "To you? Why?"

"Because of what you are," she said seriously. "And what I am."

"What I am," I repeated. "The Goblin Queen."

The Countess nodded. "There is kinship between us."

"Kinship?" I was surprised. "Who are you?"

She glanced at the Count, who met her gaze briefly, then returned his eyes back to his plate. "I presume you do not mean to ask about the illustrious house of Procházka und zu Snovin, of which my husband is the nineteenth count and I, his wife."

I crossed my arms. The Countess sighed again.

"We are—I am," she began, "the last of a line no less old or illustrious than my husband's, if not quite so noble. The Procházkas have ever kept watch over the in-between places and thresholds of the world, but my family have been the keeper of its secrets. We keep the old laws and we safeguard them, maintaining the balance between our world and the Underground."

I frowned. "How?"

"I told you that those of us touched by *Der Erlkönig* can reach across the barrier." She held her hands apart. "We can find the windows and"—she clapped her hands shut—"close them. You can do this, Elisabeth," she said, nodding toward me. "As can I."

"You?" She nodded again. I narrowed my eyes. "*What* are you?"

The Countess and her husband exchanged another glance. This time, he held her gaze and gave her the slightest of nods. She turned back to me, those eyes of hers large, luminous, and an impossibly bright green. "I am of his blood," she said in a low voice. "My foremother was the first of his brides. A brave maiden, who gave her life for the world, then doomed that very same world to bring *Der Erlkönig* back from death."

a voice from the deep places of the world called his name and Josef awoke. The sun was streaming in through windows and past curtains he had forgotten to close the night before, long past morning but not yet noon. For a moment, he thought he was back home at the inn, for the air held the faint, crisp freshness of pine and dirt and snow.

And then he remembered.

The weight of his argument with Liesl pressed heavily on his chest, pushing him back into his bed linens, a suffocating pressure that made it hard to breathe and to get out of bed.

During their entire flight from Vienna, Josef had sensed his sister's unease, her anxiety, her manic restlessness at the uncertainty of their futures. He had sensed it, and tried to care. But he didn't. Couldn't. He knew that he ought to be worried, he ought to have been frightened, for the revelations the Procházkas had bestowed upon them were alarming and unbelievable. Yet at the same time, the effort it took him to muster anything beyond vague concern was exhausting, and Josef had been tired for a long, long time.

He contemplated staying in bed all day. There were no places to go, no people to see, no auditions to prepare for.

There were, he realized, no expectations set upon him. He waited for happiness, for excitement, or even relief, but there was nothing but the same dull indifference that had plagued him since he left Bavaria. Since he left home.

But years of rising early to practice the violin were still buried deep within his muscles and bones. Josef shook off the remnants of sleep and roused himself, finding a clean set of clothes outside his door. He had not yet learned how to fill his hours without music, and the itch and the urge to play lingered in his fingers. He got dressed and picked up his violin.

Liesl was already gone by the time he left his room, and the housekeeper from the previous night was nowhere to be found. There was absolutely no one else in sight as he wandered through the wings and halls of Snovin, which suited Josef just fine. He had never been able to hear himself think in the presence of anyone else save his eldest sister and François. It was why he found playing in front of an audience so intolerable.

As Josef passed from room to room, the manor's state of decay became more and more noticeable. Shafts of light cut through the collapsed roofs and empty windows, dust motes dancing in the sunbeam like fairy lights. Winter still had its hold on this mountainous estate, but he didn't mind the cold. It was calm. Clean, despite the dirt and twigs and creatures scurrying underfoot. It put him in mind of the forest just beyond the inn, a vast change from the filthy, smelly, and crowded homes in the city. Here he could play. Here he could find communion within himself again.

But despite the ease and familiarity he felt within these inside-out walls, he couldn't find the right place to pull his violin from its case. He was searching for the sense of sacredness that had come with the Goblin Grove. He was seeking sanctuary.

"Help me," he whispered to no one in particular. "Help me find peace."

A clock chimed the hour.

To his right stood a grandfather clock, its face painted and gilded with the movement of the heavens. Its hands were not pointed to an hour, despite its sounding gong, and Josef could have sworn the spheres moving across their heavenly paths were still just a moment before. Behind him, there was a soft, grinding, clicking sound, the faint scream of rusted metal over metal. He turned to look.

A suit of armor was lifting its arm.

Tales of enchanted goblin-made armor rose up in his mind, imbued with a magic that made its wearer impervious to arrows and injuries and death. Such stories also came with accounts of fearsome fighting prowess, of the warrior defeating off hordes of the enemy with a skill in battle that was either preternatural or pretend. Not real. Not truly belonging to the warrior, but to the Underground.

Josef watched with detached fascination as the suit of armor lifted its arm, curled its fingers, and pointed down one of the corridors as if in answer to his question.

Help me. Help me find peace.

"That way?" he asked, mirroring the armor's gesture.

Its empty, helmeted head moved up, then down, then up, then down in a herky-jerky motion, a grotesque parody of a nod.

"Thank you," he whispered. "Thank you."

He followed the path of the armor's direction, walking down a long, dark, high-ceilinged corridor toward a set of large double doors, opened ajar. Light spilled in through the crack, but shakily, unsteadily, as though shadows moved in the room beyond. He reached the doors, placed his hands on the ornately carved knockers, and pushed.

It was a ballroom.

The space was empty, although shadows still danced at the corners of his vision. A circular room paneled with many large, broken mirrors, the ballroom reflecting both light and movement like a prism. The cracked marble floors rippled with growing roots, dead ivy and desiccated vine crawling down the walls like fingers reclaiming the room. Josef and the wild were mirrored over and over, a thousand boys standing in a forest.

"Yes," he breathed. If this place was not yet peace, then it was a balm to his soul: a room once dedicated to music and dance, now slowly becoming swallowed by the living, sleeping green. Twelve mirrored panels around him, like the twelve alder trees encircling the Goblin Grove; it felt both familiar and foreign. Back when he was a boy, before Master Antonius, before Vienna, before all the weight and expectations placed upon him, Josef had played his music in a place like this.

He set his case down and opened it, lifting his violin to his shoulder. He had no gloves and his fingers were cold, but Josef had long perfected the art of playing through numbness. He closed his eyes and took a deep breath, the scent of dirt and dust and deep woods filling his lungs. With the bow poised over his strings, he smiled. Then played.

And the world changed.

If there was anything left in his life that Josef loved, it was this. Music. The only thing of human invention he preferred to that of nature's creation. Birdsong and cricket choruses had been the orchestra of his childhood, but his sister's music had always been his star. His first soloist. When she sang him lullabies in the dark. When she wrote him little melodies to practice on the violin. It was as though he had learned to speak through the notes and lines and staff on the page. Language without words. Communion without communication.

The brambles and branches stirred at the sound of the violin. A sense of wakefulness came to a world deep in winter slumber, the intake of a breath before rousing. Beneath him and around him, the forest reached, stretched, grew, as though answering a call. The broken mirrored panels showed myriad boys amidst myriad trees, but Josef did not notice that all but one played the same song.

He transitioned from warmups and exercises to the largo from Vivaldi's *L'inverno,* which had been his favorite piece since he was very young. Yet as his bow sang the notes, Josef felt distant. Removed. He could no longer remember why he had loved or cared so for this movement, only that the thrill of its melody was now gone. He thought of his father then, a man for whom one drink, then two, then three, then four or five or six had ceased to be enough. Had ceased to affect him.

The memory of his father marred Josef's playing, and he hit a sour note. He stopped playing, and all the boys in the mirrors went still.

All save one.

Although Josef had lowered his instrument and his bow, still the sound of the violin carried on. Not an echo, but a reflection. The melody was familiar. Beloved. Cherished.

Der Erlkönig.

Emotion blossomed in Josef's chest—pain, fear, guilt, relief, excitement, tenderness. His sister's music had a way of opening him up to feeling, of digging up the parts of himself he had left buried back home in the Goblin Grove. He turned and searched for Liesl—to apologize, to reach out for solace or comfort—but he was alone, with only a thousand versions of himself to keep him company. A thousand blue eyes and a thousand violins stared back at Josef as he gazed into the shattered mirrors, but at the corner of his eye, one of the other Josefs moved.

He turned and turned, but as it was with the way of reflections, the perspective shifted and changed with every movement of his head. It was only when he kept still, when the other Josefs stopped turning, that he could see one of them coming closer. He tried to catch his own eye, but his reflection remained on the edges of his vision, on the edges of his sanity.

Minutes. Hours. It wasn't until *Der Erlkönig* ended that he was face to face with his errant reflection. The other Josef wore a smile on his face that wasn't mirrored on his own, and he held his violin on the opposite side. Or perhaps the correct side. He no longer knew what was left and right in this inside-out world.

"Who are you?" Josef asked, but his reflection's mouth did not move in time with his.

I am you, the other Josef replied.

"And who am I?" he whispered.

The reflection only smiled.

THE BRAVE MAIDEN'S TALE, REPRISE

he brave maiden.

I was sitting with a descendant of the brave maiden. The first of us to die, and the only one of us survive the Goblin King's embrace.

Until me.

"You . . . you . . ." I began, but my words trailed off into nothingness.

"Me, me," the Countess repeated, although there was no hint of mockery in her voice. "Yes, Goblin Queen," she said softly. "She walked away from the Underground, and lived. I am proof. And for hundreds of years, for several generations, her daughters and granddaughters and great-granddaughters were guardians and keepers of the balance between worlds, between the world above and the realms below."

The crash and thunder of my beating heart hollowed out my ears, drowning all sound and sense. I watched the Countess's lips move, but could not understand, could not comprehend a single word coming from her mouth. The notion was too big—too significant—to accept. The world narrowed to a small, singular idea.

I was not alone.

"Child? Child?" The scope and scale of my thoughts widened once more to encompass the chair I was sitting on, the room I was in, the person who was speaking to me. "My dear, are you all right? You look quite pale. Konrad, would you bring Mademoiselle Vogler something stronger than coffee to drink? A bit of sherry, perhaps?"

"I'm fine," I said in a voice that didn't sound like mine. It came from a place both far inside and outside of me, a voice so calm as to belong to another Liesl, another Elisabeth altogether. "I don't need a drink."

She watched me with those vivid, otherworldly green eyes. A jumble of half-started images and words and phrases tumbled through my mind—wife? child? *Der Erlkönig's* child? legacy family descendants found uprooted—the noise spinning into a blur of blankness. I blinked, and when I did not respond to her extraordinary claim in the manner she was apparently expecting, the Countess gave a little huff.

"Well," she said, forcing a laugh, "this is not the reception to my revelation I had hoped for."

"What was to be my response?" I asked, still in that stranger's voice.

She gave an elegant shrug. "Surprise? Shock? Gratitude? Anger? Anything other than blankness, to be honest, my dear."

The Count cleared his throat. "It is a lot to take in, darling."

He was right. It was too much for my limited comprehension to encompass wholly, so I could only pick at the details as they became clear to me, one by one.

"Are you—are you a child of *Der Erlkönig*?" Surely that wasn't possible. A goblin girl told me long ago that no union of mortal and the Goblin King had ever been fruitful. And yet. My hand went to my lower belly. My bleeding had run their monthly courses as usual when I returned from the Underground. I felt a sharp stab of . . . envy? Relief? Emptiness? Exultation?

The Countess shook her head. "No, Elisabeth. I am not a child of *Der Erlkönig*, unless you mean it in the sense that we—you, your brother, my husband, all those who believe, and I—are all his children. No," she repeated, her voice growing soft and gentle. "I am a descendant of the Goblin Queen and her consort, a man who had once been the Lord of Mischief and the Ruler Underground. A daughter of a mortal woman . . . and a mortal man." She looked to her husband, and he laid a hand on her shoulder.

"But they were both mortal . . ." I did not know how to phrase my question, or even what to ask. If what she said was true. If she indeed had powers spanning both the worlds above and below. If, if, if.

"How do I have my gift of opening and closing the barriers between worlds?" the Countess finished.

I nodded.

"Do you know the tale of Persephone?" she asked.

I blinked. "No," I said slowly, feeling even more lost and unmoored than before. "I don't believe so."

"She was the daughter of Demeter," the Count chimed in. Unlike his wife, his dark eyes were fixed on my face with a strange sort of compassion, even pity. "She was abducted by Hades and forced to become his bride."

I shuddered, but not entirely with revulsion.

"Yes," the Countess said. "Persephone ate the fruit of the

underworld and was therefore condemned to spend half the year in Hades's realm, the other half in the world above with her mother."

A sudden pang of sympathy for Persephone swept through me. Sympathy and envy. Half the year with her family, the other half with her dark beloved. If only, if only.

"But what the story doesn't say," her husband added, "is that Persephone returned from the underworld changed. Different. A dark queen for a dark realm. The ancient Greeks dared not even speak her name, for to speak of her was to call her attention. So they called her *Kore*, which meant *maiden*."

A sharp chill pierced through my numbness, sending shivers down my spine. *Her name is lost to us*, Twig had once said. The brave maiden. Nameless, and gone.

"Persephone returned changed," the Countess said softly. "And so did the first Goblin Queen. When she reemerged into life from death, she came back different. She awoke with the ability to sense the rips in the world, the cracks, the in-between spaces, and to create them and to mend them. She was both of the Underground and the world above, and she passed that ability on to her children. To me."

My heart skipped a beat. I remembered the last time I had seen my Goblin King standing in the Goblin Grove, the feel of our hands passing through each other's like fingers through smoke, like holding on to a candle flame, insubstantial and painful all at once. What would I do for this ability? To pass between realms at will, to touch and hold and embrace my Goblin King in the flesh and not in memory?

"But," the Countess said, "as you can see, I am the last of her bloodline. The last of us with this ability—this gift."

Her voice hitched, a slight tremor that would have gone

unnoticed if it weren't for the tears glimmering in her eyes. I did not know if those tears were for a child she could not have, or a child she had had, then lost. Her husband's hand on her shoulder tightened, the two of them taut and tense in their shared silent grief. Yet his features wore a troubled expression, as though this were a conversation he did not want to have.

"However," she said huskily. "It appears I am not the last after all." The Countess watched me, searching for my face for the answer to a question she did not ask. It was a long time before I replied.

"Me," I said in a quiet voice. "You mean . . . me."

The corners of her full red lips tilted upward slightly. "Yes," she said. "You, O Goblin Queen."

Silence stretched on between us. I did not know what to say. I did not know what to think, or even what to *feel*. When I made the decision to leave the Underground, I made the choice to live instead of to die, to seize what I wanted from the world instead of resigning myself to my fate. I had promised myself I would live every day as Elisabeth, entire.

But who was Elisabeth, entire? Who was the woman who had been given every opportunity and had failed to seize upon them? Who was the sister who had used her brother's pain as an excuse to run away from her problems? Who was the composer who sat before her instrument every night, unable to write? Could I find out who she was here, in the dilapidated ruins of Snovin Hall? As the successor to a secret line of uncanny women?

"Is this why you brought me here?" I asked. "To—to make me your heir?" The idea was preposterous. And yet . . .

The Countess smiled, but her eyes were sad. "You have the right of it," she said. "I thought that . . . that when my

Adelaide died, it was the end of the world." She laughed, but there was no humor in the sound, only an infinite sorrow. "A mother's grief does feel like the end of the world, it is true, but without another to carry on the legacy, the balance between worlds would fall apart."

Adelaide. Her daughter. Suddenly, I wondered just whose clothes it was I was wearing. I had put them on this morning without a second thought, merely grateful to shed the filthy, travel-stained dress I had worn for nearly a week straight. The gown and shawl I wore felt itchy, clinging, uncomfortable, as though I were wearing someone else's skin. I was wearing the trappings of a dead girl's fortune, shouldering the burden of her mother's expectations and dreams. I stood up, unable to bear another moment in the presence of my deceitful, duplicitous hosts.

"I must go," I said abruptly.

"My dear, I know it's a lot to take in—" the Countess began, but I cut her off.

"You told me I was your guest," I interrupted. "And as your guest, I would like very much to not be here. In this room. In this house. I need—I need air. I—I—I—" My words tripped over lips, running ahead of the scream not far behind. "And . . . unless you were lying and I am, in fact, your prisoner, I beg your leave. I must—I must go." My hands were shaking. Why couldn't my hands stop shaking?

"Of course, *Fräulein,*" the Count said before his wife could interject. "Our house and our estate are yours to wander."

"But Otto," she protested. "The Hunt, the unholy host? We brought her here to keep her safe."

"If she isn't safe at Snovin, then she isn't safe anywhere," the Count said shortly. "Here," he said gently, turning to me. He reached into the pocket of his waistcoat, withdrew his fob, unclipped the chain, and placed it in my hand. "Take this."

"Your watch?" I asked, bewildered. My restlessness was going to burst from my eyeballs in a rush of blood and fury if I did not leave within the next instant, Wild Hunt or no.

"A compass." The Count opened the fob, showing a beautiful compass with a golden needle spinning slowly round and round and round. "And a rather significant piece of iron, in fact. A small measure of protection against the unholy host, but moreover, it is your way back. Should you get lost at Snovin, the compass will always point you here." He pointed to the ground beneath his feet. "To this very room. It was built over a large lodestone, so the needle will always point here. To home."

Home. For better or for worse, this was home now. It would be home forever, if the Procházkas had their way. But I would not dwell on that. Could not. One day at a time. One step at a time. As long as those steps took me away from the Countess, her history, and her hopes.

"Thank you," I whispered to the Count. "I shall keep it safe."

He nodded. "You are dismissed, *Fräulein.*"

I fled.

I threw opened the glass doors of the morning room and ran onto the veranda. The snow from the previous night had mostly melted with the sun, but a light dusting remained, sugaring the tops of dead weeds and grasses with a pale, white frost. I did not know where to turn. If I had been back at the inn, I would have run to the Goblin Grove. But here, in an unfamiliar house on unfamiliar terrain in an unfamiliar country, I was lost. In more ways than one.

The grounds would have been well-manicured in summer perhaps, but now everything was a tangle of overgrown brambles, vines, and early flowers that may have tried to bloom in a thaw—all withered, desiccated, dead. In the distance, on the edges of the estate, pine trees marched in orderly fashion around the perimeter—uniform, straight, and, tall. Beyond this ring of perfectly groomed trees rose the tops of undulating forest hills. To the left, the weak morning sun glinted off the glass roofs of a greenhouse, and to the right, a bright carpet of scarlet. I squinted. It looked like a field of wildflowers. Of . . . poppies? It seemed impossible in a clime this high in the hills and too early besides, for the blooms did not blossom until summer.

But late-winter poppies were one of the least impossible things I had discovered today.

A soft breeze gently whistled about the estate, bringing with it unquiet whispers. I held the Count's compass in both hands. It was surprisingly heavy for such a small object, as though it contained magnitudes more than it revealed. I watched the needle spin aimlessly around its face, almost like watching the hands of a clock chart the hours in quarter time. As I moved farther away from the house and toward the wilds outside, the needle steadied, an arrow pointing straight behind me toward the lodestone in Snovin Hall. Where North might have been on an ordinary compass, a poppy was painted in beautiful detail. On the other side, an exquisite miniature of the melusine as seen on the Procházka crest where South would have been. The melusine put me in mind of the Lorelei in the Underground lake, her fishtail trailing in blue-green waters. Straight ahead of me, a path cut through the pine trees, disappearing into a trail up the hill.

I took it as a sign. A direction. A way. I set my feet upon the path, and walked.

It turned steep shortly after leaving the tame grounds, growing narrow and a little treacherous. The trail turned back on itself over and over, cutting into the hill face as it ascended up the slope. My breath came short and I broke into a sweat as I climbed, but the exertion and exercise calmed the unsteady turmoil and turbulence that had rocked and roiled me since the Countess's revelation about her history and my future. My step was sure, my eyes clear.

At the summit of the hill was a lake.

Its appearance was utterly surprising and unexpected, a wide expanse of vivid blue-green opening up beneath me. The path from the forest emerged onto an outcropping of rock that jutted out over the water several feet below the ledge. It was as though I had stumbled upon a secret. The existence of this lake was completely hidden from view from both Snovin Hall and the drive into the valley we had taken the day before, hardly visible even from the path I had hiked. It emerged from the forest like an enchanted gem, sparkling like a startling aquamarine against the brown and gray of the late winter woods and sky.

The surface of the lake was as smooth and as flat as glass, a perfect mirror for the ring of trees that encircled it, yet it seemed to reflect the sky of another, more vivid world. A faint mist hovered over the surface, a dreamy haze, and it seemed much warmer here than it was just a few feet below on the trail. A murmuring breeze stirred the mist atop the lake and to my shock, it was steam, not mist, for it blew warm and moist across my face.

Liesl.

I startled. The wind whispered my name, as though carrying someone's call an incalculable distance. The steam atop the lake swirled and twirled and parted in the breeze, but it did not disturb the placid, pristine surface of the water. I stepped closer to the edge, peering over the sheer drop down to the water.

Liesl, the wind whispered again.

I looked up and scanned the other side of the lake, searching for a form or figure. Stories of the Wild Hunt, of the elf-touched and elf-struck returned to me. Would I be taken? Or killed? Was I mad? Or merely suffering from a fit of nerves? In the labyrinth of the Procházkas' hedge maze, I had seen Twig and the Goblin King. Or at least, I thought I had. But there was no one else in this secret, secluded space, not even a figment of the imagination. I was alone, no one but me and my reflection in this unexpected sanctuary.

Liesl.

I looked down. A face stared back at me from the glass-smooth depths of the water, blue eyes, gold hair, apple-pink cheeks, a face I knew intimately.

But it wasn't mine.

It was Käthe's.

Startled, I drew back. Käthe's head disappeared from view, but when I peered over the edge and into the lake again, she was still there.

"Käthe?" I asked, while her lips mouthed *Liesl?* "Käthe!"

Dropping to all fours, I crawled forward on my belly, reaching for the water, for my sister, for the vision before me. Was it magic? Or was it madness? In that moment I did not care. I saw my own anguish and concern and worry for my family reflected in Käthe's eyes, the surprise and shock of the uncanny in the everyday.

François! I could see her call for the black boy over her

shoulder. *François! Bramble! Come quick!*

I could not see where she was, for beyond her I could see nothing but the blue-green depths of the lake. Was she still in Vienna, in Frau Messner's boarding house, being cared for by the Procházkas' associates? Or was she back home in Bavaria, at the inn with Mother and Constanze and the Goblin Grove? I wanted to reach through the water, to swim to the bottom, to her.

"Fräulein?"

I whirled around to see Nina standing behind me, a frightened expression on her face. Her hands were outstretched, thrown up before her as though to stop me—or to catch me. I realized then how I might appear to the house-keeper: a distressed young woman perched on the edge of a drop into a lake.

"Oh no, I'm fine, I'm fine," I said, getting to my feet and brushing the dirt off my skirts. Nina was gesturing frantically, beckoning me back from the ledge. "I'm all right," I repeated, even though she could not understand me.

I must have been here longer than I thought, for the sun was lower on the horizon than I expected. Nina gestured again, miming eating and possibly something about the Count or Countess. Not wanting to distress her further, I nodded and followed her back to Snovin Hall, but not before taking one last, longing glimpse at the enchanted lake and the mirrored world over my shoulder.

Mirrors.

Whatever I felt about the Countess and her unbelievable lineage, one thing was true. Snovin Hall was steeped in the uncanny. Like the Goblin Grove, it was perhaps one of the last sacred places left, thresholds where the world above and the Underground overlapped. I thought of what the Count had told me that morning, that the mirrors remained covered in their house to close off the shadow paths between worlds. The lake was a mirror, and a window to elsewhere. Perhaps I could open my own window to elsewhere.

In the meanwhile, I would beg of my hosts some ink and paper for a letter and write to my sister.

the wheelwright said there was a wolf-wraith in the woods.

The townspeople ignored his claims. For years the wheelwright had claimed to see fantastic sights in the woods: bears that walked on hind legs, wolves that changed into men, and goblins who stole maidens away. As vivid as these visions were in the wheelwright's mind, they left no traces on the world in which he lived.

Harmless, the townspeople reassured each other as they passed by his shop in the market square. *Eccentric.*

The wheelwright was a young widower—more youth than man—and his wife had been one of the unfortunate victims of the Great Winter the year previous, when the snow had brought with it wolves, worry, and woe. A beautiful woman, the wheelwright's wife's cheeks had flamed with youth and vitality, until the fire he treasured about her burned her up from the inside. Fever, fast and furious, first devoured her lungs and then the rest of her, taking with it not only the wheelwright's wife, but the unborn child within.

She had been one of the lucky ones. Sickness had carried her off, but the wolves had taken the others.

Grief buried the town as deep as the snowdrifts, lingering long after the spring thaw flooded the streets with emotion. The wolves had retreated along with the ice, but the beasts had left their mark. A wife here, a son there, a daughter, a grandfather, a grandchild—their absences as noticeable as a missing tooth in what had once been a long row of families whole and hale. Some soothed the pain with the usual balms—drink, whores, and God—but the wheelwright's madness was particular.

It began with the shadows, the smudges in the corners.

Tsk, tsk, tutted the wives, seeing what they took for soot on the floor of his shop.

Be kind, responded their husbands. *He's lost his wife.*

Be strong, their wives retorted. *Life goes on.*

The wheelwright ignored their whispers, ignored their words. By day he fixed their wheels, but at night he built an empire of trinkets and toys. He carved and cut, he whittled and whistled, and slowly, from scraps of wood, he founded a fantastic fairyland of goblins and bears and wolves and forests.

It was the children who noticed them first. As their parents conducted their business with the wheelwright, they picked up the goblins and bears and wolves from the scrap pile and played with them on the sawdust- and dirt-covered floor. Their parents saw only the smudges in the corner, grown now into piles of earth, loam, and the grasping, spidery roots of dead trees. But the children saw a kingdom of the possible in the wheelwright's discarded scraps of imagination, and the wheelwright, the memory of childhood still clinging to his face, brought himself down to their level and played.

At first the townspeople were charmed and not a little sympathetic by the wheelwright's childlike behavior. *A good father,* they agreed, *he will make a good father someday.* But the longer the wheelwright lingered in the realm of make-believe, the less enchanting his behavior seemed to be. The figurines he carved, at first so exquisite, now seemed grotesque, less the work of a man yearning for children than a man stunted.

The madness grew larger than the shadows in the corner. It was no longer possible to enter the wheelwright's shop; dirt covered every inch of the floor, dead branches and twigs creeping in through the windows and doors. And still the wheelwright continued to carve, adding to his collection of figurines stories that matched their outlandish shapes. Half men, half bears, wolves with human eyes, goblins shaped like alder trees.

Soon even the children came to dismiss him. They liked the wheelwright's stories, and they especially liked his toys, but the man himself made them uncomfortable. He played with them, but he was not one of them. He was too old, despite the lost look in his eyes, the look of a child abandoned. The look of an orphan. One by one, the children stopped coming to his shop and one by one, his figurines disappeared, down dirty shirtfronts and little trouser pockets. The wheelwright was left alone once more.

So when he brought tales of a ghost boy in the woods, no one was surprised. The wheelwright was lonely after all; the Great Winter had stolen his wife, his unborn child, and his parents in one fell swoop.

Just another sign of his madness, they said, eyeing the dirt now spilling from the wheelwright's windows, doorways, and lintels. *Another symptom of a mind gone awry.*

The ghost child was marvelous, or so the wheelwright claimed. A boy, a fine specimen of a lad, with wolflike grace and eyes of two different hues. *We must find him,* the wheelwright said. *We must save him.* Spurred on by his passionate pleas, searchers combed the forest far and wide for any sign of a human child in the wild, but there was nothing—not a scrap of hide nor hair.

After weeks of fruitless forays into the forest, the townspeople had had enough.

It is time, they said, *to lay the wheelwright to rest. Let him be given unto God, where he might find solace and healing.*

The church prepared a bed and the good burghers of the town marched in on the wheelwright's shop, where none had set foot for days. There was more than dirt and grime covering the windows and doorways; there were vines, roots, and dead trellis roses crawling over the walls like spidery bruise veins.

No one had heard the spectral hoofbeats pounding for days.

The townspeople called the wheelwright's name, but no one answered. They knocked, they pounded, they pleaded, but there was nothing. Nothing but muffled, ominous silence.

When at last they were able to break down the door, the townspeople found not a shop but a tomb. The wheelwright's shop was filled to the brim with dirt and loam and leaves and twigs—and the strange sight of scarlet poppies scattered like drops of blood amidst the decay and decrepitude. But the strangest sight of all, surrounded by the fractured figurines of bears who walked like men and wolves with men's faces, was a little boy with hair the color of snow and eyes of two different hues.

A wolf boy.

The townspeople caught the child, who snapped and struggled and fought like the feral animal he was, and bore him to the church, where a bed had been laid for the wheelwright. But of the wheelwright himself there was no sign. No trace of hide nor hair, nothing left but one last grotesque figurine: a willowy youth with the wheelwright's face and a goblin's pointed grin.

THE OLD
MONASTERY

"**T**ell me about your brother," the Countess said.

The day was mild for late winter, and the Countess and I were picnicking outside. It was the fourth day in a row my brother had not joined the rest of the household—such as it was—for a meal. Any meal. Breakfast, luncheon, tea, dinner, or supper, Josef was conspicuously absent from all gatherings. It was only the crumbs on his plate on the tray outside his door each morning that reassured me he was even eating at all.

"Josef?" I was surprised she had asked about him, then belatedly berated myself for such a selfish, self-absorbed thought. He was the other guest—prisoner—of the Procházkas.

The Countess nodded, slathering a roll with butter. "I've hardly seen him since we've arrived, although I have heard him playing his violin. Exquisite. Your brother has an extraordinary gift."

I flinched. Our paths had not crossed since our argument

that first night my brother and I had arrived at Snovin Hall, but I did occasionally see Josef on and about the grounds with his violin, lost in whatever private reveries that occupied his mind. His music was more of a presence than his physical self, for I often heard the high, sweet voice of his violin singing away in the abandoned hallways and corridors of the manor house.

"Yes," I said in a neutral tone. "He does."

My hostess looked askance at me. "And how is he? I know that this"—she gestured to Snovin, to the manor, to the Underground—"has all been rather overwhelming for the two of you."

Sometimes I hated those green eyes of hers, which were by turns incisive and empathetic. I did not trust her still, but there were times when I wanted to. There were times I was so lonely for a friend, a confidante, a companion, that I was nearly willing to set aside my distrust to accept her into my life. I was so isolated and removed from everything and everyone I knew and I loved—Mother and Constanze, Käthe and François, and Josef, especially Josef—that I could not help but be tempted to lean into her emotional support the way she leaned on her cane.

"I . . . I don't know," I said. "Josef and I . . . we had a fight."

I hated admitting this to her, but there was relief in it too.

"About your past as the Goblin Queen?" The Countess's voice was soft.

I looked up in surprise. "How did you—"

She laughed. "Oh, child," she said. "There will always be those envious of our gift. The touch of the Underground upon us. I adore Otto, but I cannot pretend he married me solely for love."

I picked at my luncheon. Josef's jealousy at my connection

with the Goblin King was a festering sore between us, but it wasn't the only injury slowly turning septic. My brother had more right than most to the Underground and its magic. He was *of* that magic, even if he did not know it. Even if I did not want him to know it. I was afraid of what that knowledge would do to him. To us.

"How—how do you deal with it?" I whispered.

The Countess paused mid-bite. "With what?"

"With the loneliness." I dared not look at her.

It was a while before she answered. I could feel those eyes, sharp and searching, on my face, and I did not know whether to shun or welcome her sympathy.

"You have a destiny," she said at last. "And I will not lie to you and say that it is an easy path to follow. There is no one in living memory who has done what you have done: walk away from the Underground and live. Not even I, the last descendant of the first Goblin Queen, know what that is like."

I could not swallow for the lump in my throat. I was alone. I would always be alone.

"But if your brother truly loved you, he would understand," the Countess said softly. "You are both touched by the Underground in your own ways."

I stiffened, alarm running down my spine. The truth of my brother's changeling nature was a secret I had shared with no one, not even with the one who deserved to hear it most. "What do you mean?"

She tilted her head, an enigmatic smile on her face. "He has an extraordinary gift with music. It is said that art and genius are fruits of the Underground. We are *Der Erlkönig's* own, after all."

My shoulders relaxed. "I see," I said. I bit my lip. "But is it enough?"

"For you or for him?" Her eyes were shrewd.

"Both," I replied. "Either. Jealousy can be poison."

I should know. I had been jealous of my brother his entire life.

"Only you and he can say," she said, her voice gentle. "For some, love can overcome jealousy. For others, jealousy will overcome love. Who you are and who he is is a matter only the two of you can resolve."

I stared down at the half-eaten, torn-apart bread roll in my hands.

"Come," the Countess said after a bit, brushing crumbs from her hands and skirts. "Let us go."

"Go?" I looked up to see her putting away the dishes and napkins back into our picnic basket. "Go where?"

"Where I go when I'm feeling sorry for myself." Her smile was gentle, her expression full of both pity and understanding. "Now, help me to my feet, child, and I shall call Konrad to bring the horses."

I did not ride, but according to the Countess, there was no better way to get to the monastery.

"The monastery?" I asked with surprise. I remembered my brother pointing out the burned-out building as we drove into the valley. "But I thought it was destroyed."

"It was," she said. "But the ruins are still structurally sound and it boasts some of best views of the valley."

"Is it . . . is it safe?" I did not mean the ruins.

"From the Hunt?" the Countess asked, guessing at my fear. I nodded. "Yes, as long as you're with me."

"Why?"

"Because," she said, her green eyes glinting. "There is an

ancient protection in my bloodline." Her green gaze slid to Konrad, who was bringing the horses around. "Because of what my foremother did when she walked away."

I frowned. "But the Hunt still rides after me. How did she escape retribution?"

The question had been sitting like a burning ember in my chest ever since I had first learned of the brave maiden. Ever since I had seen the gallery of the previous brides in the tailor's shop Underground, a gown on a dress form the only remaining bit of proof any of them had ever existed. I had received a story and name with each one: Magdalena, Maria Emmanuel, Bettina, Franziska, Like, Hildegard, Walburga. Women who had given themselves to death for a myriad reasons: despair, pleasure, adventure, deceit. But the very first bride—the brave maiden—her name was stricken from goblin memory, her legacy to be forgotten and forbidden by the old laws. How she did escape . . . for good?

"All in good time, my dear," the Countess said. "Now let Konrad help you up onto your horse, there's a good lass."

I eyed the beasts with fear and suspicion. Although we stabled horses at the inn, I had never ridden one before. The Countess assured me that she was a poor rider herself, and that I need not fear, for we would take it easy up the slopes to our destination.

A quarter of an hour later, I was perched precariously atop a white mare called Vesna.

"Named after the goddess of spring," the Countess said, riding up on her own horse—a dun-colored gelding—and patting Vesna on the rump. For all her claims to be a poor rider, the Countess sat astride her mount with the ease of one raised to a genteel life. She rode for pleasure, not for labor, and kept a brisk pace, leaving me and Vesna to follow as best we could. I wished I were sitting astride my horse, but Vesna had been fitted with a lady's saddle, and I did not have a lady's seat. Instead, I clung to her reins for dear life as we jostled and jounced our way up the mountain paths to Snovin Monastery.

"Beautiful, isn't it?" the Countess breathed once we reached the summit. Her cheeks were flushed from the cold and the morning's exertions, her eyes bright and sparkling. On her mount she had four good legs, and I could see how the freedom exhilarated her. I, on the other hand, could barely feel my hands for the chill and the death grip to which I had subjected them for the past hour and a half.

"Indeed," I squeaked, my throat tight with nervousness. I was held together with prayer and stiff muscles, but bit by bit, my bones stopped rattling and I was able to enjoy the scene before me.

My hostess was right, the picture before us *was* beautiful. Up close, I could see that the monastery had been built of a golden stone that still gleamed despite the ravages of time, and from our vantage point we could see around us for miles. I saw for the first time the nearby town of New Snovin, the red-tiled buildings shining bright in the afternoon sun like poppies in a field. The Countess explained that the town had been moved from its original location years ago due to plague and famine; indeed, we had passed the empty remains of several old houses and cottages on our way to the monastery. It was why Snovin Hall had seemed so isolated; the town immediately surrounding it had been abandoned years before.

We passed under a rusted iron gate into a large stone courtyard that very much resembled a village square.

"It was a castle before it became a monastery," the

Countess said. "In fact, it is the burg represented on my husband's coat of arms. But as the wars died down and the Procházkas grew prosperous with peace, they built Snovin Hall to be their legacy. We can leave the horses here," she announced as we approached what appeared to be the charred remains of a stable.

"Is it safe?" I asked, eyeing the rotted wooden beams.

"It's stood for three hundred years like this, so it can stand for at least another three hours. Now, be a dear and help me dismount," she ordered.

I scarcely knew how to gracefully get off my own horse without tumbling to the ground, but somehow I managed it without cracking a skull. I moved to help the Countess, but she seemed much more nimble than I despite the club foot.

"Otto doesn't like it when I come here alone," she admitted. "He thinks I'm not careful enough of my step." Her smile was wry. "But I love it up here. There is a certain allure to this place, some dark, shameful part of me that thrills at the beauty of death and decay."

Walking arm in arm with the Countess, I understood what she meant. The notion of finding death and decay beautiful should have sounded ridiculous and morbid, yet it resonated with me with a sort of romance of its own. I thought of the leaves of the Goblin Grove decomposing into mulch, dissolving into soil, that rich, fertile earth waiting to give way to life with the right touch of sunshine and rain. I thought of Snovin Hall, with its former grandeur slowly moldering into ruin, reclaimed by the land. The difference between sorrow and melancholy, the razor's edge that divided aesthetic pleasure and emotional devastation.

Again, I felt those green eyes upon my face. "I always knew you were one of us," she said with a smile. "Those of us who are *Der Erlkönig's* own know that we all return to the Underground's embrace in the end."

We all return in the end. I thought of Josef, and shivered. "But I thought you—she—the first Goblin Queen—escaped. Free and clear."

We passed a threshold and into a colonnade surrounding what was once a garden or a lawn. It was overgrown with weeds and wildflowers now, surprisingly green despite the light dusting of snow that covered them. I wondered where the Countess was taking me.

"The view is best from the southeast tower," she said as though reading my thoughts. We picked our way through the fallen rubble. "Nothing is free and clear," she said softly. "Not with the old laws."

I frowned. "Then how did she do it? How did she walk away?" We passed the colonnade and through the door at the base of the tower in question and began climbing a narrow spiral staircase.

Her face grew grim. "When my foremother walked away from the Underground, the Wild Hunt chased her over hill and dale, hither and yon. But she could have escaped their notice if she had been content to merely walk away. After all, a life for a life; *Der Erlkönig* could have simply found another bride."

Another bride. Jealousy, sorrow, and hope chased each other through my blood. "Why didn't he?"

The Countess smiled. "He loved her. He would have no other. And for his love, the old laws punished him."

My stomach gave a jolt. I remembered the vision I had had leaving Vienna, when the Procházkas had drugged me, when I awoke with the Goblin King's ring in my hand. The darkness crawling over his skin, the bleached-pale eyes, the horns curing from his feathery hair, the tortured, spindly, multi-jointed hands.

The covenant is undone. It is corrupting us. Corrupting him.

"Then what happened?" I asked.

"She returned Underground."

"What?" It was a twist to the story I had not anticipated. "Why?"

"There is power in a name," the Countess said. "She found his. His true name, the name he had given up when he became *Der Erlkönig*. He had placed it within her heart, so that a piece of him would live on so long as her blood still beat and her lungs did breathe. His name was the key that unlocked her shackles, and so they walked together in the world above."

My own breaths came short, my pulse skipping and fluttering with excitement, fear, joy, and not a little exertion. "How?" I whispered. "How did she find his name?"

"She cut out her heart and laid it bare before her."

I wasn't sure if the Countess was being poetic or in deadly earnest. Her expression gave nothing away, and I resisted the urge to reach for the Goblin King's ring.

I would walk the world and play, until someone called me by name and called me home. My throat constricted, and the tears that were all too close to the surface threatened to spill over once more. My austere young man, trapped Underground and being slowly corrupted—punished—for the sin of loving me more than the old laws. If I could find his name, if I could just free him . . . it seemed too good to be true. *A life for a life.* But then who became *Der Erlkönig* after the first was freed? And how?

"Ah, here we are," the Countess said.

We had reached the top of the stairs, and the space

widened around us into a long, high-ceilinged corridor. The fire seemed to have barely touched this part of the monastery. The floor beneath our feet was made of marble, and the walls were lined with a yellow silk brocade. The doors to the monks' cells were paneled with a rich, dark wood and between them stood some porcelain statues of Christ, which remained intact, as well as a few paintings.

"This room has the best view," the Countess said, opening a door at the end of the hall. "I envy the brothers who lived here."

The room was small and dark, with a small window cut some few feet above our heads into the thick outer stone wall of the tower. Panes of glass had filled that window once, but they were smashed and broken, and the wind whistled in, a high, keening sound. There were two narrow beds placed on either side, with a scant foot between them, although I wasn't sure if more than one monk had lain his head here. The bed opposite the window had a deteriorating coverlet, the threads picked clean by birds and rodents to build their own nests, and a few dusty, moldering robes were piled atop the chest at the foot of the bed. A Bible still rested on the table beside the bed, along with a half-burned candle with wax melted into a pool at its base.

By contrast, its brother bed was entirely bare. No coverlet, no pillow. No mattress, even. The Countess gestured to the frame, indicating I should climb atop it for a better view.

"I'm getting too old for such acrobatics, even without the club foot," she said. "You go ahead, child. Lean on me."

Hesitantly, I braced myself against her shoulder and pushed myself up on my toes for a glimpse through the window. I spied something scratched into the mortar surrounding the window frame. Words, etched in a surprisingly clear hand: *Wolfgangus fuit hic.* Latin. I traced my fingers over the letters, and for the briefest moment, I was connected to the brother who had left just a little bit of himself behind in this world.

Then I looked out over the valley.

"Oh," I breathed.

"Marvelous, isn't it?" Below me, I could hear the pride in her voice.

"Yes," I said. From this vantage point, I could see clear across to the mountains across the way and the sparkling ribbon of silver that cut through the valley floor. "What river is that?"

"Snovin River," the Countess said. "The Procházkas weren't terribly imaginative, I'm afraid."

I strained to see farther, toward Snovin Hall and the mountains beyond. I caught a glimpse of an intense blue-green, that enchanted mirror lake I had stumbled upon when I first learned of the Countess's lineage. "What is—what is that lake?" I asked.

"You can see it from here?" she asked, sounding surprised. I nodded.

"Lake Snovin," she said. "I told you Otto's ancestors weren't imaginative." She laughed, seeing my expression. "But we always called it Lorelei Lake, Adelaide and I," she continued in a softer voice. Her daughter.

"Lorelei Lake?" I remembered the sense of magic that lingered about the water, the window to another world I had glimpsed in its reflection.

"Yes," she said. "Family legend boasts of their descent from a Lorelei found bathing in that very lake. It's the melusine on their shield."

"Is the water always that color?" I asked.

"Oh yes," the Countess said. "And the water is always warm. Volcanic activity, I'm told, but we wanted to believe it was magic, Adelaide and I. She believed it was a gateway to the Underground." Something within her seemed to suddenly snap closed, like a trap on a mouse's neck. "Come, child," she said shortly. "Your weight is wearing me down."

I hopped down from my perch at the window and offered my arm to the Countess as we made our way back down the stairs.

"I do hope your brother will be able to join us for dinner tonight," she said in a different tone of voice as we emerged through a different door and into a wide, cavernous space. "Perhaps we can get to know him better once you are both settled."

The abrupt change in conversation startled me, and I did not know how to respond. "Where are we?" I asked, gesturing to the rocky room around us.

"The crypt," the Countess said. "Most of the brothers are buried in the cemetery at the base of the mountain itself, but their names are carved here, so that they may be remembered long after their remains rotted away."

I ran my fingers over the letters etched into stone. I thought of the day we buried Papa, of his limestone grave marker standing next to the little wooden crosses of his brothers and sisters—my aunts and uncles, most of whom had died before they had even drawn breath. In time, those crosses would wither and rot away, leaving nothing but their names in the village register behind. And even then, ink faded and paper dissolved to dust. All that remained of a person once they were gone was a legacy, which would linger only as long as you were loved or hated. Immortality was memory.

Evzen, Filip, Andrej, Victor, Johannes, Hans, Mahieu.

I paused over this last name, puzzling over its resonance with me. These were the names of monks dead and gone, their names as anonymous as the faces of strangers in this valley. Yet the name *Mahieu* rang a bell inside me, as though I had heard that name whispered to me in my sleep.

His name was Brother Mahieu.

I went still. The Goblin King's voice returned to me, our confessions to each other that last night in the chapel. I had asked him who had taught him to play the violin.

His name was Brother Mahieu.

Then the familiarity of it all unfolded before me. Why I had felt as though I had seen this place before. Because I *had* seen the monastery before. In a mirror. Underground.

Above the Goblin King's bed.

the villagers called the boy *vlček*, or "little wolf." He had a long, lupine face, a cloud of white hair like a mane about his head, and the guttural growls and snarls of a cornered animal. It was hard to say how old the wolf-child was; he was small, no more than the size of the baker's youngest, Karolína, who was three. The priest thought the boy might be older, for he was as agile as a cat, and more cunning besides.

It was a long time before anyone could come close enough to the child to bathe and tend to his wounds. A long gash ran across his chest and over his heart, inflamed and infected. The priest was afraid the cut would turn septic, but no one could approach the boy without risking a few fingers and toes. The priest himself wore a bandage and poultice about his forearm where the *vlček* had torn out a large chunk with his teeth.

Only Mahieu, another orphan of the Great Winter several seasons past and himself a ward of the church, was able to tame the wolf-child.

Faithful Mahieu, the villagers called him. The youth was good and kind, a lover of growing things and the wild things in the woods. *Touched by God*, the priest proclaimed. *Mahieu* could coax even the flowers to bloom in the snow. Little by little, like a shepherd with a recalcitrant flock, the youth called the boy out of the wolf. He taught the child the rudiments of being human, cleanliness, of posture, of manners, of clothing. The process was long and slow, the *vlček* eventually learned to use his fingers instead of claws, wear cotton instead of fur, and eat cooked meat instead of raw. When it came time for the boy to be christened, he did not struggle or resist the dunking of his head in the baptismal font. He was given the name Kašpar by the priest, recorded in the church register along with the note *Given to us by the Lord and delivered from the wild and the woods.*

The taming was complete, but for one small matter.

The *vlček* did not speak, nor did he respond to his name.

It was not that the boy lacked intelligence, even beyond the animal cunning of his wolf kin. He was quick and clever, solving the puzzles and riddles set for him by the priest, following orders, obediently cleaning the small cell in the church he had been given. He was of the age to be taught the alchemy of language and written speech in the local grammar school, and learned his letters competently alongside the other children of the village.

The boy was not dumb. When given leave to explore the village and the edges of the forest beyond, the townsfolk overheard whispered conversations between the *vlček* and the trees, between the boy and the beasts. It was a tongue half remembered by babies and babblers, a curious murmur and chatter understood only by the innocent, the mad, and Mahieu. *What was he whispering?* they wondered. It sounded like eldritch spells.

Father, Father, they entreated the priest. *There is something wrong with the child.*

The good Father tried his best to appease his flock but fear, the priest would come to know, was greater than faith.

The boy's silence was no longer regarded a symptom of a shy, retiring nature; it was the stubbornness of animal cunning. More and more, the villagers became convinced that the *vlček* could speak but wouldn't; it was in the way those mismatched eyes watched everything and everyone around them. *The* vlček *thinks,* they would say to one another in the market place. *He schemes. He spies.*

What secrets do the voiceless keep? Only their own. But the townsfolk were afraid of what the *vlček* knew. The butcher and his mistress, two years younger than his own daughter. The blacksmith's wife and her stash of stolen sweets, eaten on Lenten Sundays when the pious fasted. The goatherd and the baker, their hearts and lips still warm with the scent of each other's breaths.

On the day the old year died, the butcher's mistress was found dead in her bed.

There had been no mark upon her: no gash, no wound, no bruise. She was found blue and glassy, as though winter had turned her to ice from within.

Elf-struck! the villagers cried. *The goblins have preyed upon Ludmila in her sleep!*

The cold deepened, and with it came other deaths, other betrayals. Jakub the goatherd's flock went astray, the blacksmith's tongs turned brittle and broke, and the villagers came to understand that there was something deeply broken with the balance of the world.

It was because they had brought a monster into their midst. Who was the *vlček*? Where had he come from? Stories and rumors began to spread from house to house, tales of a kobold with mismatched eyes that stole trinkets and totems to do its owners mischief and harm.

Could it be, could it be? the townsfolk whispered.

But the *vlček* remained blameless, separate, distant. He went about his day, silent and sure-footed, a ghost among the living.

Then Karolína, the baker's youngest, became possessed of a demon.

It began with biting pains on her hands and feet. The poor child cried that a wolf was devouring her limbs in her sleep, and she awoke with red, weeping sores and deep, suppurating wounds. *Goblin bites,* the villagers said, and they sent for the priest for an exorcism.

He came with incense, he came with holy water, and he came with two companions: the *vlček* and Mahieu. But when the wolf-child approached the sickbed, Karolína screamed as though she were being burned at the stake.

It was a sign.

It's him, it's him! the villagers cried. *He's the one!*

The priest and the villagers began to crowd around the boy, who snarled and dropped to all fours, for he had not yet learned to suffer another's touch. They came with kettles, they came with pans, and the men outside went in search of pitchforks and shovels, as the cornered *vlček* lashed and kicked out in fear.

It was Mahieu who betrayed them all.

Run, Kašpar! he yelled, leaping forward to shield the villagers from the wolf-child's snapping white teeth and rolling, panicked eyes. The boy startled at the youth, his one and only friend, then ran, tearing through the crowd before disappearing into the dark beyond.

Torches sprang to life, voices were raised in eager shouts, as the fever of the hunt spread through the town like a plague, like a wildfire. While little Karolína wailed on in pain and fear, her mother and father, the priest and the mayor, the butcher and blacksmith gathered their tools as weapons and went in search of the wolf-boy.

Kill him, kill him! they chanted. *De-mon! De-mon!*

Mahieu knew where the *vlček* would go, and did not follow the others into the night. Instead he ran toward the church, toward the cemetery, toward the crypts, where a lost little boy might hide in the dark with the dead, the only humans who never asked him to speak.

Inside, Mahieu found the wolf-child hunched amidst a pile of rags, a collection of odds and ends and secrets stolen from the villagers. A little blue glass vial, the shards of a shattered sword, a goatherd's bell, last seen draped about the neck of Jakub's prize billy.

"Oh, Kašpar," Mahieu said.

The *vlček* looked at him, stubbornness writ in his gaze. He knew Mahieu was calling him, but refused to respond.

"Kašpar," Mahieu repeated, fighting against the panic rising with him. "Please. We must flee."

The wolf-child growled.

Faithful Mahieu, blessed by God to commune with bird and beast, could not find the words to reach this boy, half wild, half tame.

"I know it is not your name," he whispered to the *vlček*. "But until you give it to me, I cannot call you home."

Whether or it was the kindness or plea that undid the wolf-child, Mahieu did not know, but the *vlček* dropped his treasures and began to weep. The boy had endured much since he emerged from the beast's lair, kicking and spitting, had learned how to eat and dress and walk, but what he had never done was cry. The shine of tears had turned his mismatched eyes brilliant, and their glittering beauty stole Mahieu's breath away.

"Come," he whispered. "Come, we must flee."

He held out his hand to the *vlček*, who stared at the outstretched palm with neither suspicion nor fear on his face. The wolf-boy held Mahieu's gaze, and for a moment, eternity and a question stretched between them.

"Yes," the *vlček* said. "Yes."

His voice was rough and hoarse, his tongue thick and unused. But it was words, real words, more words than anyone had ever heard him say. The *vlček* grasped Faithful Mahieu's hand, and the two of them ran into the forest, into the beyond, and the unknown.

THE MONSTER
I CLAIM

my brother did not join us for dinner.

I hadn't expected him to show his face, yet the sting of disappointment was just as sharp this time as it had been the first. Our meal was a polite enough affair, but my hosts couldn't contain their curiosity about Josef forever. They asked several questions about his skill with the violin, about his talent, about his musical gifts. I understood that prodigies and virtuosos were marvelous and unusual, but their interest in my brother's abilities over mine picked at wounds that should have long since scabbed over.

Special Liesl. Chosen Liesl. You have always wanted to be extraordinary and now you are.

Cold, oily guilt slicked my stomach with resentment and regret, and I found I had no appetite. The remainder of the meal was stilted and awkward, and I tasted none of the food that Nina had prepared for us. The fare was simple and hearty: sausages and stews, dumplings and cream sauce, braised cabbage and hearty breads. Familiar. Comforting. But it all turned leaden in my gut.

After dinner, I returned to my quarters to find the door between Josef's room and mine still shut. I did not know whether or not he had retired for the evening or if he hadn't returned from his daytime wanderings. I undressed and climbed into my bed, though the hour was early. I was tired from our excursion to the monastery that afternoon, and I could use the rest.

Yet try as I might, I could not sleep. Silence pounded at my ears with the absence of sound. Back home, the forest chorus would have lulled me to sleep with its symphony of cacophony. In Vienna, the constant hum and drumming rhythm of human lives formed the bass line to my staccato days. But here, in Snovin, all was quiet. It was an empty sort of quiet. Once I would have sensed, would have known down to my marrow, whether or not Josef slept on the other side of a door, a window, a wall. The tether between us, woven of our love of music and magic, had frayed so badly that only the barest thread of blood tied us together.

And we weren't even bound by that.

I turned over in bed, squeezing my eyes shut as though I could shut out my own guilt.

The other times that particular disloyal thought about Josef crossed my traitorous mind, my body was racked with self-loathing and disgust. But tonight I let myself examine it. Let myself think about what it meant—what I felt—that my brother was not my brother, but a changeling.

A changeling. Before I had gone Underground, I might have been delighted. Or proud. Or even envious for many of the same reasons Josef was jealous of me now. I understood better than anyone the pain of being unremarkable. Had I not privately railed to myself about how my brother's talent set him apart from the rest of us? Music was a language we shared, and it hurt to know that not only was he better than me, he was *anointed* by Papa. To have discovered that my brother not only had a connection to the world of myth and magic to which we often escaped but an actual *belonging* to it might have devastated me.

Special. Chosen. Extraordinary. Josef had chosen his words well, for the accusations cut me to the quick. I curled up tighter into a ball, pulling my pillow over my face to blot out the last dregs of the setting sun.

But since I had walked away from the Underground, my thoughts about changelings had changed. I remembered the comely youths with whom my sister and I had danced at the goblin ball with their elegant faces and inscrutable eyes. The creature by the lake who had tricked me into crossing the barrier between worlds by playing on my homesickness and my longing for the simple pleasures of mortal life. Deceitful, tricksy, cruel. Inhuman.

Josef was inhuman. Josef was not mortal. Josef was a creature, a sprite, a thing. My entire being cringed at the notion of my brother as a *thing*. If my brother was not human, he was at the very least a *person*. He laughed, he cried, he sulked, he raged. He reasoned and felt the same as any other boy—youth—and it did not matter that his bone and blood was of otherkin, not mine.

And yet, it did. I thought of the baby who should have grown up to be my brother, the child of my parents' mortal get. The one whose name and place and life my brother stole. That Josef had been a cheerful, easygoing child, ruddy-cheeked and sparkly-eyed. My Josef was a colicky, cranky baby, a difficult and disagreeable child that I nevertheless loved.

Perhaps loved even more than the boy who shared my blood.

I should have been disgusted with myself. I loved a usurper, a thief, a monster. I turned the Goblin King's ring over and over on my finger, feeling the silver slide smoothly across my skin.

You are the monster I claim, mein Herr.

Perhaps I loved the monstrous because *I* was a monster. Josef, the Goblin King, and me. We were grotesques in the world above, too different, too odd, too talented, too much. We were all too much.

Images flashed across the backs of my eyelids. Cloud shadows passing over sun-dappled red tiles. A monastery looking down its nose at the valley below. The names of monks carved into mountainsides, the echoes of memory ringing bells in my mind. Scarlet poppies springing from white snow with a whisper and a sigh. Faster and faster and faster, a long spiral down into the labyrinth of my subconscious yet I could not sleep, could not rest. I tossed and turned, unable to stop the whirlwind carousel thoughts flying out from the center: that I should tell Josef the truth.

I kicked at the bed linens tangled about my legs, clenching my fists and teeth to hold in the urge to scream. Notes and musical phrases and melodies crashed in my head, and I clapped my hands over my ears to drown out the noise. Rage and frustration were coiled in my limbs, a tantrum building in my body ready to burst forth with a roar and whimper. The truth about my brother's changeling was a trap that could be tripped at any moment, and I would rather spring it myself than have it snap down upon our necks and break our relationship.

I should tell him.

I should tell Käthe.

My eyes flew open. Clawing my way out from under the covers, I threw myself out of bed, unable to lie still any longer despite my fatigue. I paced back and forth before the windows of my room. For the first time in a long time, I wanted to play. I wanted to sit before my klavier and work out my feelings through my fingers, through the black and white keys, through major and minor.

Your music creates a bridge between worlds.

I thought of the evening we had performed *Der Erlkönig* for the Count and Countess. The scent of ice and pine and deep woods filling the small, stuffy room. The whisper of my name across the veil. The weight of the Goblin King's ring in the palm of my hand when I awoke from the dream. The sudden itch to play scratched at me, despite the Wild Hunt, despite the barrier between worlds, despite how utterly perverse and nonsensical it was to return to my art at the moment it was the least safe.

I shouldn't.

And yet.

Why shouldn't I?

The tantrum tempest raging within me fed upon my manic irritation, growing larger and stronger to encompass Josef, my sister, the Countess, the world. I was no longer the Goblin Queen, no longer mistress of a domain that would twist and bend itself to my will. I could not tear the curtains to shreds. I could not smash the dresser beside me. I could not tear the linen cupboard doors from their hinges. I could not shatter the windowpanes with my bare hands. I was in the world above now and I could not, I could not, I could not.

Dusk deepened outside, turning the sky indigo blue and the shadows a violet purple. I walked to the windows in my quarters and looked toward the hills behind the estate and Lorelei Lake. I saw the Countess walking toward the poppy field, her uneven gait distinctive even in the darkness. One by one, stars emerged in the sky, pinpricks of light that limned the world in silver. On a night like this, my brother and I would have imagined the goblins and fey out and about, wreaking havoc and mischief upon a sleeping world. Shapes moved about in the forest beyond the edges of the estate, my imagination running wild.

Until a stark silhouette emerged from the trees, carrying a violin.

Josef.

He stood on the grounds facing the house. I could not make out anything of his face or features, but I imagined his eyes turned up to the second floor, seeing my white chemise stand out in the murky black of my window. We stared at each other—or not—for several long moments. Our first moment of connection since we had argued. Then my brother turned around and made his way back toward the poppy field and the woods.

I felt as though I had been slapped.

Fine, I thought. *You are no longer first in my heart.* I waited for guilt to flay the flesh from my bones and leave me bare, but it never did. Nothing touched me but exhaustion and resignation.

I was tired of waiting, tired of longing and hoping and wishing my brother would turn around and appreciate me. That Josef loved me, I had no doubt, but he, like so many others, had taken me for granted. That I would come running to him in Vienna to save him. To bring him home. To be at his beck and call. François and I had tried and tried and tried to put him back together after he had fallen apart, but the more we tried, the more the pieces no longer fit.

I thought of Käthe then. My sister had once called me a top spinning out of control, and that the slightest wobble would topple me. I hadn't realized until then how selfish I had been to lay that emotional burden on her shoulders. I wished Josef could see that now.

I am tired of holding your heart.

"I give it back," I whispered to my brother, lost to the shadows outside. "I give you back your heart."

Sadness washed over me. Instead of guilt or frustration or anger, in the aftermath of the tempest tantrum, I felt nothing but melancholy. Mania and melancholy, my twin demons. With sorrow came fatigue, a deep and abiding sense of exhaustion. I climbed back into bed.

"I give you back your heart," I said to the darkness. "And I wish you would give me mine."

Snovin Hall was haunted.

It wasn't haunted in the usual manner—with ghosts and sprites and spirits. Josef knew how to exorcise ghosts from a house with bells and holy water. He knew how to appease kobolds and *Hödekin* with offerings of milk and bread, how to safeguard his home from the unseen forces of the world with salt and prayers. But what he didn't know how to do was cast out the demons from his own head.

The whispers beckoned from every corner of the estate, filling his ears at night so he could no longer sleep. He had taken to wandering the halls after everyone else had risen for the day, playing his violin out in the woods where no one would hear. The playing did nothing to drown out the voiceless murmurs in his mind, but he could at least lose himself in the rigorous, tedious repetition of notes. He would play through every piece he could remember, and some he did not—once, twice, thrice. The first for feeling: the bowing languid and smooth or sharp and emphatic. The second for precision: the fingering exact, the timing rigid. The third for despair: the last resort of an unraveling mind. And when Josef had played through his entire repertoire several times over, he would fall back on his exercises. Scales. Rhythm and tempo practice.

None of it helped.

When he closed his eyes, he could still see his sister's face when he called her Goblin Queen. It had not been a term of endearment, but an accusation. He could still see the arrow land between her ribs, and the expression of shock and hurt and betrayal both shook him and soothed him. They had both gone away from home and emerged transformed: his sister a woman, he a quivering wreck. Liesl had had *Der Erlkönig* while Josef had had Master Antonius when it should have been the other way around. His sister was meant for fame and recognition and public adulation; he was meant for the Goblin Grove.

After nightfall, Josef made his way back to the manor. He was tired, exhaustion carving out blue-black hollows beneath his eyes and cheeks. He wanted to sleep, to rest his head, to forget the image of Liesl's brown eyes looking at him with such reproach. His very first memory was of his sister's eyes peering over the edge of his cradle, large and lambent and full of love. He remembered little else from his earliest childhood; in the end, it had been Liesl, always Liesl, who made him feel safe. But he could not forgive her for not being there when he had needed her most, for sending him away when every fiber of his being had cried out to stay.

When he finally returned to the grounds of Snovin Hall proper, Josef looked up at the second story window where he knew his sister slept. To his surprise, he saw her standing there, her pale chemise standing out against the darkness of the room like a ghost. He ached down to his bones, a knot of guilt and resentment and hatred and love tangled in his veins. There was no feeling but ceaseless, never-ending pain at the sight of her standing there, and he wanted to bleed himself to relieve the pressure. To leech himself of bad blood and bad thoughts.

He turned away.

In the distance, he spied the distinct figure of the Countess limping ahead. The dark was complete now, and nothing but stars lit her path, though she strode with purpose and determination. A place and destination in mind, perhaps. The faint stirrings of curiosity fluttered in Josef's breast, so slight he might have ignored them, save for one thing:

She was following the whispers.

The voiceless murmurs were strongest from the direction of the poppy field, and Josef wondered if she could hear their pulsing sighs like the breeze through weeds. *Nameless,* they said. *Usurper.*

He had ignored the whispers the way he had so often pushed away his emotions. The way he had turned away from François. If it was not Liesl's reproachful eyes he saw when he went to sleep, then it was his beloved's lips. François had long since perfected a mask of serene calm, his armor in a world hostile to those of his color, but Josef knew where to find the chinks. It would be at the corners of his mouth, tight with anger, twisted with sorrow. The weight of his sister's and beloved's feelings was heavy, and he was tired of carrying their burden. The whispers were just another load to put down.

But tonight he would follow them. Follow the Countess. His footfalls fell softly on dried grasses and broken twigs, for he did not notice the scarlet petals of the poppies wither and die in her wake. The whispers fell silent as she passed.

The stranger came, the flowers left.

It wasn't until the Countess turned to face him that Josef realized she had known he was there all along.

"Hallo, Josef," she said softly.

Her voice was lost amidst the shushing breeze, the poppies murmuring *run away, run away, run away*. But Josef did not run.

"Hallo, madame," he replied. His own voice was hoarse from disuse, but clear above the whispers.

The Countess's green eyes glowed in the dark. "Will you not play?"

He knew she meant the violin. "Have you not heard?"

She inclined her head. In the dim light of the stars above, Josef could see her mouth forming words, but they were drowned out in the cacophony of voiceless warnings. *Beware, beware, beware!*

"I'm sorry," he said. "I'm afraid I didn't quite catch that."

She only smiled. The Countess reached down to pluck a flower, and Josef flinched at the soundless scream of pain.

"Do you know why the symbol of House Procházka is the poppy?" she asked.

He did not answer.

"It is said," the Countess said, "that Jaroslav Procházka founded his house at the site of a great battle, where so many soldiers had fallen and stained the fields red with their blood." She brought the petals up to her nose, and though Josef knew the flower was odorless, he thought he could smell the slight tang of copper on the air. "The house was built to honor their sacrifice, and this field of poppies planted to commemorate their passing."

Josef glanced at the shriveled and desiccated petals at her feet, black and brittle.

"Try as I might, I never did find any evidence of a battle

here," the Countess went on. "But that isn't to say that blood hasn't been shed."

Beware, nameless one, beware.

"What do you mean?" Josef wasn't sure whether he was asking the Countess or the poppies.

"My family comes from a long line of butchers," she said. "Not nobly born was I, despite my uncanny lineage. My father was a butcher, my mother a fancy French whore. How far the first Goblin Queen's descendants have fallen. From *Der Erlkönig*'s bride to tinkers and tailors, butchers and bakers. But Snovin"—she breathed in deep the scentless flower—"was where we always returned."

"Why?" Josef asked.

"Do you know that the heir of the first Goblin Queen is always a stranger?" She laughed. "Foreigners, commoners, the lowly born. Yet we are drawn here because this placed is soaked with innocent blood, and all the Goblin Queen had been was a butcher in the end."

Run away, nameless one, run away.

"Impossible poppies," the Countess said. "Blooming in late winter. A place teeming with magic if there ever was one, and the stories say that the flower is all that remains of the souls of the stolen."

"Stolen by whom?" Fear was beginning to seep in through Josef's numbness along with the cold.

"The Wild Hunt." Her green eyes were sharp, even in the dark. "The elf-struck are dead, but the elf-touched are trapped."

He looked down to his feet, the poppies scattered across his boots like drops of blood. "Do they protect us? From the Hunt, I mean."

"The unholy host cannot be appeased by anything but a

sacrifice," the Countess said softly. "It is the ancient bargain we've struck. A life for a life. Our lives. Our livelihood."

Josef frowned. "Sacrifice?"

But the Countess did not immediately reply, kneeling down to pluck another poppy from the field. It dulled immediately between her fingers, turning purple and black with decay. She stepped forward and tucked it behind his ear.

"The gifts of *Der Erlkönig* are not to be taken lightly. But in the end, the fruits, like all bounties, must be harvested."

There was no reply but the moan of the wind through the trees.

"Go to sleep, Josef," the Countess said gently. "Not long now until spring."

He turned and obeyed, walking back to Snovin Hall as though in a trance. Darkness deepened, then lightened. The sky behind the hills lifted from densest purple to crushed, faded lavender, and the shadows retreated. Josef climbed into bed and watched as, one by one, the stars began to wink out, disappearing from the night like fireflies in summer. Silhouettes took on shape and texture, details grew clearer and brighter, and a world at peace began to stir and rise to greet the day. It wasn't until the first ray of dawn struck the foot of his bed that Josef remembered that harvest was in the autumn while planting was in the spring. Everything was inside out in this strange and unexpected place, and as he drifted off to sleep, he wondered when the whispers had finally gone silent.

the people said there were wolf-wraiths in the woods.

Tales began to spread from town to town, stories of a sighting here, an encounter there. Freshly baked pies snatched from windowsills as they were laid out to cool, stores of grain disappearing, farm animals crying. No two accounts agreed on the appearance of the wraith: some said they were ghost boys, others insisted they were wolf cubs who walked about on their hind legs. Still others—the elders of many winters past—spoke of kobolds and sprites, mischief-makers and thieves. Spidery fingers and beetle-black eyes, the usual suspects.

Goblins.

Despite these differing accounts, there was one detail all the stories had in common: that wherever these wolf-wraiths had been, red poppies bloomed in its wake.

Impossible, claimed the philosophers. *It defies natural order.*

But it was impossible to discount the evidence.

It began in the barns and stables of the farmers outside town. Doors left open, footprints in the mud and muck, frightened bleating and lowing, the impression of bodies in the hay. The first farmer to see the wraiths had woken before dawn to milk his cow to see two shadows slipping away from the stable. Fearing thieves, he ran after them, but they vanished with the last dregs of starlight, leaving no sign they had ever been there, save a handful of red poppies scattered among the rushes.

From farm to farm, town to town, poppies began springing up in the oddest of places. In a hayloft, wedged between cobblestones, twined about the gables of houses. Each appearance of the flower came with a strange tale of ethereal figures and things that went bump in the night. Locked pantry cupboards with half a season's worth of cured meats missing. Furniture completely rearranged without sound in utter darkness. A haunting shushing noise, the sound of winter branches rubbing together in the wind.

As the poppies began making appearances farther south and west, more and more descriptions of the wraith began to become similar.

Boys, the consensus ran. *Two ghost boys.*

It was always two, or so the stories said. One taller, one smaller, one as black as night, the other white as snow. Some claimed they were the spirits of two children murdered by their parents as a sacrifice to ensure a good harvest, others stated they were not human at all, but changelings escaped from the realm of the fey, looking for a home.

As the days grew longer and the nights grew warmer, fewer and fewer poppies appeared. The stories that traveled with the flowers shifted and changed as the landscape turned from rural villages to prosperous cities.

Not dead boys, they said. *Alive.*

Two children, one older, one younger. Orphans. One with hair as dark as soot, the other with eyes as pale as water. They had the haunted look of the hunted, their faces gaunt, their eyes hollow. No one knew where they came from, for they spoke no tongue the townsfolk understood.

Take them to the abbey, they said. *The monks would know.*

The learned brothers of the abbey were scholars, philosophers, musicians, and artists from near and far. Indeed, the choirmaster spoke their tongue, and understood the boys had journeyed far in search of safety. But what the choirmaster did not understand was that it was not the language of man he shared with the boys, but the language of music.

Welcome, children, the choirmaster said. *Rest, and be welcome, for you are now in God's hands. The hand of Providence has guided you to our doorstep.*

The *vlček* had followed the wolf-paths in the woods to the monastery, but what he had truly followed was the sound of singing at Sunday services. The boy had no words for melody, harmony, or counterpoint, but he wanted them. In their moments of rest on the run, in the slow breaths before they fell asleep, Mahieu had listened to *vlček* humming lullabies to himself in the wild. It was the only time he ever heard the wolf-boy use his voice, and Faithful Mahieu decided right then and there that he would learn to play music, so he could speak with his friend.

When the choirmaster asked for the boys' names, only one answered.

"I am Mahieu," said the older.

The monk glanced at the younger child. *And the boy?*

The *vlček* said nothing, only stared at the choirmaster with his piercing, unsettling, mismatched gaze.

"He . . . he has not yet given it to me," Mahieu said. The *vlček's* eyes warmed, and the smallest hint of a smile softened his face.

Does the child speak?

The boys exchanged glances. "Yes," said Mahieu. "The language of trees, of birds, of fang and fur."

But does he speak the language of Man?

Mahieu did not answer.

Then we shall call him Sebastian, the choirmaster said. *For our patron saint, and the man who cured Zoe of Rome of being mute. Perhaps the same miracle can be performed for the child.*

The *vlček* bared his teeth.

Later that night, when the monk brought the boys to their new quarters, Mahieu turned to whisper to the wolf-boy in the dark.

"Speak, friend," he said. "You understand my words and I have heard you use your voice. Why do you not reply in kind?"

It was a long moment before the *vlček* responded, first pursing his lips and curling his tongue, as though silently rolling sounds and syllables and notes and names around in his mouth. "Sebastian is not my name. And until they call my name and call me home, I shall not reply."

Mahieu paused. "What *is* your name?"

The ensuing silence was laden with pain. "I have no name."

"Then how can anyone call you home?"

The boy did not answer for a long time. "No one has given me a home."

"The wolf-paths have led you here," Mahieu said. "If the monastery is not your home and Sebastian is not your name, then what is?"

"The wolf-paths," the *vlček* murmured. "My home and my name lie at the end of them. But this is not the end."

Mahieu was troubled. "What is the end?"

The other boy did not reply for so long, Mahieu thought

he had fallen asleep. And then, in a voice so low it was almost as though the *vlček* had not even spoken:

"I don't know," he whispered. "I don't know."

CHANGELING

"**h**ave you heard yet from my sister?" I asked the Count the next morning at breakfast.

He choked on his next sip of coffee, his face turning a reddish purple as he coughed and coughed and coughed. "Hot," he managed to gasp out, setting his cup back down in its saucer. "Burned my tongue."

I waited until his fit had passed. "I sent Käthe word when we first arrived. I was wondering if she had sent any reply."

The Count stirred his coffee with a spoon, though he drank his black without any cream or sugar. "Not that I know of, my dear."

He wouldn't meet my eyes. Unlike the Countess, the Count wore every expression, every thought, every feeling on his face. He had an open countenance, and despite his shifty glances, I was more inclined to trust him than his wife.

Especially as she had stolen my correspondence before.

"How often are you able to get the post up here?" I asked. "Is there a way I can perhaps get to New Snovin to see if any letter from Vienna had been received?"

The Count continued stirring his coffee. "I will ask my wife."

I studied him. "You are the lord of the manor, Your Illustriousness," I said. "Surely you need not ask her permission."

He laughed, but it was not a cheerful sound. Instead, it quivered with nerves. "You will find once you become married, *Fräulein,* that the husband holds far less power than he would have you believe."

"Is there anything objectionable in my writing to my sister?" I asked.

"No, no, of course not," he said quickly. He took another sip of his coffee. "Ah, perhaps I will add some cream." The Count rose from his seat and walked to the sideboard.

I narrowed my eyes. "Is there a reason you don't want me to write to her?"

The creamer clattered as the Count spilled some, scattering white droplets everywhere. "Blast!"

I got to my feet. "Are you all right, Your Illustriousness?" His anxiousness was suspect, and I followed the trail like a bloodhound on the scent. Despite my exhaustion, I had slept little and ill, thoughts churning through my mind like cream into butter. Ever since I had come to Snovin, it had been one revelation after another, one heartbreak after another, and it wasn't until the distractions had fallen away that I had begun to ask questions.

If I were the bridge between worlds . . . then what was Josef?

"Yes, yes, I'm fine," he said, waving me off. "Let me call for Nina to clean up this mess."

I remembered the upside-down world I'd seen in the

waters of Lorelei Lake. On our frenzied flight from Vienna, the Procházkas had reassured us that their friends and associates would care for Käthe and François, but I had not pressed them on the details. In fact, I had asked remarkably few questions since arriving at Snovin, and had received remarkably fewer answers. Their interest in me was clear—I was the Goblin Queen—but their concern for my brother and indifference to my sister and friend were not.

Why Josef and not Käthe and François? Was it simply a stroke of misfortune that my brother happened to be with me the night the Procházkas drugged us and stole us away? Their kindnesses toward us were not insincere, but there was a disingenuousness about their compassion for our welfare at the expense of my sister's and our friend's security. Where were they? Why did I sense that the Count and Countess were doing everything in their power to discourage me from reaching out?

"No need to call for Nina," I said, walking to the Count's side and mopping up the cream with a napkin. "Or Käthe, I suppose."

He frowned. "Beg pardon?"

I set down the napkin and looked the Count square in the face. It was the first time we had looked directly at each other since Josef and I had come to Snovin, and I saw in the depths of those twinkling eyes a measure of fear and trepidation. He had the startled, panicked look of a rabbit just moments before the hawk. But who was the hawk? Me, or his wife?

"Your Illustriousness," I said softly. "Tell me what is going on. With me. With the Hunt. With my brother and sister."

He swallowed. Those rabbit eyes darted back and forth, searching for a way out, an escape. I thought of the chuckling stranger I had met in the labyrinth of his house in Vienna, the plump-cheeked man in a death's-head mask. Even then I hadn't been afraid of him; he was too cheerful, too good-humored, too frivolous to be much of a threat. He was a summer storm, all bluster and wind, but his wife was the lightning strike, beautiful but deadly. It was she I feared.

"I . . . can't," he said at last.

"Can't? Or won't?"

The Count shook his head. "Both."

"Why?"

His gaze flicked to the hallway, toward the rooms upstairs. It appeared the Countess was the hawk after all. "Because," he whispered, "it is not my place."

Irritation rose like a gorge in my throat. "Snovin is yours. Lorelei Lake is yours. This uncanny legacy is as much yours as it is your wife's. Be brave and claim what is yours."

He shook his head again. "You don't understand," he said in a strangled voice. "I dare not cross her."

I thought of the sweet gestures between the Procházkas, the affectionate teasing and comfortable ease with which they carried around the other. The pride with which the Count beheld his wife, the girlish blushes she suffered prettily beneath his charm. His fear seemed odd and misplaced.

Then I remembered his reluctance to speak of the shadow paths in mirrors. How he had gifted me with his compass against the Countess's wishes. I suddenly realized that he had not only given me his only talisman of safety from the Wild Hunt, but a measure of independence from his wife. With the compass, I need not worry about the unholy host without the Countess's protection.

There is an ancient protection in my bloodline because of what my foremother did when she walked away.

"Your Illustriousness," I said slowly. "Just what did the first

Goblin Queen do to ensure her escape from the old laws?"

Nothing is free and clear. Not with the old laws.

"It is not my story to tell," the Count whispered.

"Then why won't your wife tell me?"

It was a long time before he replied. "Haven't you heard?" he said with a bitter laugh. "That the tales from House Procházka are more incendiary than most?"

The Count refused to tell me more.

As frustrated as I was with his inability to divulge anything, I was infinitely more angry at myself. I felt like a dupe, the butt of a jest, hoodwinked by this coward of a man and his fraud of a wife. I threw down the remnants of my breakfast, not caring that it was rude or thoughtless, and stormed out of the morning room.

For a moment, I contemplated returning to Lorelei Lake, to dive into those blue-green waters and swim to my sister on the other side of that mirrored world. If my letters did not reach her, then let my body do so. Let me travel the shadow paths and escape this prison of good intentions and unholy expectations. So what if I were the last Goblin Queen? What if my decision to leave the Underground had all been for naught? I was right back where I was before I became *Der Erlkönig's* bride: trapped, stifled, smothered.

But without thinking, I became lost in the bowels of Snovin Hall instead. I had meant to return to my quarters, to wait for Josef, to plot our way out of his accursed valley together somehow, and had made a wrong turn somewhere in the house. I found myself in a room I had never seen before with a large grandfather clock in the corner and a suit of armor on the far side.

The clock chimed the hour.

Gong, gong, gong, gong. I counted the bell strikes, one, two, three, four, but they did not match the hands on its face. Indeed, instead of numbers, symbols were painted around the edge of the clock—a sword, a shield, a castle, a melusine, a dolphin, a wolf, and on and on, an unusual zodiac of eccentric objects. There was something off about the arrangement of figures around the face, and it wasn't until I counted them that I realized there were thirteen instead of the customary twelve.

All the hairs rose on the back of my neck.

After the gonging echoes faded away, there was an odd, erratic clicking sound. No second hand ticked away the moments, but moreover, the noise was coming from another part of the room.

I turned around.

Behind me, the suit of armor was lifting its arm.

Pulse pounding, I watched as the artifact moved of its own accord, animated by nothing but its own inanimate intelligence. Goblin-made, I realized, imbued with the magic of the Underground. Its fingers curled, all save one, which remained pointing in a direction down the corridor.

I followed where it led, down to a set of doors I had never seen. They were tall, reaching from floor to ceiling, and ornately carved with grotesques—leering satyrs, screaming nymphs, and snarling beasts. The doors were gilded once, but the gold had flaked and worn off with age, leaving nothing but rusted iron beneath. I glanced over my shoulder at the suit of armor still pointing its arm. It nodded, once, twice, the squeal of ancient metal grinding against itself grating on the ears.

I pushed open the doors,

Searing white brightness burned my eyes, and I threw up my hands against the light. When the world returned after temporary blindness, I saw that I was standing in a ballroom. Surrounded by mirrors.

They caught the light of the morning sun, reflecting and refracting the rays to an almost uncomfortable intensity. There were no shadows anywhere in this prism room, for even the cracked and broken floors were polished to a high shine. The forest had begun creeping in on this space years ago, and now it was as much a part of the wild outside as it was the house. Roots burst through the tiles beneath my feet, climbing up the shattered walls, and down the wooden door frames on either side —one leading back into darkness, the other into the light.

The doors to darkness slammed shut.

I jumped, but a breeze from the broken windowpanes ruffled my hair, like a reassuring sprite sent to soothe my ruffled nerves. No malicious magic here, though the ballroom was steeped in the uncanny and unknown. A thousand Liesls stared back at me from broken mirrored panels, our eyes wide with wonder, our complexion wan with weariness.

Mirrors. Every other reflective surface in the house had been covered, including polished stone and brass and copper. It seemed strange that the Procházkas had not bothered here, but perhaps it had taken too much effort. The ballroom was not much larger than the one in their Viennese *Stadthaus,* but the mirrors and ceiling height gave it the illusion of a much bigger space.

I explored the panels, lightly touching the cracked silvered glass, and discovered two walls I could slide aside like a screen. To my surprise, I found an array of old and dusty instruments as well as some chairs and music stands—a musicians' gallery. A clever construction, for the musicians could remain hidden out of sight while they played for the guests, opening up the entirety of the ballroom for dancing. I ran my hands over the violoncello and an old viol, the strings long since rotted away, leaving trails in dust as thick and as white as snow. An ancient virginal with an inverted keyboard sat off to the side, its lid closed, its bench still standing. It was likely similarly rotted and decayed inside, but I couldn't help but press a few keys despite myself, feeling a sharp pang for the clavichord I had left behind in Vienna.

The notes rang in tune.

I snatched back my hand, my myriad reflections mirroring the gesture out of the corner of my eye. Something else moved beyond the edges of my vision, half a breath later than the rest. Looking around, I searched for a rat or some other vermin scurrying about when I found myself staring into a pair of blue eyes.

Liesl?

"Käthe?" I asked, not daring to breathe.

Our images ran forward, hands outstretched, as though we could grab each other through the glass. Behind me, a thousand Liesls trailed behind, all running for my sister standing in the shadow paths.

Liesl! she said in a voiceless cry. *Liesl, where are you?*

"I'm here, I'm here," I said, choking on the salt taste of my tears as they ran down my cheeks.

Where is here? Käthe squinted, as though trying to peer into my world from the mirror.

"Snovin," I said. "Snovin Hall."

The Procházkas' house?

"Yes! I'm here, I am safe. I am well. Where are you?"

Get out of there! Käthe said, her eyes round with terror. *You must leave at once!*

"How?" I asked. "Have you received my letter? Is there any way you could send help?"

Oh, Liesl, she said. *We've been trying for weeks to send word. The night of the black-and-white ball, two people were found dead in the gardens, their throats slashed with silver, their lips blue with frost.*

"Elf-struck," I whispered.

Yes, Käthe said. *Bramble found me and François and brought us to the Faithful for safety.*

"The Faithful? Who is Bramble?"

The Faithful are those who have been touched by the Underground, like you and me. Those with the Sight, or those who have escaped the clutches of the old laws. They are keepers of knowledge, and a family bound by belief, not blood. Oh, Liesl, you must leave. You're in terrible danger!

My throat tightened. "The Faithful? *Der Erlkönig's* own?"

My sister's reflection shook her head. *The Procházkas call themselves* Der Erlkönig's *own, but they are not of the Faithful. The Faithful keep watch, but the Procházkas do harm.*

"Do harm? How do you mean?"

Do you remember the stories of the young girl they took under their wing? How she disappeared and a young man was found dead on the grounds of their country home?

A cold, sinking feeling settled into my bones, weighing me down with fear. "Yes. Rumors—"

They're not rumors! Käthe screamed, but no sound escaped her lips. *No one knows what they do up there in the remote hills of Bohemia, but they are not to be trusted. That maiden and the youth were not the first. Her name was Adelaide, and she was one of the Faithful.*

Adelaide. The Procházkas' so-called daughter. My fingers went numb.

Bramble has been teaching me of the shadow paths, she went on. *But they know, Liesl. They know to cover the mirrors, to hide their faces from the unseen world. They made a terrible sacrifice to the old laws to escape the Wild Hunt.*

"What?" I cried. "What did they do?"

Blood of the Faithful, unwillingly given, to seal the barriers between worlds.

"How do you know this?" I clenched my fists with despair. "Who told you?"

Bramble, she said. *A changeling.*

I no longer felt my heart beating in my chest. "A changeling? Are you sure?"

My sister tore out her hair. *It doesn't matter whether or not I'm sure! All that matters is that you and Josef get out of there!*

"How? Where do I go? How will you find me?"

You must— She cut herself off abruptly.

"Käthe?"

Oh no, she said, her face pale with fright. *He comes.*

"Who?"

I can't stay long, Käthe said. *Der Erlkönig will find me.* Her expression was hard. *Go. Get yourself to the nearest town and follow the poppies.*

"The symbol of House Procházka?"

No, she said. *The souls of those stolen by the Hunt. The souls of the Faithful. They protect us still, Liesl. They—* Her eyes grew wide with panic. *I must go.*

"Käthe—" But my sister was gone, leaving nothing but the stunned image of my own face staring back at me. "Käthe!"

"Liesl?"

I whirled around. Josef stood behind me, confusion writ across his features.

"Sepperl!"

"Liesl, who were you talking to?" He carried his violin case, as though he had come to the ballroom to play like a musician in the gallery.

"You didn't—did you see . . . ?" But I couldn't finish the sentence. Of course he hadn't. Even now I was beginning to doubt my conversation with my sister, surrounded by static reflections of Josef and myself—skepticism and concern on his face, fear and a crazed expression on mine. I looked like a madwoman, I realized, my hair in disarray, my eyes wild and overlarge on my face. I laughed, and even my laughter sounded insane.

"Perhaps you should have a seat," Josef said carefully. He set down his violin and pulled forth a chair from the musicians' gallery. He gently led me to it and sat me down, his touch tentative and unsure, as though I were a nervous filly about to bolt.

"Sepperl," I said, my voice shaking. "Am I going mad?"

He cocked his head and smoothed the strands of hair away from my face with calloused fingertips. "Does it matter?"

I burst into laughter again, but it sounded more like sobs. "I don't know. You wouldn't believe me if I told you."

Josef grew still. "Try me," he said quietly, pulling up another chair.

So I did. I told him of Lorelei Lake, of the shadow paths, the covered mirrors. I told him of the year I spent Underground as the Goblin King's bride, the slow death and agony of falling in love and knowing it would not last. The slipping away of my senses, the diminishment of all that was good and great in the world. I told him of the Wedding

Night Sonata, and why I hadn't been able to finish it, for the selfish act of my decision to walk away had doomed my austere young man to corruption and the world above to the ravages of the Wild Hunt. I told him and I told him and I told him, until my lips were cracked, my throat was parched, and my words had finally run dry.

My brother did not answer immediately. In the silence that followed my tale, he rose to his feet and began pacing the length of the ballroom. Although his expression was calm, there was an agitation and anger to his footsteps.

"Sepp—"

"Why didn't you tell me this before?" he interrupted.

"I didn't know how—" I began, but he cut me off with an angry retort.

"Horseshit." I flinched. I had never heard my brother swear before, and the word sounded even filthier coming from his lips. "You told Käthe."

Not all of it, I wanted to say. Not all of it at all. But I had told her enough, and it was more than what I had told Josef.

"Why?" he demanded. "Why her, of all people?"

"Because she had been there," I said tartly, unexpectedly stung on Käthe's behalf. "Because she had seen."

"I'm not talking about the Underground," he said. "I'm talking about *him.*"

Him. The Goblin King. I was taken aback, surprised by the vehemence in his tone. The Goblin King was the beginning and the end of my time Underground, yet he was also the least and most magical part of it at once. Compared to the glowing lake, the singing of the Lorelei, the twisting of time and space, the fairy lights, the glittering caverns and halls, our love seemed almost mundane. There had been no grand romantic gestures, no sweeping declarations of feeling, no fighting to be with each other against all odds. We had simply, though not always quietly, broken each other apart and put ourselves back together again. It was not a story in which I thought my brother would be interested.

"What do you mean, Sepp?"

"I mean *him*," Josef said again, punctuating the word with an emphatic jab of his bow. "And *you*." He pointed the tip of his bow at me, hovering right above my breast like a blade. "You always called me the gardener of your heart," he said softly. "But you have gone and grown your flowers without me."

It was then I understood that he had not been hurt by the fact I hadn't told him about my time Underground; it was that I had not shared with him anything about my feelings as Goblin *Queen*. We had always bared our souls to each other, our deepest thoughts and darkest emotions, often without speech. My sister had been my confidante through words and actions, but my brother had ever been the keeper of my secrets.

"Oh," I said. I did not know what else to say. "I'm sorry, Sepperl."

He shook his head. "Why didn't you trust me?" he asked, and in his voice, I heard the little boy I had thought I had lost.

I give you back your heart. Tears pricked at the backs of my eyes. "I don't know."

But I did know. He was no longer first in my heart. Josef and the Goblin King shared the space where my soul lay within my breast, along with Käthe and François and Constanze and Mother. My capacity for love had not diminished; indeed, it had only grown with each person I let in, but the formless, undifferentiated love I had felt in childhood only grew more defined with age and time. There were parts of myself I was willing to share with my sister, parts that were given to my brother, and still other parts that had been claimed by an austere young man.

Josef's stare was hard. Accusatory. "I think you do."

He always did know me best.

"What is it you want to hear from me, Sepperl?" I asked, suddenly irritated. "I'm sorry? I've already apologized to you."

"But what is it you're apologizing *for*?" he shot back. He lowered his arm, his bow hanging limp by his side. "You didn't tell me for a reason. That's why you feel so guilty. You're hiding something from me, Liesl, and I don't like that. You and I were always open with one another."

"Were we?" My eyes strayed to his wrists. His arm twitched, as though he were resisting the urge to cover himself. "Tell me, Sepp, have you always been honest with *me*?"

He stiffened. "I don't want to talk about that."

I stood up. "Then you had no right to pry either!"

"Fine!" he exploded. "Fine! What do you want to know? That Master Antonius beat me? That he subjected me to every humiliation under the sun and then some? That he twisted my longing for home, for the Goblin Grove, into a shameful, infantile indulgence? I couldn't talk to anyone, Liesl. *Anyone*. I had François to protect me, but he didn't understand. Couldn't. How the farther away from home I went, the less I felt whole. The less I felt *real*. I was a sham of a boy, the husk of a man, an imposter of a human being. It was only when I played your music that I felt any sort of connection to . . . to *life*."

Take us far from the Underground and we wither and fade.

I felt my face drain of blood. And Josef noticed.

"What?" he asked. "What is it, Liesl?"

Would it grant him peace of mind, if he knew the truth of what he was? Or would it merely serve to alienate us even further? Would he hate me for not telling him sooner? If Josef resented me for keeping the Goblin King to myself, how much more would he despite me for not giving him a piece of his own history?

"What is it?" he demanded. "What do you know?"

"It's because," I whispered, my voice catching on the edges of my emotions. "It's because you're a changeling."

His lips went white. I waited for my brother to say something, to do something—anything—other than stand there. But he was as still and silent as a statue, almost as though he had been replaced again by another entity. I hated myself for the thought.

"Sepp?" I asked in a small voice. "Talk to me, Sepp."

"How dare you." My brother did not sound like himself, and for the first time in my life, I felt as though I did not know him.

"Sepp, I—"

"Don't." He threw up his hands, his violin and bow still clenched in his fists. "Don't."

"I'm sorry." I wished the words weren't so insufficient.

"I don't want to hear it."

"Sepp—"

"Stop calling me that!"

Josef threw aside his instrument, the cherry wood body of his violin clattering across the broken marble floor, the neck snapping off from the rest. I cried out, but the bow followed soon after. "Josef, please—"

"I'm not him!" he cried. "Josef isn't real! He was never real!" He looked at me with a feral expression, the pupils of his eyes dilating to drown the blue in a depthless black. Like goblin eyes. "Who am I?" A savage cry tore from his throat. "Who am I?"

"Josef, I—"

But before I could tell him, reassure him, reaffirm him, my brother had turned and gone, vanished into the wild.

a changeling had no name, and no one to call him home. He fled from the ballroom and into the wild, leaving his sister, his past, and his name behind him. Josef. The name belonged to another boy, another son, another *human*, and he could not bear to wear it any longer. The wounds upon his wrists itched, and he longed to dig his fingers into the scars and tear off his skin, to cast off the face, the hair, the eyes of a boy who did not exist.

He did not exist.

The changeling found himself standing in a patch of poppies, the bright red blooms curled around his feet like a cat about its master's legs. *Come with us, nameless one*, they cooed. *Join us*.

As he looked up, he saw pops of scarlet, crimson, and vermillion appear like paint drops amid the gray and brown and green of a late winter wild, a river of blood cutting through the woods and up the hill.

Come, the whispers urged. *Come*.

He did not ask where, or why. The Countess had told him that these impossible flowers were the souls of the stolen, the last mortal remnants of those who had been taken by the

Wild Hunt. They were guiding him home, back to the Underground.

The changeling set his feet upon the path of poppies and followed.

Behind him, he could hear his sister calling his name—no, the name of her brother—but he paid her no heed. Josef was gone now; he had never been. The void at the center of his soul made sense now. For years he had thought there was something broken within him, that his inability to feel deeply for anyone was a defect, or a flaw in his making. He cared for his family, or the people he had thought were his blood and kin. He felt affection for his grandmother and her stories, respect for his mother and her hard work, fear for his father and his moods, and fondness for his sisters. Perhaps the changeling even felt love, especially for Liesl, insofar as he could understand it.

Love. He thought of François and waited for guilt to pool in his stomach. The changeling thought of his companion's face—the dark eyes, the tightly curled lashes, the warm skin, the full lips. It was a face that rang a bell deep inside him, that made him want to look and look and look. François was beautiful, the changeling knew, but it was not the beauty of his companion's beloved features that drew him; it was the safety he had found there. He had ever preferred the shadows to the light, and François's love was the nightfall in which he could hide.

But ever since he had come to Snovin, the memory of his beloved's face returned less and less to him. Even now the exact shade of François's skin, the scent of his cologne, and the timbre of his voice was fading, as though his companion were disappearing into mist or fog. Beloved. It was the only word the changeling could think of when he thought of

François, for he had no other word for the tenderness within him, the desire to protect, to hold, to kiss. But the changeling knew that his love was not the same as François's love, for the urge to touch was absent and the heat of passion was cold.

I love you, he had told the black boy.

And it was true, or truth as the changeling understood it.

His breath came faster as he climbed the hills behind Snovin Hall, the path narrow and steep. The poppies never ceased their whispering, cajoling, pleading, beckoning him to *hurry, hurry.* He did not know the reason for their urgency, only that he felt it too as a sort of freedom, an excuse, a reason to run away. The changeling did not care where he was running to, only that he was running at all.

He was surprised when the trail opened up into a wide vista. The poppies led him to a rocky ledge poised over a sparkling lake, a long drop. Looking down into the aquamarine waters gave him a sense of vertigo, as though he were looking up at the sky instead of into dark depths. The changeling saw his reflection below, a pale, sharp-cheeked face staring back at him with a razor-toothed grin.

The changeling touched his face, wondering if knowing the truth of who he was had rearranged his features. All his life—Josef's life—he had known his hair to be gold and his eyes to be blue. But the youth who peered back at him from the lake had hair the color of unbrushed cotton and eyes as black as obsidian. Yet the face was recognizably his: the same nose, ears, cheeks, chin.

"Who are you?" the changeling whispered.

The reflection smiled. *I am you,* it replied.

"What am I?" the changeling asked.

Lost, the reflection said.

Lost. The word resounded in the void within the

changeling. "How do I become found?" he asked his reflection.

The boy in the lake did not answer. Instead he reached for the surface, and Josef found himself reaching for the mirrored world.

Join me, the reflection said. *Join us.*

And so Josef fell, down and down and down, into the Underground.

Intermezzo

INTO THAT
WORLD INVERTED

OBLIVION

I waited one breath too long to chase after my brother.

"Josef!" I screamed. "Sepp!"

The grounds of Snovin Hall rang with my cries as I fled the ballroom after my brother, but nothing but the echoes of startled birdsong returned. Josef had disappeared, vanished, gone to earth, and I did not know how he had run so quickly and so far. No tracks trampled the tangled vines and overgrown weeds, no evidence of trespass or flight. Nothing but crushed poppy petals, scattered underfoot like drops of blood.

"Sepp!" I called again. "Sepp!"

"Fräulein?" I whirled around to see Nina standing behind me, a worried look on her face. "Is okay?"

The last thing I wanted to endure was another's presence, to keep up the mask of civility or a calm countenance. I was neither civil nor calm, and I raged and seethed that I felt compelled to maintain a straight face before her. Who would notice? Who would care? The worst Nina could do was return to the Count and Countess with tales of my rudeness, my unsociability, my erratic moods. Yet despite this, I did not want to frighten her with my monstrosity, the maelstrom that threatened to swallow not just me, but the entire world.

"Yes," I said, trying my best for a smile. The corners of my mouth shook and quivered, and I felt my lips curling in a snarl. "Everything is fine, thank you, Nina."

The housekeeper did not look reassured. Instead, she seemed even more concerned. "Is okay?" she repeated, then said something in a torrent of Bohemian I could not understand, accompanied by gestures I could not decipher.

"Yes!" I barked. "Okay. I'm okay."

I could feel the press of fury and frustration building behind my eyes, a growing headache. I was tired of keeping a tight rein on the feral beast I was inside, and I was tempted to let go, to unleash the wolves and hounds of mania and recklessness upon her. I don't know what it was Nina saw in my expression, but a strange sort of pity crossed her face. Pity was the last emotion I wanted from her, and I felt my gorge rise.

"Come," she beckoned. "I show you."

"Unless you can show me my brother, I don't care," I snapped. If she did not understand my words, she could at least understand my tone.

"Come," Nina said again. Her tone was firm, a mother's voice, and I did not resist.

She led me back into the ballroom, gently picking up the pieces of Josef's violin that he had thrown to the floor. A part of me—the part not submerged in the depths of my own feelings of self-loathing and despair—mourned the loss of such an instrument. It wasn't just that it had been a beautiful Del Gésu; it was that it had survived not only years of wear and tear and abuse, but Papa's constant pawning off to Herr Kassl's for drinking money. The housekeeper held the neck and the body out to me in separate hands. I shook my head; I did not know if it could be salvaged.

Nina gave me stern look, as though I were being a fool. I resented being treated like a petulant child by a woman I did not know, to whom I was not beholden in any way. I shook my head again, but she harrumphed before taking the neck of the broken violin and gently removing the scroll.

Ornamental scrolls were not common, and the finial of this particular instrument had been carved into the shape of a woman. Nina pressed the finial into my hand, and I wrapped my fingers around the figure. The woman's face had been carved with her mouth open in perpetual song, but in certain angles she looked as though screaming with joy . . . or terror. I was discovering more and more with each passing day that the line that divided those emotions was honed finer than the keenest razor.

"Thank you," I whispered. I said it more to send Nina away than from any sense of actual gratitude.

"Is okay?" she repeated.

No, it was not okay. I wasn't sure if I would ever be okay. The housekeeper eyed me warily, as though I were a fragile china shepherdess poised on the edge of a shelf. I forced another smile for Nina, and this time, I did not bother to swallow the growl that escaped my throat. She took the hint, and left.

I looked through the broken windows of the ballroom to the world outside. I should have gone after my brother. I should have tried to find him. I should have gone looking until my eyes went dim and my throat went hoarse, for I was afraid. For him, and *of* him. Of what he would do. To me, but to himself most of all. I should have, I should have, I should have.

But I did not.

Instead I was trapped in the quicksand of my own mind, reliving each and every mistake I had made with Josef. Every misstep revealed another, and another, and another, a long line all the way back to when we were children. I should have protected him from Papa. I should have seen how miserable our expectations made him. I should have brought him home to the Goblin Grove the instant I understood how it was killing him.

I should have told him he was a changeling.

Sooner. Better. At all. The truth of Josef's nature was not my secret to withhold, and yet I had. I hadn't wanted to tell him because . . . because deep in my heart, I knew I would lose him. He would hate me for not telling him, and the longer I held on to the truth, the more he would hate me for my selfishness. It no longer became for Josef's own good that he did not know; it was for my own peace of mind.

Was I worried he would run away to the Underground? Did he even know how? Did *I* know how? I was overcome with a sudden, fierce, unspecified anger. Toward the Underground. The Goblin King. The strange and queer and uncanny that had dogged me my entire life. If I had just been normal, if I had just been *ordinary,* none of this would have happened. I wouldn't be trapped in a house of madmen and dreamers with an unholy host at my back because I wouldn't be Liesl. I wouldn't be me.

I wanted to kick and scream. A toddler's temper tantrum crawled up my throat, and the desire to break and smash and cry made my fingers twitch with pent-up frustration. At times like these, I used to run to the klavier and pound my emotions into the keys, reveling in the cacophony of discord. I used to make noise with intent and purpose, to sound my barbaric and untamed self into the void. More than anything, I wanted that now.

Your music creates a bridge between worlds.

I hadn't tried since coming to Snovin Hall. To play. To make music. For a while I thought my reticence had been a fear of reprisal, of what my power could do to the fabric of the world. But perhaps my reticence had simply been a matter of reluctance; I had wanted so badly to leave that part of myself behind. The part that had walked the Underground. The part that had married—and loved—the Goblin King. I was so focused on being Elisabeth, alone, I had not thought about what it meant to be Elisabeth, entire.

And that meant embracing my past as well as an uncertain future. I was so determined to not wallow in my misery that I made myself *lonely*; I pushed away memories and feelings and connections not only to the Goblin King, but myself. I had mourned, but I had not let myself grieve. I had not let myself *feel.*

Don't think. Feel.

Determination and drive had returned, and with that came desire. For expression, for fulfillment, for self-destruction. I walked to the virginal in the musicians' gallery and sat down at its bench. The keys were coated in years—decades, perhaps—of dust, but the strings were still in tune. I pressed my fingers into the notes, wringing chords and phrases from the strings and plucking mechanism. The Wedding Night Sonata had lain unfinished for a long time because I had not known how the story ended. But I realized I had not known how it ended because I had not resolved my own emotions—about my music, about my

Goblin King, but about myself most of all.

The Wedding Night Sonata had been about me. My feelings. Rage, anger, frustration, fear had been the first movement. Longing, tenderness, affection, and hope had been the second.

Hatred was the third.

Hatred, and self-loathing.

I knew where to go. I was going to play. I was going to compose. I was going to open my veins and let my music run onto the keys.

I was going to open the veil between worlds.

I should have been afraid. I should have been careful. But I was a Pandora's box of desperation and recklessness; once opened, I could no longer be closed. I cared about everything and nothing, and I wanted nothing more than oblivion. If drink had been Papa's vice, then the Goblin King and the Underground was mine.

I waited for the ghostly wail of his violin.

I did not wait long.

Through the mirror, through the glass, through the veil between worlds came the high, thin voice of singing strings. I called, and he answered. A sob hitched in my throat, of both relief and fear. I had wanted to hear him, to see him, to touch him, to *hold* him in my arms forever, and the notion that I somehow could again was overwhelming. I felt the weight of that release down to my fingertips, pushing my hands into the keys of the virginal.

Yet with the hope came uncertainty. Uncertainty, or regret, for with the Goblin King's arrival came the heady scent of pine and ice and deep loam, a lifting in pressure in the ballroom.

The barrier was thin, thinning, gone.

I looked up from the keyboard to face a thousand Liesls at a thousand instruments staring back at me from broken-mirrored panels in the musicians' gallery.

In all, save one.

"Be, thou, with me," I said.

Der Erlkönig smiled.

The austere young man stands before me, violin in his hands. A soft look lights his dear, familiar, beloved mismatched eyes, and I am overcome with such longing I think I will die. My hands shake as I press the keys of the virginal, no longer aware of what notes I am playing or what melodies the Goblin King is making.

"Be, thou, with me," I say again.

He lowers his violin and his bow. The music continues on, a repeating *ostinato* of *yes, please, yes, please, yes, please.*

"Be, thou, with me," I repeat, and I rise from the virginal.

The Goblin King lifts his hand to press against the shattered glass. I walk to the reflection to meet him palm to palm, shards of silver slicing into my skin. I welcome the pain, the sharp sting of regret and want wounding me to the quick. Yes, this is oblivion. This is heaven, and this is hell.

Our fingers twine together as we reach through veil and void. His touch is cool, dry, but I feel the thrill of it down to my deepest core. I pull him to me, and he does not resist, passing from reflection into reality. My arms open and he walks into my embrace, bringing with him the scent of sleeping green, earth, roots, rock, and the faint, impossible scent of peaches. The perfume of the Underground surrounds me, and I fall into a fever dream. The ballroom wavers and flickers, the world seen through water and flame, and I am lost.

"Take me," I whisper. "Take me back."

The green and gray of the Goblin King's eyes flash white and blue, white and blue, the pupils shrinking to a pinprick of black. The corners of his lips curl, close—so close—to mine.

As you wish, my dear.

As you wish.

A breath, a sigh, a kiss, and we are met.

Ice runs through me, knife slashes of cold up and down my body. His fingertips leave searing trails of frost against my skin, and I no longer know whether or not I'm dying by fire or by freeze. Inky darkness trails up my arms and legs in whorls of black, and I can taste the sickly-sweet bitterness of opium—or blood—on my tongue. It has never hurt like this before, both inside and out. I shouldn't want it. I shouldn't crave it.

But I do.

Meine Königin.

He calls me his queen, and I drink in the words, letting them fill me inside and out. The Goblin King's hands find the seams of my gown, and I feel the laces of my stays snap one by one, the light tinkling of shattered glass as the frozen ribbons fall to the floor.

"Mein Herr," I breathe. I am excited and frightened, elated and afraid, and tears slide down my cheeks. I'm sobbing and shaking, but the Goblin King holds me even tighter, as though only he can hold me together.

"No," I whisper. "Break me. Let me fall apart."

Punish me. Destroy me. Let me suffer the consequences of being my abject, ignoble self. I was no longer Elisabeth, entire, but Elisabeth, obliterated. There is no tenderness in the Goblin King's rough touch, and it leaves me in tatters. I hated myself enough to be wiped from existence and memory, and I press myself harder against the keen edges of him. I do not deserve to be remembered. I do not deserve to be loved.

Hands wrap themselves about my throat, a cage of bones like a collar, and he claims me as his. The Goblin King's lips stretch in a feral grin, the tips of his teeth gleaming in the light like a wolf's bared to the sun. I should not have run away from the Underground. I should not have hurt my brother. I should not have doomed the world. Yes, please, yes. I am a sinner, a villain, a wretch. I am worthless, the most despicable of women.

Elisabeth.

The Goblin King's voice is changed, a desperate urgency in his tone that only stirs my blood. I feel my pulse pounding everywhere—my ears, my throat, my wrists, my chest, my thighs—a persistent rhythm echoing in my body. It sets the tempo of our encounter, but I sense him pausing, chafing, resisting.

Elisabeth, please.

The cracking, creaking sound of twigs breaking or bones snapping, and the fingers of his hands twist and gnarl. Too many joints in his fingers, too little color in the Goblin King's eyes. I stare into them, blue and white, then gray and green, as I watch the face of a man emerge from the monster in my arms.

Elisabeth.

It is the vulnerability in his voice that stops me, not the danger dressed in black with eyes of ice and death. I am holding them both, my austere young man and the Lord of Mischief, and they are one and not.

Der Erlkönig smiles.

The Goblin King cries.

With a scream, I shove him away, but I am tangled in his embrace—my skirts in shreds about my ankles, my bodice falling off my shoulders. *Der Erlkönig* laughs, a soundless cackle that makes my ears pop with pressure.

I have you now, Goblin Queen. You are mine.

Elisabeth!

With tremendous effort, my austere young man takes hold of himself, releasing me from his grip.

Go! Run!

He retreats back through the window between worlds, back into reflection, back to the Underground.

"Mein Herr!" I shout, striking at the broken mirror with bare fists. My hands leave bloody streaks against the glass, but for all my begging and pleading, the Goblin King does not return. My screams are as shattered as the panels in the ballroom, fractured and refracted in the topsy-turvy shambles of my mind.

Run, and nothing but his whispered echo remains.

HE IS FOR
DER ERLKÖNIG NOW

"**F**räulein? Fräulein!"

I felt a pair of hands upon my shoulders, and I hissed and lashed out like a panicked cat. I struck something soft, and a muffled grunt filled my ear as strong hands wrapped themselves about my wrists.

"*Fräulein?*" the voice repeated, holding my flailing limbs close. "My dear, it's all right, you're fine. You're safe." The words repeated themselves in a shushing murmur, a soothing, repetitive sound that pulled all my disparate parts back to myself.

Through my haze of fear and madness, a face came into focus. Round, rosy cheeks, black button-bright eyes, a startled shock of frizzy, iron-gray whispers framing a concerned mouth.

The Count.

"Nina! Bring the young lady something to drink. Tea, perhaps, or something stronger."

I noticed the housekeeper standing behind my host with a worried expression on her broad face. Her dark eyes widened at the sight of blood running down the broken mirrored panels, and her hands went up to cover her mouth with her apron.

"Nina!" The Count repeated his request in Bohemian, and the housekeeper snapped to attention. She bobbed a quick curtsy and bustled out of the room as fast as her legs could carry her.

"Are you all right?" The Count peered into my face, taking in my red-blotched cheeks, my swollen eyes, and unkempt hair. He then took in the ripped bodice, the tattered skirts, my general state of deshabille and the angry red welts upon my arms. "What happened?"

I had no defenses left, no strength to muster, no dignity to lose. But even so, I would have kept my mouth shut and my madness quiet were it not for the gentle sympathy and understanding in my host's expression. Nothing crumbled my armor faster than compassion and kindness, and soon every last detail of my days came spilling out. The chink in my defenses became a breach, I was open and vulnerable, and I did not care. The Count listened without saying a word to me ramble incoherently about my fight with Josef; my guilt and reckless disregard for anything other than my worthless, selfish self; my grudging longing for the Goblin King; my fears of becoming a burden, for who could bear the weight of my disgusting soul with all its attendant madness and mania? I told him everything and nothing, unable to corral my thoughts into a semblance of order.

Presently, Nina returned with a tray laden with things for tea and a small philter of a dark, brownish liquid. The Count led me back to the bench beside the virginal and dismissed the housekeeper, pouring me a cup of tea himself.

"What is that?" I asked, stopping him before he could tilt the vial of unknown solution into the brew.

"Laudanum," the Count said. At my terrified expression, he set down the vial and handed me my tea untouched. "I mean no harm, *Fräulein*, I swear to you upon my brother Ludvik's life."

I paused in sipping my drink. "Your brother?"

He nodded. "Aye. My twin brother. I was the elder by seven minutes."

I set down my cup. There was a sadness in the Count's eyes and a resignation in his tone, although his shoulders seemed tight with unexpressed tension. He was an older sibling. I felt our shared sense of responsibility and resentment as eldest children.

Then I frowned. "Was?"

It was a moment before the Count understood my question. "Oh." He went to pour himself some tea, but Nina had brought only one set. He swirled the laudanum between his fingers. "Yes. He died when we were twenty years old."

"I'm sorry," I said softly.

The Count nodded unhappily. "You understand, *Fräulein*. How you both chafe at and embrace the obligation thrust upon you. You take it upon yourself to safeguard the lives and hearts of your younger siblings, however ungrateful they might be. Although Ludvik was my twin, I was firstborn, still expected to become the next Count Procházka und zu Snovin upon our father's death. Therefore, it was my duty to watch over him."

I picked my cup back up and carefully took a small sip of tea. It was chamomile, and only chamomile. I continued sipping.

"I failed." The Count contemplated the tincture of opium in his hand. "I failed in my duty, and it was Ludvik who paid the price."

Like Josef. I reached out to touch the Count's sleeve. He did not notice me.

"He was . . . special, my brother," he continued slowly. "Elf-touched, as they would have said in the old days. Sharp-eyed and present one moment, raving and oblivious the next. He could see goblins and fairies and elves, and I always envied him that gift. Although my family had ever been the watchdogs standing guard at the threshold between the Underground and the world above, very few of the Procházkas had—if ever—been a part of the magic."

"What do you mean?"

The Count opened the philter of laudanum. I eyed it suspiciously, but my host placed the vial to his lips and drank. I started, wondering if I should stop him, if he was poisoning himself. I was no physician, but I did not think one could drink so much without poisoning oneself. Wiping his lips, the Count put the empty vial in his pocket and turned to me, his dark eyes large and dilated, lambent and shining as though wet with belladonna.

"We are the ordinary and the mundane," he said. "Perhaps by design, or perhaps by fate. Perhaps it takes a certain sort of mind to withstand the maddening uncanniness of Snovin, but my family have ever and always been seneschals and stewards to the line of the first Goblin Queen."

"The brave maiden," I said.

His lips twisted into a smile of self-loathing. "Is that what you call her? A strange notion of bravery you must have, *Fräulein*. If by *bravery*, you mean *butchery*, then I might be inclined to agree with you."

Somehow I didn't think he was speaking of his wife's illustrious forebear.

"Do you know what it takes to escape the old laws for good?" the Count asked. He forced the words through sticky lips, as though fighting his own body's impulse to silence him.

"The Countess said there is an ancient protection in her bloodline," I said slowly. Drops of nervousness were trickling down my spine, and I eyed the ballroom exits, wondering if *I* should call for Nina now. "Because of what the first Goblin Queen did when she walked away." I frowned. "But she never did say what that was."

And now I did not trust that she ever would.

The Count laughed, but the sound was bitter, raw. "Oh, child," he said, and there was genuine pity in his voice. "Nothing comes for free. A life for a life. Death for spring. You know this."

I did. The trickle of nervousness became a stream of fear. I remembered my conversation with the Countess on our excursion to the old monastery, of how the old laws had punished the first Goblin King for letting her go. Of how the brave maiden had returned Underground to save him by finding his name and setting him free. I thought of my own austere young man, of those eyes I knew so well becoming lost to cold and night and frost. Even if I did find his name and unlock his soul, there was the man I loved and the monster I craved. I did not know how to free one without losing the other.

"Ludvik was the good twin," the Count said suddenly. I was surprised by this sudden turn in conversation. "The good twin, and pure. There were those who called him elf-touched, and those meaner still who called him simple. Thickheaded. Mad."

I did not like where the story was headed, but my host

continued without a second glance in my direction, eyes fixed straight ahead, staring at something not before him, but within him.

"There were rather more of us in the old days," he said. "*Der Erlkönig's* own, that is. But science and reason have thinned our ranks, and now only the mad, the fearful, and the faithful remain. Even my own family, despite their sacred charge to safeguard the barriers between worlds, had let Snovin fall to ruin and decay. There was no one else, you see. No one else to pay the price."

"What price?"

He gave me a hard look despite the laudanum coursing through his veins. Despite the opium dreams and the poppy milk, the Count was still present, still clearheaded, still aware. Too aware. I was beginning to understand why it was he partook of the drug. The weight of belief was too much to bear alone.

"Innocent blood."

I recoiled. "What?"

A slow, syrupy smile began to spread across the Count's face like blood through water. "Elena told you of ancient protections in her bloodline. Blood is part of it, yes. But not hers. The Wild Hunt and the old laws still find her an aberration, a mistake. The first Goblin Queen cheated them not only of a proper sacrifice, but *Der Erlkönig* as well. As punishment, they would hound her and her kin to the ends of time, lest she pay in blood."

Realization was dawning within me, an inevitable, inexorable revelation I did not want to face. Not yet. Not yet.

"Whose blood?" I whispered.

The Count pulled the philter of laudanum from his pocket,

although it was empty. He gazed longingly at it, searching for the oblivion that had not yet come. "It was easier then," he murmured. "Easier when there were still those who left out gifts of bread and milk for the goblins and fairy kind. Easier when superstition ruled and science did not. The Faithful were easy prey."

With growing horror, I thought of Käthe's warning words in the mirror. *Blood of the Faithful, unwillingly given, to seal the barrier between worlds.*

I thought of the poppy field growing outside on the grounds of Snovin Hall. The souls of those stolen by the Hunt, my sister had said. The souls of the Faithful.

The souls of the sacrificed.

"But as time went on, the Faithful became wise to our ways," the Count went on. "And they went underground. Not," he said with a chuckle, "to the realm of the Goblin King, but to ground. Into foxholes, through the shadow paths, and into darkness. And so," he said, his voice thin, "we turned to our own."

My blood ran cold. "Ludvik?"

His dilated eyes met mine. "He was *Der Erlkönig's* own, after all."

I gasped, my hands flying up to cover my mouth. *Do you remember the stories of the young girl they took under their wing?*

"And . . . Adelaide?" I swallowed hard. "The girl who died . . . was she truly your daughter?"

The Count turned the empty vial over and over in his hand. He could not answer, and that was answer enough.

"How did she die?" I asked.

"She drowned," the Count whispered. "In Lorelei Lake. They always return, you know. The changelings."

I was startled. "Changelings?"

He nodded his head. "She was such a beautiful child," he crooned to himself. "Such a beautiful baby. Here, and gone. A mayfly. We tried to keep her safe, Elena and I. We tried to keep her whole. But in the end, she wanted to return home."

Josef.

"I must go," I said, rising to my feet in a panic. "I must find my brother. I must save Josef."

"There is nothing you can do for him," the Count said sadly to my fleeing back. "He is for *Der Erlkönig* now."

BRAVE MAIDEN'S END

i knew where Josef had gone. He, like me, was ever drawn to the strange, the queer, and the wild. Lorelei Lake was a threshold, a portal, one of the sacred spaces where the Underground and the world above existed together. It was where I would have gone. It was where I *had* gone, after the Countess's startling revelation about her family history.

I ran back to my quarters to retrieve the Count's compass, which I had never returned. He had claimed it granted me a measure of protection against the Wild Hunt, but I saw now that the greatest danger came not from the unholy host, but my so-called host and hostess. My benefactors, my captors. The Hunt had ever and always been the least of my worries; it had been a symptom, not the disease. I was the disease. I had broken the balance, I had corrupted the Goblin King, I had betrayed my brother, I had set the old laws loose upon the world.

And now it was up to me to make things right.

Back in my rooms, the compass was nowhere in sight. I

could have sworn I had left it on the dressing table, but when I returned, it was gone. I upended every drawer and cupboard, combed through every jewelry box and vanity, but the trinket remained missing.

"Looking for this?"

I whirled around to see the Countess standing behind me with her husband's compass in hand. I went still. She stood there with her green cat's eyes glowing in a small smile, sharp and piercing. She had managed to sneak up behind me on silent footfalls despite her club foot, or—I thought with a chill—she had lain in wait, hidden somewhere in my rooms until I returned.

"I had thought to take a turn about the grounds." I hated how my voice trembled and quavered, how my feelings and emotions would always betray any lie I told. "I didn't want to get lost."

"Surely you would have become accustomed to Snovin by now," the Countess replied.

I smiled, but it did not reach my eyes. "I'm not sure I could ever become accustomed to Snovin and its ways."

She narrowed her gaze. "You could not . . . or will not?"

I said nothing. The Countess sighed, shaking her head with a weary sort of affection. "I see Otto has been at you again."

"How could you be so cavalier about all this?" I demanded. "All those innocent lives? And for what? To escape your ancestor's fate? How could you be so selfish?"

"How could you?" she demanded. She limped forward, eyes flashing. "Think, Elisabeth. Our very existence is an abomination to the old laws. The fact that we walk the world above means that the Wild Hunt not only dogs our heels, but those we love as well. And not only those we love, but all else who are good and great and talented, for the fruits of the

Underground are art and genius and passion. Would you deprive the world of these gifts, Elisabeth? Is one life worth more than that of thousands?"

"It is when it's *your* life," I retorted. "And mine."

"What were you planning on doing, mademoiselle?" the Countess asked. "What were you intending to do once you reached Lorelei Lake? Throw yourself into its blue-green depths?"

In truth, I had not thought so far ahead. My only goal was to reach my brother before something terrible happened to him, before he was lost to me forever. To the Underground, or to death.

The Countess saw the uncertainty in my face and leaned closer. I wanted to avert my eyes, to hide my expression, but the last thing I wanted was to betray any hint of my fear. The Procházkas were not worthy of my fear. Craven cowards, the lot of them, and I felt nothing but contempt.

"It wouldn't do any good, you know," she said softly. "Ending your life. Ending mine. We are sullied, you see. Our sacrifices are worthless because we have nothing left to give. Nothing the Underground wants. Not anymore."

I did not care to listen. There was nothing the Countess could say that would sway me from going after my brother. Even if there were nothing I could do to save him, it was better that I tried and failed than to have never tried at all. I began to push past her, but the Countess stood firm, bracing herself against the bedpost in lieu of a cane.

"Why do you think you can't compose anymore?"

I paused.

"Why does the world seem not enough and too much? It is because you are of both, and neither, Elisabeth. Your mind and body are here, and your soul is elsewhere. I've felt it, child. I've *heard* it. The reason your music is a bridge between the Underground and the world above is because of your initial sacrifice. You sacrificed your music. You sacrificed your genius, your talent, and your creativity to the old laws when you crossed the threshold the first time. Any time you play, you reach across that barrier. It makes you whole and broken all at once."

Her words sailed right into the stormy heart of me, straight down the abyss swirling at the center of the maelstrom. "How—how do you know this?" I asked in a hoarse voice.

The Countess laughed, a bright, merry sound, and it was the ugliest thing I had ever heard. "I know because your face is as transparent as glass. Because you don't just wear your feelings on your sleeve; your emotions wear you." Her eyes darkened, the green turning brittle and sharp. "I know because my reckless, feckless ancestor bartered away her children's freedom, all for the sake of self-preservation. We are the forsaken, Elisabeth. The punishment for our selfishness and our greed is to perpetuate the cycle."

I pressed my hands to my mouth to muffle my sobs. *Special Liesl. Chosen Liesl. You have always wanted to be extraordinary, and now you are.*

"No," I said through clenched teeth. "No. I cannot—will not—believe that is my fate. I will not hurt others with my thoughtless actions, even if it means giving myself up to the old laws."

The Countess lifted her brows. "Even if you were as selfless as all that, Elisabeth, think you that your return to the Underground will undo all the damage you've caused? Oh, child. We can only move forward, not change the past."

I thought of Josef. I thought of the Goblin King. "I have to try," I said quietly.

"And just how were you planning on accomplishing that, my dear?" the Countess asked. She held her husband's compass before her, the trinket glinting in the light of the setting sun. "Return to Lake Snovin to . . . what? Throw yourself in? And then?"

And then what indeed. "Save my brother," I said. Then I thought of mismatched gray and green eyes consumed by white so pale as to be nearly blue.

The Countess laughed. "And then what? Save your Goblin King?"

It was the fact that she had voiced aloud the hopes I had not even dared to consider that hurt most, even more than the snide dismissal in her tone.

"I have to try," I said again.

"Oh, child," the Countess sneered. "If you think you are the one to break the cycle of sacrifice and betrayal, then your arrogance knows no bounds."

Bile began to rise at the back of my throat, acrid and bitter. "Did not the first Goblin Queen walk away?" I asked. "Did she not go back and wrest her Goblin King away from the clutches of the old laws?"

"And what do you think she left as payment?" the Countess returned.

I fell silent.

"A life for a life, Elisabeth. Death for harvest. It was she who tricked another youth into staying behind, into becoming the next Goblin King. Who then, in turn, went out into the world in search of a bride to remind him of the mortal life that was ripped from him. And in turn, that man thrust the throne upon yet another, and another, and another. It doesn't end, mademoiselle. Not for us. Not for *Der Erlkönig*'s own."

The maelstrom was closing in, the waters of madness threatening to submerge me in their depths. I could not— would not—succumb. I would not drown in despair. If there was anything I had to keep me going, it was that I believed in love—the Goblin King's for me, my own for my brother. And my sister. And the world above. I had to try, or fail my own sense of self.

"Poor fool," the Countess said softly, seeing the expression on my face. "Poor, poor fool."

I snatched the compass from her fingers. "If you will not help me," I said. "Then do not stand in my way."

She stared at me for a long moment, saying nothing, though her vivid green eyes held all the words in the world. Then she nodded, and stepped aside.

"*Viel Glück,* Elisabeth," she said as I shoved past. "Godspeed."

Once outside, I followed the path directly away from the needle onto a hidden trail, up the slopes, and to the mysterious, mirrored lake that reflected another sky. A path of impossible poppies sprang up at my feet, swaying and whispering in an unseen wind.

The souls of the sacrificed. All the hairs along the back of my neck and my arms rose up as though greeting this invisible breeze, as the whispers and murmurs resolved into words.

Hurry, hurry, the poppies urged. *It is not too late.*

It was not too late. I took courage, and ran.

The clouds overhead were heavy and gray, laden with early spring snow. Fat, wet snowflakes fell in heavy drops, half rain, half ice. Behind me, I could hear the faint drumming of hooves. Or perhaps it was the thudding of my anxious heart in my breast, beating an erratic tattoo of fear and excitement. I raced up the hill, heedless of my tread and where my footfalls lay.

The path quickly turned treacherous, the light dusting of snow turning the dirt underfoot slippery with mud. The trail was narrow, just barely wide enough for a human, even one as small as me. One misstep and I would plunge to my doom. The thought tumbled through my brain, and I could not resist looking over the ledge. It was a long, sheer drop to the valley floor several hundred feet below me, and I could not help but edge closer, lean farther out. There was ever a part of me that loved to face danger, to stare it in the eye and dare it to do its worst. I wanted the knife's edge of mortality pressed against my throat, to feel my pulse murmuring beneath the blade. I never felt more alive than when I was close to death.

Then the shelf on which I was standing crumbled.

For one piercing moment of clarity, I thought that this was perhaps the truest expression of my fate. That for all I tried to do good by those I loved and for the world, in the end it would be my own arrogance, recklessness, and mania that would trip me up. That would keep me down. That would ruin everything I touched despite my best intentions.

Vines wrapped themselves around my arms and legs, dead shrubs and mountain bushes halting my fall. The Count's compass continued tumbling to the floor below, the faint tinkle and crack of shattered glass and metal echoing up the hill. There was an audible *pop!* as something snapped in my wrist, the sound echoing behind my eyes, even as the sharp pain of it felt distant and unreal. Even my screams were stolen from me as the sudden yank preventing me from plummeting to the valley floor drove the breath from my body. I hung above the drop, suspended by roots and vines twined about my limbs, for an eternity, poised forever between life and certain death.

Then beetle-black eyes winked at me from the crevices of the hillside. Beetle-black eyes, long, spindly fingers, branches and cobwebs spun for hair.

Twig.

The brambles wrapped themselves tighter about me and slowly but surely began lifting me back onto the trail, back to safety. Hands appeared, bursting from the mud and rocks as they had when I had tried to escape the Underground, but they were helping me up instead of bringing me down.

They deposited me back to safety on a lower ledge than the one from which I had fallen, and vanished. I lay there for several breaths, trying to center myself back in my body, back to the present, to the pain in my wrist, the mud soaking into the wools and silks at my back, the pebbles pressing into my tender points. My mind was in both the past and future, all the mistakes I made and the regrets I had, and all the choices—both terrible and good—I had come so close to never making again.

When I returned to myself, I was alone.

Had I imagined Twig and the goblin hands? The agony in my wrist carved out all extraneous thought, and I cradled my left hand in the crook of my right elbow. The angle at which it sat was twisted, odd, and unnatural, and the sight of it almost made me queasier than the pain. Gasping and sobbing, I tried to move my left hand with my right, to maneuver my bones back into place. A grind, a click, an unsound deep in my body that resounded in my skull and in teeth, and then, sudden relief. The bliss flooded through me like warmth, and I found I needed to lie down to recover from the dizziness.

I could have lain there forever, succumbing to the aftermath of a whirlwind of fear and exhaustion, but the whispers tugged at me again.

Hurry, mistress, hurry, they cajoled. *It is not too late.*

I did not want to, but I must. I rose to my feet, hewing close to the hillside this time as I continued along this new path. The compass was gone, but it did not matter. Poppies sprang from crevices and rocks, guiding me to where I needed to go.

I came upon the lake.

This time I arrived at its shores instead of a ledge above its surface. Sparkling waves lapped at a ring of black sand, and light whorls of steam rose from its aquamarine depths. This close to the water, I could detect the slight hint of brimstone wafting from the lake. I shuddered. Perhaps I was wrong and this was not a portal to the Underground, but a hellmouth.

Then came the high, sweet singing of the Lorelei.

I had forgotten how strange, how eerie, how utterly seductive their music was. Tuneless, shapeless, ethereal, and hypnotic, a shimmering symphony of sound rose around me, each note bursting with a different color inside my head. Harmonies and dissonant chords wove strands of imagery, a tapestry of sensation that overwhelmed me, bringing me to my knees.

But I would not succumb.

Picking myself back up, I removed my boots, stockings, bodice, and skirts, steeling myself to wade into the water. Although I knew the lake was warm, I was still shocked by the silky-smooth heat against my skin, almost luxurious with its soothing heat. I could swim in this warmth forever. When I was far enough away from shore, I treaded water, and waited.

And waited.

And waited some more.

The last time I had encountered the Lorelei, they had been all too eager to drag me down to the depths and drown me. I did not know if it was because I was no longer Goblin Queen, or because I had nothing left to offer the Underground, but the dark, comely shapes slithering beneath the surface of the lake did not rise to meet me.

Presently, I grew tired and swam back to shore, long, pulling strokes that nevertheless did not seem to take me anywhere. My arms and legs felt leaden, my injured wrist tender and sore. It felt as though I would never reach dry land, and I began to worry that I would indeed drown. But I fought this battle every day, fighting upstream against the inevitable, inexorable pull of my own destructive tendencies, and if the body was exhausted, then at least the mind was willing.

When my fingers and toes finally scraped the gravel of the shadows, I crawled out of the lake, soaked and bedraggled and weighed down with more than water. The air was freezing against my skin, and I knew I had to get warm again, lest I die of exposure. I had to stay alive, I had to figure out a way to get Underground, I had to save my brother, and possibly, the entire world. The enormity of the task upon which I had set myself overwhelmed me, and I wanted nothing more than to lie down on the black sand of these shores and bury myself in oblivion.

I was at a loss.

The wolf's-head ring on my right hand glinted at me. I had forgotten all about it in my tumble from the hillside and just now in my swim in Lorelei Lake, but I was grateful to find it still with me. The band was too large and I had dropped it more than once, but it seemed to cling to me as hard as I clung to it. To my memory of the austere young man who had given it to me.

You may not have had Der Erlkönig's *protection as you walked the Underground, but you always had mine.*

He had always been with me. Miles away from the Goblin Grove and in another country, my austere young man had always been with me. Had always protected me. Even in my moments of reckless abandon, he struggled and fought and resisted against the tide of darkness that was corrupting him from within.

All because of me.

I knew then what it was I had to do.

With trembling fingers, I removed his ring. The mismatched gems sparkled in the waning, fading sunlight, brighter and more beautiful than the intense blue and green of the waters before me. I held it in my hands one last time, pressing it to my heart.

"Farewell, my immortal beloved," I whispered to my clasped fingers.

Then with a cry, I threw it with everything I had into the lake.

Where the silver touched the surface, ripples of glowing light spread outward, illuminating the entire mirror world in its reflection. Up was down and in was out, and a sense of vertigo overcame me at the sight of an entire realm below—above?—me. Was I looking down into the Underground, or was it looking down at me?

A dark, shadowy girl met my gaze. She had my face and my features, but her eyes were the stark, depthless black of goblin eyes. Her dark hair, unbound from the plaits I usually wore in a crown about my head, floated about her. She was naked, her body covered in shimmering scales, and it wasn't until I saw the webbing between her fingers that I recognized her for what she was.

A Lorelei.

Brave maiden, she said. *Why do you call?*

"Please," I said hoarsely to the girl in the mirrored world. "Please, I must go back."

The Lorelei tilted her head. *Why?*

To bring Josef back. To free the Goblin King. To calm the demons in my own head. "To make things right," I said.

She laughed, showing a mouth full of razor-sharp teeth. *There is no making things right, maiden. There is only reckoning.*

"Then I must reckon with those I have wronged," I replied.

She lifted her brows. *Who have you wronged?*

"My brother," I choked out. "The Goblin King. The old laws. The world."

The Underground is not a place for forgiveness, she said.

But neither was the world above. "Please," I said, holding out my empty hands before her. "I beg of you."

The Lorelei studied me, and if there could be an expression of pity in those flat, affectless eyes, I thought I detected a glimmer of sympathy.

You cannot cross the threshold of your own free will, maiden, she said. *You are taken, or you are summoned, as it was with the changeling who returned to us.*

Josef.

"Then take me!" I cried.

She shook her head. *You claim him as your brother, mortal, but we claim him as kin. He is of our kind. He belongs with us. He is home.*

Home. Tears sprang to my eyes, spilling over my cheeks to the aquamarine waters below me.

You love him, the Lorelei said with surprise. *I taste your sorrow and your tenderness.* She licked her lips. *I have not tasted such things in an age.*

"Then take them!" I clawed at my cheeks, trying to grab hold of my tears. "Take it all!"

She smiled again. *Would you give up your love for your changeling brother if I asked?*

I was stunned. Of all the things the Lorelei could have demanded of me, my love for Josef was the one thing I did not think she would claim. Was it even possible to stop loving Sepperl, the gardener of my heart?

"Could you do such a thing?"

She shrugged. *We can claim whatever it is you are willing to relinquish. Your youth, your passion, your talent. You gave us something that was as much a part of you as your eyes, your hair, your skin. What is love but another thing you claim as your own?*

The image of my brother rose up in my mind, but not as he was the last time I had seen him: tall, slim, lanky-limbed, with golden hair and eyes as blue as the sky. Instead, the memory of a sickly baby crying in his cradle returned to me, an ugly, twisted, homely thing that I had nevertheless taken into my heart as wholeheartedly as I had the rest of my family.

"No," I said. "No, I will not stop loving Sepp."

The Lorelei shrugged again. *What are you willing to sacrifice, maiden, to return to our realm?*

What did I have left to give? I had given my music, I had given that which I had held sacred and most dear. I had even given my body to the old laws, my breath, my heartbeat, and my senses. What was a person but a mind, a body, and a soul?

A mind.

My sanity.

My moods circled me like pikes scenting blood, swirling around like a vortex about a dark, dark abyss. I gripped my head, grasping at the remnants of my reason like a crown. I held my hands before the Lorelei, and cupped in my palms like a precious jewel was the last of my judgment, my sound mind.

The Lorelei smiled. Her hands mirrored my gesture, and as I lowered my sanity to the water, her palms rose up to meet mine. Her fingers wrapped themselves about my wrists, and I fell, down and down and down, until the world turned inside out.

Interlude

In a house of the Faithful sat a boy and a girl, one dark, one fair. They had traveled long and hard over hill and dale before settling down and finding a home among friends. Since their flight from Vienna, the changeling Bramble had introduced them to an underworld of actors and artists, musicians and misfits, a family bound not by blood, but loyalty. Through opera houses and theater halls, Käthe and François found work and friendship playing the fortepiano for the singers and sewing costumes for the actors.

They had escaped the Hunt.

Bramble had been careful to avoid the places where the barriers between worlds were thin, where there were no sacred spaces, following the poppies that led them to safety. If the audience found it odd that troupe members wore pouches of salt about their neck and iron keys in their pockets, then they chalked it up to the foibles and eccentricities of the creative mind.

Touched in the head, they would cluck and shake their heads. *Strange. Queer. Wild.*

The troubadours wore the badges with pride.

So did Käthe and François.

They were housed, they were clothed, they were fed, and they were even happy, insofar as they could be happy with constant anxiety gnawing at their bones. Others marveled at their productivity and work ethic, but both François and Käthe knew that the best and most efficient way to keep worry at bay was mindless repetition.

So he practiced his songs while she perfected her seams, all the while pretending not to notice the growing shadow of fear for Liesl and Josef that hovered over them.

"Play it again," Käthe said. "Play that song for me."

The girl was tone-deaf, but François knew which piece she wanted to hear. *Der Erlkönig,* composed by her sister, and performed with such exquisite skill by her brother. *Der Erlkönig* was the only time François ever heard Josef's playing sound weighty and down to earth, not ethereal, otherworldly, or transcendent. Performing Liesl's music was the only time he had ever heard his beloved's playing sound human.

Sound whole.

At first the members of the theater troupe with whom he and Käthe worked and traveled had been bemused by the piece.

I've never heard anything like this, said a troubadour.

Catchy, though, said the impresario. *Brings to mind a story.*

There was a story, but it was not theirs to tell. Käthe and François both knew it belonged to their sister and beloved, neither of whom could be found, despite the Faithful's best efforts.

It had been weeks since they had managed to reach out to Liesl through the shadow paths, weeks since they had tried to get her word about the danger she and Josef were in. Every night Käthe lit a candle before the dressing room mirror with a bath of salt water and an iron bell beside, but every morning the reflection remained empty of anything but the world in which they lived: chaotic, frenetic, mundane.

Then one morning, the bell rang.

Rehearsals for the latest play had been a disaster, with the playwright adding new lines every third scene while the composer tore out his hair and drank at having to add more bars of music to accommodate the changes. Bramble and Käthe ran back and forth between the actors, dropping pins and ribbons in their wake as they tried to finish the costumes before opening night, while François feverishly studied the new music as the pages were being rushed to him. In the midst of tumult and disorder of opening night, the ringing of the bell had been lost.

It wasn't until François returned to the dressing rooms for an older draft of the score the playwright had decided he preferred that he noticed the change in the mirror.

"Käthe!" he called. "Käthe, come quick!"

It was the excitement and astonishment in François's voice that brought her running more than his shouts.

"What?" she cried. "What is it?"

He pointed to the reflection, which showed not the dressing room, but a chamber of roots and rock. Where mannequins stood half-dressed and haphazard around them, weathered and petrified trees were draped with cobwebby lace and rotten silk. Where tables and benches and chairs sat in the world above, the mirror showed troves of gold, silver, and gemstones, a veritable goblin's hoard of treasure. The only things to remain the same in the reflection as in reality were the bath of salt water, the bell, and the candle, along with Käthe's and François's startled faces.

In the mirror, they watched as the shadow Käthe leaned

down and picked up something from the bath and dropped it into her apron pocket. The real Käthe reached into her own apron and withdrew a silver ring.

She gave a sharp gasp. "This is Liesl's!"

The ring in Käthe's palm was tarnished with age and wear, wrought into the shape of a running wolf with two mismatched gems for eyes.

"A message from the old laws," said Bramble from the entryway.

Both turned to face the changeling, who had a soft smile on his homely face.

"What does it mean?" François asked.

"It means, Herr Darkling," Bramble said, "that all is not as hopeless as we feared."

"What do I do?" Käthe asked. "How do I help my sister?"

Bramble smiled. "Keep it. Safe, sound, and secret. It was given to your care for a reason. You are her lighthouse in the dark, *Fräulein,* her bulwark against the tide. Be the anchor that brings her back to herself, for without you, she is adrift."

The girl and boy met each other's eyes, as the drumming of spectral horse hooves in the distance faded into the tapping of dancing feet upon the stage, as the audience *oo*ed and *ahh*ed at the poppies sprouting between the boards before them like magic. François placed his hand over Käthe's, enclosing Liesl's ring between their fingers, as their lips moved together in a prayer for their sister and their beloved.

Keep them safe. Keep them sound. Keep them secret.

Part IV

IMMORTAL BELOVED

Oh God—so near! so far! Is it not a real building of heaven, our Love?

—LUDWIG VAN BEETHOVEN, the Immortal Beloved letters

a monster stands on the far shore of a glowing lake, waiting for the barge bearing his bride to return.

He had stood in this very spot before, when he was a man and a king, when he played on his violin the image of a young woman through her music—her thoughts, her passions, her dreams. He had stood in this spot several times before that, greeting each bride as she made that last journey from life to death, but he never played his violin for them.

Never played their thoughts, their passions, or their dreams for them.

The high, thin singing of the Lorelei fills the cavern surrounding the Underground lake as a boat makes its way toward him, leaving a glowing trail in its wake. The multicolored light of the water illuminates the figure in the barge, laid out like a corpse with hands clasped and eyes closed. She is clad only in a chemise, still damp and transparent, her dark hair a rat's nest of tangles and snarls about her head. Only the shallowest movement of her chest betrays her breathing, and the monster curls and uncurls his twisted hands in anticipation.

He knows he should be good, he knows he should want her far from here and from him, but the goodness within him had been stolen from him by the old laws. Where once he might have felt affection, he now feels cruelty; where he had once felt tenderness, he now feels lust. His queen is not beautiful, but it does not matter. Her flesh is warm all the same.

Yet as the barge draws near, the hollowness within him rings and echoes. Where a heart might have been on a human man, the monster had only emptiness, for he had long ago torn out the remnants of his mortal self and given it away.

To her.

It is only then that the monster begins to fear.

And the man begins to hope.

THE RETURN OF THE
GOBLIN QUEEN

Sanity was a prison and now I am free, free to be shapeless, free to be formless, free to be nonsense. I wake up with gold in my mouth, fairy lights strung between my teeth like candy floss. I giggle as they light up my insides and dance, wiggling through my body like fireflies through a summer night. I am a summer night. I am heat and humidity and languidity, and I lounge upon my throne like a cat, like a queen, like Cleopatra. My throne is a bed, my receiving chamber a barrow, but I twist the reality in my mind, giving me a room full of wonders and splendors. Furniture of porcelain and glass, a hearth draped in silk and wood, tapestries woven of root and rock. My lashes are moth wings, my crown wrought of crystal and serpent scales. My royal robes are spun of spider webs and darkness, my maquillage the blood of my enemies.

"Mistress?"

I snap to attention, my body alive with the sound of a

familiar voice, tickling all the memory parts of me with a feather touch. Two goblin girls sway and tilt before me, one with thistledown for hair, the other with branches upon her head.

"Twig! Thistle!" I cry with delight.

Their faces are strange to me, for suddenly I can read the words of their emotions upon their eyes and lips. They are worried and they are frightened, and I marvel at the humanness of their expressions, and the goblinness of my thoughts.

"Have you come to bring me to the party? You should throw me a ball if there is none. Invite the changelings, invite the old laws, invite the world!"

The last time I came, there was a ball in my honor, where I had danced with the Goblin King and my sister. A goblin ball, a fairy ball, a ball of too much wine and indulgence, tasting of blackberry tongues and sin.

"*Der Erlkönig* is waiting for you," says Thistle, and I hear the twinning of her voice with another. My grandmother's snappish tone harmonizes with the goblin girl's words, saying things she would rather not have me hear. *I care about you. I am frightened for you.*

"Of course, Constanze," I reply, and float to my feet with a smile. "Take me to him!"

The other goblin girl wrings her hands, dripping her nervousness like puddles onto the floor. "He is . . . changed, Your Highness."

Changed. The man into a monster, the boy to a changeling, the composer to a madwoman. We are butterflies and the Underground is our chrysalis, a place of transformations and magic and miracles.

"I know," I say. "He is corrupted. A corrupt king for a corrupt queen."

My goblin girls exchange looks. "You are not safe," says Thistle. Contempt laces her voice but tastes cold like fear, with the unexpectedly bitter burn of concern lingering on the tongue.

"I know," I say again. My smile grows wider, my eyes madder. "I know."

"It is not *Der Erlkönig* you should fear," Twig whispers, "but the reckoning he is owed."

I open my arms wide, my robes of spider-silk and black lace billowing in an unseen wind. I am a top out of control, toppling and wobbling back and forth, back and forth, and the exhilaration and uncertainty excites me, for I do not know where I will go or what I will say.

"I am the Goblin Queen," I giggle. "I can pay whatever is asked of me." The words bubble from my lips and pop with little bursts of arrogance before me. I laugh again, feeling the tickle on my tongue.

"Even if it is the changeling boy?" Thistle asks.

My arms fall to my sides, and I fall over, the center thrown from me. Josef. How bothersome that I could not shed my love for him as easily as I gave up my reason. My heart cracks, and the pieces belonging to my brother glow and pulse through the cage of bones. I am a skeleton draped in cobwebs with a candle flame at its core. My sanity was my prison and my armor and without it, the flame flickers this way and that, buffeted by forces beyond my control. I lift my hands to cover my naked heart, but it is not enough to shield it.

"My brother has nothing to do with this," I say.

"Oh but he has everything to do with this," Thistle returns. "After all, is he not the reason you came back?"

"Yes, but I won't give him back!" Petulance forces my lips into a pout. "He's mine!"

Twig and Thistle's eyes slide back and forth, from my face to each other. *Selfish, selfish, selfish,* they seem to say. I want to snatch those beetling eyes and wear them like rings about my fingers, to shut up their unvoiced censure.

"Stop looking at me," I snap. "Stop judging me."

My goblin girls look at each other again. "As you wish, Your Highness," they say. "As you wish."

I demanded a ball, but the gathering of goblins and changelings in the enormous, glittering cavern do not look as though they are enjoying themselves. There is no music, no dancing, no feasting, no flirting. I cast my gaze thither and hither, both disturbed and delighted by the transparency of feelings upon their features. When last I visited the Underground, it was as though I visited a foreign land, the language just familiar enough to be intelligible. But now the world is not just intelligible, it is comprehensible. Comprehended. Commendable.

"I am one of you!" I clap my hands with delight, pinching the cheek of a leather-faced imp wearing a mask of trepidation. "I see you! I hear you! I understand you!"

I survey the room from the top of the carved stone stairs at the entrance to the cavern. Where once I would have seen a sea of identical faces staring back at me, I now saw individuals as clear and distinct as leaves on a tree. How have I not noticed pattern and repetition and shape of them? The veins that define them, the unique marks and branches that form them?

As I descend the steps, the crowd parts before me like the Red Sea before Moses, opening up a path straight from my feet to the figure at the other end of the cavern, sitting on a throne of antlers upon a marble dais. He lounges upon that enormous chair, inky swirls of black staining his skin, a pair of ram's horns jutting from his brow. His eyes are pale, the blue-white of blizzards and icy death.

Der Erlkönig.

A host of ghostly warriors flank him on either side of the throne, wights and *geists* and spectral horsemen, dressed in rotting scraps of flesh and fabric, holding spears and shields rusted with age and disuse. The Wild Hunt.

"Mein Herr!" The smile starts at my toes and wriggles up my body, wrapping about my lower belly, my chest, my throat, my face. The cavern rings with my voice, and all those assembled cringe from the force of it.

All save one.

Sitting at *Der Erlkönig's* feet is a fair-haired youth, long-limbed and lanky, with sharp cheekbones and an even sharper chin. Of all the changelings around me, his are the only eyes that look human. Clear as water and blue, blue, blue.

Josef.

But I don't recognize my brother. Where the expressions of the other goblins and fey creatures of the Underground are books I can read, Josef's is like trying to find words in a painting. The flame in my chest stutters and sputters with my uncertainty.

"Welcome home, my queen." *Der Erlkönig's* thin lips unfurl into a sneer, teeth glinting in the changeable, mercurial light of the Underground. "Have you missed us?" The sneer sharpens, his eyes turning glacial. "Have you missed *me*?"

"Yes," I say. "I have longed for you every minute, every hour, of my waking days."

Color flares briefly in those eyes, a lightning flash of depth and dimension. "And your sleepless nights?"

Lust ripples through my veins, my blood a murmuring brook of want. The monster before me is beautiful in his ugliness, and I imagine those corrupted hands curled around me, our skin alternating black and white like the keys of my klavier. The candle within me glows brighter.

"My nights are spent running from my desire for you. For devastation. For oblivion."

Der Erlkönig gets to his feet. "Yes." He sighs, the sound drawn out in a sibilant whisper that slithers about my loins. "Yes."

Yes, please, yes. I walk forward as *Der Erlkönig* descends from the dais. I bare my throat to him in submission, waiting for the wolf's bite that will spill my life's blood onto the floor. He wraps those multijointed hands about my arms and pulls me close, pressing his lips against where my pulse flutters beneath the skin, breathing deep the scent of my mortality.

His fingertips are licks of flame that leave chilblains in their wake, my flesh turning dead-white and deadweight beneath his touch. Claws find my every crevice, as though he can dig into me and tear me apart. I laugh with a scream.

"No!" Josef leaps upon *Der Erlkönig*'s back, breaking his grip on me. "Leave her alone! You're hurting her!"

As the Lord of Mischief steps away, I feel something hot running down my chin. I touch my face and my fingertips come away wet and red.

A nosebleed.

The world slips and slides around me, and when I lift my hands, I can see straight through my skin down to the muscles and blood and bone of my flesh. *Der Erlkönig* is stripping away who I am, layer by layer. I laugh again, and my laughter emerges from *Der Erlkönig* in a chuckle as he turns to my brother.

"Does she not deserve to be hurt? Does she not deserve to be destroyed? Have not those very thoughts crossed your own head, O nameless one?"

Josef looks to me, but I still cannot understand the words of his eyes.

"What are you doing here?" *Der Erlkönig* asks him. "Why have you come?"

"I . . . I've come home," Josef says, the pitch of his voice softer than the sound of my thoughts.

Der Erlkönig throws his head back with a roar of mirth and contempt. "Did you think it would be so easy, changeling? To shed the life of the mortal you once were? I see the strings that still tie you to the world above. To *her*."

His eyes dart my way, and I see the bonds of blood that have wrapped themselves in a stranglehold about my brother's neck and chest, slowly draining him of joy. They are tied to the candle in my own chest.

"Why do you still wear his face, *mischling*?" *Der Erlkönig* taunts. Halfling, half-blood, mongrel, I watch my brother bleed shame and agony. "Show us your real self!"

Josef pales. "This—this is my real self."

"Is it?" The Lord of Mischief steps closer to my brother, and I see Josef flinch against that bitter breath. His winter's gaze caresses my brother's face, and those broken-jointed fingers run their tips lightly across Josef's brow. "Those eyes are still human, *mischling*. Shall I pluck them out for you?"

"No!" My shout is a blade, my body a shield as I place myself between my brother and the Goblin King. "You shall not touch him."

For the briefest of moments, *Der Erlkönig*'s glacier eyes melt to reveal the man frozen behind them. His emotions take on the tang of death and mortality, not the clean, crisp taste of the fey and everlasting life.

"Would you save him?" he asks, and his voice is a kitten in my hand, soft and defenseless and vulnerable. "Would you choose him?"

Der Erlkönig's lips say one thing, but his words say another. *Would you choose me?* I hear them both, the man and the monster, and I cannot untangle one from the other.

"Why should I choose?" I ask instead. "Can I not save you both?"

The shadows writhe on *Der Erlkönig*'s skin, rustling and hissing like a nest of snakes. As one, the gathering of goblins inhales a sharp breath. The air weighs heavy in my lungs, and I drown in tension and fear as the crawling darkness gathers itself around the Goblin King's body. He screams in E-flat, iron nails of agony driving into my eardrums as he clutches his head.

Josef begins to keen in pain, a diminished second to the Goblin King's scream, jarring and dissonant and grating against where I keep my love for him. My brother claws at his eyes as shadows begin to spill from them in blue-black tears, staining them onyx and obsidian.

Behind them both, the Wild Hunt begin to laugh, clapping their rusted blades against their shields in a pounding rhythm. Shrieks and cries rise up in a cacophony of torture and torment from the changelings and goblins assembled around me, limbs cracking, fingers breaking, bodies bent and reshaped into a giant mass of grasping hands to form a mouth, a nose, eyes, a face. The unholy host dissolves into mist, and the collective face breathes in deep, the wights and riders vanishing into fog. Its eyes open, glowing blue-white in the cavernous ballroom, and I know just what it is I am facing.

The old laws made flesh.

So you have returned to us, Goblin Queen. The voice is legion, a jumble of pitches and tones and notes. If I were not already mad, I might have lost my mind at the sight of its grotesqueness.

"I have come," I say, "to claim what you have stolen."

The eyebrows wrought of fingers and eyeballs lift, the edge of a lip made of elbows and toes curling into an ironic expression. *And what is that?*

I look to Josef. I look to the Goblin King.

"My heart."

The Goblin King stirs at the words and lifts his head to meet my gaze. A kindling gaze, and it stokes the flames in my rib cage. It flickers and throbs, and I can almost hear it whisper a name.

Your heart? The old laws laugh, a hideous shriek and cackle of a myriad goblin voices. *You have but one, mortal.*

I wrap my hands around the candle in my chest. "It is big enough to warm them both. It is big enough to warm the world."

Liar. The word flies from its lips and shatters against the stony walls of the cavern, scattering sharp jibes and jeers everywhere. *Liar, liar, liar.*

Such a pretty lie. But we know the ugly truth of you, Goblin Queen. We know of your overweening arrogance, your thoughtlessness, and your utter, selfish disregard for anything other than your own feelings. We know how you walked away from this pitiful vessel before us—a finger flicks in the Goblin King's direction—*to leave him to deterioration and decay. We also know how you took this sorry changeling*—another finger toward Josef—*and corrupted him with your love.*

Josef whimpers, black ink running down his cheeks. The

whites of his eyes are already lost to the Underground, and the blue of his human irises swim in darkness.

Look at that pathetic, mewling thing, the old laws sneer. *This is what thou hath wrought, Goblin Queen.*

Madness is an escape from boundaries, from inhibitions, from my own self-doubt, but I cannot escape my self-loathing. I did not know until that moment how reason had been my shield against the worst of my own excesses, the unbridled muchness of me. Shadows coil around my wrists and throat, my fingers breaking and twisting into gnarled branches.

The covenant is broken, the old laws croon. *And it is your fault. Your fault, your fault, your fault. But you can make it right.*

"How?" I cry.

The limbs and teeth and fingers and eyes and toes that make up the old laws' face bubble and ripple, a skittering mass that breaks apart and re-forms into an enormous pair of hands, cupped together to offer me something in its palms. It is a smaller pair of hands, holding a dagger in its grip.

A life for a life, the old laws say. *It is what we are owed.*

I look to the Goblin King.

I look to Josef.

Choose, maiden. Choose your austere young man . . . or your brother.

The hands gripping the dagger stretch and grow, a branch, a sapling, a tree. The old laws offer me the blade, an ancient weapon, forged not from steel, but hewn from stone. It is simple, it is crude, it is cruel.

Choose, maiden, the old laws repeat. *Pay the price, and the other goes free.*

I take the dagger.

Yesssssssssssssssss, they hiss. *Make your choice.*

I turn to my brother. His skin is clear, his bones wrought of glass, his blood of water. Where a candle ought to have burned in his chest, there is nothing, a black hole, a swamp. Marsh light flickers there, blue and ethereal, the ghost of flame.

I turn to the Goblin King. The shadows have left him utterly, leaving him horrifically scarred and disfigured, but his eyes are brilliant, bright, full. A candle lies in his rib cage, cold and dark, as though waiting for a breath to fan it to life.

Make your choice, the old laws demand.

The Goblin King looks at me, his lips curled up like a sleeping cat, cozy and sweet. He does not speak, but I hear him anyway.

Choose him. Choose your brother.

I look to Josef. I still cannot read the language of his features, but he shakes his head. "Let me go," he tells me. "Give me up."

The dagger in my hand is more than a weapon; it is a compass needle. It points me in the direction of my heart. I press the tip to my chest.

The mass of goblins shift, hesitancy in their voice. *What are you doing?*

"I am making my choice," I whisper.

And drive the dagger deep into myself.

INSIDE OUT

there is no pain, only a sigh of relief. I cut through the cage of bones that surround my candle, and reach inside. The flame is sure and steady, and I hold it aloft, illuminating the space around me.

The cavern is gone, and I am alone. I am back in the hedge maze at Procházka House, but the shrubs are made of memories, the path of poppies. I tread on the souls of the stolen and sacrificed as I walk through the winding paths of my mind. Thoughts burst underfoot like bubbles, leaving bits of feeling in my wake as the flowers sigh their names.

Ludvik
Adelaide
Erik
Samuel
Magda

But as I wend and wind my way through the labyrinth, I realize I am walking in a river of blood, the walls of the Daedalian pathways built of bone. The hedges and bramble vines pulse and throb and breathe, warm and slick to the touch. Like skin. Like flesh.

Ich bin der umgedrehte Mann.

I am the inside-out man.

There is a glow emanating from the center of the labyrinth, and I follow the light, leaving the darkness behind me. As the corridors of the hedge maze open up, I find myself in a space very much like the ballroom at Snovin Hall—a beautiful, soaring cathedral of a space with light and glass and mirrors everywhere. The sunshine and moonlight and star glow of other worlds stream in through the windows, dust motes hanging upon the beams like fairy lights in the Underground. It is a sacred space, a sanctuary, and it is the holy hall of my heart.

In the middle of my heart is an altar, a bronze basin of oil standing upon a wooden plinth carved into the shape of a tree. I touch my candle to the oil and set it ablaze, wondering if I were to meet some version of myself like a priestess, an oracle, or a queen.

No one arrives.

There is only me, my own inadequate self reflected in the mirrors around me.

One of my reflections crooks a finger at me, beckoning me close. I obey, walking up to the girl in the mirror. I have long since made my peace with my own lack of beauty, but it is jarring to see my skin animated by another version of myself. I study my face with new eyes, as though I am a stranger to myself, finding myself both more and less critical of my features. The weak and pointed chin, the horselike nose, the thin lips are all still there, but the animated eyes and defined cheekbones are new. Or rather, they seem new, for when I speak, they are the first parts of myself I notice.

The first parts other people see.

Who are you? the reflection asks.

"I am Liesl," I reply.

She shakes her head. *Who am I?*

I blink. I remember a conversation—a game—I played with the Goblin King oh so long ago.

I am a girl with music in her soul. I am sister, a daughter, a friend, who fiercely protects those dear to her. I am a girl who loves strawberries, chocolate torte, songs in a minor key, moments stolen from chores, and childish games.

"You are Elisabeth, entire," I say to my reflection.

Her smile looks sad. *Are you?*

Am I? As I turn to peer into each of the mirrors, I see a different facet of myself: the girl with music in her soul, the daughter, the friend, the sister. These are all parts of me, entire, yet I did not know until this moment how I had fractured myself, unable to understand how to fit these pieces together into a whole.

There are mirrors, and there are windows, and through the windows I see different worlds, different lives, those precious people I have taken into myself. Mother, Constanze, and Papa can be seen through the windows to my family, while Käthe and François sit together in another. But of all these pretty pictures and vistas into other lives, only Käthe stares back.

Liesl, she says.

In her hand she holds a ring. I peer closer, and see it is the silver wolf's-head ring I threw into Lorelei Lake, the one my austere young man gave to me as a promise.

I keep you secret, she says. *I keep you safe. Until the day you return to me, I hold your heart.*

Our hands meet palm to palm through the glass, our heads nodding in unison.

The light fades in my sister's window, but a candle continues to burn.

I take a slow turn about the room then, looking through each window for glimpses of my brother or the Goblin King. But try as I might, I cannot find them, for there are myriad windows, myriad memories to sort through.

You are looking in the wrong places, my reflection tells me.

"Where should I look?" I ask her.

Not out at the world, she says. *But back at yourself.*

In the mirrors.

Then I understand.

Josef and the Goblin King are not their own, entire, but me. They are not real, but puppets of shadows and flesh. I did not see them as whole and human, for how could I, when they are the foundations upon which I stand?

Choose, the old laws told me. *Pay the price, and the other goes free.*

The sacrifice was not paid by my blood. It will be paid by my soul. To choose Josef or the Goblin King is to choose the part of me I am willing to give up: my brother, or my austere young man. The gardener of my heart, or my immortal beloved. My capacity for grace, or my potential for mercy.

For Josef is my grace. He is the unprompted, unlooked for, unplanned stranger in the night, the one I fed and clothed and loved as my own. I am a better person for loving my brother, although I have done a poor job proving it to him or myself of late.

"I'm sorry, Sepperl," I say to my reflection. Her form ripples and changes, and standing before me is a changeling. He has my brother's features and a goblin's eyes. He smiles at me and tilts his chin over my shoulder. I turn around to face another mirror.

The austere young man.

It is not the same person I left on the cavern floor with my brother and the old laws. This man is different: younger, fresh-faced, his mismatched eyes as vivid and intense as new-dyed hues. Nor is he truly an austere young man, despite the sober and somber clothing he wears. There is the sparkle of mischief in his expression, and a twist of wickedness to his lips, yet in the depths of his eyes there is an agelessness that speaks of wisdom both learned and earned.

"Who are you?" I whisper.

He nods at me. *You know who I am, Elisabeth.*

"You are a man with music in his soul," I tell him. "You are the one who showed me a way to myself, when I was lost in the woods. My teacher, my playmate, my friend." I choke a little on the sobs rising from my throat. "You allowed me to forgive myself for being imperfect. For being a sinner. For being me."

If my brother is my grace, then the Goblin King is my mercy. I look from one to the other. How can I possibly choose? I have fallen upon an ancient weapon, but how can I possibly cut out my own heart and survive?

Josef steps forward, hand outstretched. The Goblin King steps forward as well, a mirror image to my brother. I hold out my hands to each, and their shapes blur and merge, until I can no longer tell which is my mercy and which is my grace. Perhaps they are both. Perhaps they are neither.

Choose.

And still I wait. Still I hesitate, unwilling to let go of either. Both.

Choose.

the maiden's blood spilled over the cavern floor, a widening circle of crimson, scarlet, and vivid red. The changeling cried out and ran forward, placing his hands over her heart to stanch the bleeding.

"Help me!" he cried out to the man on the dais. "Help me, please!"

The man lurched upright, pale and wan and unsteady on his feet. The Goblin King. Without the power of the old laws thrumming through his veins, he looked strangely diminished. Less frightening, less otherworldly, less . . . just *less*. For his entire mortal life, the changeling had heard tales of this man—this uncanny figure—who could bend space and time and the laws of reality as the world knew it, yet the Goblin King who stood before him was not a myth. He was just a man.

And the changeling hated him a little for it.

The Goblin King joined the changeling by the maiden's side, covering his hands with his own. Together they pushed down upon her chest, feeling the *pulse, pulse, pulse* of her heart beating beneath their palms.

"Please," the changeling said, turning his eyes to the mass

of goblin hands and eyes and teeth watching with an impassive, implacable, impersonal gaze. "What can I do?"

Do, mischling? the legion of voices was amused. *Do what? Save her life? It is too late. She has made her choice.*

"She did it to save me!" He turned on the Goblin King. "How could you just let her die?"

Blame him not, the old laws said. *He is a hollow husk of a thing. We ate his soul already; he has nothing left to give.*

The changeling threw his head back and screamed.

From the crawling, writhing mass of creatures, two small goblin girls clawed and wriggled their way free. Other hands burst forth and grabbed at their ankles, their wrists, their limbs, any bit of their bodies within reach, but the girls were determined, biting and scratching as they fought their way to the changeling and the Goblin King.

"*Mischling,*" said the one nearest to him. She was slender, like a sapling tree, with a crown of branches wound with cobwebs atop her head. "There is a way to save her."

Silence! the old laws roared.

"That one," said the other, a short stout little thing with thistledown hair, pointing at the Goblin King, "has given all he can give. He has nothing left." Her black eyes were solemn. "But you do, *mischling.* You do."

The changeling looked to the man at his side. He was shaking his head, in resignation or denial, the changeling did not know what. "He should not have to bear the cost."

"What cost?" the changeling demanded.

"Eternity," the Goblin King whispered. "Unending torment."

The changeling went still. He knew then what the sacrifice would claim of him, what the old laws required.

A king.

"No," the man beside him said. "She cannot bear to lose you, Josef. Elisabeth would never forgive you."

Josef. It was a name he had stolen, an identity and a face and a life he had taken for his own. The fat, sweet little mortal child who had died of scarlatina before he had had a chance to live. The changeling had seen his opportunity, and taken it. He had become the boy in the cradle. He had become Liesl's brother.

"How?" he breathed. The changeling turned to the face wrought of nightmares. "What must I do?"

"It was never a bride who was needed to bring the world back to life," said the twig-laden goblin girl. "It was grace."

The Goblin King gave the girl a sharp look. "Explain yourself, Twig."

Twig trembled and shivered, buffeted about by fear and eagerness. "Only a person given willingly to the Underground with a whole heart understands the true price to be paid and offers it with joy."

"Grace, *mischling*," said the thistle-haired goblin, "is the capacity to love the world entire. Without regard to self. Without regard to the individual. The first Goblin King understood this."

The man beside him stiffened. "Then why a bride, Thistle?" he asked. "Why must innocent blood be spilled to wake the world to spring?" The changeling could hear the words the man did not say. *Why did I have to suffer? Why did* she?

"A sacrifice made with half a heart is worth half its value," Thistle replied. "You were tricked onto your throne, Your Majesty. The first Goblin King was tricked out of his."

"By whom?" the changeling demanded.

The goblin girls exchanged glances. "We do not speak her name," said Twig.

The first Goblin Queen.

"She loved him," Thistle said. "And she was selfish. When the Goblin King let her go, she returned to the Underground to claim him. To steal him away. And in his place she left another. A mewling, frightened lad," she sneered. "Who lasted barely a breath before finding another to take his place."

"But you, *mischling*," Twig said softly. "You understand what it is to love the world entire. You have walked amongst mortals, you have lived amongst them. You have even loved them, in the only way we fey know how. Distantly. Dispassionately. But it does not mean it is any less deep."

The changeling stared at the dagger in his sister's hand, still wet with her blood. "But I have no soul to give," he said.

"She gave you a name," Twig said gently. "And you took it to forge your own soul."

Sepperl.

The man beside him was shaking his head, but did not say a word in protest. The changeling took the weapon from his sister's hand.

"Oh, Josef," the man said. There were tears in his mismatched eyes, and there was great compassion in their blue and green depths. "You don't have to do this."

But he did.

"Take care of her," he whispered to the man beside him. "She deserves to be loved."

The man nodded his head, but could not speak. Josef heard him anyway. *I will.*

The old laws were silent and watchful as the changeling took the dagger.

And pierced his own heart.

A WHOLE HEART AND
A WORLD ENTIRE

the shadows shift and stir, and my brother separates himself from my reflection, from my thoughts, and emerges as himself, whole and entire beside me.

"Liesl," he calls softly.

"Sepperl. Is it you? Or are you me?"

"I am you," he says. "And you are me. We are the left and right hands of a single fortepianist. We are part of a larger whole, greater than us, greater than the world."

My sanctuary is dark, for not even the flame atop the altar can lift the despair around me. The candle I had cut from my cage of bones lies discarded, cold and dead, beside the plinth. "What do I do, Sepp?" I say in a hoarse voice. "How do I choose?"

"You don't," he says simply.

"What do you mean?" I can still hear the echoes of the old laws in my ears, ringing with such force and authority. *Pay the price, and the other goes free.*

"You don't," he repeats. "For the choice is mine."

"No!" I lunge forward and take my brother by the hand. "You can't."

"Why not, Elisabeth?" The Goblin King stands beside Josef, his form and figure as I had always known him. His mismatched eyes a faded green and gray, his face lean, his hair in silver-white-gold disarray about his head.

"Because . . . because . . ." But I cannot find the right words to say. This choice should be mine. It had always been mine.

"Stop being so selfish," Josef teases. "Let us take on the burden for once."

"I'm trying not to be," I say in a small voice. "Selfish, that is."

"Have you learned nothing from your time Underground?" The Goblin King stoops to pick my candle off the floor. "What was it I asked you oh so long ago?"

"When will you learn to be selfish," I whisper. "When you will learn to do anything for yourself?"

"And when will you learn to let others do things for you?" The Goblin King hands my candle to my brother, who re-lights my flame with the marsh light in his own heart.

"Is this real?" I dare not voice the question louder than a murmur.

"What is real?" the Goblin King asks.

I shake my head. I do not know.

"Reality is what you make of it, Elisabeth," he says. "The same as madness. Whether or not this is real matters not to me, but it matters to you. Therefore, which is it? What would you rather have it be?"

The feel of his skin against mine, the scent of his musk, the taste of his lips. The Goblin King has height and breadth and *weight* in my hands, and I watch the rise and fall of his chest as he breathes in and out. In and out. I have a sudden memory, or rather, a vision of the future, but one so closely lived as to be memory. I remember the two of us lying in bed, side by side, our bodies sticky with satisfaction and wrapped in the warm glow of easy comfort. I remember how the features of his face grow sharper with age, the skin thinning to reveal the fine lines and bones beneath. I remember the silver-white-gold of his hair turning white with frost, true white now, not the enchanted glitter of magic and the Underground. I remember how we grow old together.

"Real," I say.

"Then name me." His eyes are solemn. "Give me back to myself, Elisabeth."

"But I do not know your name," I tell him, my tongue tripping over my tears.

"You have always had it," he replies. He presses his hand against my chest. "You have carried it ever and always, bringing remnants of me back into the world above."

The monastery. I think of the names hewn into the stone walls of the catacombs, brothers long dead and gone. *Mahieu*, I remember. But that is not the Goblin King's name. I realize then that I *do* know it, in bits, in pieces, in dreams. A wolf-boy, a feral child, a name carved into a windowsill.

"How . . ." I trail off.

He laughs softly. "The Lord works in mysterious ways."

"I really do wish He would be a little less mysterious and a lot more forthcoming," I say irritably. The Goblin King chuckles.

"You gave me a name," Josef says. My brother's smile is tender and sweet, and I do not think I can bear the pain. "Now give him his."

He takes my hand and places it in the Goblin King's. My austere young man. My—

"Wolfgang," I whisper.

Josef returns my candle to me, lit not with the fire from my altar, but from the marsh light in his own chest. His soul, my soul. I reach forward and light the candle in the Goblin King's chest.

The shadows fall away.

"Go," Josef says, and he points toward a window, where a girl with sunshine hair and summer-blue eyes stands with palms outstretched, waiting to take me by the hand.

"Käthe," I murmur.

Behind my sister stands François. My brother and his beloved lock eyes. What is said in that long, quiet gaze is unknown to me, for although theirs is a language of love, it is not the language I speak. After a moment, François nods. It is not a nod of resignation or defeat, but of acceptance. Of farewell. Josef nods his head in return.

"Go," my brother repeats. "Go, and play your music for the world. Be the self you are meant to be, Liesl, just as I am the king I choose to be."

"But how can I play without you?" I don't bother to wipe away the tears streaming down my cheeks.

"You have him," he says, tilting his head toward the Goblin King. Toward Wolfgang. "But you will always have me too. Your music is a bridge, Liesl," he says. "Play it, and we shall always be together. Play it, and I shall always remember. You. Life. What it means to love. For your music was the first and only thing in this world that kept me human, the first and last thing I give back to you."

I am crying so hard I can barely speak. "I love you, Sepperl." Great, heaving sobs, and I cannot breathe, cannot gulp enough air to say this last goodbye. "I love you, *mein Brüderchen*. With my whole heart."

Josef smiles, and the tips of his teeth gleam in the flickering candlelight. "And I love you, Liesl," he says softly. "With the world entire."

a baby cries in a cradle before stopping, the red fading from its overflushed cheeks.

It grows very still, pale, and wan.

Josef?

A little girl walks into the room. She is sallow-skinned and skinny, with dark hair and eyes that seem to take over her entire face. She leans over the cradle and touches her brother's cheek.

The baby opens its eyes. They are a flat black. Goblin's eyes. Changeling eyes.

Sepperl?

There is worry in her voice, and love. At the sound, the black in the baby's eyes dwindles, and a pale blue appears in its place. It reaches out a tiny hand to the little girl, who holds it tightly in her own. The little girl begins to sing. A lullaby, a melody of her own making. It moves something within him, something new, something different, something marvelous.

A memory.

His memory. The first he could truly call his own, for it did not belong to the Underground, or to Liesl, or to anyone but himself.

Der Erlkönig.

In the distance, music plays. It is the sound of his sister's voice, reaching across the veil between worlds. And as he had done when he was a baby in a cradle, Josef reaches back.

Their souls touch, and it is a bridge. He had a name. He had a soul. He had grace.

Der Erlkönig remembers what it is to love.

And brings the world back to life.

Finale

To Anna Katharina Magdalena Ingeborg Vogler
Care of the Faithful
Vienna

My darling Käthe,

We have arrived safe and sound back in Bavaria with Mother and Constanze. Despite our fears, the inn has prospered without us, a steady flow of business filling our coffers instead of Papa's debts. Our grandmother is as irritable and irascible as ever, although she did rouse herself from her quarters to greet Wolfgang. Like everyone else we've met on this journey back to the Goblin Grove, she is relentlessly charmed by him, although she would furiously deny it if asked.

"Where did you find such a young man?" she demanded. "How was such a small, plain little thing like you able to ensorcell him into marriage?"

"The Lord works in mysterious ways," was Wolfgang's reply, an answer that endeared him to Mother's churchgoing sensibilities, but unfortunately distanced him from Constanze's rather heretical ones.

"Pah," she said. "He is not one of Der Erlkönig's own, I see."

"Alas, no," he replied. "I am my own, I'm afraid."

Everyone looked at me as though I were mad as I laughed and laughed and laughed.

Our small, provincial village was just as shocked as Constanze to find me returned with a husband, and perhaps none more so than Herr Baumgärtner. I confess to feeling a measure of petty satisfaction to note how much more handsome than Hans my Wolfgang is, even as I know that is beneath me. I give you permission to tease me about it later, Käthe. I know.

I paid our respects to Papa's grave in the old church cemetery. The old rector is gone, vanished from his bed last winter with nothing but poppies left in his wake. I noted another headstone beside our father's as we left, new to me, but old and weathered as though it had been there for years.

Franz Josef Gottlieb Vogler
Gone Too Soon

I left a poppy behind.

Tomorrow I shall venture to the Goblin Grove one last time with our offerings. The locks of hair from you and François have thankfully survived the journey, and I shall bury them in the grove. And then, as the sun sets in the west on the first night of summer, I shall play <u>Der Erlkönig</u> upon my new violin.

Wolfgang had it refinished with the finial of the carved woman that had been in our family for generations as a wedding gift. I can't believe you and François found it in your dressing room.

When I was younger, I could not decide whether the woman's face was one of agony or ecstasy, but now that I am grown, I understand her expression for what it is:

Joy.

I have not heard word of the Prochászkas since we departed Vienna, but rumor is that Snovin Hall is overgrown. Sometimes I think of that blue-green lake hidden in the hills above their estate and wonder.

We shall return once the sale of the inn is final. Mother has been beside herself with excitement to see you again, and even Constanze seems eager to leave this place behind.

"The place is full of so many ghosts," she said. "And I cannot rest for their relentless chatter."

The villagers think she has lost her mind, but I understand better now how our grandmother thinks. Those of us with one foot Underground and one in the world above are ever privy to the uncanny and unseen. Is that madness? Or merely another way of being?

Give my love to François. Tell him I look forward to how the troupe has staged the opera when we return, and how much I have appreciated his guidance and his tutelage on the writing and composition. The story was mine to tell, but the music was a work of collaboration.

Before we leave, Wolfgang insists we debut the Wedding Night Sonata for the villagers, so they might have something to remember us by.

"So they understand the whole of you, Elisabeth," he told me. "So they understand the entirety of us."

I don't know what the butcher and baker will think of the music, but I fancy they'll enjoy a performance nonetheless. The ending of the Wedding Night Sonata keeps changing, and I imagine it will change still further, on and on and on until I die. But that is the way of a life's work, and I am happy to keep composing, to keep writing, until I find the right finale.

One last thing before I end my letter. I know you would rather have me keep the wolf's-head ring, or at least have it appraised for its value. But in the end, a promise is without price. When I step into the Goblin Grove for the last time, I will leave it for our brother, along with your locks of hair and our love.

Yours always,
Composer of Der Erlkönig

Where I am, you are with me.

— LUDWIG VAN BEETHOVEN,
the Immortal Beloved letters

Coda

Once there was a little girl who played her music for a little boy in the wood. She was the genius, he was the interpreter, and they were each the gardeners of the other's heart, taming, tilling, and tending the fertile soil of their souls until they blossomed into a far-reaching forest that encompassed the world.

Their grandmother had taught them the old ways and the old laws, but the little girl and boy were not afraid, for they were both *Der Erlkönig's* own.

Don't forget me, Liesl.

And the little girl did not reply. Instead she played her song for the Goblin King every spring, every year, to bring the world from death back into life. And when the little girl's gnarled and aged fingers could no longer hold her bow, her children and students picked up her song and continued to play, one long, unbroken melody that stretched across time and memory. On and on and on, for as long as the seasons turn and the living remember all that is good and beautiful and worthwhile in the world.

For love is our only immortality, and when memory is faded and gone, it is our legacies that endure.

A GUIDE TO NAMES AND TITLES

CONSTANZE: *Kohn-STANTS-eh*

DER ERLKÖNIG: *Dere ERRL-keu-nikh*

ELISABETH: *eh-LEE-za-bet*

JOSEF: *YO-sef*

KÄTHE: *KEI-teh*

LIESL: *LEE-sul*

MAHIEU: *MAY-yew*

MEIN HERR: *Mine Hehrr*

PROCHÁZKA: *pro-(k)HASS-ka*

SEPPERL: *SEPP-url*

SNOVIN: *SNO-vin*

VLČEK: *VLI-chek*

A GUIDE TO GERMAN PHRASES

AUF WIEDERSEHEN: *Owf VEE-der-zayn*—Until we meet again

DANKE: *DAHN-keh*—Thank you

FRÄULEIN: *FROI-line*—Miss, maiden, a form of address

GROSCHEN: *GROH-shen*—A unit of currency

HÖDEKIN: *HU-deh-kin*—A sort of sprite, similar to the British brownie or pixie

KAPELLMEISTER: *Kah-PELL-mai-ster*—The highest position in a nobleman's orchestra, the person responsible for finding and producing new music and directing productions, as well as conducting and playing

LÄNDLER: *LEND-ler*—A folk dance

MEIN BRÜDERCHEN: *Mine BREW-der-khen*—My little brother

VIEL GLÜCK: *FEEL GLYOOK*—Good luck

ZWEIFACHER: *ZVAI-fahkh-er*—A folk dance

A GUIDE TO
MUSICAL TERMS

ADAGIO: A tempo marking meaning a piece should be played slowly

BASSO CONTINUO: The bass line or accompaniment to the melody in a piece

CHACONNE: A short composition, often with a repetitive bass line, used as a vehicle for variation; can also be a sort of warm-up or exercise for a musician

CONCERTO: A piece of music written for a solo instrument to be accompanied by an orchestra

DECRESCENDO: A musical term indicating that the phrase should be played with increasing softness

ÉCOSSAISE: Originally a Scottish dance, a short, lively piece that accompanies a social dance (like a waltz)

ÉTUDE: A short musical composition written for a solo instrument, usually of considerable difficulty in order to practice various technical skills

FERMATA: A musical notation indicating a note should be held longer than its usual duration

F-HOLES: The holes on the body of a violin, shaped like the letter f

FORTEPIANO: A precursor to the modern piano

GLISSANDO: A musical notation indicating that there should be a glide from one note to another

KLAVIER: A general term for an instrument with a keyboard

LARGO: A tempo marking indicating a piece should be played very slowly

OSTINATO: A repeating musical phrase

PIZZICATO: A playing style which involves plucking strings with fingers instead of bowing

PRESTO: A tempo marking, indicating a piece should be played very quickly

RITARDANDO: A change in tempo indicating a gradual slowing down

SCORDATURA: The tuning of a stringed instrument different from its standard tuning, e.g., a violin is tuned to G-D-A-E; the scordatura referenced in *Wintersong* is the retuning of the strings to G-G-D-D

SONATA: A musical composition written to be played (as opposed to sung), the definition and form of which has changed over the years

SONATINEN: The plural of sonatina, or "little (short)" sonatas

SOTTO VOCE: Not actually a musical term, but it means the dropping of one's voice for emphasis

VIOLONCELLO: The precursor to the cello

ACKNOWLEDGMENTS

First books are a dream, but second books are a nightmare. If you were to page through the acknowledgments of nearly every author who has ever had the privilege (punishment?) of writing a second book, you'll likely see multiple variations on the same theme:

WRITING IS REALLY, REALLY HARD.

Debut novels are not always the first novels written; *Wintersong* was certainly not my first. But I consider *Shadowsong* my first Real novel—the first written under contract, the first written under deadline, and the first written knowing it *will* be published and read by people other than myself. If *Wintersong* was the book that introduced me to a wider audience, then *Shadowsong* is the one that made me a Real writer.

No book is ever written in a vacuum, and I would be remiss if I did not give a nod to all the people who helped me through the strange and wondrous process that is publishing. First and foremost, I need to thank my editor,

Eileen Rothschild. Eileen, being with you is like coming home. You knew me as a friend, a peer, and a colleague before you knew me as a writer, and I am grateful for your guidance in shaping this manuscript. Here's to many more!

And as always, thanks to Katelyn Detweiler, agent and author extraordinaire, as well as everyone at Jill Grinberg Literary Management who helped bring *Wintersong* and *Shadowsong* to the world: Cheryl Pientka, Denise St. Pierre, and Jill Grinberg. Thanks also to Tiffany Shelton, Brittani Hilles, Karen Masnica, DJ Smyter, and everyone else who worked on my books at St. Martin's Press and Wednesday Books.

Art and commerce are strange bedfellows; a shout-out to all my fellow authors who helped me navigate the boundaries. Thanks and coffee whiskey are owed to Roshani Chokshi, Sarah Nicole Lemon, and Renée Ahdieh for the career advice and commiseration, but moreover for keeping me grounded and sane, and for being my lighthouses in the storm. Hugs and drinks are also owed to Marie Lu, Vicki Lame, Kelly Van Sant, Leigh Bardugo, Sabaa Tahir, Carrie Ryan, Beth Revis, everyone in Fight Me Club, and all my fellow Pub(lishing) Crawl members for the laughter, the shoulders to cry on, and the much-needed doses of reality.

To my readers, thanks and glitter for everything. It's so wonderful knowing I am not alone in my love of all things goth and David Bowie.

Last, but certainly not least, all my love and gratitude to my family. For Grandma, Uncle Steve, Aunt Robin and Scott, thank you for all your support and pride in my work. For my mother, father, baby brother, and Halmeoni, you are my bedrock and my anchor. Thank you for the gift of my life.

And for Bear. Thank you for showing me how the monstrous can be loved. I am loved. I love you.

ABOUT THE AUTHOR

S. JAE-JONES (called JJ) is an artist, an adrenaline junkie, and an erstwhile editrix. When not obsessing over books, she can be found jumping out of perfectly good airplanes, cohosting the Pub(lishing) Crawl podcast, or playing dress-up. Born and raised in Los Angeles, she now lives in North Carolina as well as many places on the Internet, including Twitter, Tumblr, Facebook, Instagram, and her blog.

www.sjaejones.com

WINTERSONG

S. Jae-Jones

All her life, Liesl has heard tales of the beautiful, dangerous Goblin King. They've enraptured her and inspired her musical compositions. Now eighteen, Liesl feels that her childhood dreams are slipping away. And when her sister is taken by the Goblin King, Liesl has no choice but to journey to the Underground to save her. But with time and the old laws working against her, Liesl must discover who she truly is before her fate is sealed.

"This is a world you will want to stay lost in"
Marie Lu, #1 *New York Times* bestselling author

"Lush, sexy, and gorgeous"
Laura Lam, author of *Pantomime & False Hearts*

"A darkly lush and dangerous tale"
Kate Elliott, *New York Times* bestselling author of the Crown of Stars series

A DARKER SHADE OF MAGIC

V. E. Schwab

Most people only know one London; but what if there were several? Kell is one of the last Travelers—magicians with a rare ability to travel between parallel Londons. There's Grey London, dirty and crowded and without magic, home to the mad king George III. There's Red London, where life and magic are revered. Then, White London, ruled by whoever has murdered their way to the throne. But once upon a time, there was Black London...

"Marvellous"
Publishers Weekly starred review

"Spellbinding"
Starburst

"Smart, funny and sexy"
Independent

A GATHERING OF SHADOWS

V. E. Schwab

Kell is plagued by his guilt. Restless, and having given up smuggling, he is visited by dreams of ominous magical events, waking only to think of Lila. As Red London prepares for the Element Games—an extravagant international competition of magic—a certain pirate ship draws closer. But another London is coming back to life, a shadow that was gone in the night reappears in the morning. Black London has risen again—and so to keep magic's balance, another London must fall.

"Fantastic"
Publishers Weekly **starred review**

"Mighty storytelling"
Io9 on *A Darker Shade of Magic*

"Excellent worldbuilding"
SF Signal on *A Darker Shade of Magic*

A CONJURING OF LIGHT

V. E. Schwab

Londons fall and kingdoms rise while darkness sweeps the Maresh Empire, and the fraught balance of magic blossoms into dangerous territory while heroes struggle. The final book in the Shades of Magic epic fantasy series, *A Conjuring of Light* sees the newly minted *New York Times* bestselling author V. E. Schwab reach a thrilling conclusion concerning the fate of beloved protagonists—and old foes.

"Compulsively readable"
NPR on *A Darker Shade of Magic*

"Inventive fantasy... One for Neil Gaiman fans"
Guardian on *A Darker Shade of Magic*

"Roller-coaster plot twists"
The Independent on *A Darker Shade of Magic*

TITANBOOKS.COM

ALL THE BIRDS IN THE SKY

Charlie Jane Anders

Childhood friends Patricia Delfine, a witch, and Laurence Armstead, a mad scientist, parted ways under mysterious circumstances during middle school. But as adults they both wind up in near-future San Francisco, where Laurence is an engineering genius and Patricia works with a small band of other magicians to secretly repair the world's ever growing ailments. But something is determined to bring them back together—to either save the world, or end it.

"Dazzling... profound... wondrous"
Michael Chabon

"Lively, sexy, scary, weird and wonderful"
Karen Joy Fowler

"Everything you could ask for in a debut novel"
Cory Doctorow

SPARE AND FOUND PARTS

Sarah Maria Griffin

In a city devastated by an epidemic, where survivors are all missing parts—an arm, a leg, an eye—Nell has always been an outsider. Her father is the scientist who created the biomechanical limbs that everyone now uses. But she's the only one with her machinery on the inside: her heart. Then she finds a lost mannequin's hand while salvaging on the beach, and inspiration strikes. Can Nell build her own companion in a world that fears advanced technology?

"Reads like a piece of mechanical poetry, an intricate machine with a fierce and fearless heartbeat"
V. E. Schwab, author of *A Darker Shade of Magic*

"A sweet and darkly hopeful tale of what it takes to build love"
Kiran Millwood Hargrave, author of *The Girl of Ink and Stars*

"A dark and fierce thing"
Joseph Fink, co-author of *Welcome to Night Vale*

TITANBOOKS.COM

For more fantastic fiction, author events, exclusive
excerpts, competitions, limited editions and more

VISIT OUR WEBSITE
titanbooks.com

LIKE US ON FACEBOOK
facebook.com/titanbooks

FOLLOW US ON TWITTER
@TitanBooks

EMAIL US
readerfeedback@titanemail.com